SECRET THE
PLACE

SECRET
THE

PLACE

CAMILLE EIDE

This is a work of fiction. All characters and events portrayed in this novel are either fictitious or used fictitiously.

THE SECRET PLACE

WhiteFire Publishing
13607 Bedford Rd NE
Cumberland, MD 21502

ISBN: 978-1-946531-99-5 (print)
    978-1-941720-39-4 (digital)

ALSO BY CAMILLE EIDE

NOVELETTES

Savanna's Gift
The Healer

CONTEMPORARY FICTION

Like There's No Tomorrow
Like a Love Song

HISTORICAL FICTION

The Memoir of Johnny Devine
Wings Like a Dove

This book is dedicated to the One who sees all, knows all, and still loves me no matter what.

My frame was not hidden from you
when I was made in the secret place,
when I was woven together in the depths of the earth.
Your eyes saw my unformed body;
all the days ordained for me were written in your book
before one of them came to be.
— Psalm 139: 15-16

CHAPTER

-1-

But in the end it's only a passing thing, this shadow.
Even darkness must pass.
—Samwise Gamgee

June 9, 2003 – McKenzie River, Oregon

On the last day of fifth grade, just as the sun dipped below the canyon's western rim, Nadine and Josie Norris left the river's edge and toted their fishing poles up the spongy bank, away from the deafening sound of rushing water. Like twin yearlings, they scrambled with ease over mossy tree roots, ferns, and jutting rock, until the sloped ground leading away from the McKenzie leveled out. From there, they headed for the old, covered bridge.

Their old, covered bridge.

With the same wiry build, same honey-gold hair, same freckles, and same green eyes, it would have been nearly impossible for people to tell them apart—if not for the fact that they never dressed alike. Aunt Libby had made it clear from day one how absurd she thought it was for twins to wear matching outfits. The fact that they were identical and pageant-pretty drew more than enough stares already, she'd said. No need to add to the novelty by parading them around like some circus side-show act.

Above the river, they followed the hidden path through thick ferns and underbrush. Few locals knew about the trail or what it led to, and dumb tourists definitely didn't know about it.

As usual, Josie was stuck carrying both the tackle box and the creel.

Nadine beat Josie to the covered bridge—also typical. She tucked her pole through the gap in the shrubs covering the bridge's undergirding, then slipped between the bushes and disappeared.

Josie checked to make sure no one was watching, then ducked inside. The summer before, they'd found the abandoned fort beneath the bridge, and since Josie and her sister had recently decided to be river pirates, they had spent afternoons and weekends filling their new lair with booty. Josie had long ago learned that kids raised by a no-nonsense aunt and a kooky grandma weren't likely to have anything even remotely cool, so a top secret place all their own was basically sacred.

Nadine plopped down on the rug they'd found in the recycle bin behind Wally's Mini-Mart, pulled off a shoe, and shook dirt and pebbles from it.

"Stink's finally gone, thank God."

Josie sniffed and wrinkled her nose. "Nope, I can still smell it." Definitely skunk.

Nadine slipped her eye patch into place, then leaned back, arms behind her like a pillow. "Nope. You just remember it, so you think you still smell it. It's all in your head."

Josie scoffed. "You have no idea what's in my head."

"Probably not much." Nadine rolled to avoid the pinecone Josie chucked at her.

"So what kept you so long after the bell?" Josie asked. "You took forever to come out."

Nadine shrugged.

Josie laughed. "Seriously? I totally thought you would've been the first one out the door screaming 'freeeeedomm!' at the top of your lungs. But when you came out, you never said a word."

With a frown, Nadine lifted her eye patch. "I didn't want Aunt Libby going down to the school and causing drama, like she did last year with Miss B." She plucked a fiddle fern and wrapped it around her finger. Then she let out an exasperated growl. "Miss Parker wanted to chat. Weirdo. She asked how I liked being raised by a couple of spinsters. And if I miss my parents."

"What?" Josie's face puckered. "Why'd she want to know that?"

Nadine snorted. "Because she's stupid. And nosy. Just like all the others."

All her life, Josie had heard countless comments about her and Nadine, about their odd family, the absence of a "real" mom and dad. Whispers about Gram, Aunt Libby. Speculation about who the girls' parents really were. Josie wished the small-town busybodies would be satisfied with just the basics about Josephine and Nadine Norris, and leave it at that.

Because just the basics was all the girls had ever known.

"And then she asked me if Libby was a lesbian. Or a communist. Or a mushroom-picking hippy, like Gram."

Josie scoffed, then stared at her twin. "I hope you said our family is none of her business."

"I did." Nadine replaced the eye patch. "Right after I told her Libby smokes weed and dances naked in the moonlight."

Josie's jaw dropped. "No way! Did you really?"

Nadine rose to sit cross-legged. "Yep. And then I told her off."

"Good." Josie giggled, ignoring a guilty twinge of relief that the teacher had cornered Nadine instead of her. Nadine had no problem speaking her mind. Which often landed her in trouble.

"But don't tell Libby," Nadine added.

"Why?"

Nadine shrugged one shoulder. "Just not a good idea."

This from the girl who thought diving out of the hayloft with a rope tied to her ankle was a good idea.

"Nadine! Josephine!" Aunt Libby's voice startled Josie.

Nadine leaned in closer. "I mean it, Feen. Promise you won't tell her."

"Okay," Josie said as she sprang to her feet. Libby despised hollering.

Her twin stood and faced her. "*Say* it."

"Let's go, girls." Libby sounded stressed.

"Okay, I promise. Come on," Josie said, picking up the tackle box and creel. The longer they took to appear, the more annoyed their aunt would be.

Nadine grasped her sister's biceps and met her with a dead-level, one-eyed glare. "In fact, I want you to promise me that everything we tell each other in this place stays in this place."

Josie replied with another eye roll. They were eleven. It wasn't like they had earthshaking secrets, nothing Gram and Libby didn't already know.

"Swear on the greatest, most sacred mystery of the universe."

"Which is…?"

"Twin telepathy. Promise!"

"Okay, okay, I swear on twinsy-telepathy."

Nadine spit into her palm and held it out, the look in her lone eye grim.

Josie did likewise, and they shook. Goose bumps prickled her skin, partly because Josie knew her aunt really did not like having to call them like hogs, and partly because of the sudden, strange solemnity in her twin sister's face.

But then she told herself Nadine was just being dramatic, as usual, and scurried out ahead of her sister into the waning sunlight.

CHAPTER
-2-

Courage is found in unlikely places.
—J. R. R. Tolkien

September 4, 2019 - Twin Falls, Idaho

Bad boys, bad boys...whatcha gonna do...whatcha gonna do when they come for you?

The COPS theme song coming from the TV cut straight through Josie's focus, nudging a tingle down her back. She set the laptop aside, clambered off the beanbag, and peeked into the bedroom.

How a four-year-old could sleep with arms flung wide like a soaring eagle never ceased to amaze her.

She tiptoed over to Kennedy's bed. Toothpaste breath escaped his parted lips. Tiny beads of sweat glistened on his brow, pulling his brown bangs into dark little clumps, thanks to record-breaking humidity. The AC was just for looks, apparently. One of the things she'd learned about "affordable" apartment life is that it was anyone's guess what fixtures—if any—actually worked.

She could just hear Aunt Libby saying something pithy about how little trials like this were God's way of reminding Josie that she'd wandered off the path of his provision and blessing.

Opening a window in this neighborhood was not an option, so she brought the janky fan from the other room and turned it on low. She brushed a tiny kiss on Kennedy's temple and then cracked the door of their shared bedroom a few more inches. Nothing trained a mommy's superpowers like a child sleeping in the next room.

Returning to the beanbag, she repositioned her laptop and resumed her work. A career in freelance graphic design had its perks, like the ability to work from home so she didn't have to leave Kennedy with a sitter. Portability, so she wasn't tied down to one location. And anonymity, which allowed for a quick vanishing act if needed, as well as the benefit of avoiding face-to-face contact with clients. Which could be either pro or con, depending on how long it had been since Josie had spoken to anyone above three feet tall in sentences that didn't require answering more "why" questions than she ever knew existed.

Since today was Friday and her Monday deadline loomed, she focused on the layout her client was waiting to see, but the thought of her aunt reminded Josie they hadn't talked in a while, not since Libby had taken the job of custodian at her church. She said she did it to escape from Gram a few hours each week, but Josie was afraid the real reason was that her aunt and grandma needed the money.

Hoping it wasn't too late, Josie pulled out her phone and dialed her aunt's cell. A while back, Gram had voiced her suspicions that Libby and Josie didn't use the landline because they were sharing scandalous secrets. But even though she was notoriously odd, Gwendolyn Buckley was no dummy. In her day, she memorized Shakespeare for a living. So Libby and Josie admitted nothing. What Gram didn't know, she couldn't worry about. Or accidentally tell anyone.

"Josie?"

"Hey, Libby."

"Hey, yourself." The relief in her aunt's sigh traveled across the miles as clearly as if they were standing hip to hip, shelling peas in Gram's kitchen. "It's about time."

Josie could always tell when Libby was worried, even though she hid it well. Actually, Liberty Buckley hid everything well. Which was a quality Josie had lately come to value very highly.

"You okay?" she asked. "How's Captain America?"

"Growing like a weed. I can hardly keep him in clothes that fit. Good thing it's still warm enough for shorts. Hides my mom fails." She could hope, anyway.

"Oh, Josie."

"What?"

"Quit being so hard on yourself."

Who was she kidding? Chapter one in *Motherhood for Dummies* probably began with "Welcome to second-guessing yourself now and for all of eternity."

"You sound tired," Josie said, heading toward the bedroom again for another peek.

Another sigh. "Keeping up with my mom is a full-time job."

Josie smiled even though she knew her aunt wasn't kidding. Gram was a young girl in an eighty-year-old body and knew no stranger, whether it had two legs, four, or—to Josie's never-ending horror—eight. Gram was the quintessential *Friend to All Living Things* but absolutely needed to draw the line at spiders. That was so many kinds of wrong. But to her credit, Gram always had a cat named Peaseblossom. Josie was pretty sure Gram was on Peaseblossom #27.

"How's Gram?"

"Fixing to run me into the ground."

"Whatever. Since when are you afraid of work?"

Libby's prolonged pause spoke volumes. "It's not the work, Josie. She's…" Another sigh. "You need to come see for yourself."

Josie could think of nothing she'd love more. The Buckley home on the McKenzie River was the only place she'd ever felt anchored, like part of something sturdy. And if there was ever a time she craved sturdy, it was now. But at this point in Josie's life, home was a comfort she couldn't afford. Home wasn't safe for Kennedy, not now. Which Libby knew full well.

She peeked at her mini-superhero to make sure he was still asleep, then took her phone into the kitchen and lowered her voice to a near whisper. "Has Nadine come around?"

"No."

"Has she called? Has she asked about…?" She sucked in air and held it. She still couldn't say it.

"No, we haven't heard from your sister in a long time."

The air Josie held leaked out with a hiss. But the reassurance in Libby's answer was short-lived. The one thing you could count on about Josie's sister was that you couldn't. Nadine Norris had never stuck with a plan for more than twelve minutes in her entire life.

Josie had always wished they were more alike—and not in the freckled, green-eyed blonde sense. Physical appearance was where their similarities began and ended. In fact, they couldn't have been more opposite. Nadine was the striking one. Even as a kid, she'd always had this *Hey! I'm here!* way of exploding into a room, a feral charisma no one could ignore. She was all about making sure the world stopped and took a good look at her.

And then there was Josie. Good old, dependable Josephine—resident worrywart and vibe-killer. When their mom woke up one day and decided she was done being mom to twin preschoolers, Josie had naturally assumed the role of Nadine's mother. She was always her lookout, always cleaning up her messes, always defending or bailing her out. And Nadine always got a kick out of baiting her—she even admitted it.

Despite all that had happened and all the damage Nadine had done, Josie still loved her sister. Nadine would always be an inextricable part of her. But that didn't change the fact that Josie was now prepared to do whatever it took to avoid crossing her sister's path—even if it meant living in exile.

"Josephine?"

"Sorry. I'm here."

"Sounds like you need to get some rest."

"What I need is to land a ginormous contract and become filthy rich."

Libby said no more on that subject—she knew. Josie promised to check in again soon and ended the call on a livelier note than she was feeling.

Saturday afternoon, the sound of someone pounding on a window yanked Josie's attention from her laptop to the LEGO empire on the kitchen floor beside her, which now lay abandoned. Heart hammering, she jumped up, maneuvered bare feet between tiny instruments of torture scattered across the linoleum, and hurried to the front room.

Balanced on a stack of still-packed boxes, Kennedy, dressed in his usual Captain America garb, held the curtain open with one hand and knuckle-rapped on the window with the other.

Josie's relief was replaced by a fresh wave of apprehension. She tucked a long lock of hair behind one ear and forced her tone light. "Hey, buddy, who's out there?" *Since we don't know anybody in Idaho.*

"Squirt gun war! Look!" He opened the curtain as wide as his little arm could stretch.

A reminder about staying away from doors and windows died on her lips. She leaned closer to the glass, taking in the shrieking neighbor kids playing outside in the dwindling hours of daylight, and wrapped an arm around his wriggly body. The boyish energy bursting to be free stabbed at her heart.

"Did you see that?" he said. "That guy shot all the way across the street!"

"Yeah, that was awesome."

Kennedy turned to her, doe-eyes wide beneath his red and blue hero mask.

She could only fake smile. *Someday,* she wanted to say, *you'll play carefree like all the other kids, I promise.*

"Can we get squirt guns?"

She crossed her eyes and touched her forehead to his. "What do you think?"

"I think I need one!"

I think you're four going on fourteen. "We'll just have to see about that."

"Then I can shoot the bad guys when they come to get me."

Her breath caught. He was far too perceptive for a preschooler.

Baby, no one's going to get you because I'll do whatever it takes to make sure the bad guys never find you...

"Whatever it takes" had come to include a number of skills Josie had never dreamed she was going to need. Like the art of traveling light and owning only what her twenty-year-old Outback could hold. Trusting no one. Dating no one. It also included leaving God and everyone she loved behind because the role of protecting Kennedy was a 24/7 job that fell squarely on her.

Kennedy palmed the window with both hands.

Time for a diversion.

"Know what?" Josie asked. "When I came in here just now, I thought you were the *real* Captain America."

Turning, he lifted a corner of his mask and eyeballed her.

Josie's brows rose to add authenticity. "Serious."

He studied her, thoughts churning. "Naw," he said finally, shaking his head. "You're lying."

"Me? Never."

Well…

He leapt off the boxes, still packed since the move from Ogden two weeks ago. The thought of unpacking made Josie's brain hurt. Besides, who knew how long before a grocery checker or apartment manager told her some sketchy-looking guy was asking about them, and they would need to move again.

Another noise pulled her focus back to the kitchen. Kennedy was tiptoe on a chair, reaching as high as he could into the cupboard.

"Whoa, buddy, let me do that. I don't want you to get hurt."

"Watch this." He flicked a box so hard that it bounced against a can of Dennison's and popped off the shelf. He hopped down, opened the box, and with a dimpled grin, held up a package of microwave popcorn. "Orbull Red and Buckers. Perfect every time."

Josie smiled without a word as he unwrapped the cellophane. It was actually the generic store brand—she couldn't afford the good stuff. What kids didn't know wouldn't hurt them.

You sure do tell yourself that a lot…

She helped him set the timer on the microwave and let him push the button. So what if she'd withheld some useless information from him? If it was a crime, she was prepared to do the time. Kennedy would never be like a piece of luggage somebody wanted one day and tossed out the next. He'd never have to deal with bonehead teachers and their insensitive questions about who his parents were. It wouldn't take him decades to figure out that the mean kids at school don't actually know what they're talking about and that he was no weirder than anyone else.

He would never know what not worth keeping felt like. Not as long as Josie had a heartbeat.

The microwave timer beeped in sync with the ringtone on her cell. Libby's name appeared on the screen. That was odd, since they had just talked the night before. What if Gram had fallen in the woods, or had a stroke, or…?

Heart thumping, she answered. But it was not her aunt's soothing alto. It was her grandma, her little kitten voice garbled.

"Gram? What's wrong? What are you saying?"

"Liberty…" Gram was sobbing so hard she could hardly speak. "They took her away…in a helicopter…"

Josie went instantly numb. "What? Why?"

"She's bleeding. Oh, Josephine, they said her brain…she's in a coma!"

Aunt Libby? In a *coma*? Josie's legs felt like noodles. "W-what happened?"

Panic pressed her chest tight as Gram gasped and stammered out the details like pieces of a nightmarish puzzle. Libby had fallen down the basement stairs while cleaning her church. Hit her head on a concrete ledge. Lay in a pool of blood for who knew how long. Brain bleeding and rapid swelling. Acute trauma.

Tears blinded her. She gulped air. "Where are they taking her?"

"I don't know…McKenzie-Willamette? I don't remember."

Please, God, please. Not Libby.

"They said she might…might not…make it." More pitiful, choking sobs. This was far too much reality for Gram. "I need to be with her. Can you come?"

"Yes, of course, I'll be there as soon as—"

Nadine.

"Gram, does Nadine know?"

"Who? No, I don't know where your sister is, but Liberty needs us." She sobbed. "Please come?"

"Yes, I'll leave right now. I'm about eight hours away, but I'll be there as soon as I can. Just hold on, okay?"

Gram said she'd try to hold on, but Josie suspected her grandma was losing it, and fast.

Josie hung up and stared at her phone.

Acute brain trauma.

What if Libby didn't make it?

Icy fear paralyzed her.

Snap out of it, Josie. Move.

She grabbed a hoodie and stuffed it into her duffel bag. On second thought, she went to the bedroom and grabbed jeans, T-shirts, undies, and other random stuff. Just in case. It was about eight hours to McKenzie Bridge, and then another hour to the hospital in Springfield, then no telling how long they would have to wait for news, or for—

"Mommy, what are you doing?" Kennedy stared at her with a deepening frown.

Tears blinded her. She blinked hard, sucked it up. "We're going for a surprise drive, buddy."

"Ahhh!" He flopped onto her bed, his groans right up there with a wounded walrus. "Again?"

Josie grabbed his backpack and stuffed in some of his clothes and a pair of tennis shoes, then grabbed whatever toys were in reach.

"Hey! Why are you putting Captain America in my tool belt?"

Good question. "It's going to be kind of a long surprise drive, so let's take your pillow and blanket too."

"But where are we going?"

"We're going to see my Gram and...my aunt." Her aunt who could NOT die.

Please, God, please. Libby is the closest thing I have to a mom. You know that, right?

"Will your Gram like me?"

Heart twisting, Josie paused and met Kennedy's cocoa brown gaze. She had studied that sweet face countless times since the moment he was born, but suddenly, she was seeing him anew, through an old woman's eyes. What would Gram see when she looked at him? What would she say?

Josie always assumed Kennedy got his dark hair and eye coloring from his father—whoever that was—because he certainly didn't take after his mother.

"Of course. Gram's going to be so surprised to meet you." Epic understatement. Josie had no idea how Gram would react to learning she had a great-grandson. But what choice did she have? Josie needed to be there, and, therefore, so did Kennedy.

She crammed everything she could think of into the bags, then raided the fridge and pantry, which she was surprised to find actually contained anything portable. Pop Tarts, string cheese, granola bars. Half a box of cereal.

Fact: Josie was no food snob and was definitely not above munching on Cap'n Crunch to stay awake.

"What's a 'aunt'?" Kennedy hollered from the bedroom. "Do I have one?"

Now there was a loaded question.

She could barely focus on what to pack, much less tackle that topic. Hands shaking, she stuffed her laptop and cord in her duffel, grabbed her keys, and then froze. A giant, numbing cold hit her like a brick wall, and Josie was suddenly too limp to stand. Her brain wanted to power down into some kind of jellyfish mode.

Move, Josie. Now!

She dragged in a deep breath. "Okay, bud, ready? Let's hit the road."

She tossed everything in the back of the Subaru, smooshed it down enough to see out the rear window, then buckled Kennedy in the backseat and made sure his water, blanket, and the Captain were within reach.

As she drove away from the apartment complex, she glanced in the rearview mirror, nagged by the feeling that she was forgetting something really important. But Kennedy was buckled in, his pillow beside him. Beyond him, the apartment building, trash bins, and graffitied street signs shrank until they disappeared. It was like Idaho was swallowing up everything she hadn't crammed into her car.

God, I know I haven't exactly been keeping in touch lately, but Libby can't die. Please?

Losing Libby was something Josie had never even considered. At fifty-six, Libby was strong, healthy, and full of endless stamina. Josie had given no thought to her aunt's health or how long she'd be around. She'd always been there. She was supposed to always be there.

Thick, suffocating fear pressed in.

Libby was the tough, sturdy one, not Josie. Libby was the one who stayed calm and reasonable when things got crazy.

Tears flooded her vision, turning passing cars into a blur.

And what if Nadine found out and decided to come—

She couldn't. She just couldn't.

Gram said doctors weren't sure if Libby would make it through the night. Getting to her was Josie's only focus, her only concern right now.

She would just have to worry about her sister later.

CHAPTER
-3-

*Aunt Libby has zero tolerance for Nadine's "crappola"
and gives her extra chores when she cops an attitude.
Her current chore list is gonna take her till she's like forty.*
—Josie Norris, age 12

Kennedy was finally asleep, still clutching Captain America—which Josie had once made the unholy mistake of calling a doll, earning her a sharp correction and a *How Could You* look that only a four-year-old could produce.

Before he'd fallen asleep, he'd plied her with endless questions about where they were going.

We're going to visit my old home on the river, where I grew up.

Did you have a rowboat?

No.

A raft?

No.

A tree fort?

Sort of. I had a secret hideout beneath the covered bridge.

Did you build it?

No, I found it. Someone else built and abandoned it. I just fixed it up.

Did you have a snake?

Gross, no. But there were frogs. And tons of fish.

Fish? Cooooool. I want to catch a big fish. Like a shark. Or maybe a narwhal.

At the time, Josie was grateful for the distraction—his chatter kept the panic from gnawing at her sanity all the way from Twin Falls to Caldwell. But once they'd passed into Oregon, it occurred to her that they were not only in another state, but another time zone. She didn't even remember crossing the Snake River. Now, in the silence, a mental slideshow kept looping through her mind, of things like Libby teaching her how to fish off the banks of the McKenzie. Teaching her and Nadine how to ride a bike. Her obsession with her garden, and her insistence that Nadine and Josie know how to handle a table saw, a tiller, and a shotgun.

You know, just in case they ever needed to shoot an intruder, build a coffin, and bury it in the garden.

Liberty Buckley was unlike any woman Josie had ever known. She carried herself with a deep, quiet reserve that rarely let up—at least, not that Josie had ever seen. She might have shed a tear once, and Josie may have seen Libby crack a genuine smile four or five times, tops. She wasn't cold or hard—she just had no use for displays of emotion. Sap, she called it. Josie remembered trying to get a laugh or at least a smile out of her once by hamming it up with some getup from Gram's old theater trunk. Josie must have been about eight or nine. She could still see the look on her aunt's face. With a sigh and a shake of her head, Libby had simply said, "You're just like your mother." At that age, Josie was starving for any crumb of information she could get about Geraldine Norris, the woman who had dropped her children off like a Goodwill donation and left without a backward glance. Whenever Josie had asked Libby *how* she was like her mother, Libby just shook her head or sighed.

But one time, she surprised Josie by saying, "Gerry was needy, too."

Shrugging off the memory, Josie checked the rearview mirror. Kennedy was baby-snoring, his little mouth gaped.

Libby calling Josie "needy" had stung, but it also taught her to simply accept whatever she could get from a surrogate mother who was doing her very best, and not ask for more.

Josie didn't fault Libby for being frugal with her emotions. She probably hadn't asked to be saddled with the job of raising someone else's kids, and yet she had risen fully to the task.

Why Liberty Buckley never had a family of her own was a mystery. Maybe a kooky mother and a pair of messed-up nieces was more than enough family for her. All Josie knew was that while Libby was reserved, she'd always been there, offering her quiet strength, frank advice, and steady guidance. Gram was fragile and kooky, but she was also gentle and kind to a fault. Josie had no doubt that Gram loved her.

But Libby *knew* her.

After she passed the sign saying they had entered the Willamette National Forest, the highway began to bend like a snake through the dense wilderness. In a few more weeks, this area would be crawling with hunters, but now, Josie and Kennedy were pretty much the only ones on the road. In daylight, the dark, velvety green foothills and the snow-capped peaks of the Three Sisters mountains would have offered a breathtaking, frame-worthy view, even after the long, dry summer. But at nearly midnight, all Josie could see was her own headlights cutting feeble swaths into the blackness.

She smacked her cheeks a few times to help her stay awake, then checked the rearview mirror to make sure she wasn't actually slapping herself red. She forgot to grab a hair band, and her long hair was now a tangled mess from the air coming in her window.

Josie was using every trick she knew to keep her eyes from closing—including crunching on dry cereal like theater popcorn. Her cracked window filled the car with the pungent scents of fir and fall foliage, lake algae, pine, and fallen leaves, and the occasional whiff of smoke from some distant forest fire. She hadn't passed a town or gas station that sold coffee in hours, and of course she hadn't thought about the need for caffeine as she left Bend and headed west. Now, she'd give her left kidney for a double mocha frap.

Actually, she hadn't been thinking about anything besides getting to Libby as soon as possible, which was probably why it hadn't occurred to her until she'd hit Central Oregon's long, straight stretches of silent highway that she was heading—at well above the speed limit—into a double dilemma.

Dilemma one: Josie had a four-year-old, which would come as a huge shock to Gram.

Surprise! You're a great grandma!

Dilemma two: There had been good reason to keep his existence a secret from Gram, and that reason still existed: Kennedy was far too young to learn the truth. A cruel truth that Josie had been shielding Kennedy from at all cost—which may or may not have included her eternal soul. She had kept him from Gram because there was a very real possibility that her sweet little grandma would tell someone, and that was too risky. And far worse—she could slip and mention it in Kennedy's hearing.

That could never happen. Ever. So Josie would definitely not be telling Gram the truth.

But if Josie tried to make up some cover story about who Kennedy was in hopes of sparing Gram's feelings, Captain Smarty-pants would catch on and blow that cover, adding more spark to an already highly flammable situation.

So, Josie was left with only one solution: A half-truth. She would have to tell Gram that she had a great-grandson she never knew about, which would surely hurt her feelings. She would also have to give Gram the same vague, airbrushed story about his origins that she'd given Kennedy and pray it satisfied her. But even if Gram bought the story, how could Josie keep her Just-Give-Peace-a-Chance grandma from telling Nadine that Josie was home? If Libby thought it was too risky for Gram to know, then surely—

A sudden flash of tan in her headlights gave Josie's heart a triple jolt. She braked and swerved to avoid the deer, but the animal doubled back. Josie whipped the wheel hard to the right, praying the deer wouldn't switch back again. She would either hit the creature or find out what was beyond the edge of the road.

Fortunately, her car just barely missed the deer.

Unfortunately, her connection with pavement ended. They were airborne, headlights splaying out into the blackness.

Josie screamed—stomach in her throat—and kept screaming.

Oh dear Jesus, we're falling—

They landed with a horrendous scraping sound, bounce-thunked five or six times, then came to an abrupt, screeching halt.

When she finally stopped screaming, she could hear Kennedy whimpering.

"Did we crash?"

The engine was dead. The dash lights were still glowing, and the headlights beamed straight ahead, but Josie couldn't see anything. She was surrounded by blackness. She held her breath, still waiting—for who knew what, zombies maybe—and listening.

Nothing.

"Mommy?"

Josie pivoted slowly in her seat. "I'm right here, baby. You okay?" She could barely make out his shape in the dark.

"I dropped Captain America."

"Okay." Thank God, they weren't hurt. "I'm just gonna..." See what in the name of Kitty Hawk she'd just done to her car. She unfastened her seat belt.

"Are we there yet?"

Josie belted out a laugh, she couldn't help it. Laughing at this point was good. Maybe.

She opened her door slowly, just in case they'd landed atop an angry she-bear or a wolf den. Because that would be just her luck.

She extended her foot, but there was no ground, which she was pretty sure was *not* good. She reached as far as her leg could stretch, and finally connected with something. Pointy and hard, like sharp rock.

Bless me, Betsy, I've landed on a mountain. Where the deer and the antelope play. And Coyotes. And hairy little critters of every evil kind.

She yanked her foot back and slammed the door, shuddering.

"What is it? Is it a bear? Can I see?" She heard her brave boy fumbling with his seat belt.

"No bears, Ken. How about you stay put until I figure out where we are."

Think, Josie.

Flashlight.

She fished around in the glovebox and grasped the flashlight, turned it on—thank goodness the batteries were still good—opened the door, and shined the light onto the ground outside. All she could make out was very lumpy black rock about a foot or two below her door. Excellent. She'd landed on the moon.

She shone the light fartherand saw more of the same. She aimed the beam behind her, in the direction from which they had come, and then finally saw the road a few dozen yards above them.

"Hang on a minute, Ken. I need to check on something. Can you sit tight for me?"

Carefully, she climbed down onto the jagged stuff and shined the light around. From what she could tell, they were completely surrounded by porous, black rock. Her twenty-year-old Subaru was perched peacefully on a mini mountain of lava. Her all-terrain tires were having a jolly time spinning in the breeze, not touching a blessed thing but air.

They were perfectly high-centered. In a million years, she could never have intentionally pulled this off.

"Mommy?" Kennedy poked his head around the driver's seat.

"Hold on, buddy, I just need a minute to figure out what to do." Because this car wasn't going anywhere without help.

Odd, but the only thing that came to mind at that precise moment was how not *one* of the Subaru commercials with the tanned, sporty couples in shiny new Outbacks bounding from one adventure to the next ever showed the vehicle flying off the road and into a lava bed.

She needed to call for help—if she was lucky enough to get a signal way out here. And if 911 even responded to calls in the wilderness in the middle of the freaking night.

"Kennedy, I need you to grab my bag and then I'm going to lift you down, okay?"

She heard rustling and the sound of metal jiggling.

"Be careful!"

"Got it!"

"Good boy, now just—"

"I found Captain America."

Right. "Okay. Now I just need you to find my bag, and my phone."

Once boy and phone were safely on the ground, they picked their way over jagged volcanic rock and clambered up the bank until they reach the road. It was black up there, too. And silent.

This was so great.

"We climbed a mountain!"

"We sure did!" Josie said, punching in 911.

Someone actually answered. And no, unfortunately, Josie couldn't give the county sheriff's dispatcher her exact location. But she could tell her about how long it had been since she'd passed the junction of highways 20 and 126.

Then the woman suggested Josie call a tow truck.

Excellent advice, under normal circumstances. Taking a deep breath, Josie told the woman as calmly as she could that perhaps she didn't hear her over the howling from the wolves closing in on them, but it was well past midnight, she didn't know where to find a tow truck at that hour, and that she and her baby were *stranded* in the *wilderness*. The kind with bears and cougars and such.

This was met with silence.

The dispatcher took her number and said she would get back to her.

Josie hung up, pulled Kennedy close, closed her eyes, and fought back tears. She had a pretty good feeling they would be walking the last twenty miles to Gram's and coming back for the car some other time—if they weren't eaten on the way.

Normally, at a time like this, Josie would be dialing Aunt Libby for a dose of calming words and wise advice.

"Are we there now?" Kennedy asked.

Josie sighed. "We're close, but our car is stuck."

"You should call a fireman."

Her mouth tugged at a smile. "I called for help, but I don't think there are any firemen out here." And if there were, they would surely have more important things to do than drag a Subaru off a mini volcano.

Her phone buzzed. It was a different lady—a nicer one, this time—calling from the McKenzie River Ranger Station. Thankfully, this lady knew right where the lava fields were and she was going to try to dispatch someone, told Josie to hang tight.

"Help is on the way," she said to her boy, half laugh, half sob.

CHAPTER
-4-

A real man does the right thing, even if he's the only one doing it. And even when no one's expecting him to. And even when no one's looking. Especially when no one's looking.
—William K. McKnight, age 32

Ranger Will McKnight finished cordoning off the crime scene with yellow tape marked *USFS*, then stepped to the edge of the clearing and swept his flashlight over the area for one last look around. A long, heavy sigh left him flat, like he'd just emptied the last of his reserves. Whoever had set up this deadly little science fair project had left in a hurry, and his best guess: the scumbags would be back. But he was the only officer patrolling a half million acres of forest, and even if it wasn't nearly midnight, HAZMAT was at least an hour and a half away. He was neither equipped nor inclined to dispose of the hazardous materials by himself. After five years on patrol with the Forest Service, he knew what battles to pick, and which ones to turn over to the State Troopers.

He climbed into his vehicle, and wrote an entry in his logbook: *Cordoned off meth lab on Forest Road 3442 near milepost 22. Reported to OSP.*

He put the logbook away and started his truck. On autopilot, he grabbed his coffee from the cup holder, took a swig, and then grimaced. Cold, and not in a good way. No surprise, he'd just put in a thirteen-hour shift—the fourth this week.

Which would have easily explained the weariness dogging him

lately. But long hours wasn't even the half of it. He was tired of the crime, the trafficking, the looting. The constant struggle between the law and the lawless. That would drain anyone, but his fatigue wasn't just the job. And he wasn't surprised by it, not anymore. It had just taken a while to realize he'd missed the warning signs.

Wasn't that the story of his life.

He was over Kristi Lockwood; that wasn't the problem. Breaking up with his girlfriend on his thirty-second birthday hadn't been as painful as it should have been. The problem was how long he'd been oblivious to her true nature. Good old fleshly desire had allowed it. Cultivated it, even. It had taken time, but he finally recognized his mistake. He'd allowed himself to be blinded by the intoxicating beauty of an ambitious, shallow, self-absorbed woman.

That would never happen again.

He just wished the bitterness didn't still rush in like sea water over sand, returning with tidal force and swift ease. He'd taken that bitterness to God so many times that the Lord was probably sick of hearing him by now.

Will reached for the hand mic and signed out with dispatch, then turned and headed west for the twenty-mile drive home.

Home. A place that had lately become far too quiet. It wasn't like Dad had ever been much of a conversationalist, and especially not in those last three agonizing months, but at least he'd been there. Now, the cabin they'd built together felt like someone had sucked out all the oxygen and replaced it with a flat, stifling silence. Watching his dad suffer 24/7 and feeling powerless to ease his pain had been excruciating. But even after Dad passed, the relief Will expected to feel hadn't followed. Even after seven months, he was still getting used to the idea that Keith McKnight was, not is.

Between grief, bitterness, and the role he'd inherited as Grandma McKnight's guardian, he felt like a pack mule after a long mountain climb. His job as Ranger was a game of *Call of Duty* by comparison.

Static crackled over the radio, then Darcie's voice. "Hey, McKnight? You still on the road?"

He debated whether or not to answer. A call from dispatch this time of night was likely someone up to no good. Probably a prank call, or worse, a diversion. Or another looter. He'd already apprehended four this week, with several more still at large. For some reason, the Willamette National Forest had become the new hot spot for thieves.

"Yeah, but I'm heading home."

"Sorry," she said, "but we've got a distress call, stranded motorist. Broke down on Highway 126 at the lava field south of the junction."

He blasted out a hiss that probably registered red on the jerk meter. "Can't you call a tow?"

A hesitation. "I would, but the caller says the vehicle is stuck on top of a volcano."

Volcano? Perfect. A drunk looter.

With a growl, Will turned his rig around and headed north.

After finding a boulder where she could sit with Kennedy snuggled on her lap, she left a message on Gram's home phone letting her know that she'd met with a "slight" delay and would be there as soon as she could. She didn't mention what had happened, that would only add to her grandmother's distress. But it was odd that Gram wasn't sitting by the phone waiting for updates on Libby. This either meant that she couldn't stay awake, or couldn't wait for Josie any longer and had gone ahead to the hospital. Which was no simple feat, since Gwennie Buckley had never driven a car in her life.

Not a single vehicle had passed in nearly an hour. But the upside: the moon was higher now and shone clear and bright, painting a dim, blue silhouette of the Sisters mountains and casting a faint, milky glow on the landscape. Which was good since Josie had run the battery down on her flashlight and needed to keep an eye out for bears and cougars. Of course, moonlight was useless for seeing hideous little eight-legged demons, but she forced herself to block that thought.

She heard a vehicle in the distance, followed by the spreading glow of headlights coming around the bend. Kennedy was asleep on her shoulder, so she struggled to her feet about as gracefully as a newborn calf, trying not to disturb him. A white pickup with a big star emblem on the side approached, then came to a stop. Someone got out, leaving the headlights aimed at her, the engine running.

"Ma'am?" A rumbling male voice. "Are you the one that called for help?"

Really? Were there a bunch of women sitting in the middle of the national forest at two a.m.? "Bingo. That would be me."

The guy came closer, but with the headlights blinding her, all she could see was a tall, broad-shouldered silhouette wearing a dark ball cap.

She shined her flashlight at him, which would have been super useful if it wasn't dead.

"I'm Ranger McKnight, U.S. Forest Service. Dispatch said you broke down." He looked up and down the road. "So, where's your vehicle?"

"Um, actually it's more stuck than broke down." Kennedy squirmed on her shoulder, so she lowered her voice to a whisper and gestured with her head. "It's right over there."

He took a flashlight off his belt and aimed it out across the lava beds. "What were you doing out there?"

"Four-wheeling?"

Silence.

Work with me, Ranger. Levity is the only way I can keep from freaking out. "I swerved to miss a deer and went off the road."

Make that flew off the road like a drunken goose.

"Wait here, please." He went to his truck, and Josie could hear him on his radio. Then he headed over the embankment and disappeared.

Squinting, Josie could make out the USFS Law Enforcement emblem on the truck. Odd. In the fourteen years she'd lived in this area, she never knew there were cops in the national forest. What kind of laws did they enforce? Speeding badgers? Disorderly deer?

The officer returned, and he didn't look happy. "Where did you say you were coming from?"

"Idaho. Why?"

"What brings you to Oregon?"

Okay, this guy was rude and getting ruder by the minute. "Family emergency," she said through gritted teeth. That had better satisfy him, because if she let herself say more, she would tear up, and she refused to cry in front of some overgrown Boy Scout who spent his time staking out beaver dams and ticketing raccoons.

He looked toward her car, then faced her, hands on hips. "I just spent twelve hours chasing down campground looters. The stuff in your car looks like it was shoved in there in a hurry."

"Well, there's stuff shoved in there in a hurry because emergencies don't always give you time to arrange things all nice and tidy." Her face burned. This rescue wasn't looking so good.

"What kind of emergency?"

Darn it! He just had to ask. Her chin jutted as an achy knot gathered in her throat. "My aunt suffered a traumatic head injury and she's…" She swallowed hard, but the tears came in a rush anyway. "They took her by Life Flight. She might not make it. I don't even know if…" Tears spilled now, big ones. And worse, she was fixing to ugly cry. "She and my grandma need me."

The officer just stared at her, as best she could tell, since she could barely see his face.

"Yeah, I heard that chopper call," he said slowly. "We've got a lot going on. In addition to the looting, we've had a string of wildfires, plus some illegal drug activity." He peered at her car again. "That's going to need a winch. Best to call a tow truck."

Perfect. Back to square one.

Josie closed her eyes and dried a cheek on Kennedy's shoulder.

"I'll have dispatch call in a tow for you," he said. "Meanwhile, let's get you two home."

"Really?" Josie looked up, but the officer was already halfway to his truck.

Thanks for being so courteous. Your concern warms my heart.

Shoulder cramping under thirty-seven pounds of sleeping boy, she followed.

About ten minutes into the ride, Kennedy woke, blinked at Josie a few times, then stared at the uniformed man behind the wheel. "You're not a fireman."

"Nope, I'm LEO—law enforcement officer." His voice was a low rumble, and his eyes never left the road. "Ranger McKnight, U.S. Forest Service. What's your name?"

Kennedy turned to Josie, eyes wide. "I can talk to him, right?" Then in a starstruck whisper, he added, "He's a Ranger."

Josie nodded. They finished introductions and even shook hands, which totally irked her for some reason. Fully awake now, Kennedy wasted no time firing off a round of questions, and Josie was far too exhausted to stop him.

Are you a real cop?

Where are your handcups?

Are we gonna 'rest someone?

Where's your dash cam?

Josie winced. It was probably time to lay off the late-night episodes of COPS until she was sure he was asleep. But "Ranger McNugget"—as Kennedy had already dubbed him—didn't seem to mind, and, in fact, was answering every question with a patient smile.

Okay, so maybe there was a decent guy under the uniform. An insanely cute, decent guy, now that she could see him up close. His hair was a light, sun-kissed brown, and his eyes reminded her of a caramel mocha. She could also see that he wasn't wearing a ring—not that she was looking. Because even if the past eleven hours hadn't left her looking like something that would send a zombie crying for its mommy, an insanely cute cop was definitely the last thing her crazy life needed.

They passed the McKenzie Bridge Ranger Station, then drove two more miles to Gram's driveway. The old birdhouse mailbox was so weathered that the name *Buckley* was barely legible now. They turned in and passed between maples lining the long drive like bystanders at a homecoming parade, their branches touching to form a fiery canopy overhead, and for a second, Josie felt like a prodigal returning home.

The truck pulled up in front of the house, but even before it stopped, Josie could hear the powerful, steady rush of river. She closed her eyes and was instantly transported back in time. The smell of fall foliage, the damp air, the whispering woods. She'd forgotten how much she missed the aliveness of this place.

The passenger side door clicked open suddenly, jerking Josie's focus back to the present and into the steely gaze of Ranger McKnight. He stepped aside and waited while she got out and unfastened Kennedy. She could feel him watching her as she hoisted her sleeping boy out, simultaneously stroking his hair, bouncing, and shushing him back to sleep while she rearranged him on her shoulder, a hard-won skill that had saved her many an hour of lost sleep.

Josie snagged her duffel and turned. Cute But Cranky Ranger Guy was still staring, and not in a good way. It felt like an appraisal of some kind.

Well, let him. It was nearly three a.m. and she was reeling from the ordeal she'd just been through, and trying to brace herself for what lay ahead. She couldn't care less how she measured up to some uptight detective.

"I'll have the tow company give you a call," the Ranger whispered, with a knowing nod at her sleeping child. "It shouldn't be long."

"Thank you," she whispered back, swallowing her hostility along with her assumptions. She offered him the best smile she could muster, since exhaustion was about to take her out at the knee. "And thanks again for the ride. That twenty-mile hike would've been brutal."

"Glad to be of help." He nodded, then glanced at Kennedy and added softly, "Tell the Captain it was nice meeting him."

CHAPTER
-5-

To thine own self be true, and it must follow, as the night the day,
thou canst not then be false to any man.
—Hamlet

Josie watched the Forest Service truck as it headed back to the road, then she inhaled, slow and deep. She needed to collect Gram and then somehow get to Libby, but for some reason, she couldn't move. Moonlight set the McKenzie River canyon aglow. The trees on Gram's property were much bigger than they were the last time she was here. Which was…the summer after her freshman year at the U of O. Had it really been nine years? The rope swing still hung from the enormous oak on the west side of the house to the right. The potting shed on the other side was overrun with wisteria vines and dozens of randomly placed bird feeders. Mums and dahlias in every color spilled out of the boxes lining the front of the shed like glad little faces that couldn't stop smiling.

Glowing feline eyes peered out of the shed, joined by at least two more pairs. They saw Josie and disappeared.

Typical.

The old farmhouse seemed to be gazing thoughtfully at Josie, holding its breath, waiting. Daring her to touch a toe to the first step, the same way it had more than two decades before. And, oddly, the hesitation gripping her now was the same one she'd felt on that sweltering day back in 1996. She and Nadine had stood side by side, staring up at the old farmhouse, then at their thin, sweat-soaked mother as she dragged a large, battered suitcase up the steps and dropped it with a clank beside the front door. Looking back, Josie hadn't thought to ask what two four-year-old girls could possibly need for a weekend at Gram's farm that would make the big suitcase so heavy. They'd had no reason to question the amount of stuff their mommy had packed, until a weekend stretched into a week, then a month.

Then forever.

Gram, whom the twins had met only once before, cried and hugged them both, tight. Too tight. Then she declared them too thin. On the other hand, Aunt Libby, whom the girls had never met, didn't say anything. The younger woman's silence made Josie want to shrink like a slug when you salted its slimy body. But somehow, even at four, Josie had the idea that her aunt's silence was its own distinct form of communication, and the message she sent was heavy, like an elephant sitting on them all.

And that weight hovered over the farm during the coming weeks and months, as Josie and Nadine asked vaguely answered questions, as they swallowed their tears and confusion and waited for their mother to return. The weight felt like a shapeless, silent intruder, and it wasn't until the twins' eighth birthday that Josie finally began to see the weight take shape.

Gram and Libby had spoken in low tones while they worked on the lopsided chocolate birthday cake, unaware that Josie could hear them from the dining room where she was doodling.

Gram made abrupt, snuffling sounds, like she was crying but trying to hold it in. "I just don't understand, Liberty. How could she give up like that? I died a thousand deaths when I lost your father, and even I could never go that far." More snuffling.

Libby snorted. "She could have gotten help. Real help. And not that 'let's circle the chairs and talk about our navels' crap."

"What if she tried but simply lost her way? Even darkness must pass."

"She didn't try, Mom. She bailed."

Gram sobbed openly then.

"I know it hurts, but it's true." Libby sighed. "Life will try to beat the living daylights out of you. You have to grab the nerve to stand up to it."

"Like you did," Gram whispered. "Finally."

A silence filled the room so thick, it felt like Aunt Libby's elephant was back.

"But you could lose heart," Gram said. "Like Geraldine did."

"Nope. Not as long as my shotgun's loaded and my aim is steady." Another long silence, then Libby's voice softened. "Mom, I would never, ever do that to you. Or those girls. Ever."

At eight, Josie understood that bailed meant taking one's own life. And doing that, in her Aunt Libby's view, was the coward's way out.

Josie shook off the memory along with the bitter ache attached to it, and took another look around. Little had changed, but one thing was new: the dilapidated log border that once surrounded the vegetable garden had been replaced with a chest-high cyclone fence. Well. It seemed that Libby had finally won the battle over the deer getting into her garden. Gram could not have been happy about that. She preferred a few politely placed, fallen tree limbs over the obscenity of metal.

But then, she also preferred the idea of Middle Earth over the real world.

The rock pond in front of the house was still home to a dozen koi, and tree frogs still sang their husky chorus from the grove beyond the woodshed.

Josie smiled. It was still here—the magic. Kennedy was going to be in pure heaven—for a little while, anyway. They couldn't stay long, because the longer they stayed, the higher the risk of running into Nadine.

As if he sensed she was thinking of him, he lifted his head. "Mommy, I gotta pee."

Josie heaved a sigh. "You and me both. We'd better get inside."

The door was unlocked, as usual, and the rarely used living room was dark, but Josie could hear the tick of the ancient grandfather clock. The story, according to Gram, was that Peter Buckley had sent for it all the way from London right after he saw the enchanting Gwendolyn LaPlante playing Hermia on stage in Ashland for the first time.

It was a story Gram never tired of telling.

Kennedy tugged her sleeve. She led him past the narrow stairs to the bathroom in the center of the hall, then to the right and into the kitchen at the back of the house. The kitchen was also silent but for the hum of the ancient Frigidaire, and, of course, the endless rush of the McKenzie about fifty yards or so beyond the house.

Josie had forgotten how much she loved that sound. The river's strength, the constancy of it.

Her quick visual sweep paused on the sink full of dirty dishes. How odd. Libby was obsessive about keeping everything tidy. Maybe she'd been working more hours than she let on, or maybe they'd had company recently and hadn't had a chance to clean up.

"What's that?" Kennedy frowned, head cocked.

"What's what?"

"I hear something. It sounds like 'shhhhhhhh.'"

"That's the river."

She lifted him up to see the McKenzie from the long kitchen window. The view of the river was still unhindered by curtains, although now, an assortment of hand-painted jelly jars and clay pots had turned the windowsill in to a mini jungle of herbs, succulents, and various plant starts.

A slight movement in the trees beyond the woodshed bench caught Josie's eye, but whatever it was, it disappeared. Probably the latest critter from Gram's menagerie waiting for a handout.

Then she heard a sound, like a cough. She followed it through the dining room, then circled back around to the foot of the stairs.

"Liberty?"

Gram's girlish voice, but faint. And it wasn't coming from upstairs. It sounded closer, like from the room at the end of the hall.

Josie towed Kennedy past the staircase and hung a left toward the parlor—a term she'd never understood since the room had served all sorts of purposes over the years including art studio, indoor terrarium, and library.

She and Kennedy reached the parlor doorway and stopped. In the center of the room, Gram lay on a rollaway cot, dressed in her typical combo of gauzy dress, knobby sweater, and moccasins, with an orange tabby curled up at her side. Her eyes were closed.

"Gram, it's me, Josie." She moved closer to the bed that had taken over the spot where Gram's velvet fainting couch used to be, the one bequeathed to her at the end of her troupe's seven-year run of *A Midsummer Night's Dream*. Her wrinkly face was so pale it nearly matched her paper-white hair, which was flowing freely instead of plaited in her trademark side braid.

Eyes still closed, Gram exhaled slowly. "What angel wakes me from my flow'ry bed?"

"No angel, Gram, it's just me. I'm sorry it took so long. I hit…a slight detour on the way." More like a major close call. A ginormous *Thank You, Jesus*, was probably in order. That launching off the road thing could have ended so much worse.

"What day is it?"

Good question. She checked her phone. "Well, now it's about three a.m. Sunday."

"The gods forbid." She rose to sitting, but it was an effort.

Josie set her bag down, motioned to Kennedy to stay put, and went closer to Gram. "Why is there a bed in here? Are you sick?"

Gram inhaled slowly. "Be a love and help me up."

Josie grasped Gram's arm and helped her to her feet, her features strained. This was new, and Josie didn't like it. "What's going on?"

Gram closed her eyes. "Just some bits and pieces wearing thin, blossom."

From the looks of her, all her bits and pieces had worn thin at once, but Josie kept that to herself. "Have you heard anything from the hospital?"

"Mommy?" Kennedy had suddenly docked at Josie's hip.

Gram's eyes widened.

"Um, Kennedy, this is Gram." Josie had to force her lips to move. "Gram, this is Kennedy, your…" She swallowed, her throat suddenly dry. "Great-grandson."

Time stilled as Gram and Kennedy locked into a slow-mo stare-off.

Josie waited, unable to breathe.

"Surprise!" Kennedy threw his hands up with a triumphant grin.

"Oh!" Gram blinked, then offered him a genuine smile. "Kennedy. Now there's a name I haven't heard in ages. So tragic, that Irish clan and their accursed Camelot. Come closer and let's have a good look at you."

While Kennedy moved closer to Gram, Josie forced herself to breathe, since passing out would probably make things a lot worse.

Gram aimed a confused look at Josie, the curiosity in her raised brow off the chart. Josie felt a tiny prickle of relief. At least Gram had no clue. Libby had given her solemn promise not to tell anyone, including Gram, and Libby was tighter than Fort Knox.

"And what do you do, Sir Kennedy?"

"I fight bad guys."

"Do you ride with the Knights of the Round Table?"

"No, but I have a light saver and a magic tool belt."

"Well, sir. You must tell me of your adventures on the way to the hospital." She reached for a gnarled walking stick that Josie had never seen before and shuffled out of the room.

Josie followed. "Do you need me to grab you some breakfast for later, or a snack, or—"

"No." In the front room, Gram tugged on a crocheted purple hat with an enormous orange flower. "All I need is to be with Liberty."

Josie went out to check on the vehicle situation and *voila*. Her lucky streak was still holding out. Libby's ancient Ford pickup was here, meaning either some kind soul had brought it home, or she had walked to work at the church, which was not uncommon. Either way, Josie didn't have to wait for the tow truck, which was a bonus because she had no idea if her car even ran.

A bonus that Libby would no doubt call a blessing. Well, if it was a blessing from God, it was totally for Libby's sake. The Lord didn't usually bless people who kept their faith in storage like the box of keepsakes Josie toted from town to town that never ended up getting unpacked.

While Gram shuffled out to the pickup, Josie stuffed three apples and a sleeve of Ritz in her duffel. Then they loaded up and hit the road, following the river toward Springfield.

As they made their way west, Gram told her that someone had called her earlier in the evening and said Libby was in the ICU and still unconscious. Gram had brought a fresh change of clothes for Libby in her tapestry bag, insisting clean undies would be the first thing Libby would ask for when she woke up.

Josie nodded but said nothing, because she had no idea if Libby would wake up. Gram was hopeful to a fault, but Josie suspected Gram was going to need that hope in a steady IV.

The winding road had Kennedy conked out between the two women within minutes. Fortunately, the twisty road also meant that

Josie couldn't make eye contact with Gram. She decided to fill the span of travel time with the story of her moon-landing adventure while pretending not to notice Gram's steady gaze boring into her cheek, but even with adding the part about the rude Forest Service Ranger, she was running out of ways to prolong the story.

When Josie hit a ten-second loss for words, Gram made her move.

"As long as you're telling tales, perchance you'll tell the one about your son."

Dang it! She was trapped in the cab of a '79 Ford with the woman who had dealt with Josie's ten-year-old hunger strike by swearing that if Josie was going to die a tragic death, Gram would die alongside her, just like Romeo and Juliet. Aunt Libby had rolled her eyes and called them both drama junkies. Josie had wimped out after a mere twelve hours, right after Libby pulled a batch of homemade cinnamon rolls out of the oven and left them on the counter to cool, filling the house with their evil sweetness. The sly pair could've aced Survivor with an alliance like that. Josie couldn't remember what her tantrum was about. All she could remember was the sinking realization that she would never be able to outwit or outlast those two.

"Somehow, I missed this story." Gram tilted her head to watch the sleeping boy.

Josie took a deep breath. "He's four and a half. He's super smart." She lowered her voice to a whisper, even though what she was about to say wasn't anything Kennedy hadn't heard before. "The father is non-existent. Totally out of the picture. Didn't stick around."

She frowned. Fathers not sticking around was a running snag in this family's tapestry. Nadine and Josie had never known their father. Her grandfather, Peter Buckley, had died young in a logging accident, and since Gram never remarried, Libby and Geraldine had also grown up without a father.

"Where was the noble young knight born?"

"In a hospital."

Gram stared at her. Josie focused on the winding road and pretended not to notice.

"Methinks I see these things with parted eye, when everything seems double."

Josie glanced at her. "That's really about it. End of story."

With a nod, Gram faced ahead, lips pinched. "Elves seldom give unguarded advice, for advice is a dangerous gift, even from the wise to the wise," Gram whispered.

Shoot. "It's not that I don't trust you, it's just…" Ugh. She was so wrecking this. "Things in my life are super complicated right now."

Gram sighed and fixed her gaze on the road.

Heart sinking, Josie stole a glance at Kennedy. "Gram, I need to ask you a huge favor. It's really important." As if holding out on the woman wasn't bad enough; now she was adding insult to injury by asking favors. "I wouldn't ask, but I have no choice."

"What favor?"

"Don't tell—" Her lips clamped. She couldn't say her name. She didn't even want to use the word "sister" in his hearing. He was asleep, but she couldn't even take that chance. "Please don't tell anyone he and I are here. I mean nobody. Can you promise me?"

Gram glanced at Josie. "But rosebud, I already have."

Josie nearly slammed on the brakes. "Who?" she blurted, heart thumping.

"Liberty's reverend. He called to ask if anyone was coming to help us. I told him you were on your way."

Relief rushed through her. Nadine probably wouldn't remember that Libby had started going to church during the twins' senior year of high school. It was highly unlikely that Nadine would ever call or run into Libby's pastor.

"You're sure that's the only person you've told?"

Gram cocked her head and squinted at Josie like she was some strange, new species of beetle she'd never seen before. "Of course I'm sure. I'm not senile."

No, of course not. "And will you promise not to tell anyone else?"

Gram continued her scrutiny. "On one condition, fair maid."

Josie stopped at a four-way and waited, engine idling. When Gram didn't go on, Josie forced herself to glance over. "All right. What's the condition?"

Her grandma's gaze was steady. "Sooner than later, I would like to hear the story about the great-grandson no one told me about."

CHAPTER
-6-

Nothing in life is worse than finding out you're not worth keeping.
—Josie Norris, age 24

Fact: Kennedy Norris weighed twice as much when he was asleep. It probably had something to do with the fact that the kid could eat double his weight in peanut butter toast.

Josie shifted him and his blanket to her other shoulder and leaned back, ignoring the cramp in her neck and the heaviness in her heart. The chairs in the lobby were cold and hard. Maybe because comfort was the last thing people waiting outside ICU were thinking about. Which she could attest to, because all Josie could think about was how wrong it was that Libby was lying in a bed a few feet away fighting for her life, while she and Gram were stuck in the waiting room about as useful as dryer lint.

It was nearly six a.m., and emerging sunlight was coloring the room in shades of rainbow sherbet. Finally, some guy in scrubs came over and asked Josie and Gram to follow him. No news, no update, just come.

Heart in her throat, Josie lifted her sleeping bundle and matched Gram's measured gait down the hall toward the cubicle. It had been around sixteen hours since the accident, although no one could be sure since no one knew how long Libby had lain unconscious in a pool of her own blood.

Josie inhaled sharply, then braced herself for what she'd see.

Inside the cubicle, two women worked near the bed, along with a man in a white coat. Gram let out a gasp that was more of a sob. Josie waited in the doorway with her boy-bundle and let Gram go first. Because whether or not Libby needed her mom, Gram needed to be with Libby.

And because what Josie could see from where she stood made her stomach lurch.

Libby looked like she'd taken a violent beating.

She lay lifeless, with a tube coming out of her mouth and taped to her cheek, her eyes a swollen mass of purple, green, and yellow. Gram held Libby's hand while a nurse worked nearby, jotting on a chart, adjusting the drips and checking beeping equipment. Josie could hear the doctor speaking to Gram, who nodded vaguely as he spoke, but her eyes weren't tracking. With one hand over her mouth, she cried silently and couldn't stop petting her daughter's shoulder.

Poor Gram. She looked so small, so frail. So lost.

Josie came closer. As the doctor continued to fill them in, Josie tried to reconcile this bruised, bandaged stranger with the tall, regal beauty who had raised her. Libby was in a coma, suffering from brain trauma and multiple skull fractures. They had gotten the bleeding to stop but were still trying to control the swelling inside her skull. The doctor said they were doing everything they could, but they needed to prepare themselves. If she survived the next twenty-four hours, she might have a chance. But even if she did, only time would tell the full extent of the damage to her brain.

"She'll get better, now that you're here, Josephine," Gram whispered, tears rolling down her face unchecked. "She needs you."

Josie said nothing, because they both knew that was a lie. Liberty Buckley never needed anyone.

A nurse brought in another chair and helped the three of them squeeze into the corner of Libby's cubicle. Then a sweet lady from the volunteer squad who looked older than Moses brought coloring stuff and snacks, which kept Kennedy occupied for the moment, a good thing because Libby's condition still hadn't changed, and all anyone could do at this point was wait. Gram and Josie hung in a restless, silent limbo while machines did for Libby what her body could not.

God, you know Libby can't die, right? Please, please heal her.

From the chair beside Josie's, Gram sat, gaze fixed on her daughter. "They think she fell all the way down the stairs," Gram whispered. Tears continued to spill from her once-blue eyes, now dulled by age and grief. She wiped them with an embroidered hanky.

Please, God. Libby needs a miracle.

As if God would listen to Josie. But she was hoping he could look past the sinner doing the asking and see the saint in need, the woman who often sang "Just as I Am" while she worked in her garden. The one who had come, late in life, to trust him with all of her being.

When Libby first began attending the little church down the road one spring, she'd tried to get Josie and Nadine to go with her, but of course, since the girls had just turned eighteen and were aiming to finish their senior year on a high note—each in their own very different way—they'd had far more important things to do. Nadine had death-defying stunts to pull. Josie had a 4.0 GPA to maintain, and Nadine to keep alive and out of detention.

Which Nadine made as absolutely difficult as possible.

But eventually, Josie became curious about Libby's newfound faith, began to take note of the changes taking place in her aunt and the quiet peace radiating from somewhere inside her. The glimpses of Someone at work, even in a woman so reserved.

Libby and Josie had discussed the Bible and Jesus and faith a number of times, and that winter, Josie decided to attend a youth camp, where she received Christ as her Savior. But then so soon afterward she moved to Eugene to work and attend college, and then came Kennedy, and then, a life that kept Josie far from home for far too long.

If only we'd had more time.

Josie told herself not to go there, not to cry, not now. It wasn't over, not yet. God could still bring her through.

She glanced at Gram, whose eyelids were drooping. The poor old girl had to be beyond exhausted. Josie didn't even know how Gram was still upright. Josie hadn't slept in 24 hours, and Kennedy's blanket was starting to look mighty good.

But how long this vigil would last was anyone's guess.

Josie hoped Gram wouldn't press for the rest of Kennedy's story. Aside from the need for secrecy, it was just far too complicated. How could she possibly explain to her emotionally fragile grandmother the life she now lived, the shift in the universe that had permanently tilted her world onto this new axis, the race she now ran and the constant focus to stay miles in the lead?

The story of Kennedy began long before the day he was born and placed into his mother's arms. It had begun the day Nadine showed up at Josie's dorm at the beginning of her senior year at U of O. The stark whiteness of her sister's face was even more pronounced by her dyed black hair and the dark hollows beneath her eyes. It was the stricken look in her eyes that had Josie guessing the truth even before her twin spat out the words, *I'm pregnant.*

Josie also understood her sister's anger and frustration over discovering she was pregnant at twenty-two. The jerk that knocked her up had vanished. Neither of the sisters were the motherly type, nor were either of them looking to settle down and do the typical family thing. But even though Josie knew Nadine wasn't interested in having kids, it had come as a shock to find out that she wanted to abort.

Josie told Nadine that she was just angry about being used by some skuzzball, that she wasn't thinking but was responding out of hurt. When Nadine didn't disagree, Josie seized the hesitation and insisted Nadine take some time to think it through, to consider the options. Like going home to Gram's until the baby was born. But Nadine didn't want Gram or Libby to know.

"They have to know, you goob," Josie said. "They'll get over it and they'll be totally supportive."

"Right. Just like they've always been." Nadine crossed her arms tightly around her slender torso, like she suddenly needed to keep herself from flying apart. "That's coming from your vantage point, Jose. We're not the same person. Which you seem to keep forgetting."

"They wouldn't judge you. And I'm sure they'd much rather see you deliver than abort."

Nadine refused to go home to Gram's farm on the river, but she did agree not to go to the clinic and to consider other options.

Relieved, Josie finished the semester and then visited her sister in Albany at Christmas break. Nadine was six months along by that time and working at the Pancake Shack off I-5. She was starting to cave in, but Josie encouraged her to hang in there and finish the race, she could do it, only three more months.

Then a month later, Josie got this text:

CAN'T HANDLE IT ANYMORE. HEADED TO THE CLINIC.

Josie bolted out of class, broke a dozen traffic laws getting to Albany in record time, and met Nadine outside the clinic. She sat her sister down in her Subaru and pointed out that in the span of her entire life, two more months of heartburn and itchy skin was just a tiny speck, a minor disruption. A few more weeks of her life versus someone's entire existence. A temporary situation versus a permanent act that could never be undone. It wasn't that Josie wanted to control Nadine; it was that Josie knew her sister, and in fact, knew her better than anyone, including Nadine. She knew without a shadow of a doubt that Nadine would regret it for the rest of her life if she went through with it. She told her there were lots of good people desperate for a child. She pleaded and promised to help Nadine with the birth and afterward with everything, no matter what direction she chose to go from there. She promised to be there every step of the way, to be her rock.

Finally, Nadine relented and agreed to go full term.

Josie cried in relief all the way back to her dorm. Nadine wasn't able to see it just yet, but Josie could. It wasn't just a bump, it was a person. It was someone. A defenseless someone dependent on the brief inconvenience of another, with nothing to offer in return—yet—except pure potential. Someone not yet able to speak up for himself, to voice his hopes and dreams, to be allowed a choice in his own destiny. Someone who just needed a "reserved" sign placed on the path in life that God already had all planned out for him.

The person her sister carried was someone worth keeping. Worth knowing. And Josie believed that as soon as Nadine saw her baby in all his tiny, sweet perfection, she would totally agree. Idiot that she was, Josie had assumed that being discarded by their own mother had sparked the same empathy in Nadine as it had in Josie. After what they had suffered, how could they not feel a kindred compassion for the unwanted?

But apparently, Nadine hadn't been affected by the fact that she once belonged to a woman who woke up one day and decided her children weren't worth another minute of her time.

When Nadine went into labor on the first of March, Josie was there, sweating right alongside her, and helped deliver a healthy six-pound boy. He was the most beautiful thing Josie had ever seen. She could still remember the powerful awe she felt the moment he was born, could still see his tiny purple face, still hear his gusty little cry. She could still remember falling instantly in love.

She had just finished winter quarter and was one semester away from her degree, but she took a break from school to help Nadine, as promised.

Nadine was a hot mess, naturally, with her hormones ricocheting all over the place, plus she was clueless about babies, especially newborns. But she was rocking it, Josie kept telling her. She stayed with Nadine, and they took turns getting up with him and feeding him, learning how to read his cries. And holy moly, that kid could *cry*. He'd scream for hours sometimes. Nadine couldn't handle it. So Josie focused on staying calm and calling advice nurses and learning how to swaddle him and carry him like a football to soothe his tummy while Nadine went out for "breathers." But the breathers got longer and longer, and by the time Kennedy was two weeks old, Josie was taking care of him 24/7.

What an idiot she'd been to think that Nadine would get the hang of it, would come to feel the same way about her baby that Josie did. How blind she'd been.

Which was probably why, when Nadine announced that she was "done," Josie didn't believe her at first. She figured it was just wacky hormones and exhaustion talking. Because who could touch those perfect little fingers and toes in all their velvety sweetness, see those cheeks and those dark, inquisitive eyes, look at his little face and not fall madly and forever in love?

But Nadine kept saying she'd never wanted to be a mom, wasn't cut out for it, and since Josie was the one responsible for him being here, he was her problem. She turned her two-week old son over to Josie and wanted nothing more to do with him.

Josie withdrew from school and found a cheap apartment. She was already working in graphic design and had all the freelance work she wanted, so she and Kennedy started their new life. Josie worked when he napped. Single motherhood was a major adjustment, but she was already used to taking care of him day and night, and they quickly fell into a routine. It wasn't easy, but they managed, and as he grew, it got easier.

And dummy that she was, Josie kept thinking Nadine would level out at some point and come around. She figured it might take some time, but she held out hope. Josie loved her tiny nephew to pieces but she certainly didn't see this arrangement as permanent. She did have to ask Nadine to sign some papers at the county courthouse giving Josie temporary guardianship so she could take care of his medical stuff, which Nadine wasted no time signing.

And then her sister fell off the grid.

For the next several months, Nadine spun off into a downward spiral. And while Josie hadn't seen or heard from her, she heard from a mutual friend that Nadine looked like death and was totally strung out. Josie didn't believe it at first, until she was downtown one day and caught a glimpse of her. Josie barely recognized her twin. Her hair was bleached to a frazzled crisp, she was skeletal and covered in sores and bruises, and she was flanked by two guys who looked like they'd done hard time.

Later, Libby told Josie that Nadine had come to the farm looking like that, about six months after Kennedy was born. Libby encouraged her to stay and rest, get her strength back. And Libby believed Nadine wanted that. She stayed three days and was trying to detox, but then some "twitchy-looking guys" showed up, and Nadine vanished. They hadn't seen her since.

And then, there was the "mommy" thing, which made everything a whole lot stickier.

It started off innocently enough. Most babies babble the word "mama." It was only natural for Kennedy to call her that. At the time, Josie saw no need to correct him. He was growing and thriving, and she was focusing on getting through each day. She didn't know how long their little dynamic duo would last. She wasn't thinking long term; her only thought was to get through the first few weeks and months. They were managing, and she didn't want to rock the boat.

But then the months went on and on. By the time he was nearing his first birthday and it occurred to her that she needed to correct what he was calling her, things suddenly got way more complicated.

After nearly a year with no word from Nadine, she started calling out of the blue. The first time she called, she was stoned out of her mind. She spewed hateful things that made no sense. And she called a few more times, more of the same. When Josie stopped answering, Nadine started leaving messages. Weird, awful messages, like how Josie had totally ruined her life and how someday soon, she was going to find out just how much. One message said she and her boyfriend were going to take Kennedy somewhere for his first birthday—like to a carnival, get him some ice cream and cotton candy. Josie called back and told her she could come, and she and Nadine could take him somewhere, but the boyfriend wasn't invited.

Nadine cussed her out and hung up.

Then she called again on his birthday, barely coherent, wanting to FaceTime him. Josie told her to call back when she was sober. She swore she was going to steal the baby and that Josie would never see him again. That was when Josie realized she was dealing with something deeper than intoxication or even addiction. Nadine was mentally unstable, irrational, and clearly a danger to herself and to Kennedy.

While Nadine had become unstable, Josie had changed as well. She was no longer filling a role or playing a part—she had settled firmly into motherhood. First, it had been out of necessity, to raise and nurture the child. But by the time Kennedy was eighteen months old, everything had changed. She had started off as his stand-in mama, but now, in both her eyes and especially in Kennedy's, she was "Mommy."

By the time Kennedy was two, Josie was living on high alert, and life was growing increasingly tense. She kept him away from public places and was highly aware of anyone taking an interest in him. Until Nadine got sober and got her head on straight, Josie didn't want Kennedy exposed to her. She had no idea what was going on with Nadine, or why, or who she was with, or how long it would last.

As it turned out, months would pass without a hint of Nadine, and then Josie would get another message threatening to take him, or she'd see some sketchy-looking guy lurking around the neighborhood. Charlon, a grocery checker in Ogden, Utah, had told her some strange people were asking specific questions about Kennedy. And if Nadine's friends were the kind of people Josie suspected they were, they were capable of abducting a child. She moved whenever she felt they were being watched or followed.

Once Libby asked why Josie hadn't involved the police, or tried to get custody.

Josie struggled with these questions a lot more than she cared to admit. Josie could hardly explain it, but Nadine had always been and always would be a part of her. Growing up, Josie had always looked out for her. For as long as she could remember, Josie had felt a deep sense of responsibility for her sister. No matter what Nadine did, Josie could never get her into trouble. She simply couldn't. Besides, Nadine wasn't technically doing anything illegal.

Custody would have involved investigating Nadine, and Josie couldn't bring herself to do that. It hadn't been an issue, in the beginning. Nadine had given temporary guardianship, which was all Josie wanted at the time, and only out of necessity. At twenty-three, neither of them had given a single thought to doing anything permanent or legal; there had been no need. Legal terms had always been for grumpy, bored adults. It was only going to be temporary—at least, in Josie's mind.

But when things became complicated, and ugly, and then downright dangerous, everything changed. As critical as it was to protect the boy from physical harm, Josie was even more determined to protect him from emotional damage. So determined, in fact, that she was willing to live a lie. Which was wrong, she knew. Lying to a child and everyone she met was surely a sin. But she had a good reason. If God insisted on punishing her for the lie, she was willing to pay the penalty.

Josie had become singularly focused on protecting him until he could handle the painful truth, at some later time when it might not so badly scar him and rob him of his self-confidence and self-worth. Someday. Like when he was fifty, maybe.

"You'll know when the time is right," Libby had once told her over the phone.

But that was just it. Was there even such a thing as a right time?

So, Ken, is now *a good time to tell you that your mom tried to do away with you, not once but three times, and when you finally arrived, she couldn't get rid of you fast enough?*

There was no way Josie could let Kennedy go through life messed up as she had been, constantly questioning his worth. Wondering what was so defective that his own mother didn't want him. Spending decades convinced there was something lacking or terribly wrong with him.

Tears snuck down Josie's cheeks. She swiped at them, thankful Gram was still dozing in the chair beside her. The whole thing was a train wreck, Josie was well aware. She knew she was lying to a trusting child. She was a liar, a fake.

But she also knew to the core of her being that nothing in life was worse than finding out you weren't worth keeping.

CHAPTER
-7-

My mother hasn't eaten meat in years. Asking her to eat meat would be like asking her to boil one of her cats. Or vote Republican.
—Liberty Buckley, age 34

As Josie scrolled through stock photos on her phone for an upcoming design project, it occurred to her that maybe it was a good thing, in a backhanded way, that she knew what it felt like to be discarded. She understood all the sucky ways the truth could wreck Kennedy. In someone else's care, Kennedy might not have been protected half as well.

Fact: One person's baggage could be someone else's blessing.

Meanwhile, Gram seemed to be enjoying the novelty of being a great-grandma and was apparently making up for lost time. Josie had grabbed some breakfast from the cafeteria and brought it up to Gram and Kennedy out in the waiting room, where Gram promptly challenged Kennedy to an oatmeal duel.

Josie bit back a smile but said nothing. If Gram thought Kennedy was one of those kids who needed to be coaxed to eat, she was in for another shock. The child could easily eat his oatmeal and hers, plus a side of beef.

Libby's doctor came through on his rounds and reported that while she was still in a coma, she was showing signs of improvement, which was nothing short of miraculous. That was the actual word he used, miraculous. She was still unconscious, but the brain bleed was under control, and the internal swelling had not only stopped, but was beginning to recede.

Gram had some questions for the doctor, and Josie pretended to listen, but she was still processing what the doctor said, particularly how surprised he was about her remarkable turnaround.

This was good. Libby wasn't awake, but she was healing.

Okay, God. I'm totally crediting this one to You. Thank You. Thank You!

That evening, after getting dinner in the cafeteria, Josie, Gram, and Kennedy returned to Libby's cubicle and found her much less purple, and her eyes were now slightly open.

"Liberty?" Gram hurried to her side, took her hand, and rubbed it.

"She has begun responding to stimulus," the nurse said, smiling. "They'll do more tests to assess the damage and her brain function. But this is good. She can't speak, but we think she can see a little, and hear."

"She can't talk?" Josie asked. "Is that permanent?"

The nurse shrugged. "With brain injuries, it's difficult to say. There is a lot we don't know, but we do know that she is semi-conscious. Go ahead, talk to her. It's actually helpful, speeds up healing of the brain."

Gram stroked Libby's cheek tenderly and spoke softly to her, while Josie remembered her manners and thanked the nurse.

Kennedy tugged on Josie's sleeve and whispered, "What's that lady doing?"

Josie watched the nurse's activity. "She's giving Aunt Libby an IV. It's a sack of liquid hooked up to a tube in her arm that gives her food and water. And that's how they give her medicine."

He frowned at the IV, clearly disturbed. "It looks like water."

"Well, not exactly food, but it's stuff she needs."

Alarm filled Kennedy's face. "She can't have real food?"

His tone was so appalled, Josie had to bite her tongue to keep from laughing. Just the urge to laugh brought a small measure of relief. "They have to feed her that way because she can't chew or swallow right now. But if…" She winced and snuck a glance at Libby, wishing she could take that last word back. "When she gets better, then she can have all the food she wants."

She *had* to get better.

He was still frowning at the IV, shaking his head slowly. "I would not like that."

"No," Josie chuckled. "I'm pretty sure you wouldn't."

Gram motioned them over. "Come, come, noble knights and fair maidens. Let us sing to our beloved lady. Music calms the beast and heals the soul." Poor Gram. She looked more hopeful than she had since Josie arrived.

Kennedy looked at Libby's half-mast eyes and pinned himself to Josie's side, shaking his head slowly.

"Maybe we could talk to her," Josie said. "Tell her what we had for dinner."

"Bad idea, Mommy."

"Why?"

He shot her a wide-eyed look and pointed at the IV, lips pressed tight.

Josie smacked her forehead. "Yikes! You're right! What was I thinking?"

Gram smiled, her eyes shining. "It sounds like she's out of the woods."

"Woods?" Kennedy peered at Libby with sudden admiration. "Did she fight a grizzly bear?" He moved closer, and Josie followed.

"Sing to her, Josephine," Gram said. "She always loved your singing."

Since when? Gram must have been brewing tea from the wrong kind of mushrooms again. But then, singing to her probably couldn't hurt.

Josie leaned close and took Libby's free hand. *I'm going waaay out on a limb here, Libby. I sure hope you appreciate this.* She scratched around in her brain for the words to one of her aunt's favorite hymns. Cleared her throat. Felt self-conscious and hopeful and nauseous all at once.

"Just as I am, without one plea," she started, her voice rusty. "But that Thy blood…was shed for me…"

Gram massaged Libby's arm while Josie studied her aunt's face, trying to remember the next line.

"And that Thou bid'st me…come to Thee, oh Lamb…of God, I come. I come."

There wasn't a single sound except the steady blip of monitors.

"That's all I can remember, Libby." Josie leaned closer to her aunt and spoke into her ear. "You're going to have to help me with the rest." She didn't move. Not even a blink.

"Well, you know, not right this minute. But next time, I expect you to sing."

It was probably just her imagination, but Josie thought she could hear extra pressure in Libby's exhale. As if to say singing sounded like a monster task, but she'd give it a try.

Or not. But Josie was taking it all the same.

The next few days merged into a blur of waiting, praying, and waiting some more. On Tuesday, her old Subaru finally arrived via tow-truck. It was a little banged up and sporting some wicked scrapes from the moon landing, but, as luck had it, the engine ran just fine.

Now that Libby was breathing on her own, and now that Josie had a vehicle that didn't burn through more fuel than a 747, the three of them slept at Gram's and made the hour-long commute to the hospital and back each day.

The downside: days of driving and hanging out in a hospital was giving Kennedy a serious case of the whines.

And then there was Gram.

Josie knew Gwennie Buckley was getting old, but she wasn't prepared for how slow she moved now, and how easily she tired. Of course, Josie hadn't been around in a while, but still. It was rude to age that much while people were away. As best they could, Kennedy and Josie helped Gram catch up on chores around the house and in Libby's garden. Dishes and laundry had already piled up, plus they needed to make some portable meals since neither of the women could take one more day of cafeteria food. And they stank. She and Kennedy didn't have a lot of clothes, so she laundered at night.

On Thursday, Gram noticed Josie's limited wardrobe and suggested that she borrow some of Libby's clothes. This seemed reasonable—

in theory—but the minute Josie opened her aunt's closet, something about what she was doing hit her all kinds of wrong and she burst out crying. And it wasn't because five-foot-nine Libby's jeans were five inches too long for Josie. It was the idea that Libby wasn't here wearing them herself. Wasn't in the garden showing Kennedy how to harvest cucumbers.

Wasn't conscious.

Which probably explained why Josie was crying in Libby's closet.

She wiped her eyes, sucked in a deep breath, then reached to close the folding door, but something caught her eye: a stack of thin, matching notebooks on a small built-in shelf.

She pulled one out.

It looked like a small ledger, musty-smelling and worn around the edges.

She opened it, and the first page was inscribed with the date September 7, 1996.

Odd—that was around the time Nadine and Josie had come here to live.

Flipping through the book, she saw that the pages were full of handwritten sections, each one beginning with a date. She pulled out the other notebooks and it occurred to her that they were an ongoing series of dated ledgers. All in Libby's elegant cursive.

She opened the first page of the first book again and read:

September 7, 1996

Dear Diary,

This is stupid. I haven't kept a diary since I was ten. But Mom insists that we—meaning ME—keep a journal in case the latest drama with my sister becomes our new normal and the twins end up staying a while. Because I have a really bad feeling that the four of us have just seen the last of Geraldine Norris...

Josie let out a sharp gasp. This was no ledger—it was Libby's personal diary.

And just what do you think you're doing, young lady? Josie could almost hear Libby saying over her shoulder.

Fumbling, she stuffed the notebooks back on the shelf.

Libby kept a diary? And not just one, but a series? Josie never saw her writing in them, at least, not that she was aware of. She couldn't picture her doing anything like that.

Which made Josie wonder just how well she even knew her aunt.

She glanced at the notebooks. Tried to ignore the fact that the answers to all her unanswered questions were probably in there. Just sitting there waiting to be read.

She stepped out the doorway of Libby's bedroom and listened. Gram and Kennedy were downstairs in the kitchen packing a lunch and discussing the IQ level of pigs and how some humans could be trained to understand them.

Pulse quickening, Josie stepped back inside the closet and slipped the first notebook out again, but then stopped. It was strange, but here, in this room, she could somehow feel Libby's presence even more than when she was with her at the hospital. It was like Coma Libby was just a shell. Her real essence was *here*.

With a sigh, she slid the volume back in place and left.

Libby was making slow but steady improvements, surprising the medical staff. She could swallow liquids and was moving her arms and legs. Her eyes were fully open, and she could look around. It was hard to tell what or who she recognized, if anything, but at times, she seemed to be focused on the three of them. She made motions with her hands. She muttered. Not words anyone recognized, but clearly, she was trying to form speech. As bizarre and uncharacteristic as this behavior seemed, the nurses said this was a very good sign. Josie and Gram could only trust them and hold onto this hope, because it was all they had.

On Thursday, Pastor Dennis from Libby's church stopped by the hospital to pray for Libby—a "real" prayer, thank the Lord—which lifted a burden Josie didn't even realize she was carrying. Now, Libby would be getting legit prayers by someone who actually had any business talking to God.

Later that evening, Gram handed Josie an envelope.

"What's this?" It was addressed to Josie at her old address in Utah, which had been crossed out and forwarded to McKenzie Bridge.

"I found it in my cookbook. I'm sorry, rosebud, but someone called looking for you, oh it's been ages now. Some kind soul in Utah. Your landlord, I think. She said this came in the mail and looked important, so I told her to send it here. I stuck it in a cookbook and alas, there it stayed."

The return address read *Domestic Relations Unit, Lane County Circuit Court.* And the postmark was dated almost a year ago.

Josie racked her brain. The last time she'd had any contact with Lane County, it was to try to get them to change her temporary guardian status to permanent. Maybe they'd finally gotten it changed.

She ripped open the envelope, hoping the judge hadn't changed his mind since it had been sent so long ago. She pulled out the pages and scanned through the legal mumbo jumbo, confused, then stunned.

The letter was not about granting her permanent guardianship. Apparently, Nadine had formally filed to terminate Josie's guardianship altogether.

She let out a snort. Fat chance. Nadine's history would be more than enough to tip off any judge to deny such a request. But then maybe the court didn't know that Nadine was crafty and shouldn't be trusted, or that her on-again-off-again interest in her child was not a factor that Kennedy needed in his life. At all. Or that Nadine had a habit of falling in with scary, ruthless people who were willing to kidnap a baby when Nadine was in one of her *Okay, Now I Want Him* manic moments. Or that Nadine had a habit of going back to people who probably hurt her.

Plus, Nadine didn't even know the child.

Clearly, she would never be granted such a request.

Josie was about to toss it in the trash, but caught a line about "hearing" and "to confirm the welfare of the child" and read on. A date had been set for an in-chambers meeting so that the judge could hear facts and then grant or deny Nadine's request. That date had long ago come and gone.

And she hadn't known, so she hadn't shown.

Well, it wasn't like actual court, or they would have served her a summons or something.

Right?

But even so, not showing up for a judge—even if you didn't know about it—did not sound good.

"Did you get any other mail for me? Anything else like this?" Josie asked.

"Hmm?" Gram shook her head. "No, just the one."

Josie nodded. Well, no sense stressing about something that long past.

Six days after the accident, the doc was confident that Libby was stable enough to move to a rehab facility where she could begin occupational therapy.

Fortunately, Riverbend Care Home was not only a reputable nursing and memory care facility, it was less than a mile from the Buckley farm. Which was a huge relief. Because while Libby's progress was good, the travel back and forth was taking a toll on Gram's strength. Josie suspected that sheer adrenaline alone was what had kept Gram going the first few days, because now that Libby was out of danger and showing signs of improvement, Gram suddenly looked pale and depleted.

Josie asked her how long this *wearing thin* thing had been going on. Gram sighed and mentioned her age again. Josie wasn't sure if age was the whole issue. But then, what did she know? She'd never been eighty.

The weird thing was, since Josie had been home, she had discovered something odd about Gram. Well, something more than her normal odd. Because in the fourteen years she had lived at the Buckley farm, Gram had always done kooky stuff, like conversing with plants and stepping around tree roots. She was widely known for rescuing critters of every kind and was notorious for picking up spiders—in her *hands*. Once, when Josie was a teen, she bumped into Gram as she was carrying a hairy spawn of Satan outside. Josie had hyperventilated and passed out.

She was used to Gram's peculiarities—her Spiderwoman thing topping the list—but now, she noticed that Gram would sometimes disappear for a while, and when Josie asked where she went, Gram said she was just stretching her legs.

One night, Gram had been out "stretching" for nearly an hour.

Kennedy was asleep, so Josie went outside and searched for her around the house and garden. There was no sign of Gram anywhere, so she crossed the yard and headed for the barn. The door was ajar. Before she reached it, she could hear someone speaking in low, hushed tones. Weird. Gram had always been known to talk to herself. And she always had at least a dozen feral cats at any given time. She was always stressing out over their litters. She was probably in there with them now, discussing family planning.

Gram stepped out of the barn and saw Josie. "Oh!" She poked the door shut with her walking stick and backed up against it. "Good heavens, rosebud. What are you doing out here?"

Josie's brows lifted. "Looking for you. You've been gone a while, and I was starting to, you know, worry." *Since you keep reminding me of your age.* Josie craned her neck, listening. "Who were you talking to?"

"Talking?" Gram's eyes rounded.

"Yeah, I thought I heard someone talking."

"Oh. I was just singing."

Gwendolyn Buckley could perform Shakespeare without missing a beat, but she couldn't lie to save her life.

Josie listened some more, not at all sure what she hoped to hear. Something? Nothing? Did she dare give voice to the fear churning in her gut?

"Gram, you'd tell me if Nadine had come around, wouldn't you?"

"Of course." The old woman took hold of Josie's elbow like a dinner escort and steered her toward the house, leaning heavily on her arm. "'What's gone and what's past help should be past grief.'"

"*Macbeth?*"

"*The Winter's Tale.*"

Josie sighed. She could never keep those plays straight.

As they trudged back to the house, the scent of river algae wafted across the path, and for a second, Josie thought she heard whispering. A shudder traveled down her spine.

CHAPTER
-8-

*I rescue every creature I meet because I can't bear
to lose another living soul.*
—Gwendolyn Buckley, age 61

Early Saturday morning, Gram, Josie, and Kennedy headed over to visit Libby at Riverbend, which was located exactly where you'd think: at a bend in the river. The first thing Josie noticed, besides how much better Libby looked, was that her room had a window overlooking the McKenzie. Libby, much less swollen now and nearly normal in color, looked comfortable and seemed to be asleep, although brain trauma had taught Josie that looks could be deceiving.

On the other side of the room, a lumpy quilt covered another twin bed. The wall above it displayed what looked like family picture collages and a child's work of art. The walls above Libby's bed were bare, of course. There was no telling if Libby would be at the facility long enough to bring in pictures, but Josie was praying for her speedy recovery. Because the sooner Libby came home, the sooner everything could return to normal, and the sooner Josie and Kennedy could move on and avoid her sister. While Nadine hadn't been around in a while, Josie wasn't taking any chances.

While Gram settled into a chair near Libby, a grim-faced Kennedy stood at the foot of the bed, surveying the room. Probably bracing himself for more long days of hospital prison.

"If you're thinking about poking me, you better think again."

Kennedy and Josie stared across the room at the other bed, which was producing a really good imitation of Minnie Mouse.

"I'm a lot stronger than I look," Minnie went on.

On closer look, the lumpy quilt was concealing a tiny person.

Libby mumbled something.

Gram leaned in, and Josie stepped closer to her aunt to hear. Once in a while, Libby would say a word or two that they understood, but today, she was just mumbling.

Kennedy plopped down on the end of Libby's bed and emptied his pockets of a large cache of Hot Wheels.

"Shog-gun," Libby muttered.

Gram bent closer. "Liberty? Can you hear me?"

"Beagle." Libby's eyes were still closed, but she was frowning slightly.

"She wants a bagel," Kennedy said, lips pursed. "Prob'ly cuz she's starving."

A gloved nurse in a flowered smock came in with a glass and a little paper cup. She smiled at the three of them, then went to the other bed and pulled the cover back.

The tiny occupant turned toward the wall.

"Oh, come on, Miss Ellie. It's such a beautiful day. Let's not start it off like this."

Minnie Mouse didn't budge.

Josie glanced at Gram, but she was preoccupied with Libby's muttering, which still made zero sense.

"Miss Ellie."

"Nope," Miss Ellie squeaked.

"Sweetie, you know I have to give you your meds," the nurse said.

"Don't sweetie me." The tiny woman yanked the quilt over her head.

"Please? If you'll take this now, we could get it over with and save him a trip."

A long string of muttering came from beneath the blanket.

"What's that?"

"And same goes for all those other bingo-pushers." Miss Ellie's teeny voice had risen. If she was going for intimidating, she was actually having the opposite effect.

Kennedy giggled.

The nurse heaved a sigh. "All right, Eleanor. Have it your way." She took the items and left, shaking her head as she passed by Libby's bed.

Libby moaned.

Gram glanced at Josie, her look troubled. "Do you think she's in pain?"

Josie leaned down and examined Libby's features. "I don't know, Gram. I hope not."

"I do wish she could tell us." Gram stroked Libby's cheek.

Josie powered up her laptop, while Kennedy made roads for his cars in the wrinkle-folds of Libby's blankets. Josie wasn't sure how Libby would feel about that but had to weigh her options and immediate needs. Keeping Kennedy happily occupied scored higher at the moment than Libby's thing for tidiness.

While Gram read Dickens to Libby, Josie worked on the second draft of a new design, applying the client's latest feedback. It was a logo for a counseling clinic specializing in child psychology, and while Josie worked, she pressed down a familiar twinge in her gut.

What would a child psychologist say about the way Josie was raising Kennedy? She was pretty sure that dragging a kid all over the place like a refugee was frowned upon by the juvenile mental health community. It wasn't like Josie wanted to live this way. It was for his greater good.

But her stomach knotted again as she scrolled through photos of happy little kids at play. Kennedy had no friends. What if she was ruining his life? She had to protect him from emotional damage, but what if she was just exchanging one injury for another?

Which brought up the other nagging issue she could never shake.

Good moms didn't lie to their kids.

Josie watched Kennedy spin a tiny airplane in the air. She was pretty sure that lying was a sin. How big a sin, though? And did it matter if you had a good reason?

She had once asked Libby if God would judge her for lying to Kennedy, or if he understood that she had no choice. Libby of course said she couldn't answer for God, that was something Josie would have to discuss with him herself. But she did point out that God was usually better at his job than Josie was, and that when our plans didn't match his, we could assume that his plan was the better of the two, always.

Josie wanted to trust God, but she didn't trust Nadine. Not for a minute.

She tried to focus on her work, but the twisty feeling in her gut would not let up. How did all those cool, confident moms Josie saw at the park choose between what was right and what was best for their child? And how did they live with their choices without constantly worrying or second-guessing themselves?

If you were his real mom, you'd know the answer to that.

Kennedy climbed up on Gram's lap as she read and watched her lips move, fascinated. Josie watched them and reminded herself—again—that she had good reasons for the choices she'd made. But no matter how good her reasons were, she still couldn't shake that relentless sense of guilt.

"So, Grandma, what's this I hear about you giving Ashley a hard time?"

Startled by the familiar male voice, Josie turned.

Ranger McKnight, in uniform, was heading for the other bed, a small grocery bag in hand. He stopped short when he saw Josie. "Oh, sorry, I didn't—"

"Ranger McNugget!" Kennedy hopped down and ran to the officer. "Remember me?"

"Hey, Captain America." He smiled at him, then nodded at Josie. "Hello, again."

She smiled and forced her tongue to work. "Hi."

And there they were again—those eyes that could make a girl forget her name. In the light of day, their color was even richer, warmer. Like molten caramel. How inconvenient.

"I hope things turned out okay with your car." He had a deep, rumbling kind of voice that messed with Josie's ability to focus. Definitely inconvenient.

"Oh!" Gram blurted. "Speak again, bright angel! For thou art as glorious to this night, being o'er my head as is a winged messenger of heaven!"

Josie shot a death glare at Gram, who was totally oblivious to the warning, then turned to the Ranger. "Yeah, I got it back. Sadly, its beauty pageant days are over, but it still runs like a tank. Thanks again for arranging the tow, and for the ride home."

"No problem."

The covers on the other bed flipped open and Miss Ellie sat up, her stiff, white hair standing in twenty different directions. She saw the uniformed officer and her jaw dropped. "Did pansy pants call the cops on me again?"

"No, Grandma, it's me, Will. How are you doing?"

She shook her head, arms crossed. "I'm going to need to see some ID."

With a sigh, he pulled out his wallet and showed it to her. She eyeballed him, and then the bag in his hand. Her brow creased with worry. "What's that for? You're not trying to shanghai me, are you?"

"No, ma'am." He chuckled. "It's just a little Ben & Jerry's." He pulled a half-pint carton from the grocery bag bearing the name *Wally's Mini-Mart*.

Ellie's tongue darted out, wetting her lips. "Chunky Monkey?"

The Ranger smiled. "As a matter of fact, it is."

The old woman studied him. "Well, if you're going to bring that on this school bus, I sure hope you brought enough to share."

He glanced at his watch and then sat on the edge of her bed. He pulled the spurned medicine cup from his pocket. "I'd be happy to share, right after you take your medicine."

Ellie's brow furrowed. "Is your name Keith?"

Will shook his head slowly. "No, ma'am. I'm Will. Keith was my dad, your son."

"Where is he? He was supposed to bring me a milkshake."

"He's, uh." Will winced, seemed to be searching for words. "He can't come today, Grandma, so he sent me."

She nodded. "Well, that's okay. He's probably out on a forest fire. Okay, Columbo, pass me those pills. These kids need to get to school." She tossed back the medicine and chased it with water. "Now, what about that ice cream?"

With a chuckle, Will pulled a plastic spoon out of his uniform vest pocket.

As he offered her a scoop, Kennedy whipped around and shot Josie a wide-eyed look she could only guess meant *ice cream for breakfast?*

"Willie," Ellie mumbled around a mouthful of ice cream, "Why in heaven's name are you dressed like that?"

"I was on my way to work when your nurse called me."

She frowned. "Well, just between us, my roommate over there is a showgirl." She nodded toward Libby's bed. "From Vegas. She's had a little trouble with the law, if you get my drift. If you're going to come aboard this bus, you'd better play it cool."

"I'll play it cool, Grandma, but if you'll take your meds without a fight, then I won't have to come here while I'm on duty. Deal?"

Eleanor's gaze narrowed.

Will offered her another scoop with a wink at Kennedy, then he glanced at Josie, who suddenly realized she was full-on staring.

Awesome.

She yanked her attention to Libby.

Fact: Josie's life had zero room for romance.

Nadine stood across the river like a zombie, staring at Josie. Then she beckoned her to come across.

Josie's heart raced. *How?* she shouted above the roar of rushing water.

Nadine didn't answer, just kept beckoning.

Are you crazy? Josie could hear the break in her voice, the fear. *I can't swim across this!*

Her twin pointed west, at something downstream.

Josie followed her gaze and saw the covered bridge. *Why should I?*

Nadine folded her skinny arms tight and glared at Josie, her honey-blonde hair dyed inky-black and covering half her face like a curtain. The river was so powerful, Josie could feel the current from where she stood on the bank, shaking the ground with its roaring strength.

Her sister beckoned again.

What do you want from me? Josie shouted.

Nadine glared at her, then turned and disappeared into the woods beyond the river.

Josie tried to call out, tell her to come back, but she couldn't say her name—

"Mommy. Mommy. MO-meeeeeeee."

Josie woke with a jolt. Kennedy was bathing her face in moist, warm boy breath.

Where was she?

It took a second to remember she was at Gram and Libby's, sleeping on her old bottom bunk. The ground-shaking in her dream was probably Kennedy climbing down from the bunk above, Nadine's old bed. He was just standing there now, one brow high, one low, and rocking an impressive case of bedhead.

"What?"

"You were going, 'Deennneeeeee!' That was weird."

"Oh, sorry." She snagged her lower lip in her teeth. *Deenie* was a nickname for Nadine that she hadn't used in nearly two decades. And definitely not since high school when Nadine was on her *Amputate Josie* campaign.

So now Josie was sleep-talking. Awesome. As soon as Libby was recovered enough to function, Josie needed to get away from this place, from the memories. They were too real. Too three-dimensional. This place was so full of Nadine, it felt like she could reach out and touch her.

Half an hour later, as Josie and Kennedy were cleaning up their breakfast dishes, Gram came in from the parlor and joined them. She waved away the oatmeal Josie offered, which was unfortunate, because it looked like she could definitely use it. Actually, Gram was so thin, what she really needed was a quarter-pounder with extra cheese. But all Gram wanted was her nasty tea, which she brewed in a black kettle. Josie fought the urge to ask Gram if she got the recipe from Macbeth. The smell alone made her want to hurl. She had no clue what went in it, and quite honestly, was afraid to ask.

Josie gathered her laptop, water bottle, and snagged some snacks for the day, while Gram and Kennedy went outside to pick apples and pears from the trees, and water the plants and critters and whatever other wild thing Gram was convinced couldn't survive half a day on its own.

Josie took her bag out to the car and then halted in her tracks.

A small pig wearing an inverted cone around his head ran past her and disappeared into the shed.

"Romeo? Romeo!" Gram was trying to catch it but could barely walk herself, much less keep up with a speedy little swine. She saw Josie and stopped to lean on her stick, flushed and breathing hard. "Oh, rosebud…the cone of shame is…too cruel a punishment. He hides himself away all day long. I told Liberty it will…crush his little spirit, but the vet…insists he keep it on." She shook her head, took a deep breath. "Poor fellow! I've never seen him so distraught." She tottered toward the shed, still calling out to the runaway Romeo.

Josie took a quick glance around the property fully expecting to see a snout-nosed Juliet, but no such damsel appeared.

Once Josie had everything they needed stowed in the Subaru, she waited for her boy and his great-grandmother to feed the koi in the tiny pond. Kennedy was loving the farm—no surprise. And he was enjoying being Gram's right-hand man.

He saw Josie and ran to her with a big grin. "I did a mission," he said, looking all pleased with himself. "It was top-secret."

"Way to go. What was it?"

He frowned, clearly offended. "Don't you know what top-secret means?"

"Okay, so you were just taunting me."

His frown deepened. "What's that mean?"

"You come up bragging about your secret mission so I'll be all dying to know what it is, and then you don't even tell me. That's taunting."

"Oh." His grin stretched to reveal a perfect row of baby teeth. "Yeah. I'm taunting."

"Whatever." Josie reached out to tousle his hair, but he tried to duck out of reach, so she lunged and caught him, then tickled the daylights out of him until he begged for mercy.

That'd teach him.

As the three of them walked down the corridor to Libby's room, they could hear her speaking loudly, like she was telling someone a story, but Josie knew she wasn't talking to her roommate, because they passed Miss Ellie in the main room where other residents were watching TV.

When they entered Libby's room, she was chattering away to no one. As they moved into her line of sight, the stream of her narrative shifted.

"And then a small man with a backpack walked by…on his way to the zoo…"

Kennedy hesitated, then shrugged off his backpack full of toys slowly, watching Libby.

"He took off his parachute. He was…" She sighed. "A circus monkey."

He spun back to Josie, eyes alight. "She's making up a story about me."

"Skipperrrr. Giiiiiilligan," Libby murmured, closing her eyes.

Gram gave Josie a worried look. They'd been told Libby's rambling was due to the scramble her brain took when she hit her head, and that this increased verbalization was a sign of progress, but still, it was so odd. Josie was trying to reconcile the stoic, no-nonsense Libby she'd known all her life with the goofy woman lying in this bed. New Libby chuckled and jabbered, two things Old Libby would never do.

What no one could tell them was if Libby would return to normal and how long that would take, or if this version of Libby was her new normal. Medical staff had told them that brain injuries are complex and extremely varied, making the time and the extent of recovery impossible to project. So all they could do was wait, engage her, talk to her when she was awake, read to her. Gram brought the book Libby was reading before the accident, a novel by her favorite author, Francine Rivers.

"Oh, look, Josephine—a radio!" Gram pointed to a boom box on the bureau. "We could bring Liberty's favorite music."

"Josephine?" Libby said faintly.

Josie's breath caught. She leaned forward. "Hi, Aunt Libby. I'm right here."

"Right here," she echoed softly. She heaved a sigh and closed her eyes. "Forgive your sister."

Josie froze.

Gram leaned close and took her daughter's hand. "It's okay. Shh now, baby girl."

Libby nodded. "Baby."

Concern crossed Gram's face. She fiddled with the tip of her braid and glanced at Josie.

"Mama, go get Daddy's shotgun."

What? Josie stole a glance at Kennedy who was setting out LEGO blocks, oblivious.

"He's coming."

"Oh!" Gram said, eyes wide. "No, no, all is well, dearest love. You're safe."

"Safe." Libby inhaled, relaxed.

Josie forced her shoulders down, willed away the tension in her neck.

"We made blackberry jam," Libby said, suddenly eyeing her mother.

Gram patted Libby's hand. "Yes. We had so much we took some to Dr. Jenson to pay down our bill, and we also bartered with Farmer Reynolds for a big crock of butter. Do you remember?"

"Butter," Libby muttered. "We picked a ton of berries."

Josie smiled, but her mind drifted. Near the end of summer every year, she and Nadine would pick buckets of the wild blackberries that grew along the road. And now, the warm September air was thick with the scent of them, the sweet, cloying aroma of ripe, smashed berries baking into the hot asphalt, taking Josie straight back to childhood.

"We ate more than we picked," Libby murmured.

Josie frowned. Libby didn't pick them—that was Nadine and Josie's job.

Gram cocked her head at Libby. "Yes. You made yourselves sick."

"So sick." Libby let out a groan. "Oh, no…"

"Oh dear. Are you queasy?" Gram felt Libby's forehead.

Josie looked around for a barf pan. She hated puking.

"No more," Libby moaned.

"No more what?" Josie asked. Was she in pain? Should they call the nurse?

"No, please, not again." Libby wept, her face streaming with tears.

Josie's breath caught. She had never seen tears from Libby. Ever.

"Oh, sweet love," Gram sobbed. She lay down on the bed beside Libby and held her, shushing her as if she were a child. "It's over, blossom. Shhh, you're going to be fine, shhh…"

"No…" Libby's voice rose, then she opened her eyes. "Mom?" She looked around her. "What happened? Where am I?"

Gram continued to hold Libby, anguish filling her pallid face. "You're safe now, Liberty."

"What happened? Where is he?" Libby lifted her gaze and caught Josie square in the eye. "Where's the baby? It's not safe here—"

"Whoa, whoa, whoa—" Josie shouted, leaping to her feet. She went to Libby, but what on earth could she do? It wasn't like she could cover her mouth.

She glanced at her boy.

Wide-eyed, Kennedy was staring at all three women, a forgotten action figure in each hand.

CHAPTER
-9-

Oft in lies truth is hidden.
—J. R. R. Tolkien

Later that evening, while Gram kept Kennedy at home, Josie returned to Riverbend and waited while Libby dozed, hoping she would wake up soon and let Josie feed her something, since she hadn't eaten all day. Josie and Gram both agreed that Libby needed their help if she was going to get her strength back. Josie wanted to be on hand providing some extra vigilance, since the staff always seemed to be running and didn't have time to monitor her closely. They'd give Libby an Ensure, if asked, but they didn't have time to sit with her and make sure she ate.

It just wasn't fair. Libby, the one who would move mountains to get the best care possible if it was Josie or Gram in that bed, was now unable to advocate for herself.

Josie also wanted to stick close by for an extra measure of vigilance over Libby's tongue. Libby was talking more now, but wasn't making a lot of sense, and worse, the things she was saying now seemed to be out of her control. What was to keep her from blurting out secrets she wasn't supposed to tell?

God, please heal her, body and mind.

No one had any solid answers. But one thing Josie knew was that she couldn't leave McKenzie Bridge—not yet. Not until she knew Libby was back to herself and on her own two feet. Gram sure didn't have the strength to assist Libby at home. What if she didn't get any better? Would she be in a nursing home indefinitely?

She couldn't think about that possibility, not yet.

Josie wanted to help Gram and Libby, but she also wanted to guard what she had entrusted to Libby until her aunt returned to her right mind. If she ever did.

She *had* to.

But would staying close to Libby mean Kennedy would hear things she didn't want him to hear? All she could do was keep him occupied and hope and pray that didn't happen.

Eyeing her bag, she considered taking out her laptop, but she was in no frame of mind to focus on work. Besides, there was something else in her bag, and it was calling to her.

Who was she kidding? The journal had been beckoning to her like an open bag of M&Ms since she'd first laid eyes on it. Normally, Josie would never dream of reading someone else's diary.

Normally.

But this diary, as far as she could tell, was a chronicle of sorts, an account of the time she and her sister had come to live with Gram and Libby, and well beyond. There were things in there she needed to know—she was sure of it.

Chewing her lower lip, Josie pondered her aunt, then her bag.

Taking a deep breath, she slipped the notebook out and opened it to the first page. She did the math, and at the time of the first entry, Libby would have been thirty-three.

Dear Diary,

This is stupid. I haven't kept a diary since I was ten. But Mom insists that we—meaning ME—keep a journal in case the latest drama with my sister becomes our new normal and the twins end up staying a while. Because I have a really bad feeling that the four of us have just seen the last of Geraldine Norris.

But then again, maybe a journal will be useful. Maybe when they're old enough to handle it, Nadine and Josephine will want to read about the year their mommy dumped them on me and Mom and then split. But that's not really fair, is it? Maybe I could have stopped the demons from chasing my sister off to find the nearest ledge. Maybe.

(I never blamed Ger for what happened. Is it my fault she feels responsible?)

I think Mom is hoping that I'll keep clawing up and out of the hell that's been my life for the past nine years, but what she doesn't understand is that some of the clawing happens on the inside. Some grieving is silent.

"Everyone can master a grief but he that has it."
—William Shakespeare. (Yes, Mom, that one's for you. Right back atcha.)

But maybe this journal can be a way for me to gather little nuggets of joy and store them up for later, like acorns. For the barren winters that never seem to end. Or, maybe, years from now, these ramblings will give me, Mozart, and a half-gallon of merlot a jolly good laugh.
-Libby

Libby moaned, and Josie nearly dropped the journal. She held her breath, but her aunt was still asleep. She could hear *The Andy Griffith Show* blaring in the adjoining room. Actually, anyone within a five-mile radius could hear it—except a good portion of the elderly residents in that room.

Josie glanced at the next dated heading. Just one more, she promised herself. That was it.

November 12, 1996

Dear Diary,

Nadine laughed today. The sound surprised me, partly because I'd never heard it before, and partly because it sounded like a cross between a surfer dude and a chipmunk. And her laugh coaxed a big smile from her sister, although it took Josie a few seconds, as if she had to make sure smiling was okay.

Good heavens, those poor babies.

Then, Mom had to go and make a major production out of it by bringing out a secret stash of marshmallows—which were not even remotely vegan, the hypocrite—and made us gather sticks to roast them in celebration of this "first."

Sheesh. What the girls are sure to remember about this day is the magic of burnt marshmallows, their Gram's girlish giggles, and their Aunt Libby nagging them to brush their teeth. SOMEbody has to keep them from becoming toothless hags. Whatever. I know the girls think I'm the fun police. That's fine. Since Mom clearly isn't planning on being the grown up, the job falls to me.

-Libby

Josie covered a snort, nodding. Okay, this was the Libby she knew. She didn't know who first coined the term "fun police" for their aunt, but Josie and Nadine had used it countless times.

And she remembered the marshmallows, but she didn't remember it being a celebration. She didn't remember that neither she nor her sister had laughed for their first two months at the farm. She couldn't even remember their lives before they came to Gram's. She did vaguely remember clinging to Nadine for weeks and being overwhelmed by the creaky old house, the damp forest smells, the loud river. But before that, she remembered very little. When Josie tried to picture her mother, all she could see was a pale, dark-haired mannequin.

"Must be some fascinating reading," a deep voice said.

With a jerk, Josie fumbled and dropped the book. As she scrambled to retrieve it, she accidentally kicked it even farther away, sending it straight to the feet of Ranger McKnight, dressed in jeans and a T-shirt, hands on hips and barricading the doorway.

The feisty little blonde came toward him for her book, but on impulse, Will scooped it up. He studied it. Plain cover. Some kind of ledger.

Then he looked at her.

Her eyes had gone huge and round, arresting him instantly. He'd never in his life seen eyes like that. Luminous green, like the color of young leaves caught in a shaft of sunlight.

Cheeks aflame, she held out a hand that trembled slightly. "May I have that back, please?"

He studied her flushed face and body language and instantly bristled. She showed all the classic signs of guilt. But then, every female he'd ever known, except maybe his sister, had some moral defect or other in her DNA.

Take a day off, for crying out loud.

He handed the book over. "Since your aunt and my grandma are sharing a room, it looks like we'll be running into each other."

"Lucky me." She held the book close to her chest in her tightly crossed arms.

He frowned. "Okay, listen, I know we got off to a rocky start—"

"Rocky?" She snickered, then turned and stuffed the book into her backpack. "That's clever."

Okay, she was definitely mocking him. And he probably deserved it. "Look, I owe you an apology."

"For...?"

He sighed. "Sometimes, the job gives me tunnel vision. I... shouldn't have assumed you were a looter."

One shoulder lifted in a shrug. "It's okay. I get that a lot." She puffed out a tiny laugh from her nose. "Really, don't worry about it."

His brows rose. "Okay, I just don't want running into me to be a problem for you."

"I don't think that'll be a problem," she said, going slightly pink again. "But it does help that you're not in uniform."

Ah. He nodded, fascinated by the color of her eyes. He really needed to stop staring.

"I was beginning to think it was tattooed on," she added.

It took a second to register what she meant. The uniform. He couldn't help but smile. "Pretty much."

She smiled too, the refreshing kind—full and genuine. No playing coy, no holding back. There was something about this girl. Aside from her clean, unassuming kind of pretty. Maybe it was the spray of freckles across the bridge of her nose. It was like an added touch of authenticity that made her seem straight up. Real.

"Just so you know, my grandma wasn't always the person you see now," he said, glancing at Grandma's empty bed. "She was a teacher, and a pastor's wife for over fifty years, until my grandpa passed away."

"Wow. You don't see that kind of commitment much these days."

"True."

"Check," the woman in the bed murmured. "Your move."

Apparently, the green-eyed girl's aunt was in a delusional state. At least she was enjoying an imaginary chess game, nothing traumatic. The brain could do weird things. Hopefully, her condition would improve and wouldn't lead to the fear and aggression he'd seen in some of the other memory care patients here. Reasoning with them was challenging enough for staff, and even more for loved ones. It was just one more reminder that life wasn't fair. But then, the job had shown him that the pursuit of justice was an endless uphill battle.

Will studied the niece. This situation with her aunt had to be hard, like being in limbo and trying to hold everything together. He stuck out a hand. "How about a do-over? William McKnight, but everyone calls me Will."

She seemed surprised, then took his hand and smiled. "Josephine Norris, but everyone calls me Josie." She glanced at her aunt. "My aunt Libby is also not the person you see now. She's here for rehab for her brain injury. We don't know how long, or how much she'll recover, or if…" She met his gaze and held it, her eyes glistening. "We're just taking it one day at a time."

"Sorry." He nodded. "That's tough. If there's anything I can do to help, let me know."

She peered into his eyes, clearly surprised by the offer. "That's really nice of you, Will. But you already came to my rescue in the middle of the night. Giving me and Kennedy a ride home was a huge help. Thank you."

"My pleasure. And I think I've met your aunt before."

"Really?"

"I visited her church a couple times when they had a missionary guest. I usually go to the Baptist church in Blue River when I can, if I don't get called in on my day off. Which is pretty often."

She frowned. "Wow, you must work a lot."

"Yeah, especially this time of year. If I get even one day off a week, I'm lucky."

"But you still make time to come here." Josie looked across the room at Grandma's bed. "Your grandma is…"

"A handful, yes, I'm aware."

She giggled. "I was going to say lucky."

He glanced at the collection of photos on the wall and on Grandma's bureau. "Eleanor McKnight was once a very intelligent lady. She taught middle school for forty years before she retired. But dementia has altered her personality a lot. And it affects her health. Her brain and body signals are haywire. She refuses food and water and then hollers in the middle of the night that they're trying to starve her. We have trouble keeping her hydrated, which can be serious, and lead to a sudden decline. She can go comatose within twenty-four hours if we don't catch it."

"Wow. Don't the nurses check on her?"

Will nodded. "They try, but they're super short-staffed. With shift changes and her refusing food or fibbing about what she ate or drank, they can't always keep track."

"So this is where you come in."

"Yeah, literally. I stop by at some point every day to make sure she gets something in her."

Josie's brows rose. "Like Ben and Jerry's."

"With dementia, you pick your battles." He hesitated, gave his tone a chance to lose any trace of defensiveness. "If I can get some calories in her, I don't care what kind they are."

She smiled. "I take it her caregivers don't approve."

He shrugged. "Let's just say if Grandma's protein shake comes in a DQ cup, most of the staff here turns a blind eye."

"Probably because most of the staff here is female—" A hand flew to her mouth, her eyes suddenly huge.

He fought to keep a straight face. Apparently, Josie Norris was transparent to a fault. How interesting. And totally refreshing.

She shook her head, then stammered on, "I mean, they probably know it can't be easy for you, fitting in visits with your work schedule. She's lucky to have you."

"It's what family does." He shrugged again. "You take care of each other."

"In a perfect world, maybe," she said lightly. "Where nobody bails on the vulnerable ones."

Ah. So she'd experienced that, too. It was a feeling he knew all too well.

"Well," he said, slowly, "you came here all the way from Idaho to take care of your family. And here you are now, sitting by your aunt's side." He dipped his head so they were eye level. "I believe my point is made." He smiled.

She stared at him, a dozen mysterious thoughts churning in those luminous eyes.

"Checkmate," Libby murmured.

CHAPTER
-10-

My mother lives in a polite bubble of her own creation. Sometimes, I envy
her for being allowed to escape to her sorrow-free world.
Must be nice to hide from reality.
—Libby Buckley, age 48

It had been eleven days since Libby's accident, and Gram still insisted on being at Libby's side every minute of every day. But even with Libby closer to home, the long days were wearing Gram out. On Josie's insistence, Gram agreed to take turns with Josie and visit on alternate days. That way Gram could get some rest, and Kennedy could spend some time at home and outside.

Oddly enough, Kennedy wasn't hating the nursing home now. On Tuesday, Josie had caught Miss Ellie teaching him names he could use on "stinky" people. One of the nurses told Josie that people with dementia have to make up names for people because they can't remember actual names. It was the brain's way of dealing with broken memory paths. But Josie wasn't sure poor memory was the only reason Eleanor made up names for people. She and Kennedy were getting way too big a kick out of calling Josie *Bossy Britches*.

On Thursday, it was Josie and Kennedy's turn to stay with Libby. Since the weather was warm and clear, they walked to Riverbend on the forest trail that followed the river. It was one that Josie knew well, since she and Nadine had spent every spare moment at the river. She'd almost forgotten about the little fishing hole halfway between Riverbend and Gram's farm. As she and Kennedy passed by the path leading down to it, she pointed it out.

"Did you catch a hundred fish there?" he asked.

"Not a hundred, but a bunch."

"I wanna try."

"This time of year, stock trout are mostly fished out, but we can give it a shot. We just have to let the fish go if they're not the right kind to keep."

"Can we go today?" He stopped and faced her, eyes bright. It had been too long since he'd had something fun to look forward to. Poor baby.

"Not today, bud. It's our Libby day. But soon."

"Tomorrow?"

"Soon, I promise. We'll have to check the rules and get the right bait and lures, and I'll need to find our old poles." Too late, she realized her slip. "I mean, my pole."

Kennedy kept walking, oblivious. "Gram said we can't use worms."

Josie's brows rose, but she didn't respond. She knew where this was headed.

"She says they're exploded."

She cracked a half grin. "I think she means *exploited*."

"Yeah." He nodded. "What kind of fish are we gonna catch? Sharks?"

"No sharks in the river, bud. It's salmon season right now."

"What do we catch 'em with?"

"Lures, probably. And maybe worms, but don't mention it to Gram or she'll turn us in to PETA. I'll check with Lucky Jack at the Hook and Reel. He's a well-known fishing guide. He'll know what they're biting on."

"I wanna stay here."

He kept walking, but Josie's steps slowed. He could have meant stay here along the river instead of going on to the nursing home, but she knew better. He probably meant stay at Gram's. To live. Her gut knotted again, right on cue. He was probably sick of being on the move. What kid wouldn't be?

"I wanna build a fort. Can I see your fort?"

Josie opened her mouth to give an answer but didn't have one. The fort she had shared with her sister was probably massacred by now. Raccoons or later generations of river pirates would have taken it over long ago. Trashed the whole thing, probably, memories and all.

"Is it by the fishing hole?"

"No, it's the other direction, upstream. Under the covered bridge."

"I wanna see it."

Naturally. But the question was, did Josie want to see it? She couldn't remember the last time she'd been there, but it felt like a hundred years. She'd almost forgotten how special it had been, how sacred it had felt.

She had almost forgotten, but not quite. Because there was a time when she and Nadine had been inseparable, which was impossible to forget, even after all that had come between them. There had been a time when one twin would seek out the other, even if she didn't need anything. They would often rest in the quiet of each other's company, sometimes with words, sometimes with nothing but the sound of their breathing.

That was a time when the give-and-take roles they'd fallen into worked well for them, a time when Josie's incessant need to rescue Nadine had not been resented. Why that changed, Josie never fully understood, but eventually, Nadine was no longer interested in sharing quiet moments or her thoughts and feelings with Josie. The gulf that began as a tiny crack in junior high had blown wider than the Grand Canyon by high school.

What started the gradual rift was never really clear. But the ugly scene that blew them completely apart was still painfully so.

It was one day in the spring of sophomore year. Josie had found her sister skipping class and smoking pot with the dark-clad, stoner crowd behind the football bleachers. Josie didn't even say anything critical to her at the time—she knew better than to embarrass her in front of her new friends.

"Come on, Deenie. Let's go." Josie didn't have to state the obvious. Nadine had to recognize the stupidity of what she was doing.

"Take a hike, Josephine. I'm not your shadow. It's not like we're attached."

That stung. Nadine had never once, in their entire lives, called her *Josephine.*

"Nadine, just come with me, we need to talk." She prided herself on keeping her cool, on not getting dramatic or reacting like a kid. On being the adult. As usual.

She waited, nostrils itching from the stink coming from the snickering band of dopeheads.

"Fly away, Glenda," Nadine muttered. "And take your magic broom with you."

Josie's jaw dropped. She ignored the tittering laughter that followed. Nadine was just showing off, but that crack was totally uncalled for.

Then Nadine took a step closer, sweeping dyed-black bangs out of her eyes. "You know what? We're way too old to be part of a matched set. Way past that twinsy—aren't they *sooo* cute—stage. Well, guess what? I'm tired of being pepper to your salt. I'm sick of being paired with you."

The punch to her gut might as well have come straight from Nadine's fist. Josie's identity had always been tied to Nadine. They had always been attached. Always had each other's backs. But as much as it hurt, Josie just stood there like a dumb dog you have to yell at to go home, to stop following.

And Nadine wasn't even done.

"You and I may share a face and freckles, but our similarities end there. We are *not* identical. I'm not like you. I'll *never* be like you. You don't get it. What I do bothers you, but what you do has zero effect on me. None. Get it? Go do your own thing and leave me alone. I don't care what you do with your life. Stop caring what I do with mine!"

Reeling, Josie turned and ran home sobbing, stopping a few times to catch her breath, feeling like she would puke, wishing she could, wishing even more that she would wake up and find it was just a bad dream. Wishing it didn't feel like she'd just been dumped again by the one person who was supposed to love her forever—

"Can we go see the fort?" Kennedy was on the verge of whining. "Pleeeease?"

"Um, maybe we can go tomorrow." If Josie could muster the nerve.

Libby was awake when they arrived and was pleased to see them. Josie brought Mozart and Bach for the CD player. The music seemed to calm Libby, to leave her less prone to ramble and a little more able to focus. She tired easily, so Josie tried to gauge how much conversation she could handle. Mostly, the things she talked about were random, with normal things sprinkled in, like things about her garden and the farm.

Pastor Dennis came to pray and read some scriptures to Libby, which calmed her quite a bit. And the aides had been getting her up for therapy with a walker, a few steps at a time.

While Josie helped Libby eat her lunch, Kennedy sat with Miss Ellie, who wanted to read him a book about whales. Josie wasn't sure why, but those two clicked like Batman and Robin. She kept an ear out, just in case Miss Ellie got kooky ideas about teaching Kennedy any questionable phrases. But she suspected that whatever he learned from Miss Ellie couldn't be any worse than what he might learn from Libby.

After dinner, she and Kennedy said their goodbyes, then headed for home. As they crossed the parking lot and aimed for the river trail, Josie saw a white U.S.F.S. pickup pulling in. Her steps slowed and her pulse sped.

Stop that.

Will got out and nodded their way. He was wearing jeans and a zip-up hoodie, so maybe he just got off work, or maybe he drove his work rig all the time.

"Ranger McNugget!" Kennedy took off and bore down on him like a torpedo, caution to the wind. He'd clearly decided that Will was a friend, whether Will liked it or not.

Yes, a friend. Nothing more.

Will came toward her with Kennedy glued to his side. Both in jeans and matching strides, they looked like quite the pair. Like they belonged together.

Stop it!

Josie spied a white, grease-stained paper bag in Will's hand. Her brows rose. "Contraband?"

His expression turned sheepish—a look she had not seen on him before but one that was definitely going on her list of favorites. Not that she was keeping a list.

She sniffed the air. "Cheeseburger? Onion rings?"

Kennedy leaned close and smelled the bag. "Donuts."

"You nailed it, bud. Raspberry jelly-filled from the mini-mart. Grandma's favorite."

Josie raised a brow. "Um, if you're planning on taking that aboard, I think you're going to need to bring a lot more than one donut."

He nodded. "Good call. I'll have to slip this to her on the sly."

She couldn't help but grin. Who was this guy, anyway? Did they even make them like this anymore?

And now, he was just staring at Josie, completely unaware that Kennedy was tugging on his sleeve.

"Sorry, buddy, what?" He turned and crouched down.

"We're going fishing," Kennedy told him. "But first Mommy has to find her pole. We can't explode any worms but that's okay, we're going to make bait from some old fishing guy."

Will belted out a laugh. "That sounds interesting." He glanced up at Josie with a half grin.

Blast those eyes! And the pesky thrill that zinged through her every time he looked at her. She was not going to develop a crush on Will McKnight. She was not!

"Actually," she said, mussing Kennedy's hair, "we'll spare old Lucky Jack this time and just ask him what the fish are biting on."

Will nodded. "Even better. Just remember to check the regs. You don't want to tangle with the game warden."

Kennedy frowned. "Is he a bad guy?"

"Good guy."

"Are you a game warden?"

"Nope, different department."

"You wanna come fishing with us?"

Josie sucked in a breath. She should have totally seen that one coming. But there was no way a guy like Will was interested in fishing with a single mom and her kid.

Will's gaze rose from Kennedy to her. "I'm on rotating shifts and my day off is pretty hit and miss right now, so it's hard to make any solid plans. But if you're ever going early in the morning, I wouldn't mind tagging along."

"You wouldn't?" she gasped. "I mean, good. Great."

They said goodbye, and as she and Kennedy headed for home, she tried to pay attention to her boy's chatter, but was mostly wondering how deep of a hole she was digging herself into.

CHAPTER
-11-

light reflecting on rapids
sunlight glinting through green leaves
scent of fern, damp earth, fir bark, pinecones
river rocks and salamanders
old dead wood, damp and mossy
huckleberries
silver trout shimmering in a mountain stream
—from the essay "What I Love" by Will McKnight, age 14

Friday was Gram's day to visit Libby, and after getting dressed, eating the oatmeal Josie forced on her, and giving Kennedy a list of things to take care of outside, Gram finally allowed Josie to drop her off at Riverbend. Now that it was just the two of them, Kennedy insisted it was his job to gather the chicken eggs, because *Gram said so.*

Okay, then.

Josie asked if she could tag along and was surprised when he actually let her. On the way to the coop, he told Josie she had to be really, really quiet so she didn't scare the chickens.

"Dude. I know all about chickens. I grew up here."

Kennedy stopped at the coop and threw her a confused frown.

She nodded. Maybe grew up didn't compute to a four-year-old. "Yep. I lived here from the time I was your age until I was a grown up."

Well. As grown up as she could have been at eighteen, when she got the brilliant idea to move to Eugene and spend a year getting *life experience* to give her art more authenticity. Libby caught on to what she was doing and told her she'd better experience getting her tiny hiney into college before her special scholarship offer ran out. She could get authenticity after she got her degree. Which she ended up not getting, after all, thanks to Nadine.

"You lived here when you were a kid?" Kennedy frowned. "Always?"

"Yeah."

Kennedy lifted the little door and took out an egg, then set it carefully in his basket. "You didn't have to always pack up all your toys and drive far away?"

Her jaw dropped. He was describing his life. The only life he'd ever known.

Josie swallowed hard. "It was different then."

Lord, how do I explain this?

He took out two more eggs, then did the same at all the other doors. Then he looked up at her. "I wish *I* could stay here all the time."

"Uh…" was about all she could say. "Maybe we can talk about—"

"Shhh," he said, finger to his lips. He was looking at a crumbling, moss-covered potting bench near the edge of the woods. It looked like something that belonged in the Shire. When Josie looked more closely, she noticed something on top of it: a small bundle wrapped in wax paper and tied with string.

"What's that?" she whispered.

Kennedy leaned close and whispered, "The secret mission. But don't tell Gram I told you."

Josie nodded, crossed her heart, and whispered, "But why do we have to be quiet?"

Eyes wide, he pointed into the woods. "The elves might hear us. They'll come out if we leave a present, but only if nobody is around. So we gotta go before they see us."

Josie felt her brows raise. "Okay, then. Guess we better scram."

He nodded solemnly.

A few hours later, as she made PBJs for lunch, she looked out the kitchen window. She wasn't sure what she expected to see, but the bundle was still sitting on the potting bench. Naturally. What on earth was Gram thinking, telling a little boy a story like that? Next he'd be having nightmares about dragons coming out of the woods to snatch him up and carry him away.

Kennedy was so obsessed with the Lincoln Logs Josie had found in the old toy chest that she could barely get him to take the sandwich she offered him—a phenomenon in itself.

Since he was totally engaged, she slipped outside and made her way to the potting bench, neither seeing nor hearing a single elf. But then, she never did when she lived there, either. Gram had her own theories about nature. Our relationship with it, what we may and may not disturb, that sort of thing. Josie had no clue where Gram had gotten such ideas—maybe from her parents. The LaPlantes were French Canadian; her mom, an actress; her dad, a painter and poet. Josie had always assumed her artistic streak had come from Gram's side, since she was clueless about her Norris genes. All she knew about that side was a partial name on her birth certificate: N. Norris. For all she knew, she and Nadine were related to Chuck.

Which they had milked for all it was worth in middle school.

She stood in the yard for a full minute, and while no elves appeared, she did have a creepy feeling that she was being watched. Which wasn't totally paranoid. Deer, raccoons, squirrels, birds, and at least forty-seven cats mooched off Gram daily.

With a glance at the window to make sure Kennedy wasn't watching, she stepped closer to the potting bench and peeked at the "top-secret" bundle.

It was a little bigger than a deck of cards, wrapped in wax paper and tied with string. She looked closer. Beside the bundle was a note held in place by a small, empty bucket. In Gram's block print, the note read: PICK UP PINECONES.

Josie moved closer and thought she smelled onion. She glanced over her shoulder again. Her little guy didn't appear to be watching, so she peeked inside the wrapper.

It was a toasted onion bagel stuffed with cream cheese. The one Josie had seen Gram making that morning, which she'd assumed was going to be Gram's lunch. Odd that she'd left it out here. Along with a to-do list and an empty bucket.

Of course, everyone knew Gram was a little cuckoo. But still, this was extra weird.

Shaking her head, Josie returned to the house.

Since she was already guilty of snooping, she figured she might as well make a day of it. She took out Libby's journal. She didn't know what she hoped to learn, if anything. She was just drawn to the possibility that this book might give her some sense of connection with the woman she was missing more with each passing day. The strong, wise woman Josie was beginning to fear might never come back.

June 9, 1997

Sorry, Diary. Not this year. You're not ready and neither am I. Maybe next year.

Not ready for what? And why did she bother making an entry if she wasn't going to write something? Strange.

She read on.

September 9, 1997

Dear Diary,

I guess it's been a while. Let's blame summer. And those blasted deer. Someday I'm going to put up a cyclone fence. (Sorry, Mom. I'm NOT putting in all that work just so Bambi and his freeloading friends can eat their fill.)

J & N have been with us for about a year now. I guess they're here to stay, and just between us and the chickens, I'm fine with that. They're full of grit, sass, and sweetness. Well, that depends on the day. And which twin. Nadine makes sure you KNOW she's there. I have to watch her from the corner of my eye, because if she thinks I'm watching, she tries even harder to be outrageous. And while I secretly get a kick out of her spunk, I'm afraid she's going to hurt someone someday. Most likely herself.

Based on my last conversation with the state hospital, I don't think we'll ever see my sister again. They told me the last time Geraldine checked out, she said she was

*"going out to face her demons" one last time, and she took
a white flag. As in she was literally carrying a white flag.
She told the staff she was tired of trying to keep her head
above water and was ready to call it quits.*

*Sorry, Diary, I can't find the words to explain how I
feel about that. Catch me later, after the shock wears off.*
-Libby

Josie set the book down, stunned.

Like Libby, she had no idea how to articulate how she felt about
her mother taking her own life. There were so many sharp edges rolled
up inside that act. There was the pain of abandonment, the loss, and
the long-standing sense of fear mingled with a lingering sense of guilt
that Josie was to blame for her mother's inability to face the world
another day.

Guilt was a pushy parasite. It didn't need an invitation, and it sure
didn't care that it might be undeserved. You could tell yourself a thousand times it wasn't your fault, but guilt would still hang on like a fishy
smell in your clothes you couldn't get rid of.

Josie wasn't sure how she ought to feel. But she was surprised that
hearing this through Libby's voice made her feel sad. And sorry. Sorry
for the pain her mom had caused others. Sorry that Josie never really
knew her mom. Sorry that Geraldine felt she had no other choice but
to end her life.

But to be brutally honest, which Josie actually could be when it
mattered, she was mostly sorry her mom didn't find Josie and Nadine
worth living for. She was sorry that they weren't reason enough.

That Josie wasn't enough.

"Mommy? What's wrong?" Kennedy was staring at her, uncertainty filling his brown eyes.

She probably looked a hot mess. Josie wiped unchecked tears from
her face, then tugged her boy close. Held him tight. Inhaled the scent
of him.

"Ow!" he said.

"Sorry," she whispered.

So sorry. For the pain I already have—and probably will—cause you.

CHAPTER
-12-

You think you're alone, but God sees you. You can't hide your sin with good works, or your pride with false humility, or your loneliness with a cheerful smile. You can't fool him, you can't hide your failings, and you can't be free of them without his help. He's a good, loving Father, so just surrender and let his joy into your life. He's already right there.
You're never alone!
—Eleanor McKnight, age 56

The dream began the same way it always did. Holding Kennedy's hand, she urged his tired little legs to keep walking across the desert, ignoring her thirst while painfully aware of his. She glanced down. His eyes were dull, listless. The heat beat down on his puffy little red face. His lips were cracked. He needed water soon or he wouldn't make it. And they needed to find shade. She searched the horizon for a clump of trees, or even a single tree fed by a stream or underground spring—something.

As she scanned the desert, the air shifted and danced, the rising heat sending up waves that morphed the flat horizon into a writhing blur. There was nothing. No water, no oasis, no relief.

I'm so thirsty. God, are you even there?

I am. You know where there's shade. And more water than you could ever possibly need.

But he's in trouble. Please, just send a little water, that's all I ask.

Mommy...

She looked down but Kennedy was gone. Instead of his hand, she was clutching Nadine's, and her sister was tugging hard to escape Josie's grasp.

Let me go, Josie!

No, Deenie. Stay with me so I can take care of you.

You don't care about me! You just want me to be like you.

No. You don't understand. I'm the mom now. I need to protect you.

You need? What about what I need?

You can't go! You'll get lost!

Let me go! I'm thirsty!

Mommy...

Josie awoke with a gasp. Kennedy was standing beside the bed, rubbing his eyes.

"Mommy, I'm thirsty."

"Okay, buddy, just a sec."

She went downstairs, got him a drink, tucked him back in, then returned to her bunk, marveling at how quickly the kid could fall asleep. At how oblivious he was to the smallness of their lives. At how completely he trusted her. Believed her.

Believed the lie that she was his mother.

She shushed the familiar whisper of shame. Stuffed it away, put a padlock on it. She knew—of course she knew—that this whole setup was so far from ideal. But what choice did she have? The truth was ugly. And painful. And useless.

The truth was that some people just weren't enough, no matter how hard they tried. And that was a truth no four-year-old should ever have to hear.

Shielding him from the truth had to be the right thing to do.

When Josie arrived at Riverbend on Saturday, Libby was dozing. Gram had kept Kennedy at home again, and while Josie was hesitant to leave him alone with Gram too much, she couldn't deny that he was far happier at the farm than he would be at the nursing home.

Gently, she brushed Libby's white-blonde hair from her forehead. The two weeks since the accident felt more like two years, but in that time, the swelling and discoloration around Libby's eyes and forehead had become barely visible, and her skin had regained its smooth, golden glow. Libby had never worn makeup, which Josie found cosmically unfair, because even without it, she was a beautiful woman. Her quiet demeanor and sapphire blue eyes gave her an air of mystique. And she had that naturally elegant bone structure that models would trade organs for.

The only notable thing that Josie possessed (inherited from the Norris side, obviously) was her green eyes that often made people stop and do a double take. And of course freckles, which had been such a bonus as a teen.

Apparently, the Buckley women were good at guarding things, including their beauty genes.

Libby moaned and seemed to be waking. "You moved your rook while I wasn't looking," she muttered, then sighed. "Come on, Jenny, your turn. And no cheating."

Josie had no idea if *Jenny* was real or imaginary, but at least Libby hadn't forgotten how to play chess. Which was unfortunate, because she was a wicked and merciless opponent.

Seeing Libby's Bible on the nightstand, Josie said, "Would you like me to read to you?"

Libby sighed. "Yes, please."

Josie opened the Bible to the center. Psalms—it seemed as good a place as any. She read a few chapters, marveling at the mentions of God's faithfulness, his nearness. Josie couldn't decide if King David was delusional, or a guy who actually knew God personally.

A few minutes into the reading, Libby opened her eyes wide and looked around the room. "Where's the baby? Who's watching him?"

Uh oh. "He's fine, Libby. He's with Gram." *And we don't discuss him in public, remember?*

Her aunt leaned back, closed her eyes. Tears slipped down her cheeks, which Josie still could not get used to seeing. "I didn't get to kiss him goodbye."

Aleah, one of the nurses, came in with water and medicine. "Hi, Josie." She stepped close to the bed. "Hello there, Libby," she said loudly, probably wanting to make sure she was awake. "How are you doing, gorgeous?"

Libby's eyes fluttered open.

"I've got your meds," Aleah said with a cheerfulness that Josie found contagious. "And some ice-cold apple juice, your *faaaavorite.*"

"Where am I? Am I in the hospital again?" Libby said slowly, frowning.

"Not exactly," the nurse said, adjusting Libby's pillow. "You're in a place where we can take care of you while you heal."

Libby drew a deep breath. "I told her I tripped and hit my face on the woodstove." A tear slipped down her cheek.

Told who? Was this real or delusion? Her speech seemed awfully clear...

Aleah raised the head of the bed and got Libby to swallow a pill, then checked her vitals.

"She didn't even question me this time." Libby sighed, then looked at the nurse, her expression strained. "I think Mom knows."

"Moms always know," Aleah said. "I could never hide anything from my mama. Still can't." She chuckled.

"Mom knows what?" Josie asked, stroking hair away from her aunt's wet cheek.

She groaned. "No more, please."

Josie stopped stroking but suspected that wasn't what Libby meant.

"I hate him."

The nurse raised a brow at Josie, who had no idea if "him" was an actual person. Should she ask? Or were these just random delusions plaguing her poor injured brain?

"Who do you hate?" Aleah asked. Nothing like diving right in.

Libby fidgeted suddenly, her legs twitching like a toddler working up to a tantrum. "He's going to come looking for me, Mom." The twitching increased.

Josie froze.

"I need to get Daddy's gun."

Josie stroked her shoulder. "Shh, Libby, it's okay." Regardless of who was coming, if anyone, it wouldn't do her any good to get agitated in the state she was in.

"Sorry I asked," Aleah whispered to Josie. "What's she talking about?"

Slowly, Josie shook her head. "No clue. Whatever it is, she's never mentioned it before."

"Poor thing!" Aleah looked genuinely concerned. "Of all the rotten luck. If a girl's secrets aren't safe in her own mind, they're not safe at all, are they?"

Josie stared at the nurse. *If a girl's secrets aren't safe in her own mind...*

Libby had always been a vault, and not just with Josie's secrets, but with life in general. Josie had never considered the possibility that the subconscious mind could surface in such a vocal way. How eerie to think that someone could lose control and speak freely without any of their usual filters, with no idea that they were spilling all their private thoughts and secrets.

Was Libby talking about something scary in her life recently? That didn't seem likely, because even though her aunt was good at keeping secrets, Josie believed she would have sensed something wrong during their phone conversations. So was this something that had happened in her past? Had Libby actually feared for her life? If so, from whom? What "him" did she hate, and why? And if this was real, would Libby be saying these things if she were in her right mind, if she knew people were listening?

And what other secrets did she have that everyone might now hear?

God, if she could pray, I think she'd ask you to heal her brain, and also guard her tongue from telling us things that are no one's business but her own.

Hoping to create a diversion, Josie leaned close to her aunt. "I never met my Grandpa, Peter Buckley. What was he like? Do you remember?"

"Of course." Relaxing, Libby smiled, then turned toward Josie. "Daddy was big and strong and always smelled like motor oil. And sawdust."

Aleah winked at Josie as she clipped an oxygen meter on Libby's finger. "Good call."

"She's still in love with him." Libby snorted.

Josie smiled. "Gram? Yes, I think you're right."

Libby frowned at her, then yawned. "Josie? When did you get so blasted big?"

"Me? Gee, thanks." Josie huffed. "You always said I had to eat all my veggies if I wanted to grow tall like you."

"She hates green beans," Libby said with an exasperated sigh. "I forgot about that."

Josie frowned. Everyone in the family loved Libby's homegrown green beans, slathered in butter. "Who hates them?"

"Your little sister. She hides them in her napkin and feeds them to Othello when Mama's not looking."

Nadine? She didn't remember her ever doing that. "Who's Othello?"

"Mom's pig."

Ah. Possibly a predecessor to Romeo, maybe even related. He must have joined the menagerie after Josie moved out.

"'Do not plunge thyself too far in anger,'" Libby murmured. "The only one it hurts is you."

A line of Shakespeare. Excellent—Libby was turning into Gram.

As the nurse gathered her things and left, Josie wondered if Libby really knew what she was saying. It was so hard to tell.

"You have to forgive your sister."

Lucky for Josie, Kennedy wasn't here today. She didn't know how long she could dodge the sister question, especially now that Libby was rambling about her.

"So what's the secret to forgiveness?" Josie didn't expect a rational answer, but she waited all the same.

Libby gazed at her through heavy-lidded eyes. "God sees everything. You can't hide. No matter where you go, he still sees you. Like Hagar. He's always here. In fact, he's here now."

Goose bumps crawled along Josie's arms. She turned and glanced at the open doorway. She wasn't sure what she expected to see, but there was nothing out of the norm, just a big room down the hall with upholstered chairs and some dementia patients watching TV or dozing.

"He knows every hair on your head."

Josie could hear the frustration in her sigh as she turned back and met her aunt's veiled gaze. "I know. You've told me a hundred times, I can't hide anything from God."

And this had always bugged her, though she had never really stopped to consider why. It wasn't just because she'd been living a lie, which was always the big, fat elephant in the room between her and

God. No, what bothered her was that apparently he'd been watching Josie all her life but hadn't lifted a finger to prevent crappy things from happening.

Yep. That was what bugged her.

"He will help you forgive, but you have to make the first move. You have to choose to forgive," Libby whispered. "If you don't, you'll wind up mean and nasty, like Miss Belden."

Josie burst out laughing. *The B*, as Miss Belden was otherwise known by generations of school-aged kids, had been terrifying children since the Jurassic Age. The normally reserved Libby, God bless her, had stormed down to the school and chewed out the woman the year Josie and Nadine were cursed to have her as a fourth-grade teacher.

It still made Josie smile. "After you told her off, Miss Belden never had the nerve to speak to a single member of our family again."

Libby's eyes closed. She shook her head side to side, slowly. "Let it go, blossom. It'll rot you inside out. Make you nothing but a hollow, useless shell."

Josie frowned. Libby was definitely echoing Gram now. She really didn't want to ask, but then again, she couldn't stand not knowing. "All right. Who do you want me to forgive?"

"Your sister," Libby said under her breath, as if all this advice was suddenly taxing her strength. She heaved a weary sigh. "Geraldine."

CHAPTER
-13-

As a single mom, I should probably learn some kind of self-defense, since my most impressive move is a thirty-five second diaper change in the dark. Definitely a mugger's worst nightmare.
—Josie Norris, age 25

The next day, Josie promised to take Kennedy fishing, as soon as his chores were done and they had dropped off Gram. Josie still couldn't get over how easy it had been to get him to do chores. As a little girl, she used to balk at anything that got in the way of playing, or as a teenager, getting down to the river. It was a good thing Libby had always been patient with Josie's silent grousing and shortcut taking, a patience that Josie could now see from an adult's perspective, making her both ashamed of herself and more appreciative of her aunt.

While Kennedy gathered eggs, he actually let Josie feed the koi, as long as she promised not to overdo it. As she carried out her privileged duty, Josie chuckled and watched from across the yard as he carefully lifted the egg doors so as not to frighten the hens. So her boy was a little farmer at heart. In fact, she just realized he hadn't been wearing his Captain America stuff, not even the cape. Apparently he'd found his new superpower.

A rustling in the woods drew Josie's attention. She didn't see anything but felt that sensation again that she was being watched. She squinted, and there, beyond the potting shed, she saw movement. Too tall for a deer, and the undergrowth was pretty high.

Then, in the shadows, she saw the silhouette of a person.

Josie gasped. The person was small and slender, about the size of— *Nadine.*

She dropped her sack of dead bugs and rushed to Kennedy. Heart pounding, she reached his side and looked back, but there was no one there. She checked all around, but the figure was gone.

"I can't play tag right now, Mommy," Kennedy said, shaking his head at her. "I'm busy. Maybe later."

"What?" Josie's jaw dropped. "Whatever." She glanced into the woods again and stuck close to Kennedy as he carried the eggs into the house.

It couldn't have been Nadine—she had a presence that was impossible to miss. So either it was a robber, or one of Gram's elf friends.

With a groan, Josie rubbed her temples. This place was making her nuts.

In the kitchen, Gram was brewing a cup of what she called "tea." The murky, dark green concoction smelled like a cross between boiled toadstool and river mud. And the stuff she emptied from the tea strainer looked worse, like something Josie had stepped in while cutting through a neighbor's dairy farm. Gram removed the spent mushroom gunk into a tin cup, and then carried it out to the mudroom between the kitchen and the back porch.

Josie followed.

Gram added the gunk to a crock, which probably contained more of the same, and which Josie was positive she did not want to smell.

"Gram, do you ever see people walking around in your woods?"

Her grandma turned to her. "Of course, blossom."

Josie shook her head. "No, I don't mean your fairy friends. I mean *real* people. I just saw someone in the woods, near the potting shed."

Gram replaced the lid. "I'm sure you did."

Okay, aaand? Josie waited. When Gram didn't answer, Josie probed. "Do your neighbors take shortcuts through there?"

"We don't have many neighbors. And those we have don't darken our door much."

Right. "Well, then, who was it?"

For a moment, it seemed as if Gram wouldn't answer. "Jenny," she said, finally.

Josie frowned. "I've heard that name. From Libby. She said something about a chess game."

Gram nodded. "They play on the big stump. The one from the giant oak that my lover cut down in 1967."

Josie stared at her grandma, sorting through this information, not sure how much was real and how much was fairy tale. "Libby and Jenny play chess on an old stump?"

"Yes, love. They have been at it for quite some time."

"In the woods?"

"Ay." Gram shuffled slowly back into the kitchen.

Josie trailed her. This was getting weirder by the minute. "So where's Jenny from?"

"The forest, like others of her kind."

With an eye roll, Josie inwardly kicked herself. She should have seen that one coming. At least Gram's brand of bizarre was consistent. "Is she homeless?"

Gram stared out the window, fiddling with the end of her braid. "She dislikes walls, they frighten her," she said softly. She rinsed her tin cup and set it on the drainboard. "Caged, she calls it."

"So I'm guessing the food you leave out is for her."

With a deep sigh, Gram nodded.

Well, at least Josie could rest easy that the lurker wasn't Nadine. Or some robber.

After Josie dropped Gram off at Riverbend, she came back and made a lunch for their fishing trip while Kennedy built a farm out of LEGO bricks.

As she washed two apples from Libby's tree, Josie glanced out the window, wondering if she would see the woman again. Something about all this felt off. Creepy. Maybe she shouldn't be too quick to dismiss the possibility that Jenny was a robber or on the run from the law. Gram was way too trusting. Why else would someone lurk around in the shadows if they weren't hiding something?

But then, it sounded like Libby played chess with Jenny, and Libby was no dummy. She would be onto the woman in a heartbeat if there was anything shady going on. Libby was clearly unable to give Josie any solid answers at the moment, but hopefully, that would change soon. In the meantime, since Josie was here for a while, maybe she would do a little sleuthing. She was observant and could be pretty sharp when she put her mind to it. *Ranger McNugget* wasn't the only one around here who could play detective.

Maybe you should get together with him over dinner and compare notes.

She gasped and nearly dropped the apple. She glanced at Kennedy, who hadn't noticed, and then shook her head. *Are you insane? High on the fumes from Gram's brew?*

Maybe now was a good time for a refresher from the textbook of her life, entitled, *Josie Norris: Single & Totally Fine With It.* Starting with a pop quiz.

Fact: Will McKnight is—

a) Male. (Check. Guys have been off the table for the past four years, in case you haven't noticed, so NO.)

b) An eagle-eyed cop. (Check. He enforces the law, which it turns out there's a chance you might actually be breaking, so a big fat double NO.)

c) Kind, confident, and insanely cute. (Check. He has zero interest in a sassy, freckle-faced single mom. Triple NO.)

d) Normal. (Check. As in he has a life, and you bounce around like a caffeinated gypsy. Big fat hairy NO.)

If you checked all of the above, congratulations, you passed. Proceed to the next chapter: *Knitting Your Own Underwear & Other Fascinating Ways to Occupy Yourself for the Next Fifty Years—Alone.*

It took some hunting, but Josie finally found two fishing poles and her old tackle box. The sounds and smells of the barn were like stepping into a time machine and traveling back fifteen years. She almost expected to see Nadine come flying down from the loft to scare her, or hauling her bike to the top of the nearest hill to launch herself down at break-neck speed.

She looked over her shoulder, just checking to make sure Nadine wasn't actually there, for the fortieth time. This was becoming annoying. The more time she spent here, the more she could feel her, could feel what Nadine used to be. Bright, bold, big-hearted, and full of sass.

And Josie's best friend, once upon a time.

With a sigh, she loaded the gear into her car. Since the fishing spot she had in mind for Kennedy was about a mile hike along a stretch of highway with too narrow a shoulder for a small kid to safely walk, she decided to drive there.

A mile later, the bridge came into view. For decades, the old, covered bridge had been revered by locals and tourists alike, and included in numerous books featuring photos of America's bridges. There was just something about a covered bridge that gave people a feeling of connection, a living link to the past. A bridge in more than one sense of the word.

Though the fishing wasn't as good as it was in the pools farther downriver, the current here wasn't as swift along the shoreline and didn't make Josie quite as nervous about taking Kennedy so close to the water.

She parked on the shoulder and headed to the trail that led down to the river. Kennedy was still pouting about the neon orange life jacket.

"Sorry, bud," she said in response to his wrinkled-up nose. "I know it's not as cool as your cape, but it'll keep you safe."

She carried the poles and tackle down to the bank of the river where she'd spent a good portion of her childhood. Kennedy forgot all about the vest when they reached the water.

"Whoa!" he yelled. "It's loud!"

"I know," Josie hollered back. "Watch this."

With all the volume she could muster, she sang the chorus of "Let It Go." She stilled and listened for the song to repeat downstream.

Kennedy grinned and tried it, sending his little kid voice dancing across the rushing current as well.

Josie smiled, then wondered what kind of a man Kennedy would turn out to be, with only a mom to teach and guide him. Would a dad be doing this? Teaching his son to sing the *Frozen* song across the water on a fishing trip?

If there was something more Josie should be doing for him, she wanted to know what it was and at least try to do it. As she showed him how to rig up his pole, she silently renewed her vow to do her best to raise him into a good man, no matter what it took.

But what if she was setting him up for failure? What if her best wasn't good enough? What if she wasn't enough?

She needed to talk to someone about this, but the only person she could confide in about Kennedy was still recovering from a brain injury. If Libby ever became coherent enough, Josie intended to ask.

She helped him cast his line into the water and then showed him how to watch it, holding part of the line between his fingers to feel for a bite. She cast her line in, but then his snagged, so she set her pole down and worked to free his.

After about a dozen snags, Kennedy's shoulders were drooping. They needed a bite soon or they'd have to try another spot.

Then, Josie finally got a nibble. Kennedy wasn't looking, so she set the hook with a quick tug, then tested it. Fish on! Perfect.

"Hey, Ken, could you come over here?" she said. "I need you to hold my pole for a sec."

Kennedy reeled in his line and stared cross-eyed at the nightcrawler swinging at the end of it. "You're not doing a very good job, worm." He set his pole down, then came to Josie and took hers. She turned away and acted like she was looking for something in the tackle box. It took a few seconds for him to feel the tugs on the line.

He squealed. "Hey! I think I got one!"

"Really?" Josie came over and checked the line. "Yeah, you sure do."

"What do I do? What do I do?"

"Give it a little tug to set the hook, then reel him in."

"Okay! Hold on, fish!"

He jerked so hard, she was surprised the fish didn't come sailing out of the water.

"That's good, Ken, now crank the reel."

"I am! I am!"

Grunting, he cranked the handle as hard as he could, his tongue poking out at the corner of his mouth, eyes fixed on the end of his pole. "What if it's a shark? Can I keep it?"

She smothered a chuckle. "There aren't any sharks in this river, bud."

He tipped the pole up higher and kept cranking. "Man, this is hard! My hand's getting really tired. Fishing's hard work!"

She laughed out loud, couldn't help it.

"Keep reeling, you're doing great," a deep male voice said.

Josie nearly buckled at the knee. *Stop fangirling like a twelve-year old.* She turned. Will McKnight was coming down the path toward them, in faded jeans and OSU T-shirt.

He was a Beaver? Oh, they definitely could not be friends.

Kennedy saw him and quivered all over. "Ranger McNugget! I got a fish!"

"Way to go, Ken. Reel it in and let's see what you got."

Please, dear Jesus, that fish had better still be on the hook.

As the end of the line came closer, the thrashing fish broke the water's surface.

"Mommy!" He jumped with both feet. "I see it! Look!"

"Yep, you're almost there! Keep reeling!"

"You got him!" Will said.

When Kennedy brought the fish close enough, Josie helped him lift it from the water.

"Good job," Will said. "Looks like about a twelve-incher."

"A *twelvinger*!" Kennedy was nearly hyperventilating while Josie steadied the line and held the trout up for him to see. "It's really wiggly!" He gave it a tiny poke.

Josie smiled so wide it almost hurt, filled with breathless joy at the sheer delight on his face.

Thank you, God.

"Do you want to take it off the hook, or do you want me to?" she asked.

Kennedy frowned. He looked up at Will. "What would you do?"

Will crouched down to Kennedy's level. "Well, if I were the fisherman that caught it, I'd finish the job and take that sucker off myself."

Kennedy turned to her. "Okay, Mommy. Gimme that sucker."

She laughed and couldn't keep from grinning as she crouched to their level. "Here you go. He might be slippery. Just holler if you need help." She winked at Will. "Ranger McNugget is itching to get his hands slimy."

He gave a *why not* shrug. "You bet."

Kennedy tried to hold the fish, but the minute he took hold of it, it did a double backbend and slipped out of his grasp. He groaned.

"It's okay," she said. "If you want, I could hold it still for you, and then you could take the hook out."

He looked at Will again. Josie could tell by the battle on his face he was torn between accepting help and impressing his new hero with his fishing prowess.

Will eyed the fish. "That's a pretty slippery one. If someone offered to help me hold it, I'd accept."

Josie was both thankful for Will's help and irked that Kennedy was so quick to defer to a man for the final decision.

No matter what it takes, remember?

Kennedy took the line holding the wiggling fish and towed it close to Will. "Will you hold him for me?"

"Sure." Will held the fish and talked Kennedy through the hook removal. Josie tried to ignore the poignant image of man and boy together, heads bent over their shared job. But the frame-worthy image singed itself on her brain anyway, stirring a deep, desperate craving for something she knew better than to crave.

Stupid photographic memory.

Once that job was done, they cast their lines again. Kennedy offered to share his pole with Will, who politely declined. She thought he would leave, but he folded arms across his chest and stood beside them, his stance relaxed, just watching the river. Kennedy was totally braced and ready for action, centering every muscle on catching another fish.

At least one member of the Norris family could concentrate on fishing.

Josie glanced at Will. "You don't have a pole?"

"I wasn't planning on fishing. I saw a car parked on the shoulder and came down to see who was poaching."

Crud. She didn't have her fishing license on her. Her pole suddenly felt like lead. "Um, honestly, I *do* have a license, but it's—"

"I'm kidding." He smiled. "I recognized your car."

She lifted her brows. "Oh. So you thought you'd just crash our family fishing party."

"Sorry," he said, frowning even as his face flushed. "I didn't mean to intrude—"

"Kidding." She grinned.

He nodded, then a tantalizing smile hitched up on one side. Holy moly, did the guy have to be so beautiful? He cocked his head and kept watching her, doing that scrutinizing thing he did. "So, is his dad not part of the family?"

"Uh." She always had a standard answer for that one, but at the moment, it totally escaped her.

"I mean, I noticed you don't wear a ring, so I assumed that's why his dad's not here doing this."

"Yeah," was all she could squeak out. What an idiot. What was wrong with her?

"Not that you're not doing a great job. You obviously know what you're doing."

She smiled. "Thanks."

He waited.

What? Was he asking about a dad because he was a cop? Or because he was interested and wanted to get all the cards on the table?

Josie. There is no table. Remember? You gave up dating when a six-pound mini-hunk became the center of your universe.

"His dad was never part of our lives." *That's all I can offer, Ranger Man. Do with it what you will.* Chin poking out, she waited, holding her ground, trying to play it cool when she felt anything but.

"Too bad for him," Will said gently. "Ken's a great kid."

She let out a steady breath and glanced at her boy. "He is. I don't deserve him."

Whoa, whoa, whoa—you're skating on thin ice.

Time for an emergency diversion. "So, do you know anything about a homeless woman in the area named Jenny?"

Will nodded. "A little. We think she's dealing with some mental illness, but she seems harmless enough."

"Is there a way to see if she has a record or something?"

He frowned. "Do you suspect her of criminal activity?"

She shook her head. "I don't know. I saw her lurking around the farm. Gram's being kind of weird about it, but it's hard to know what's actually weird with Gram since she lives in a world of fairies, elves, and Shakespeare."

He rubbed his jaw. "She's pretty much a drifter. We have to wake her up and roust her out of her makeshift camps once in a while. Library breezeway, the marina, people's barns."

"Should I do something about her lurking around Gram's place?"

"Well, like I said, she seems harmless enough. But it wouldn't hurt to keep an eye on her and let me know if you see anything that looks suspicious. Does your grandma keep valuables around the place? Tools, small equipment?"

Oh. She hadn't thought of that. "I don't know." With a stab of shame, she realized there was a lot she didn't know about the day-to-day operation of Gram and Libby's lives.

"It's really good that you're there. Must be a huge relief to your grandma."

She smiled. "I hope so."

He nodded and just stood there, studying her face without a word.

Mesmerized, she stared back, vaguely aware of the flush creeping into her cheeks.

"Fish on."

She nodded, still caught in that long-lashed, caramel-colored tractor beam. "Will do."

"No." Barely restraining a smile, he nodded toward the twitching tip of her pole. "I meant you've got a bite."

CHAPTER
-14-

Patrolling a half million acres of forest all alone and then going home to
an empty cabin is a great way to get sick of your own company.
—William McKnight, age 32

Once Will finally had Grandma convinced that it was really root beer and not arsenic in her Beavers drink cup, he promised to come back tomorrow, then said goodbye and headed for the exit. He checked his watch. It was only 10:00 a.m., so he still had time for a run before heading to work. Only six more months until the rebid, and with any luck, he'd get straight days and be done with rotating shifts. He might even be able to get some weekends off. If he got lucky.

As he crossed the parking lot, he glanced toward the river trail, the one Josie and her son had used, and stopped. He still wasn't sure why he'd crashed their fishing party at the river. He definitely wasn't looking for a relationship—Kristi had thoroughly cured him of that. His plan going forward was to follow his dad's footsteps and live out the rest of his life as a bachelor.

Running into Josie and Kennedy was just about the fishing. Nothing more. The kid wanted to learn. He didn't have a dad and probably needed a little male role-modeling.

That was it. There was nothing more to this interest.

Except there is more to it. Way more. Admit it.

Nope. Josie Norris was only in town to help her family. She wasn't sticking around. Which was fine with him. Because he wasn't looking to date, and definitely wasn't looking for a family.

"Hey, handsome!"

He turned. "Mandy?"

His sister hurried to him, carrying bags of what was probably her usual contraband for Grandma and the other Riverbend residents.

Mandy hugged him best she could with her arms full. "Aw, you're leaving? Dang it! I didn't know you'd be here, or I would've come sooner. I'm really glad I caught you though, I have something for you. Come over to my car."

He followed her to where she opened the back door of her Suburban and lifted out a thick leather book. She handed it to him like it was a ceremonial baton or something, then sucked in a deep breath. "I finally got it done. Only took me seven months."

Will knew exactly what the book was, but he wasn't eager to open it. He and his dad had always been tight, and then Will had been Dad's full-time caregiver for the final months of his life. He didn't need a photo album to remember him by.

Mandy lifted her chin. The resolve in her eye was not lost on him. "Part of the reason it took me so long to finish was because Mom had some of the photos I wanted to include."

Will stiffened.

"I know. But I'd really like you to keep it for a while. Take it home, and then when you're ready," she shrugged, "then look at it."

He was shaking his head before he was even aware he was doing it. Flipping through photos of the good years they'd had and the reminders of how strong and healthy Dad was before cancer's double assault turned him into a pasty scarecrow would be tough enough to see. But what he really dreaded was the idea of seeing old photos of his mom. Images of all four of them together, looking like a family, looking whole. *Happy.* Because if the photos in this book showed a happy wife and mother, they lied. He wasn't interested in fake memories of a fake family.

Mandy laid a hand on his forearm. "I know it'll be tough. But these are really good, Will. There are some great memories in here."

"You and I don't share the same memories, remember?"

When their mom had chosen to take twelve-year-old Mandy with her in the divorce and leave her fourteen-year-old son behind with his dad, she not only severed a family, she'd also damaged the bond between a brother and sister.

But Will knew better than to bring it up now. As adults, Will and Mandy had carefully mended their relationship, and that had taken time, prayer, and a lot of grace. He wasn't about to jeopardize what he and his sister had now over a bunch of dumb photos.

Her dark eyes glittered. "I'm sorry." She was working up a brave smile. "I just thought it might, you know, help."

He nodded. "I appreciate it. I'm sure you worked really hard on this."

"Dude. You have *no* idea. This scrapbooking stuff is serious business. You should see the section of the craft store. It's like a major league sport. Scrapbookers do not mess around." Brows raised, she cocked her head at him. "So, you'll look through it?"

A slow hiss escaped him. For a thirty-year-old soccer mom, she was way too perky. He shook his head. "I don't know. Maybe."

She scoffed. "That's the best you can do?"

Will frowned. "Look, I know you put a lot of work into sorting through photos and like decorating them or whatever it is women do to these things. But I have a feeling you have some other motive."

"Motive?" Her face scrunched. "What, now you're going all detective on me?"

He heaved a sigh. "I know what you're doing. But you need to stop. You don't need to make up for anything. The choices she made are all on her. It's not your responsibility to fix what she broke."

His sister opened her mouth, probably to fire off some sassy comeback, but seemed to think better of it and clammed up. Tears filled her eyes.

Ah, great. That was two women he'd made cry this month. He was on a roll. Next, he'd probably run over some kid's pet bunny.

"I can't help it, Will. You're my big brother, and I'm sorry if I caused you pain by getting something you missed out on."

He shook his head. "You've done nothing of the kind."

Her dark brown eyes were unconvinced.

Will shrugged. "I could tease you and pull your hair, make it even."

She burst out with a snort. "You could try that, if you want to show up to work with two black eyes and a serious limp."

He winced. "Dang it. Forgot about the black belt."

Mandy grinned. Then sobered. "Mom has been asking about you."

Will shook his head, long and slow. "Sorry, sis, but I really don't care. Which you know." He heaved a sigh. "You're persistent, gotta hand it to you. But I'm onto you."

"Yeah, yeah, once a cop, always a cop. But I love you anyway." She gathered up her goodie bags. "Oh, and you'll never guess who I ran into."

Will groaned. He could guess.

"Your ex. And get this: Kristi said she hopes you find what you're looking for, because apparently what you really want is some hillbilly girl next door with a big butt and zero ambition." Mandy rolled her eyes. "She was with some poor guy. I told him he'd better plan on or-biting her 24/7 or she'll turn on him like a cobra."

Will's eyes drifted closed. "You didn't."

"I did. And she just laughed. The bimbo."

He groaned again. Mandy definitely talked too much.

"Have I told you how glad I am that you broke up with her?"

"About five-thousand times."

"I'm not going to ask what you ever saw in her."

"Thank you."

As two people emerged from the river trail, Will's breath seized. Crud. Of all the days.

Kennedy saw Will and came running. "Ranger McNugget! I brought Jenga to play with Miss Ellie, but I fink you can play, too. Okay?"

Mandy nailed Will with a wide-eyed, *whoa, bro, back the train up* look.

"Sorry, buddy, but I'm on my way to work. Maybe next time."

Mandy shaded her eyes and watched Josie approach, much like a hawk spying its prey.

Lord in heaven, if you have any compassion at all…

"Hi." Mandy smiled at Josie as she caught up with her son. "I've been trying to come up with a nickname for my brother, but 'Ranger McNugget' tops them all. Best ever."

Josie smiled and ruffled Kennedy's hair.

Will introduced his sister to Josie and Kennedy, and as he gave a brief recap of how they'd met and why they'd been crossing paths at Riverbend, Mandy just smiled and nodded, not even bothering to hide her head-to-toe scrutiny of Josie.

It wasn't until Will stopped talking that he realized he was sweating like a pig on a spit.

"So, I gotta run—literally—before my shift. Mandy, thanks for the photos. I'll call you."

"Yep," she said, still smiling at Josie like a Cheshire cat.

Lord...

Josie wondered about Will's sister as she and Kennedy went inside and headed for Libby's room. Mandy Stafford seemed really nice, and clearly curious about Josie. Of course, Kennedy's adoration of Will was obvious, so it wasn't surprising that his sister might wonder about Josie.

But there was nothing to wonder about. Nothing here to see, people. Josie was not crushing on the ranger who had rescued her in the middle of the night and who was adorably kind and patient with her boy and who was even slightly fun when he decided to loosen up.

And who was a cop. Which normally wouldn't be an issue. But when Josie did a little digging, she found out that the family court hearing she'd missed was kind of a big deal. She probably wasn't in any serious legal trouble. But now was not a good time to expose herself by contacting the court to try and clear up what was just a dumb technicality. Right now, Libby was vulnerable, and unpredictable, and no one knew if she would recover. Josie hoped and prayed Libby would be herself again, and soon. Meanwhile, it just wasn't safe for Josie to run around drawing needless attention to herself. It was probably risky— and Josie really hated risking getting into trouble—but it was a chance she would just have to take.

The nurse on duty at Riverbend warned Josie that Libby had woken in a mood, which didn't improve with hearing her novel, her Bible, or Mozart. She seemed extra tired and cranky. Her speech was less coherent and more troubled. It was days like this that made Josie wonder if Libby was actually making any progress at all. Josie helped her eat a little and did the best she could to make Libby comfortable, but by day's end, the added tension had pulled her shoulder muscles into knots.

The next day, Josie promised Kennedy they could see the fort, or at least, see where it used to be. She warned him that the brush was probably so overgrown there might not even be a fort, but he didn't care. He brought his "light saver" just in case there were any bad guys around.

She hadn't thought about that. It was highly unlikely, but of course, the idea sent her imagination spinning. A rush of images of Nadine came to mind, good and bad, crashing together, throwing her off.

The closer they got to the bridge, the more her nerves crackled.

They took the overgrown path to the underside of the bridge, then poked around, hoping to find a way in without getting scratched by the thick underbrush. They found a narrow break in the bushes, but Josie made Kennedy wait until she could see what lay ahead, like things that were coiled and ready to spring. She pushed her way through and found the space beneath the bridge just as she remembered, and much the way she and Nadine had left it.

Josie told Kennedy to be careful of what he touched, then scoffed at herself. When had she become such a wuss? When she was a kid, no one cared about things like catching rabies from racoon poo.

She tried to remember when she and Nadine had been here last. Eighth grade? Summer before high school? And had they known that it would be their last time together in this place, as sisters, as friends? She hardly knew.

Kennedy asked a million questions, and Josie mumbled answers, but was lost in a fog. Everything about this place screamed Nadine. This had been their sanctuary. The place they could rest and regroup and make plans to stand up to the injustices of life and mean, nosy teachers and rotten, pranking boys and snotty, spoiled girls who thought they were better because of the label on their jeans. They had discussed and agreed on ways they would stick up for each other. In this place, they had made solemn vows.

What happened, Nadine? Why did we grow apart? When did we stop wanting the same things? Why did we stop having each other's back?

Kennedy had unearthed an old rug and was shaking it out, and Josie suddenly realized that it was Nadine's, the one she'd found in the bin behind Wally's market. Now Kennedy was about to use it. Like he was stepping into his rightful place as heir of the pirate kingdom his mother had once co-ruled.

And all at once, Josie was back in middle school. She and Nadine were fishing on the bank several yards to the east. Brody, a boy they'd known since first grade, was inside the covered bridge and waving at them through a side vent. He hollered something at them, but the river was too loud to hear what he was saying.

Nadine, hunting for the perfect skipping rock, rolled her eyes. "He won't leave me alone, he's always bumping into me every time I turn around, like a puppy. He probably followed us here. What a turd. Just ignore him." She kept picking through rocks.

Josie cocked her head and listened, curious about what sort of things a lovesick twelve-year-old boy hollered upriver to his true love.

She frowned. "Deenie? It sounds like he's calling for help."

Nadine stopped and stared at the bridge, listening intently, then sprinted toward it full speed. Josie tried to keep up, but Nadine had always been faster. They stopped on the bank below the bridge and Nadine hollered up at Brody, but before he even answered, they saw what was wrong.

His little sister had fallen through the gap between the bridge's floor and outer wall and was clinging to a beam beneath the bridge, dangling high above the rushing river. Brody was trying to grab her but couldn't reach her from above.

Nadine sprang to action and climbed up and into the bridge's underbelly, moving deftly, as if her feet automatically knew all the footholds. Josie yelled at her sister to be careful, knowing full well it wouldn't be heard or heeded, then covered her ears. Then her eyes. Then she uncovered them, because as gruesome as it would be to watch her sister and another girl fall to their deaths, she had to know what was going on.

She watched, heart pounding, while Nadine scurried like a monkey to the spot where the girl was, hooked her legs around a beam like a gymnast, then yelled something at the boy. One end of a belt came down through the gap. Nadine took it and wrapped it around the girl's chest, then hollered again. She pushed while Brody hoisted the girl up through the gap and out of sight.

Josie held her breath as she waited for her sister to come down. Seconds felt like hours. Then the boy shouted and Josie turned. Brody and his little sister had emerged from the north end of the bridge on the road above. He hollered his thanks as he led his sobbing sister away.

Laughter made Josie spin around. Nadine was now upside down, hanging by her knees beneath the bridge.

"Knock it off, dork!"

"Want to see me fly through the air and do a dismount? Like the Olympics?"

"No!"

"What's the matter, Feenie? Don't like heights? Fraidy cat."

Josie crossed her arms and waited.

With a sigh, Nadine climbed down. "That was fun. You ought to try it sometime." Nadine passed Josie and slipped into the fort.

Josie followed. "Weren't you even a tiny bit scared?"

"Pfff." Nadine shook her head. "Climbing doesn't scare me."

"Nothing scares you," Josie muttered.

"Not true." Nadine took her spot in the corner and laid back on her rug, closed her eyes. "Libby's green Jell-O scares me." She shuddered.

Josie put on her eye patch. "Well, even if it was dangerous, I'm glad you rescued Brody's little sister. She could have fallen and gotten really hurt. Died, even."

Nadine nodded. "Yeah."

Josie grinned. "I bet Brody brings you flowers and candy tomorrow."

"Eww! Gross! No thanks."

"He'll probably even try to kiss you."

"*What?*" Nadine bolted upright, eyes wide. "The psycho better not even think about it."

So there *was* something Nadine was afraid of.

Seeing Kennedy in the fort now, taking Nadine's place, struck Josie with a strange feeling she couldn't quite name—a discordant kind of déjà vu. But while Kennedy depended on Josie, he was nothing like Nadine. During their earlier years, Josie and Nadine's roles were an unconscious given. Josie was determined to keep Nadine alive and keep her from being a total social outcast. And apparently, Nadine was determined to give Josie a heart attack. In time, Josie had grown more aware of their differences, which increased as they got older. The harder Nadine tried to break her neck, the more determined Josie was to protect her. She knew she could be a pain and maybe sometimes smothering. But if anyone was to blame for that, it was Nadine.

It was funny how Josie hadn't wondered, until that moment, why Nadine was always so outrageous, such a daredevil. Maybe they were more alike than either would admit. Maybe Josie's determination to achieve, and Nadine's determination to shock, were both a means toward the same end. Maybe they were both trying to force the world to see and accept them. To stake their claim and establish their right to simply *be*.

Later that evening, Gram disappeared again.

When she was sure Kennedy was asleep, Josie slipped outside. Moonlight cast shadows from the trees, leaving patches of darkness that no eighty-year-old woman had any business venturing into. Seeing no sign of her grandma around the yard and garden, Josie headed straight to the barn.

Light spilled out from around the edges of the door, and as she got closer, she could hear voices. Definitely more than one this time.

Josie peered through the cracked door and saw the shapes of two people inside. One was Gram, and the other one was a very slender woman...

...of Nadine's height and build.

Shock numbed Josie, but she forced herself to breathe, then think.

It was probably Jenny, the lurker. If so, why all the secrecy? Was the woman running from the law, maybe? Up to no good? If Josie was going to help Gram and Libby, she needed to know what was going on around here.

She opened the barn door and stepped inside.

Gram turned toward her and froze. "Oh!"

The thin woman also froze, dropping a large bundle of fabric that looked like a blanket. She took two steps backward and looked to Gram, her face a mask of panic.

"There, now, Jenny," Gram said quickly. "No one's going to bother you. She's a friend."

But Jenny continued to watch Josie with growing alarm. She was rigid, as if braced for something, but since she was so frail, Josie thought a small gust of wind could knock her down. Her haggard face was wrinkly and brown, like rawhide. Like she'd been exposed to the elements for a long time. Her sparse, gray hair was pulled up into a meager bun on top of her head. As frail and weathered as she was, the best guess Josie could make on her age was somewhere between forty and eighty.

"Shh, rest easy, dear one." Gram spoke gently in her girlish voice, trying to soothe the disturbed woman. "Peace upon you."

Jenny stared at Josie, then pulled the drawstrings on her hoodie so hard that the hood closed tightly around her face, leaving very little exposed. She held a small, ratty bundle the size of a football close to her chest, never taking her eyes from Josie.

"Oh, dear," Gram whispered, turning to Josie. "She's going to fly." Gram picked up a small package from an overturned crate and held it out to Jenny. "Don't leave without your dinner, fair lady."

Jenny blinked at the food Gram offered, then shook her head. "Haven't earned it," she muttered, her voice low and creaky, like the sound of a rusty old gate rarely opened.

Slowly, Gram took a half-step closer and held out her offering, the same way Josie had seen her coax an injured bird or squirrel to eat from her hand.

Without warning, Jenny turned and bolted away.

With a deflating sigh, Gram stared down at the sandwich in her hand as if it would tell her what to do next. "She might come back and take it. She has before. I'll leave it, just in case."

"Gram, what's her story?"

She set the bundle back on the crate, and it took her a moment to answer. "She's…just lost. Another poor lost, wounded creature."

"So she does little jobs for you in exchange for food?"

Gram nodded. Slowly, she stooped and picked up the wadded

blanket Jenny had dropped. "She was going to fix this quilt for me. It's missing a couple of stitches."

From what Josie could see, the tattered thing was far beyond the help of a few stitches. It needed an incinerator.

Apparently, Gram had been trying to tame the poor woman for quite some time. But since Jenny wanted to work for food, it seemed unlikely that she was a thief, setting Josie's mind a little more at ease. A little.

CHAPTER
-15-

Sometimes, true love slips in late and is forced to take a seat in the front row, in the shape of a brawny lumberjack surrounded by ethereal beings, so out of place and yet strangely at home, because the girl of his dreams is suddenly right in front of him, so real that his heart nearly breaks at the sight of her. Oh yes, I believe in true love at first sight.
—Gwendolyn Buckley, age 24

Hours after everyone else had fallen asleep, Josie stared at the underside of Ken's bunk, trying not to toss and wake him. She was frustrated at her inability to sleep, but worse, she was frustrated with herself. It bothered her that Gram had befriended a homeless woman, but then, that was Gram. As Josie lay there, it occurred to her that if you were going to be suspicious of every raggedy stranger, you'd likely miss the chance to help someone truly in need. The poor, deranged woman was probably just hungry and wasn't looking to steal. Gram had said Jenny didn't like confinement. Will had said there was some mental illness involved, which was not uncommon among the homeless. And while she didn't understand, it wouldn't kill Josie to lighten up. If she got another chance, she would try to speak to the woman, see if there was a way to help her.

Now if only she could help herself get to sleep. Which was all the more difficult with Libby's journal tucked beneath her mattress, calling to her.

With a sigh, she slipped it out, switched on the flashlight from her phone, and read.

March 3, 1998
When Daddy died in a logging accident, I was 5,
and Gerry was only 2, barely talking. Mom was only 29
then—6 years younger than I am now. She's been on her
own ever since. She's never once even looked at another
man. She's still madly in love with Peter Buckley.

Josie closed her eyes, trying to imagine what it was like to love someone with all your heart like that, in such a consuming way that the guy didn't even have to walk the earth any more for your heart to still beat like crazy for him.

Will McKnight's face came to mind.

She gasped.

You're pathetic. You don't even know him.

She read on.

September 8, 1998
N & J started first grade at Riverside Elementary
today. While Josephine made sure her sister's hoodie and
backpack were hung beside hers in the hall outside the
classroom, Nadine launched herself like a torpedo into
a cluster of girls with perfectly tidy ponytails. That stunt
went over like a lead balloon. Of course, Josie smoothed
things over by introducing herself and bragging about
how her twin, Nadine, could shoot water through her
teeth and hit a spider ten feet away. This did not have the
desired effect on the little snobs, but I don't think our girls
noticed. I'm pretty stinkin' proud of them. What a pair.

Josie smiled. She remembered that day. And in her memory, Aunt Libby never even raised an eyebrow. Why was Libby so closed when it came to showing her feelings? Josie wished she had known the depth of her aunt's affection.

November 14, 1998
From the start, we told the girls their mom was sick
and needed to go away and get well, and they didn't
question it. I guess at four, they already knew that much,

anyway. But they're six now and they still ask about her sometimes, things like when is she going to be well enough to come back and get them. I don't know if that means they want her to take them, or if they're afraid she will. I don't want to ask. I guess because I don't want to know. And anyway, it hasn't come up in a while. So I'm just going to let the subject die, right along with Ger.

The girls have settled into the routines of farm life so well you'd think they've always lived here. Life with the four of us feels so normal now. The Buckley homestead is teeming with life again, just like it was when Ger and I were growing up, helping Mom in the garden, learning how to tell the difference between a tomato plant and a weed, picking beans and putting up pickles and gathering eggs.

This was her childhood as she remembered it, but oddly, now that she was seeing it through adult eyes, it felt whole. Full. Steady and stable. A wave of homesickness struck her without warning, and she fought back tears.

Josie pushed aside the hollow ache in her heart and read on.

February 14, 1999

Josephine and Nadine turned seven today. They're so in sync with each other, they totally astound me. They seem to understand what the other needs without words, and they take care of each other. Nadine turns on the bathroom light for Josephine and checks first to make sure it's spider-free (I finally found out why Josie is such an arachnophobe—she found one in her hair when she was four and it thoroughly traumatized her). Josie distracts Nadine when she's in a funk and always saves the last brownie for her, even if Josie wanted it for herself.

I've heard twins have some sort of telepathy, and I believe it. I've watched them when they're together, which is pretty much all of the time, since they rarely leave each other's sight. No surprise, after all that they've been

*through. Lord only knows after seeing the shape Gerry
was in when the girls came to us. I'd rather not think
about that. The vacant woman who gave her children
to me was not the Geraldine I knew. In fact, I hardly
recognized her.*

Josie held her breath, caught off guard by this unexpected glimpse
of her mother, unsure if she was ready to learn about her from an
adult's perspective, or dreading it, or both.

*Geraldine and I always had trouble understanding
each other growing up—with or without words. She was
all about needing approval, and I didn't give a rip about
that. I loathed the way she was always trying to earn approval, mainly because I thought the people she was trying so hard to win weren't worth it. With Mom's reputa-
tion (Tree Hugger, Loopy La-la, Spider Whisperer, etc.)
all I cared about was being taken seriously, and since
Ger had no self-respect, she couldn't understand that. The
harder I worked to be "normal," the more disconnected
Ger and I became. Ah, Geraldine. If only I'd known how
deeply insecure she was. How bottomless was that black
abyss beneath her tightrope. Not that there was anything
I could've done about it.*

Josie closed her eyes. She could easily hear Libby's voice, hear her
saying these things in her matter-of-fact tone. How different those two
sisters were from each other. How strange to hear these kinds of details
about the mother she never knew. And poor Gram. How difficult life
must have been for her as a young widow and mother of two, running
the farm all alone.

Josie had never really thought about that.

June 9, 1999
*Okay, Diary, this probably isn't the place for this,
but I need to vent, and it's not like anyone's actually going to read this thing anyway.*

It's been eight years and my arms still ache. It's not fair. It's no one's fault. It's no one's fault.

It's NO ONE'S FAULT.

And that's the crappy part. Without someone to blame, I have nothing. No occupation with seeking justice, no way to fill the hollowness that echoes inside me. It's a miracle I haven't filled it with booze or bar hopping—not that I will ever, EVER want a man in my life again, and even if I somehow lost my mind and did, men who frequent bars looking for women hold absolutely zero appeal.

But now, as I watch Josephine and Nadine giggling and fishing on the riverbank, it suddenly occurs to me that there IS a way to permanently fill the raging emptiness. My salvation is right in front of me.

Maybe that was my sister's plan all along—warped as that sounds. And since she's most likely dead, and these girls desperately need a mother, pouring my energies and focus into them is a no-brainer. It's not like I don't already love them to pieces.

Her eyes were finally beginning to droop, but Josie didn't want to stop. So at one time, there really had been a man in Libby's life. But who? Was he the man in her ramblings at Riverbend, the "him" she had feared was coming? Apparently, this person was real, and since Josie had no knowledge of him, she fought sleep and kept reading.

I don't know how much longer I can keep this up. Mom would snap like a feather if I weren't here to help keep this place going. But I'm so blasted restless. And so tired. Tired of the pain. The anger. It's been eating me slowly from the inside out ever since that day. I don't blame her, even though a part of me still can't help but wonder if anything more could have been done, or if it would have even made a difference. Or if my being there would have changed anything.

No, the life-sucking anger is all for him. How could a human be so completely heartless, so absolutely brutal? How can a man hit a woman, again and again and again? How can a man hurt the one he claims to love? He has to be a monster. And it takes a special kind of monster to beat a woman while she's carrying his child. And not once, but many times.

And what woman would stay and let it continue? Far too many, I fear. Some women fear for their lives if they leave. I've known that fear. Some believe the lies and the apologies and the promises. And unfortunately, sometimes, believing the lies gets them killed. I was one of the fortunate ones. My babies were not.

Josie covered another gasp, heart pounding. Dear, dear God! Libby had been beaten by her own husband? Josie had never suspected that Libby had even been married, much less so brutalized.

And she'd been pregnant. And her babies had not survived the beatings.

Oh God oh God! Poor Libby.

Weeping in silence, Josie fumbled around in the dark for a tissue and blew her nose, but she couldn't stop crying. This explained so much about her reserved, stoic aunt. And maybe why she was so tough. If not for Libby's strong backbone, would she even be alive now?

Josie read the last entry in the first ledger:

Okay, Mom, you were right. You were always right about him. And you were right when you suspected that my story about tripping over the hearth was a lie. You were painfully right. I'm so sorry that all the loss in both our lives has become more than you can bear. I don't blame you for retreating to the Shire in your mind. It's a kinder and gentler place than the real world.

I'm so sorry.

-Libby

CHAPTER
-16-

I'm an embarrassment to my teenage daughters. I pretend that I don't know. And that it doesn't break my heart.
—Gwendolyn Buckley, age 43

Mommy?"

Josie fought her way up through the deep, powerful currents of sleep and forced her eyes open. Kennedy was watching her, munching on a bagel, his little cheeks smeared with peanut butter.

"Oh, sorry, buddy. Did I oversleep?"

He shrugged, then offered her a bite.

She smiled. "Thanks, but not yet. You know the drill."

"Yep. Coffee first. But Gram made you tea."

She shuddered. "No, thanks. I'll be down in a sec. Why don't you start on your chores while I get dressed so we can go see Libby?"

"I already did my chores." He hopped up. "Now I'm gonna go outside with Gram to see the new baby kittens."

Josie nodded, frowning. What time was it? She checked her phone. It was after eight? She hurried and got dressed. Downstairs, she grabbed coffee and an apple, then headed out to the barn, slowing her steps to draw in all the scents of river and pine. Maybe she could figure out a way to bottle the aroma and take it with her when she left here.

Because sooner than later, she really did need to leave.

Heart heavy, she went inside the barn. Kennedy was sitting near a pile of straw, and Gram was bending over, doing something beside him. The sounds of mewing kittens softened the crusty vibe of the century-old barn. Thanks to Gram's cats, mice had never been a problem around here.

Gram straightened and turned around slowly, her hand cupped as though she carried a tiny bird.

No…what she held was too small for a bird.

Oh, no. Please, God, no.

"Welcome to your new home, sir," she crooned into her hand. She walked toward Josie. "They tell me you're not welcome in the realm of man, ignorant peasants. Terrible injustice."

No. No. No…

Before Josie even saw what was in Gram's hand, she could feel her blood pressure spiking.

Kennedy stood and followed Gram. "Who you talking to?" He peered into her hand. "Whoa! That's a big spider!"

Josie screamed, tripped backward—apple flying—and stumbled against the riding mower. She covered her mouth but couldn't stop the next scream. Or the one after that.

Kennedy ran to her. "What's wrong, Mommy?"

Was he kidding? Couldn't he see that their psycho grandmother was holding a spider? She panted but couldn't catch air. Panic was closing in.

"Oh, dear," Gram said, coming closer with the devil himself in hand. "Are you going to faint? Try putting your head between your knees, rosebud. That's what the director always had me do."

Josie pointed at Gram and tried to tell her to take the hairy little beast away but all she could say was, "Gaaaaaa!"

Frowning, Kennedy peered at her. "Are you crying?"

"Gram!" Josie finally spit out. "Get that thing out of here!"

"But all of God's creatures are welcome in this mortal realm."

"That—" Josie sucked in air and pointed— "is not God's creature! That came crawling straight from the pit of hell!" She shuddered violently at the graphic image her words just conjured up. Why, in the name of all that was holy, did her sweet Gram have to touch them?

Gram shuffled out the barn door, shaking her head.

Kennedy came closer and stared at Josie, his brow wrinkled. "It's just a pet."

"*Pet?*" She shook her head, drenched in sweat. No. A pet was a wagging thing with a cute face and no more than four legs and didn't make Josie nearly wet her pants.

Once Josie's heartrate and breathing had returned to sort of normal, she took Ken inside the house to choose some toys to bring for their visit with Libby, and then found Gram at the kitchen table. She checked first to make sure Spiderwoman didn't still have the blasted beast, then edged closer to her.

Her grandma's cheeks were damp with tears.

"Gram? What's wrong?"

"I am sorry, lambkin. I meant no harm."

Crud. Josie threw arms around her. "No, I'm sorry. I probably scared the daylights out of you, screaming like a lunatic. And I'm so sorry I snapped at you."

Gram patted Josie's arm. "All's well that ends well, fair maid."

Josie nodded, then drew a fortifying breath, determined to fill in the missing pieces of Libby's journal. Libby had protected her nieces from the horrors of her past, but Josie was no longer a child who needed to be shielded from the truth.

"Gram, was Libby married?"

Her grandma's brow pinched, but she didn't answer, only wrung her knobby hands.

Josie waited, giving her time to answer, while Kennedy packed his backpack.

"She was. But Dean Allen was a foul fiend."

So, the jerk had a name. Josie inhaled, forced herself to wait.

"Oh, he was a charmer. Quick at flattery, and even quicker to explode into a fit of rage." Her little voice wavered. "He was controlling, a vicious bully. Liberty never told me because he... he..." Her voice trailed away.

"Oh, Gram." Josie leaned closer. "He threatened her if she told?"

Trembling, Gram nodded, tearful.

"And he beat her?"

Gram nodded again.

"And she miscarried a baby?"

"Two." Gram's voice broke, and she burst out sobbing. "Two precious little angels." She covered her mouth to muffle her crying.

Tears filled Josie's eyes. How devastating for Libby. And how horrid to be married to such a beastly man.

Gram wiped her cheeks and looked across the room. "Liberty was so young, only twenty-eight. About your age."

"How did she get away?"

Gram glanced down, smoothed the fabric of her gauzy skirt slowly, repeatedly. "When she finally gathered the courage to come home, she walked into this kitchen, loaded her father's shotgun, and then she waited by the front door." Gram gazed across the room toward the front of the house, as if seeing it afresh. "And soon after, the villain arrived in a hurricane of dust, just as she expected."

"Did you call the police?"

"Oh, no," Gram said. "Not Liberty. She was out on the porch before his foot hit the ground, her father's shotgun pumped and aimed at his head. Dean saw her and actually had the sense to stop. His gaze narrowed, and he just stood there for a long time, sizing her up. As though deciding whether or not my girl was bluffing."

Josie could barely get the words out. "What did Libby do?"

Gram drew a deep breath, eyes closed, as if what came next was too difficult to recount. She exhaled slowly. "She said, 'Only a coward would beat up a girl. Come on, Dean. Take another step so I can blow your head off. After all you put me through, prison would be a vacation. I'd gladly go to jail if it means you can't hurt anyone else. Go ahead, come and get it.'"

Josie gasped and stared at Gram, processing what she'd just heard. The scene played out clearly in her mind's eye, like a movie. "Then what?"

"He cursed her and left," Gram said. "My Liberty sank to the floor, quaking like a hunted rabbit, poor baby. And then she waited by the door for a week, gripping that shotgun, but he never came back."

Stunned, Josie just sat there, staring at Gram, her tears hot and unchecked. She'd had no idea. She wiped her face. By the time Libby was Josie's age, she had already lost two babies at her husband's brutal hand. It wasn't hard to picture Libby taking a shotgun to an intruder, but to be hunted down by her own husband? How had she gotten through it all?

She suddenly remembered Libby's terrible bruises the first few days after her accident and how she looked as if she'd been beaten.

"Gram, is there any chance that Libby's head injury could have been from Dean?"

"Oh, no. He drove drunk one night and killed himself in a ball of flames."

Still numb, Josie checked on Kennedy to see if he was ready, and as she splashed water on her blotchy, tear-stained face, she saw her aunt in a new light. Libby was far more complex than what Josie had believed her to be. Far more than simply a reserved woman who had lived a quiet life raising her twin nieces and tending her garden.

For some reason, even though Gram looked pale and was moving even slower than usual, she decided to accompany Josie and Kennedy to visit Libby.

After reliving that story, Josie didn't blame her.

At Riverbend, Miss Ellie was thrilled to see Kennedy and challenged him to a game of checkers. Libby was sitting up in a chair, listening to music.

Josie smiled, relieved. Her aunt looked peaceful today, which felt huge and momentous. Knowing Libby's history seemed to cause a major shift in the atmosphere. Josie felt as if she was seeing her aunt through a different lens now, or from a new vantage point. How strong and unshakable Libby had seemed all those years while Josie was growing up. How ignorant Josie and Nadine had been of their aunt's pain and suffering.

What was it like for Libby to raise someone else's kids instead of the ones she'd lost? The thought made her heart swell to the point of breaking.

Josie pulled a chair close to the bed for Gram, then sat on the bed facing Libby and forced a smile, though it felt so inadequate. "Look at you, all up and perky. And it looks like someone fixed your hair today."

"I'm ready for my close-up now, Mr. DeMille." She smiled.

Josie chuckled at the ancient joke that Gram had often interjected over the years. "How do you feel today?"

"Spectacular, darling."

Josie shook her head. This new version of Libby would take some getting used to. She offered to read and Libby accepted, so she read a chapter of her novel, then Libby asked her to read the Bible. Josie opened to Psalms again and read from the first verse she saw.

"Where can I go from your Spirit? Where can I flee from your presence? If I go up to the heavens, you are there; if I make my bed in the depths, you are there."

"True." Libby fixed her gaze directly at Josie, her sapphire eyes shining. "God is always with you. You can't outrun him, and you can't leave him behind. You keep forgetting that, Nadine."

Josie gasped, then shot a look across the room at Kennedy. He and Eleanor were focused on their checker game, oblivious to Libby's blunder.

"Libby," Josie whispered. What could she tell her? How could she make sure Libby didn't slip again?

"Grandma, are you decent?"

Will McKnight strode into the room carrying a paper sack and nodded at the visitors on Libby's side. "And before you ask," he said, locking eyes with Josie, "Yes, I brought enough to share." He cracked a half grin.

There was that darn tingle again, right on cue.

Will pulled up a chair beside Kennedy and pretended to study the checker game, but he was acutely aware of Josie's presence, like a live wire putting off an electric current in the air. He offered Grandma a Klondike bar, asked Josie if Kennedy could have one, then offered one to each of the three women on the other side of the room.

Josie's grandmother shook her head. She looked frail, or like she'd been crying, or both.

"Sounds divine," Libby drawled, "but I'm late for rehearsal. Some other time, maybe." She sighed and turned to her mother. "Read to me, Hermia. And no more Longfellow."

"I brought sonnets today, fairest," the older woman said, digging through a big cloth bag that looked like something from the stagecoach days. The older woman always sounded like someone who watched way too much PBS.

Will offered an ice cream bar to Josie, but she shook her head.

"None for me, thanks," she said, her voice low. She seemed down, quieter than usual.

"No problem, all the more for me." He checked to make sure Grandma Eleanor was faring well with hers, then unwrapped a chocolate-covered square and took a bite.

Josie watched him.

"Oh. You must be a granola girl. I can feel the disdain in your eyes from here."

"Me?" One brow arched. She made a scoffing sound. "I could put away three of those suckers without batting an eye."

He leaned back, surprised. "Really. Duly noted. And I stand corrected."

Her chin stuck out. If she was trying to look tough, it wasn't working. She just looked sort of adorable.

Even so, something about her was off. Not that he knew her well enough to know that, but she seemed down, subdued.

He turned to watch Grandma and Kennedy's game, but the boy was now dumping all the toys out of his backpack with a vengeance. The poor kid was probably bored out of his mind.

Will got up and went down the hall to the nurses' station and refilled Grandma's cup with fresh apple juice, still wondering about Josie. And her son. The little guy was cooped up inside all day with a bunch of loony old women. An idea came to mind. It might be a little left field, but what would be the harm in it? The worst she could do was say no.

He returned to Grandma's room and said, "Josie? Can I talk to you for a second?" He motioned to the hallway with his head.

She followed him out, staying within watching distance of her son and the others.

He turned to her. "Are you doing okay? Getting enough rest?"

Her mouth gaped. "Wow. I must look worse than I thought."

Way to go, McKnight. "Uh, no. I just thought...you have a lot on your plate—taking care of your aunt, your grandma, and your son. It's probably hard to get any down time."

She attempted a smile, but it seemed stiff and didn't quite reach her eyes. "I'm just trying to focus on getting through one day at a time. I probably need to try harder to get some sleep."

"Try harder to sleep?" He let out a chuckle. "Kind of an oxymoron."

She smiled again, but this time, it was real, like her heart was in it. "That's me. An oxymoron."

His gaze lingered on her smile, obliterating every other thought. Everything except that light dusting of freckles across the bridge of her nose, like a sprinkle of cinnamon sugar.

"So…was there something besides how haggard I look, or was that it?"

He cleared his throat. "Yeah, actually, I was just thinking that if you and Kennedy were up for a little R and R, I have a boat, and I'm off on Saturday, if you're free. Maybe we could take him out on the river and do a little fishing."

Her eyes widened. "On a boat? Seriously?"

He nodded, pleased. He'd guessed right.

She glanced at the others, and while she was clearly intrigued by the idea, she was waffling.

"I'm not a creeper, if you're worried about—"

"No, it's not that. Far from it, actually."

What, then? He waited.

She turned and met him with those stunning eyes, nearly taking his breath away. "Can I be honest?"

"Please."

She drew a steady breath. "It's really kind of you, and it's a very tempting offer. But my life is kind of complicated, and I'm really not looking to date anyone right now."

Whoa. "Oh, no, it's not a date. And as long as we're being honest, I'm not interested in dating you, either. I have no desire to put the moves on you. At all."

Her brows arched. "Wow. Point made. Thanks."

Good one, idiot. "No, that's not what I meant, sorry. Any guy would have to be totally braindead not to want—"

And getting better. You should stop now.

Her eyes widened, but her astonishment relaxed into a flushed smile.

He hissed through his teeth. "I'm wrecking this, aren't I?"

"Pretty much," she chuckled.

It was a soft, musical sound, and he found himself wanting to hear more of it. A pleasant buzz stole over him. "I get it. My life is complicated, too. I just thought you could use a friend. But the last thing I want to do is add more stress to your life."

She studied him, boring into him with her vibrant gaze, like she was measuring his every word against what she saw in his eyes. He couldn't remember ever being sized up so thoroughly by anyone.

"And like I said, the invite includes Kennedy, so it would be a party of three."

Josie looked over her shoulder again, at the others.

"You can even pitch in for gas, if that makes you feel better."

She turned to him and busted out laughing. "Wow, you really know how to sweeten a deal."

Something in his chest squeezed at the sound of her laugh.

"Okay, Will, you drive a hard bargain. We accept."

"Excellent." He told her what time he'd pick them up on Saturday morning, but as he followed her back in to join the others, it dawned on him that he'd been fooling himself, and what he'd said wasn't exactly true.

In fact, telling Josie he didn't want to date her was a flat-out lie.

CHAPTER
-17-

They think I long for another world because I wish to escape this one.
But they don't know I simply long for all that is precious
to stop slipping away from me.
—Gwendolyn Buckley, age 71

Gram was spending Thursday with Libby, so Josie stayed at the farm. The weather was so warm and mild, she suggested that Kennedy bring his Hot Wheels outside and find a place to make a town and some roads while she caught up on work. They scouted around Gram's backyard and beyond until Josie spied a mound of dirt next to a big, flat stump, near the woods.

As they reached the pile, Kennedy said, "Look! It's a game. Can we play?"

On closer look, the stump had a chessboard carved into its surface, and there were several painted rocks set around the board like chess pieces.

Libby and Jenny's chess game, most likely. Something about the idea of Libby playing chess with a homeless woman made her tear up again. She sighed. She longed to be able to talk to Libby. There was so much she never knew about her aunt.

Kennedy was examining the board and rocks, but Josie called him away. "I think someone is still playing their game, so we probably shouldn't disturb it."

He threw her a pouty look. She steered him to the dirt pile and got him started making roads, then found a grassy place to sit and fired up her laptop. The breeze was perfect; not too chilly, just enough of a flow to bring a hundred familiar scents wafting in, of pungent pine and fir and wild grasses warmed by the sun, surrounding her like a loving embrace. The sun also warmed her skin, which would mean more freckles, but who cared? She'd finally come to the place of accepting the way she looked, freckles and all. Why not? The good Lord had made her the way she was, and there wasn't a lot she could do about it even if she wanted to.

What Libby had said about God always being with her had been lingering in the back of her mind. She knew God wasn't one to look past her pretense with a blind eye.

As she edited a photo to match her client's color palette, she wondered again what God must think of her life, her lie. And her very good reasons for her lie.

If they were such good reasons, why wasn't she trusting God to fix the situation?

That was just it. It had always been Josie's job to fix things. To take matters in hand and help those she loved. To smooth things out, to make wrongs right, to make everything perfect. This had been her job from the earliest moment she could remember. From the beginning, she and Nadine had been so inseparable that whenever Nadine was in some jam or another, Josie had been right there, the one Nadine could always count on. It was a given, like an unspoken rule. Even as Nadine got older and became the brash tornado, the daring force, the one who thrived on defying death and intentionally pushing Josie beyond the point of frustration. Josie had simply adapted and ramped up her rescue skills to keep up with Nadine's chaos.

So now, she lived with the consequences of adapting to her sister's latest chaos. The life Josie lived as Kennedy's mother was a life that had begun like a tiny seed falling to the ground, but had quickly taken root as the child grew until it became too hard to explain, too deep to uproot, too big to turn back, and by then, too late to change.

Right? Wrong? An overlapping of the two? Josie hardly knew anymore. The lines of love and loyalty had grown too fuzzy for her to be sure of anything. All she knew was that Nadine was no longer rational or trustworthy, so the job of handling everything remained Josie's.

God, I don't know what you would have me do differently, but I can't allow this child to be damaged. I just can't. If that means you want nothing more to do with me, I understand. I'm used to being discarded. I guess I'll get over it.

Movement from the corner of her eye grabbed Josie's attention. A slender, baggy-clothed figure lurked in the shadows, swaying slightly, like a stiff gust of wind could carry her away.

Josie stilled. Gram hadn't left food out for Jenny in a while. Josie had an apple with her. She sat still, just watching as the woman hovered in the shadows. Maybe since she'd seen Josie with Gram, she wouldn't be afraid now.

Trying to sound casual, Josie said, "Hi, Jenny," then focused on her work and pretended not to notice the woman, hoping she would see that Josie was not a threat. She held her breath and waited.

Slowly, the woman stepped out of the trees and edged closer to the stump.

Josie took a sidelong glance at her. Jenny wore deeply sagging sweatpants and several layers of sweatshirts, worn thin and colorless.

She still carried the bundle of rags she'd had with her the other day.

"Are you hungry?" Josie asked. "Because I have an extra apple, if you want it." She held it up to show her.

Jenny's gaze flitted to Josie. Her eyes were a pale shade of blue, her skin brown and leathery, her hair sparse and graying. Her clothes hung so loosely that it was hard to tell what condition she was in, but her features were so sharp and her face so gaunt that Josie could only imagine how thin the woman must be.

The woman took a step closer, then glanced at the chess game. "Where'd she go?"

"Libby? She's been sick, but she's getting better now." Josie wasn't sure how much reality the woman could grasp, or how she would react to the news of Libby's accident and the extent of her injuries.

Jenny moved to the stump, then with great care, she set the pile of rags down close to her feet.

As Jenny examined the position of the chess pieces, Josie took a closer look at Jenny's pile and saw that the bundle was actually a tattered receiving blanket wrapped around a filthy baby doll.

Dismay and sympathy shuddered through her.

Jenny moved one of the rocks to a new position. "It's her move now."

"Good, I'll let her know. She's probably got the next one all planned out." Josie hesitated, then stood.

The old woman stumbled back a step and squinted at Josie, her body suddenly taut. "What do you want?"

"I just wanted to give you this." She held up the apple.

Jenny studied Josie. Then she saw Kennedy playing with his cars in the dirt. She made a weird sound, like a wounded cat, then snatched up her doll and clutched it to her chest. "You're lying. You're trying to take my baby."

Josie shook her head, struck with sorrow for this frail woman plagued with delusions and fear.

"No, Jenny, I would never—"

Muttering, Jenny turned and shuffled off toward the woods.

As she watched her go, Josie felt rattled. It was so unsettling, that someone could wander alone through life like that, exposed to the elements, foraging for food. Gram had said the woman didn't like confinement, felt caged by walls, but Josie suspected she was already trapped in a prison that no one could see.

Later that night, after Kennedy was asleep, Josie made Gram a piece of brown sugar cinnamon toast and a soft-boiled egg, then joined her with a cup of herbal tea. Good thing Libby knew what tea was supposed to look like—sealed in a little bag that you dunked with a string—and kept a stash of lavender chamomile on hand.

"I spoke to Jenny today."

Gram paused mid-bite and blinked at Josie. "Did you? How strange. Woodland folk rarely show themselves to humans."

"Really. Then what does that make you?"

Setting her toast down, Gram wiped her mouth with a cloth. "Titania."

Josie laughed. "Gram, you are no more Queen of the Fairies than I am. And come on, you know there's no such thing."

"What gave you cause to speak to the lady?"

Josie drew a deep breath. "I was trying to give her an apple, but she took off before I could convince her to take it."

Gram shook her head. "She will not take food from you. She believes she must earn it."

Ah. The note about gathering pinecones came to mind. "Not even if she's hungry?"

"Nay." Gram heaved a sigh. "She is determined to work, but I fear she will never rest, poor soul. Not on this earth." Her eyes glistened with tears. "It's a wretched thing, to wear the shackles of the unabsolved."

"Have you tried to get her help?"

Gram pushed her plate away, her food barely touched. Then she grasped her stick and rose to her feet. "She will accept no help."

"What about getting her into a shelter or a home where they treat mental illness?"

"We tried. It drove the poor soul away for months. But then one day, she reappeared." Gram turned to go, then stopped. "At least this way, we can watch over her, and know how she fares. Which is better than the alternative, methinks."

That night, Nadine returned again in a dream.

Come on Josie, come over to my side of the river.

No, you need to come back to me.

Why?

So we're on the same side.

But that's the problem. We're not the same.

Josie stared at her, trying to understand.

Just come, Jose. Why won't you come with me?

The river is way too strong to swim across.

But there's a bridge, remember?

Josie looked downriver, but the bridge was gone. Now there was only a single rope stretched across, like a tightrope.

Bye, Josie.

Wait, Nadine, don't go.

But Nadine turned and vanished into the woods.

CHAPTER
-18-

I can't remember the last time I saw my mom smile.
—Will McKnight, age 13

Will signed off from Friday's conference call, then sat back and rubbed his eyes. Wildfire season was already on top of them, and the Northwest Coordination Center just confirmed everyone's suspicions: The better part of the state was critically low on firefighting personnel and desperate for recruits. Will was going to spend at least a week or two at the Umpqua National Forest two hours south, and since he was still line-qualified, he'd most likely be working on an actual fire crew.

He was no stranger to battling forest fires, and he was ready. Before being hired as LEO, he'd spent several years working as a woodland firefighter. He'd learned a lot and he'd learned fast, which was no surprise, since he'd grown up seeing it firsthand. Keith McKnight had spent many years as a Hot Shot and a Smoke Jumper before becoming a Zone Management Officer. Will had always known he would follow in his dad's footsteps.

He clocked out, and as he drove home, memories flooded in of the first time he worked on a fire crew right after high school. He could still see the glow of pride in his dad's face when he came home covered in soot, exhausted, and ready to go right back out.

Of course by that time, Mom and Mandy were long gone.

As a kid, Will was used to his dad being gone for weeks at a time; he understood it was part of the job. When Keith was home, Will's friends would often come over to hang out and beg him to tell his smoke jumping stories. They practically worshipped him.

But for reasons Will never understood, the Keith McKnight fan club never included his wife, Linda.

Will could still remember the tension in the house when Dad was gone and how uptight his mom would get when he was away. The tension only increased over time. He couldn't remember his mom ever being happy, but she seemed downright agitated whenever Dad was out working a fire.

And to Will, this made no sense. Dad was already a firefighter when Mom married him. Hadn't she known that fighting forest fires was his job? Didn't she know he'd be gone for weeks at a time? And that he wouldn't be able to call home while out in the forest?

Back then, communication from fire crew was little to none, and Will sometimes wondered if his mom's tension was from worry about Dad's safety. But then the day she packed up and left shot that theory down.

Eventually, Will had stopped wondering why his mom was so unhappy. At some point, he'd figured the loss was all hers. He and Dad had managed without her.

And yet, he still felt bitter. Not for his own sake, but for his dad's. Keith had always been a fun, upbeat guy, someone known for lighting up a room just by being there. He had this endless joy from somewhere inside him, like a natural spring. But when his wife left, the light and joy in Dad faded, and he was never the same.

That was hard to forgive. Not just hard, but pretty much impossible.

Will pulled into his driveway, parked in front of the cabin, and then carried his gear inside. He started a fire in the stone fireplace, then waited while the kindling crackled and popped. Will's pastor had often said that there was no point stewing about the actions of others. No good could be gained from it. The best thing to do was to make peace with the past and lay it to rest. Which Will had honestly tried to do. But peace was such a hollow, wimpy replacement for bitterness. Bitterness had weight. Substance.

If he had to be honest, peace was nowhere near as satisfying.

He stoked the fire and checked his calendar. Two weeks out of town for him was a long time. He needed to figure out what to do about Grandma Eleanor. Mandy could probably come a few times, but he knew she couldn't make the trip from Sisters every day.

Without thinking, he pictured Josie visiting her aunt at Riverbend, and then quickly dismissed the image. Favors created entanglements, and entanglements created…tangles.

As he heated chili on the stove, thoughts of Josie kept returning.

Okay, this was insane—he hardly knew her. It was insane to be consumed with thoughts of someone he hardly knew.

Insane.

Even if her smile was like sunlight warming the ground after a long, suffocating rain.

Yep. Definitely insane.

It's just fishing.
We're just friends.
Just two friends fishing.

Despite giving herself several stern talkings-to, Josie couldn't wait for Saturday to arrive, and when it did, she actually overslept. Waking in a panic, she threw on clothes, pulled her hair into a ponytail, then tossed cereal bars, two pears, and a milk box into Kennedy's backpack.

Will arrived before dawn and had just gotten out of his truck as Josie stepped outside, flustered and breathless, with a backpack on one shoulder and a sleeping child on the other.

"Hi," she whispered. "Sorry, I—we overslept."

He took one look at the sleeping boy. "Hey, it's okay," he whispered back with a smile. "It's not a fishing derby, just a lazy day off, remember?"

Josie heaved a relieved sigh, grateful that Will wasn't expecting Kennedy to man-up to the rigors of pre-dawn fishing. While Kennedy was thrilled to be doing big guy stuff with a real grown-up guy, he was still a little boy who cried when he was tired and needed snuggles when he was sad. She wasn't ready for him to be all grown up just yet.

They headed out on the highway west, along the river. After a few miles, they turned onto a narrow road that wove for a quarter mile through a deep wall of fir. The sun was just coming up, and light filtered through the evergreens surrounding a log cabin in the center of a lush patch of grass and brilliant autumn foliage. The cabin looked exactly like it belonged here, like it had just sprung up in the middle of the clearing, surrounded by ferns and rhododendrons and gorgeous masses of copper-leafed shrubs.

"Wow," Josie breathed, drinking in the cabin's rugged charm and the beauty of its carefully handcrafted logs. "Is it yours?"

Will simply nodded, then led the way around to the back of the cabin and to the river beyond. As they approached the water, Josie saw a dock jutting out, with a sixteen-foot Starcraft moored there.

"Are you serious? You have your own dock?"

"Yep. It's pretty handy."

She got Kennedy fitted in his life jacket while Will fired up the Evinrude, then they set off upriver, toward the rising sun. Kennedy still wasn't completely awake and said the wind was too cold, so Josie snuggled him on her lap with the blanket Will offered and gave him a cereal bar.

Will wore a Beavers baseball cap, well-worn jeans, and a thick pullover sweatshirt, the sleeves pushed up to reveal tanned, muscular forearms. Josie watched as he navigated the river like someone born on the water. He gave a nod to some of the other boats anchored near the banks.

As they headed east, the rising sun lit the upper rim of the canyon that sloped up and away from the river on either side. The water stretched out ahead like a glistening trail of topaz and sapphire.

When they finally reached the spot he wanted to fish, Will dropped anchor and helped her and Kennedy rig up, then they cast their lines and waited.

Josie drank in the sights, the sounds, and the smells of the McKenzie. "I haven't been on the river in a long time, and I don't even remember the last time I was out in a boat. We—uh, I mean I always fished off the bank."

Idiot. She needed to be more careful about slips like that. She blamed it on being here, at home, on this river, in this colorful canyon packed full of old memories and happy times and Nadine.

Will reached for a thermos. "Coffee?" he asked.

"Yes, please."

Kennedy held his line between his fingers, just like she had shown him. "If I catch a fish, can I keep him?" he asked.

"If he's got a notch on his fin and he's big enough," Josie said.

He leaned forward and squinted hard at the end of his pole.

"What are you doing?"

"I'm gonna watch till it wiggles."

"Interesting," Will said, scratching his unshaven chin. "I've never tried that. Does it work?"

Kennedy nodded, never taking his eyes from the pole.

Josie bit her lip to keep from laughing.

They fished that area for quite a while with only a few nibbles, so Will pulled up and headed for a different spot, where Josie got a bite but didn't hook anything. Will suggested they try trolling for a change.

"Want me to watch your line while you steer?" Josie asked.

"Sure, thanks." Will seemed relaxed, at home. At peace.

This was nice. So nice, in fact, that Josie felt a tug of guilt that she was here relaxing and not with Gram and Libby. But it wasn't like being on the river was all that different than being at home in the yard working on her laptop. But still. It seemed wrong that she could run off and have fun when Libby was stuck in that little room 24/7.

"You okay?" Will asked.

She found him watching her. "Yeah, I'm good. This is really nice, Will. Thank you."

"My pleasure." His rumbling voice set off a rush of warmth inside her.

Stop that.

Kennedy was fascinated by the way his line dragged behind them in the wake as they trolled slowly through the water.

"I think somebody's in sheer heaven here," Josie said. "I really appreciate this."

He nodded. "Like I said, it's my pleasure. In fact, I should be thanking you."

"What for?"

"Inspiring me to take a break. I don't do this. Ever. Work is really busy right now, and when I get a day off, I usually spend it…" He sighed. "Not doing this."

She chuckled. "I'm glad to give you a reason to cut loose, then. From whatever it is you would have been doing."

He glanced ahead, slowed the throttle, moved slightly to let another boat pass. The wake rocked them gently side to side. "It's been a pretty rough year. My dad passed away in February, and I've been sort of picking up the pieces ever since, trying to figure out where they all go." He frowned at the horizon.

"Oh, Will, I'm so sorry." Sadness for him washed over her in waves. "That must be so hard. Was it unexpected?"

He shook his head. "Cancer. He'd had it a few years ago and beat it, but then it came back. He was trying to fight it, but nothing worked." He heaved a sigh. "It wouldn't stop spreading. My dad's always been a fighter, but he finally threw in the towel. I moved back into the cabin with him and did what I could, but he declined pretty fast."

Josie's heart ached. Losing a parent that way had to be a heavy ordeal for anyone, especially someone so young.

"So your cabin, that's where he lived, too?"

Will nodded. "He and I built it together when I was fifteen. The logs came from the clearing, then we milled each one by hand."

"Wow," she breathed. "It's gorgeous."

"Thanks." He checked Ken's line and slowed the throttle a bit more. "Getting any nibbles there, buddy?"

Kennedy shook his head, heaved a sigh. "No. Stupid fish. I fink they're not hungry."

Will pursed his lips. "I think I know just the spot. Let's reel in and head back downriver a ways."

Once they'd reeled in, the boat picked up speed, and Will drove a few miles back the way they came, near his cabin.

"You and Mandy grew up here?" Josie asked.

Will shook his head slowly, but didn't say anything. He pulled closer to the river's edge, then helped Kennedy cast into a little eddy. "My parents split when I was fourteen and Mandy was twelve. She went with our mom."

"Really?" Josie frowned. "I never would have guessed. It looks like you two stayed close, anyway," she said.

He dropped anchor, then turned to her, frowning. "It does?"

She laughed. "Seriously? She clearly adores you."

Will's eyes met Josie's, and for a moment, she thought she saw something deep and unguarded, but it quickly vanished.

"The truth is," he said, "my sister and I have come a long way. We both struggled for a while with the way everything happened, and because we were young, there was a lot we didn't understand. Including how we each felt about the split. She still feels..." He shook his head. "Sorry. I don't know why I'm talking so much."

"No, not at all! How does she feel? I'm all ears."

He eyed her, then huffed a laugh. "I forgot. Girls live for this stuff."

Josie grinned. "True."

Will's gaze lingered on her smile for a long moment, then he went on. "Mandy feels like she got something I missed out on, even though I tell her it's not true, and she knocks herself out trying to make up for it, even though I tell her it's really not necessary."

"Guilt is a powerful habit to break," Josie said softly.

He looked away, seemed to be considering her words. "Yeah, I think you're right," he said. Then he turned to her. "Spoken like an expert."

"Well. I mean, you know. Who doesn't have regrets?" *Careful where you tread, Josephine.*

He nodded slowly. "Enough about me. What about you? You seem pretty close with your aunt and grandma." He dropped his line a few feet away from Kennedy's.

Josie reminded herself to put up some verbal caution tape. "They raised me," she said. "Well, mostly Aunt Libby. She was way more of a mom than an aunt." A mom in more ways than Josie had truly understood until recently.

"What happened to your real parents?"

It was a question she'd been asked countless times, and yet, it didn't feel intrusive or nosy, coming from Will.

"I never knew my father, and my real mom—" She drew a deep breath, measuring each word carefully before she spoke. Will was safely turned away from her, so she went on. "She dropped me off at Gram and Libby's when I was four and I never saw her again."

It was odd how much it still stung, how thoroughly it still reminded her that she was dispensable. Forgettable. Josie turned and looked away, across the stern, to avoid revealing more than she cared to. It was probably written all over her face. *Not enough. Not worth your time. Not worth keeping.*

"So you know how that feels, too."

Josie turned back and found him watching her intently. "What?"

"The hurt. The questions. Wondering what you'd done wrong, why you weren't enough."

"Yes! My gosh. You too?"

He nodded. "It does things to you. Messes with your head."

"It does." She looked away again. This fishing trip was turning into a full-blown therapy session.

"Josie?"

She faced him.

"I don't know if it makes any difference to you, but the way you care for your son and put him first is remarkable. You're obviously nothing like the mother who left you. The way you love him makes that very clear."

Tears blurred her vision, and an achy knot burned her throat. She didn't trust herself to speak, didn't trust the reservoir of guilt not to rise up and spill over. "Thank you," she whispered, her voice barely audible. "You have no idea what that means to me."

He nodded. The way he was regarding her was unnerving, but in a strangely thrilling way. Like she'd been plugged into an electrical current.

Enough of that. "You seem to have a thing for putting others first as well," she said with a smile. "Your dad, and your grandma."

He shrugged. "They're family. Dad moved Grandma into the cabin after Grandpa died, then about two years ago, when her dementia got to be too much for him, Dad moved her into Riverbend, and he went to see her every day. She used to be super independent, but dementia changed that. She didn't feel safe anymore, and she really leaned on my dad. He was the only one who could make her feel at ease. He bore that burden by himself a lot longer than he should have." With a frown, he turned away and reeled in his line. "I should have stepped up sooner."

"You're doing it now, Will. Don't let guilt drag you down. It's a bad habit, remember?"

He glanced at her over his shoulder, his mouth hitched up on one side. "Right."

"You're doing an amazing job."

He let out a sigh. "Thanks. Actually, it turns out I'm going to be a slacker for the next couple of weeks. I'm scheduled to work out of town. Mandy's going to check on her, but she can only come on the weekends."

"Why are you leaving?"

"Fire season doesn't cut us much of a break. For Forest Service personnel, it's all hands on deck."

"Oh no!" Josie blurted out, too loud. "That sounds dang—"

Kennedy swung around, wide-eyed.

She didn't want to use the word dangerous in front of him. "That sounds intense."

Will shrugged.

"Is it? I mean, you know, dangerous?" she whispered.

"Only if I do something stupid."

Josie nodded as she watched Will's face, looking for any hidden signs that there was more to it than he was saying, but he didn't show anything. Typical male. Take a nap, eat a sandwich, battle a forest fire, no big deal.

She drew a steadying breath, trying hard not to imagine the worst-case scenario. "Will?"

"What?"

"Don't do anything stupid."

He chuckled lightly. "I'll try not to." And there it was, in his face. Something *was* off.

"Are you stressed about going?"

"No. Well, not about the work, anyway. But I hate to leave Grandma not knowing if she's getting her liquids. If they miss it for even a day or two, things can get bad for her pretty quick."

Wow. The man was more concerned about his grandma than he was about heading into a deadly fire zone. That hit her with gale force intensity, and suddenly, she found it difficult to breathe. She could not, could not, could not fall for this man.

Could. Not.

"I don't know how much longer I'll be here," she said, "but it will probably be at least a couple of weeks. I can make sure Eleanor's getting food and liquids while you're gone, if you'd like."

His face sobered. "Really? You don't mind?"

"Not at all."

"Wow. I'd sure appreciate that. Thank you."

She shrugged. "It's the least I can do, after the volcano rescue."

With a frown, he studied her, then heaved a sigh. "Josie, you don't have to pay me back for that."

"I don't?" She feigned surprise. "The way you were acting all cranky when you came that night, I just thought—"

"Cranky?" His jaw dropped.

She giggled.

His eyes narrowed, but a twinkle appeared. "Are you mocking me?"

Fully laughing now, she nodded.

"What's so funny?" Kennedy asked.

"Your mom," Will said, eyes never leaving hers. A slow smile formed. "She's a real joker."

"No, she's Wonder Woman." Kennedy reeled in his line.

Josie raised a brow and crossed her arms. "Did you hear that?"

"I think I have to agree." His amusement faded. "But I mean it, you don't owe me anything."

"I know that. But you put yourself in harm's way every day to protect the forest and the people who depend on you for safety and the people you care about. It's the very least I can do." She looked into his eyes. "You'll have enough to deal with, Will. You don't need to be worrying about your grandma, too."

His expression instantly sobered. He swallowed hard and held her gaze, his eyes intense. "That really means a lot to me, Josie. Thank you."

When they returned to Gram's, Kennedy was tired but so excited about his two fish that he hopped out of the truck and took off at a run to tell Gram, forgetting that she was at Riverbend.

Josie turned to say goodbye and found Will leaning on his truck, watching her.

Her heart raced for no good reason. She couldn't begin to read his mind, but she sure hoped he couldn't read hers, because all she could think about was how he was leaving and she might not see him again and that she didn't want to say goodbye. Not now, and certainly not when the time came for her to leave for good.

Don't be dumb, Josie. You can't fall in love with Will McKnight. You just can't.

Kennedy turned around and ran back to Josie. "Forgot my fish!" He took the creel out of her hand, then looked up at Will. "Hey, are you sad? Is it because you didn't catch any fish?"

Will chuckled and ruffled his hair. "Naw, I just don't like good-byes." His gaze rose and met Josie's.

"Oh," Kennedy said. "Me neither. But you can just call me on your radio." Then he took his fish and ran into the house.

Josie fought a ridiculous urge to hug Will. And the way he stood there watching her, as if he was also feeling the same magnetic pull, was making the battle twice as hard.

"Did you want to exchange phone numbers?" she asked.

He nodded. "Yeah. I'd like that."

"I mean, for Eleanor," Josie added quickly, cheeks warming.

"Right. For Eleanor."

CHAPTER
-19-

Peter can't bear to wait, so we're going to elope. Not to hide our love, but because I want to spare Mama and Papa sorrow. They don't believe in love at first sight and they fear I'll be unhappy. But I think what they fear is love itself, the wildness of it.
—Gwendolyn LaPlante, age 23

On Monday, Libby's doctor came to Riverbend for a checkup and evaluation, then took Gram and Josie aside. He reported that her brain function had shown significant improvement, and her ambulatory time was steadily increasing. He was pleased with the progress she'd made with occupational therapy and was optimistic that she would continue to improve. How fully she would recover was something only time could tell, but he was confident Libby would be released to home care very soon.

Home!

This was excellent news, and yet it left Josie and Gram with a list of people to contact and decisions to make. Going home would be better for Libby on so many levels but would also create new challenges. The doctor said Libby would still need assistance, and that a county caseworker could help them find out if home health care was available. Libby also would need occupational therapy, which may or may not be available in home. If not, Libby would need to be transported to rehab three times a week.

Josie knew that Gram was not capable of setting up appointments with the health agency, nor was she physically capable of assisting Libby or driving her anywhere. Nor was Libby capable of taking care of herself, Gram, or the farm.

They would clearly need a lot of help, and possibly, for some time.

What Josie needed to find out was how much help was available from the county. Would it be enough? Josie would love nothing more than to stay at the farm indefinitely and help them, but how long could she stay and still keep her whereabouts hidden from Nadine?

Josie and Gram returned to Libby's room. Someone had brought her a lunch tray, but she wasn't eating. Gram moved in right away and did her thing, coaxing Libby to take bites.

"That stuff is disgusting," Libby murmured. She leaned back against her pillows.

Gram frowned. "But you like mashed potatoes and gravy."

"It's gross." Libby spied a cup with a lid and reached for that instead. "Did you remember to feed Oliver?"

"Who?" Gram asked.

"My rabbit."

Gram screwed up her face as though she were racking her brain. "Oliver, the rabbit." She thought some more. "Dearest, Oliver was your rabbit when you were six."

"*I* want to see the rabbit," Kennedy said.

"If you sit really still by the huckleberry patch," Libby murmured, "you'll see lots of them."

Kennedy turned to Josie. "Mommy, I wanna go see them. Can we?"

Josie mussed his hair. "Sure, maybe we'll go out and look for them tomorrow."

"Don't forget his hat. The sun isn't good for babies."

Josie stilled. Any mention of Kennedy as a baby put her instantly on edge. The sooner Libby came to her senses, the better.

Please, God. She needs her brain back. She needs to be whole. We all need her to be whole.

"Please keep a close watch on my baby."

Josie's heart hammered.

"Shh," Gram whispered. "All is well, sweet love. Shh."

Gram continued to console Libby and offered to read to her. Meanwhile, Kennedy had contracted a serious case of the fidgets, so

Josie decided to take him outside for a race around the grounds and maybe burn off some of his energy.

Eleanor was in the TV room along with Mandy and two young girls. Earlier, when Josie had first arrived, she'd given Eleanor a root beer float, which the older woman had accepted without a fuss, to Josie's relief.

"There she is again," Eleanor blurted out when she saw Josie.

Josie stopped, brows raised.

"That's Josie, Grandma," Mandy said. "Will's friend."

"The hussy."

Mandy gasped. "Sorry, Josie! Pay no attention to her, she gets things mixed up."

"I know." Josie smiled. "No worries."

Kennedy was staring at Mandy's girls, whom she introduced as Amelie and Scarlet. Both girls were talking to Kennedy at once and trying to get him to play. He just stared, then finally responded by taking a toy truck out of his pocket and showing it to them. That bashfulness would last about a second and a half.

"For the life of me I don't know why Willie keeps that phony baloney around."

Josie's eyes widened.

Mandy shook her head, then glanced at Josie. "She means Will's last girlfriend." She turned to Eleanor. "He's not with Kristi anymore, Grandma. They broke up. Remember?"

"I hope he dropped her like a sack of bricks."

Mandy chuckled. "Pretty much."

"Bleach-blonde string bean."

"Um, actually, she looked like a supermodel," Mandy added.

Josie couldn't help feeling a rapt fascination by the topic of Will's love life, but she wasn't sure he'd appreciate it. Actually, she wasn't even sure she wanted to take part. But then, maybe the more she heard about him dating a supermodel, the sooner she'd get a reality check, and the sooner she could get her focus back.

Fact: Will McKnight, local knight in shining armor and all-around good guy, was a supermodel magnet.

"Break ups are hard," Josie said, fully aware that she was angling.

"Yes. It was really hard on him, even though he was the one that ended it."

"Because she was too skinny."

Mandy burst out laughing. "Grandma! He didn't break up with her because she was too skinny."

"Well, he should have."

Mandy just shook her head, then eyed Josie. "Will hasn't had the best luck with women."

Josie nodded, knowing she should make a polite exit and leave them to their ruthless dissection of Will's love life, but she'd swallowed the bait and was now thoroughly hooked.

"She was a piranha," Eleanor said in her teeny voice.

"True," Mandy said. "And for the longest time, everyone else saw it except Will. The big, glaring moment of truth for him was finding out she was two-faced."

Josie cringed. "She was cheating on him?"

"No, she was cheating at work, stealing sales accounts from co-workers. But even worse, she made it look like another girl had screwed up a big account, and it cost the other girl her job." Mandy shook her head. "I think the worst part of all was that when Kristi finally admitted it to him, she acted like it was no big deal. She said anyone with an ounce of ambition would have done the same. She didn't even care that she'd gotten someone fired."

Josie gasped. "That's awful! Good thing he found out before it was too late."

"Colombo can spot a phony baloney a mile away," Eleanor chirped.

Mandy heaved a sigh. "Will's been burned too many times, poor guy. He has zero tolerance for deception. And even though it jaded him, I can't say I blame him."

"No," Josie said weakly. "Can't blame him."

She said her goodbyes and gathered Kennedy but couldn't get outside quickly enough to escape a face-off with the obvious.

Fact: Will McKnight hated liars.

Another Fact: Josie Norris was a liar. A phony baloney. And therefore, she had no hope of being anything more to Will than a one-time acquaintance.

But what else had she been hoping for? Even if he didn't despise her for lying, Josie was in no position to date anyone, much less pursue the kind of relationship her heart desperately craved when he was near—both in person and in her thoughts. Kennedy's well-being was solely in her hands, and as long as the full weight of that rested on her, she would have no other priority, no other focus. No other man in her life. Crushing on gorgeous Forest Service rangers with a soft spot for kids and kooky old folks was definitely out.

After dinner that evening, Josie bagged up leftovers into little freezer meals for Gram and Libby, which turned out to be the perfect chore for Kennedy. When he discovered he could stuff cooked noodles into Ziploc bags with his bare hands, he was ecstatic, and by adding a scoop of Ragu and a couple of meatballs, he was proud to discover that he now knew how to "cook."

Gram had gone to bed right after picking at her dinner, and while Josie and Kennedy worked on their task, Josie couldn't shake a nagging sense of sadness. The way Libby fretted at times was hard to watch. Why was she so unsettled? Will said his dad had a way of easing Eleanor's disordered mind. How? Was there a trick, something Josie could do to set Libby's mind at ease?

Longing to hear Libby's voice, Josie waited until Kennedy was asleep, then took out the second journal and cocooned herself in the comforter on Libby's bed.

> *December 20, 1999*
>
> *I wish I could remember Daddy. I've been thinking about him a lot lately, probably because Mom and I are trying to raise two little girls the best we can without a father. There are no male role models in sight, so these girls are stuck with the spinster version of The Odd Couple for parents.*
>
> *And I'm afraid that's just not enough. I'M not enough. I suspect that growing up fatherless left me missing something vitally important. I'm sure that if Daddy had been alive, I never would have been stupid enough to fall for that yellow-bellied piece of trash.*

It's almost Christmas. There are a lot of things I'd like to give these girls, but the one thing they need most, I can't give them. Girls need a father to give them the confidence and worth they'll need out in the world. A girl needs to believe in her soul that she's worth sticking up for.

I'm afraid that's never going to happen for Josie and Nadine. The best I can do is teach them how to wield a shotgun and a few choice swear words.

Mom's been wondering lately if there's Someone kind and fatherly in charge of everything, but then, she gets things mixed up. If there is a God, I wish he'd show up. These girls are going to need all the help they can get.

Oh, I fear for them. You have no idea how much.

-Libby

Josie stopped and re-read the last lines again, stunned by Libby's concern. It wasn't until several years later, when Josie was in high school, that Libby discovered there was a God that she would know and trust. She had found the father she'd been missing. No wonder Libby had tried so hard to get Josie and Nadine to come to church with her.

October 16, 2001

I just spent a half hour at the grade school yelling at that flabby, four-eyed sow, Miss Belden, who has absolutely no business teaching kids. What she needs is a serious butt kicking. If I didn't think I'd end up in jail, I'd do it myself. But I did get in her face and tell her it was her turn to be schooled. Her beady little possum eyes went huge.

Then I said, "This isn't some game where the biggest bully wins. Belittling children in front of the entire class for not knowing the answer to a question that YOU failed to teach them is proof that you're nothing but a petty tyrant. You have no business teaching nine-year olds. If I ever hear that you've ridiculed Nadine or any other child again, I'll demand that the school board revoke your credentials and I'll press charges. I still have a half a mind to."

I guess I made my point. The coward just stood there, quaking. I think she may have wet herself.

Any adult who would pick on a child had better be prepared to deal with someone their own size.

Okay. If anyone needs me, I'll be in the garden. With sharp things. Be warned.

-Libby

Josie remembered that day and that she'd wanted to kick Miss B in the shins herself. It was one of the few times Josie had ever seen Nadine cry. She also remembered how furious Libby was and how Miss Belden had never looked Josie or Nadine in the eye after that.

She had no idea that Libby had felt inadequate as a mom or that she worried that her fatherless nieces were missing something, but Josie wanted to reassure Libby that she'd grown up feeling totally safe. She'd never doubted that there was someone strong and fearless who always had her back.

February 14, 2002

The twins turned 10 today. They don't mind sharing their birthday with Valentine's Day because there's always candy. Today, when they brought home their valentines, it dawned on me how different Nadine and Josie are becoming. Josie took all her valentine cards out of the little mailbox she'd decorated and read each kid's name one by one aloud, God help us, along with every idiotic, generic Valentine message. Nadine on the other hand tossed hers into the trash, grabbed a handful of pretzels, and flopped down on the sofa. When I peeked in the trash later—hey, I have a right to know what's going on around here—I saw that Nadine had gotten twice as many valentines as Josie. I don't know if she trashed them because she didn't care about them, or because she didn't want Josie to feel bad for not getting as many. I'm not going to ask. I'm sure I already know.

Good grief, those two remind me of me and Ger more and more each day. I just hope Nadine figures out that there's nothing wrong with liking respect. It's like she goes out of her way to make sure no one takes her seriously because she's afraid they won't. I get it. But truth be told, I think the only person on the planet whose love and respect she cares about is Josie's. Must be a twin thing.
-Libby

Love and respect.

Josie re-read the last few lines. Maybe there was a time that was true, when she and Nadine were young. She hardly remembered. The changes and estrangement of later years was like someone placed a blurry filter over the entire photo gallery of their earlier years.

Had Nadine really wanted to avoid hurting Josie's feelings? If that was true, what had changed her so much?

She read on.

June 9, 2003

Today was the girls' last day of fifth grade. I'm sure they wanted to celebrate their freedom by fishing and hanging out in their fort under the bridge. But I just couldn't bear to have them out of my sight, not today. Sorry. I know they think I'm a shrew, and that's okay. I didn't have the heart to tell them why I need them close to me today. I don't know that I ever will.

Today, he would have been twelve. Leonardo Joseph Allen. God help me, I still miss him. He was the most beautiful baby I've ever seen. He was absolutely perfect in every way, the best thing I've ever done. I miss him so much it hurts.

Mom forgets that today would have been Leo's birthday. Probably because the four months that he lived is part of that harsh reality that Mom has neatly folded up and tucked away, out of sight where she doesn't have to face unbearable sorrow. It's just too much for her.

So, Diary, it's just you, me, and a glass of gin.
Happy twelfth birthday, Leo, my darling son.
-Libby

Josie gasped. Libby had a baby that lived? A son?

As she re-read the entry, sadness washed over her, dulling her senses. Libby had given birth to a child? She'd actually had a child of her own?

What had happened to him?

Crying, Josie pushed the book away. Libby had been so closed off, so quiet about her own life, her loss, her pain. Why? And how had she motored on through life so steady, so strong? How had she shifted, without complaint, into the role of raising her two nieces?

Her phone dinged with a text alert.

Will.

Her heart tripped.

> Will – 12:33 a.m.
> Hi. Just talked to Mandy. Please forget everything my grandma says about me. Btw, Amelie thinks Kennedy is "sooo cute." I won't tell you what Mandy said about you—it'd make you blush.

> Will – 12:33 a.m.
> In a good way.

> Will – 12:33 a.m.
> Sorry, that went way off course. Thanks for taking Grandma a root beer float. She said it was the best whiskey sour she's ever had—not that she'd know. Thanks again. Sleep well. See you in a week or two, Lord willing.

> Josie – 12:34 a.m.
> Don't worry about a thing, I've got you covered. Just take care of yourself. Please be careful—I mean, don't do anything stupid. ☺ Kennedy is begging non-stop to go fishing on your boat again.

Will – 12:34 a.m.
Tell Kennedy I'll come back in one piece so I can take him fishing, but only if he promises to let me catch more fish! I can't have a four-year-old smoking me on my own boat.

CHAPTER
-20-

I had no intention of being a mom. I've never had that calm, cool mojo that real mommies have. I cuss in my head when I can't get the lid off the pickle jar. I'm afraid of moldy bread and IKEA instructions. And don't even get me started on spiders. Yet here I am raising a mini superhero, totally wrapped around his sticky little fingers and melted by his goofy, sweet smile.
–Josie Norris, age 26

Josie woke Tuesday feeling a blanket of sorrow pressing on her. Something was horribly wrong. Then she remembered: Libby had a son who only lived four months. Was he Dean's child? Was his death a result of Dean's abuse?

Her heart ached at the thought of all that Libby had lost.

According to the journal, Gram knew about Leo, and it was sheer willpower that had kept Josie from waking her grandma at eleven o'clock at night to ask about the baby. That is, if asking would get anywhere, because as Libby had said, Gram had a way of tucking painful things away in a mental padded room that she kept locked tight.

Which explained a lot, actually.

Josie checked Kennedy's bunk, but apparently, he was already up, so she padded downstairs in the pj's that she'd finally gotten the nerve to borrow from Libby.

Kennedy was standing on a chair that he'd pushed over to the counter. He turned to her. "I'm cooking breakfast." He reached his hand into the box of Cap'n Crunch that Josie had picked up at Wally's, then pulled out a fistful and sprinkled cereal on top of whatever was in the three bowls.

Josie came closer for a peek. Each bowl contained a scoop of Libby's homemade applesauce, garnished with curled up peelings of string cheese, and topped with bits of cereal dotted with Crunchberries. She bit back a smile. "Wow. Look at you, Mr. Chef. Protein, fiber, and… sugar. All the food groups. And so fancy. Do I get one?"

"Yep." He nodded. "Here you go. Oh, wait." He added a spoon.

"Thanks." Good thing for him she wasn't picky. "Looks good."

He grinned and carried one of the bowls to Gram's spot at the kitchen table.

"Is Gram outside?" she asked.

Kennedy nodded. "She had a job for the fairy lady." His nose wrinkled. "She's weird."

Josie took a bite of applesauce and crunched thoughtfully. "She's just confused. And lonely. That's how people get sometimes when they don't have any family." Or all their mental faculties.

"Well, I have a family. You, Gram, and Aunt Libby. And Miss Ellie. And Ranger McNugget."

"Whoa, dial it back, buddy. Miss Ellie and Ranger Will are just friends. Family are the people you're related to. That means the people who…uh…"

Okay. She needed to think this through better.

"Who eat breakfast together," he finished.

Josie nodded. "Yes. Okay. That's a start. We can talk about biology and genes when you're a little older." Among other things.

It was Gram's day to visit Libby, which meant Josie didn't have a lot of time to get answers before dropping her off. She went outside and looked around the potting bench, but Gram wasn't there. Though Josie didn't see anyone lurking, she had that creepy feeling again that she was being watched. She headed to the barn and found Gram inside, talking to an orange tabby who was nursing her litter.

"Have you met Peaseblossom?" Gram asked Josie.

"Yes, I have. She's got her hands—I mean, her paws full."

"Does she look peaked to you?" Gram said, her brow furrowed. "I don't think she eats enough. She's not very bright. I worry about how her children will fare."

Speaking of which… "Gram, I need to ask you about something."

Gram stroked Peaseblossom's head, then straightened and took hold of Josie's arm, grasping her walking stick in the other hand. She leaned on Josie as they made their way out of the barn. The sky was cloudless and blue, the perfect backdrop for the brilliant reds and golds scattered throughout the canyon, mingling with the evergreens.

Josie drew a fortifying breath. "Gram, is it true that Libby had a baby boy?"

Gram's steps faltered. Trembling, she shook her head. "It's too much sadness," she whispered.

Sad, and incomprehensible. Josie couldn't begin to imagine all that Libby had suffered. "Was he Dean's child?"

Aiming her gaze far away, Gram spoke in hushed tones. "Yes. He'd robbed her of the first two. When a third child was on the way, something inside Liberty snapped." Gram met Josie's gaze. "She refused to lose another, so she came home." She set out again toward the house.

Josie followed. "So, she was pregnant with Dean's child when she left him?"

Gram nodded again as they reached the porch. She took one step at a time, slowly.

"And she lived here with you when Leo was born?"

Pausing on the second step, Gram glanced across the yard, her chin trembling. "We don't speak his name."

Obviously.

"I know it hurts, and I'm sorry to bring it up. I just wish I'd known."

This explained a whole lot about Libby, the woman Josie had always assumed had no family except her two nieces and Gram. But now, it turned out she'd had a husband and a son, as well as two other babies who never saw their mommy's face.

"Libby has made her peace. I respect her wishes and leave it be."

"I understand."

Well, not exactly. Was it Libby who didn't want Leo's name mentioned, or Gram? It seemed that both women were trying to protect each other from pain. Josie hated to continue prodding Gram, but she had no other choice. "Was the baby sick?"

Shaking her head, Gram went inside, and Josie followed. Gram took her kettle to the sink, filled it with water, then put it on to heat.

"He was not sick, not that any of us knew. One afternoon, as he napped, he just didn't wake." Her voice broke in a sob.

"Oh no! He died in his sleep?"

Gram sat down, lifted part of her broomstick skirt, and wiped tears from her cheeks. "He was perfect. Dark haired like my Peter, so handsome. So pink and healthy."

So he hadn't been sick or abused. It sounded like it might have been a case of crib death. What a heartbreaking outcome for any parent to deal with, and especially for Libby who had already lost so very much.

How tragic that a child of Libby's had finally survived, only to die from SIDS.

"Poor Aunt Libby," Josie whispered, tears clogging her throat.

"We must speak of it no more," Gram whispered, fiddling with the tip of her braid. "It is too, too painful."

On Wednesday, Gram and Kennedy were busy painting flower pots, so Josie went to Riverbend alone. When she arrived, she learned that the occupational therapist had taken Libby on a walk around the facility, so Josie spent some time with Eleanor and gave her the option of root beer or apple juice. She chose both.

When Eleanor finished, Josie tracked down Libby. Her aunt was getting tired but had walked farther than she had before.

"There you are," Libby said to Josie. She leaned heavily on her walker. "I had a dream you came home and slept in my bed."

Josie fell into slow step with Libby and her aide. The odd thing was, she had actually fallen asleep in Libby's bed, reading her journal.

Libby winced. "I need to sit for a minute."

"Just a few more steps, Miss Libby," the aide said. She signaled to another staffer to bring up the wheelchair that was trailing them a little ways behind. "You can do it. Three, two, one, there. You did it!" They helped her into the wheelchair and then let Josie wheel her back to her room.

"You went a lot farther today," Josie said, as they wheeled along the hallway.

"We can't go too far," Libby said. "It's against the rules."

"When have you ever let that stop you?"

"Darn right." She looked at Josie sleepily. "Hey, did you get enough to eat?"

"Me?" As Josie steered Libby into her room, she remembered the banana peanut butter toast she and Kennedy had decorated like teddy bears that morning. "I don't think you have to worry about that."

"You were always so picky."

Frowning, Josie eyed her aunt cautiously. She had never been picky. Nadine had been the picky one, another way the twins differed. Maybe it was time to set things straight.

"Aunt Libby, do you know who I am?" Josie held her breath.

Libby nodded. "Feenie."

Relieved, Josie chuckled. "Wow. I haven't been called Feenie in a long time. Not since—"

Feenie and *Deenie* were nicknames that she and Nadine used for each other.

The aide met them in the room and transferred Libby from the wheelchair to the chaise chair in the corner.

Josie decided to bite the bullet. She pulled a chair close and lowered herself to sit facing Libby. "I heard a story today."

"Oh, I'd love a story."

"This one was about a little boy."

"Little Boy Blue, come blow your horn…"

"No, younger," Josie said, biting her lip. She had been mulling over what she'd read in Libby's journal, trying to figure out how to learn what she could about baby Leo without distressing Libby. Josie didn't want to mention his name, but maybe there was a way she could work up to it.

Mozart was playing on the CD player, which seemed to keep Libby's mood even.

"Why don't you tell me a story," Josie said. "Tell me about…when you came back home to live with Gram. What was it like, just the two of you?"

"Mom? Oh, honestly. She's always quoting that infernal Hermia. Did you ever see her costumes?"

"Yes," Josie said. She and Nadine had spent countless hours in

Gram's old theater trunk and had about worn out all her costumes playing and creating some gloriously ridiculous characters. She'd have to take Kennedy up to the attic sometime and show him.

"I bet you wore them when Gram wasn't around." Josie snickered at the absurdity of that. Libby never did anything silly.

Libby shook her head. "No way. I was enormous."

Josie's breath caught. "As in…pregnant?"

She nodded. "I looked like a pumpkin on stilts."

"Tell me more." She prayed she wasn't pushing too hard. It wouldn't do Libby any good to have an emotional meltdown in her current mental state.

Her aunt's face sagged, and she slowly shook her head. "No. I know what you're trying to do, and I'm not falling for it."

Josie's eyes widened.

"You're trying to get me to dig it back up, and we've worked way too hard to put it to rest."

Josie's heart thumped.

"But I finally let go of the anger."

"Anger?"

"Yes. We talked and talked until I was finally free of it."

Josie frowned. "Who did you talk to?"

Libby leaned back, closed her eyes, and expelled a long sigh. "Jesus."

Josie waited to see if she would say more, but sleep had taken over.

CHAPTER
-21-

The only way to find out if people really care about you is to do something crazy. If they don't care about that, then they don't care.
—Nadine Norris, age 13

On the first of October, the call came that they had been waiting for: Libby's doctor was releasing her to home care.

Gram was thrilled, but Josie wasn't sure how she felt about this. Libby was partially mobile and using the bathroom on her own now, but her mind and energy levels were not even half her normal. She was still very dependent and sometimes confused. She would receive in-home health care twice a week. Josie had no idea what to expect with Libby at home, but there was little she could do but roll with it.

Someone from the county brought an adjustable lounge chair for the living room, and a hospital bed that they set up in the parlor, next to Gram, meaning she and Libby would be roomies. This could be interesting. Josie wasn't sure how that would work, but again, all they could do was take it one day at a time.

On Friday, Libby came home at noon, and with the caregiver's help, Josie got her set up in the living room. Then Josie tried to get Libby to eat a little soup, but the move completely wore her out. All Libby wanted was to nap in her chair.

Meanwhile, Gram fretted about the fit Libby would throw when she saw her garden so overgrown, so while Libby napped, Josie and Kennedy took baskets out to the garden and worked steadily, harvesting cucumbers, carrots, potatoes, and onions, plus more apples and pears from the trees. Josie's mouth watered at the thought of Libby's pear butter, and she wondered if she could find the recipe and try to make a batch without totally destroying Gram's kitchen.

A car pulled into the drive.

Josie froze and stood in front of Kennedy, blocking him from sight, totally out of habit.

Two women got out of the car, bearing steaming casserole dishes covered with foil. The older one looked familiar. A former school teacher, maybe?

Surely not Miss B.

The woman came closer and smiled at Josie. "Hi. We brought dinner for Libby and her family. Is this a good time?" The aroma of herbs and tomato sauce wafting from the dishes could have put an Italian restaurant to shame.

"Wow, that's really nice of you. Please come in," Josie said. Confused, she ushered them into the house. The younger one, a pretty dark-haired girl about high school age, carried a fresh loaf of homemade bread wrapped in cloth.

Oh-my-garlic-and-asiago. The aromas smelled even more authentic inside the house. Josie led them to the kitchen, then turned to the older woman. "I'm Josie. Sorry, you look familiar, but I can't remember where from."

"That's okay. I'm Charise Duncan. We met at the hospital."

"Oh, right. You came to pray for Libby."

"Yes, and this is Kristen Brooks, Pastor Dennis's daughter. We know Libby from church. We wanted to do something to help while she's getting settled in at home. I hope you like Olive Garden salad, I try to copy it." She smiled and greeted Gram as she joined them.

"I can promise you we'll love it," Josie said, salivating.

Hallelujah—real food!

"This is so incredible, and it all smells amazing. I don't even know…"

What to say to such kindness.

While Charise and Kristen unpacked steaming dishes, paper plates, and plastic silverware, Josie went to the living room and checked on Libby, who was still dozing. When she returned, Kennedy had climbed onto a chair and was watching the women.

Kristen glanced over her shoulder at Kennedy. "Hi. What's your name?"

He scooted off the chair and darted over to Josie.

Kristen smiled at Josie and tucked long, dark hair behind one ear. "Your little boy is *so* cute."

Kennedy pressed himself to Josie's thigh and stared at the girl.

"He can be shy some—"

"I'm four." He stepped away from Josie and held up the correct number of fingers. So much for shy. He went on to tell Kristen about painting flowerpots with Gram, how he could eat four pieces of jelly toast and get only a little tummy ache—news to Josie—and about the fish he caught all by himself.

Josie looked for serving spoons while Charise took the foil off the dishes.

"Except Ranger McNugget helped me a little."

Kristen laughed. "Ranger McNugget? Oh my goodness, you are so adorable."

Gram thanked Charise but seemed confused by the food. "Did you say a church sent you?"

"Yes, everyone at church has been praying for Libby, and we just wanted to help. We do that when someone's been in the hospital or recovering from surgery, that kind of thing. Just a little something to help lighten the load if we can."

Gram nodded. "Liberty will appreciate your goodwill."

"We just feel so bad about the accident," Charise said, her eyes tearing up. "Is she up for visitors, do you think?"

"I don't—" Josie hesitated. Everyone looked to her, clearly waiting for her to finish, but she wasn't sure how. "I don't know if she's ready for visits yet. I mean, her recovery from the injury has been slow. Her conversation isn't always sensible." Or safe.

"Ah." Charise said, sympathy filling her face. "My father suffered a head injury once. It took him nearly three months to fully regain his faculties." She nodded. "I understand. If you think she wouldn't be comfortable seeing us, we'll just come back another time. Maybe later when she's ready."

"Mom? What's going on?"

Everyone turned toward the soft, low voice. Libby leaned against the kitchen doorway in her robe and gown.

"Libby!" Josie rushed to her and the others followed. "What's wrong? Are you okay?"

Libby turned and looked her in the eye. Sweat sparkled on her upper lip. "Where did she go? I was just talking to her. Down at the river."

Josie cringed. She'd gone loop-de-loo again.

"Hey, Aunt Libby, I went down to the river too," Kennedy said. "I caught a twelvinger."

As Kennedy chattered about his life jacket and his wiggly fish, Josie felt a prickle of dread. Libby could be feverish. The nurse said that was something they needed to watch for.

Libby looked around the room, then shuffled to the kitchen table and grasped a chair. "Something smelled so good I had to come and see what it was. I didn't know we were going to Olive Garden. I would've put on something more fashionable."

Charise smiled and helped her into a seat. Kristen went to her side and gave her a shoulder hug. "Good to see you up and around, Libby."

Libby nodded and looked at each person in the room until her gaze landed on Gram. "Mom? You saw her too, didn't you?"

Gram frowned. "Who?"

"Nadine."

No, no, nooooo!

A burst of panic shot through Josie. She went straight to Kennedy, who was still basking in Kristen's attention and hadn't seemed to hear Libby. Everything in Josie wanted to scoop him up and take him out of the room before she spoke again, but she couldn't move.

Gram wrung her hands. "Would you like to say grace, Liberty?"

Libby closed her eyes and breathed in deeply. "Thank you, Jesus! I was really hoping heaven would have Italian food. Amen!"

Nice diversion, Gram. Let's just hope it sticks.

Libby smiled at Charise, then at Kristen, as if she were just now seeing them for the first time. "Hi. I didn't realize it was Sunday. Did I miss the singing? Are we having a potluck? There was a dish just like this last time. You remember, Mom?"

Gram's brows shot straight up. She'd never been to a church potluck in her entire life.

Kristen got a plate for Kennedy while Charise insisted Josie and Gram sit down and let her dish up for them. Josie couldn't remember the last time she'd been served.

The cannelloni was bursting with herbs, garlic, tomato, and cheese, and the salad was crisp and better than any she'd had in a restaurant. And the bread. Mercy, that woman could bake.

"Charise, this bread is so good I could live off of it. How do you do it?"

Cheeks pinking, Kristen smiled and said, "I made it."

Josie stared at her. "Really?"

She nodded. "I make it all the time."

Kennedy speared an entire cannelloni and tried to lift it to his mouth. Josie helped him cut it into bites.

Gram chewed slowly, still staring at the two women.

"Elves." Libby dipped a piece of bread in marinara sauce. "Tiny ones. They bake bread all night. In their tree house."

Kristen's brows shot up, her gaze meeting Josie's. Josie just shrugged.

As soon as he was finished eating, Kennedy took Kristen around the house and explained every random thing he knew and some things he didn't, then he asked her to give him a piggyback ride. Meanwhile, Charise prayed for Libby, and when the women finished their visit, they offered to bring more food and to come help if needed.

Josie didn't know what to say, so she thanked them again. After they left, she turned to Gram. "They're so kind."

Gram shuffled to the stove and started her tea kettle. "Most elves are."

CHAPTER
-22-

Mom moved out today and took Mandy with her. She said I need a dad more than I need a mom, said it's "better" this way, and it's not about me. What a liar.
—Will McKnight, age 14

As Josie climbed into bed, she fired off a text to Will, even though it was probably too late to hope for a reply tonight.

Josie – 11:27 p.m.
Libby's home. Some ladies from her church brought dinner. Omigosh! I hope they come back.

Will – 11:27 p.m.
What'd they bring?

Josie – 11:28 p.m.
Italian. I acted like I knew what Bolognese & al dente meant but I'm clueless.

Will – 11:28 p.m.
Sweet. Now I'm hungry.

Josie – 11:29 p.m.
Sorry! Your Grandma seemed good today but didn't tell me anything embarrassing about you. ☹ I'm going to ask her for highlights from your middle school days tomorrow when I bring her DQ. Stay smart (aka safe).

Will – 11:30 p.m.
Thank you for sticking with Grandma. I REALLY appreciate it.

Josie – 11:30 p.m.
No problem!

Will – 11:30 p.m.
And I'll pay good money to keep you from asking Grandma for stories. Especially middle school. Name your price.

Josie couldn't sleep. There was still a fluctuating gulf between Loopy Libby and Good Old Normal Libby. Josie missed her aunt. She longed for her steadfast wisdom, to be able to lean on her. Having her at home now, in this condition, only made it more obvious that she was no longer herself. Would she ever be? If she didn't completely recover, not only would her life be limited, but there would always be the chance she'd give Josie's secret away. If this was the case, Josie needed to get Kennedy far away from here.

But then who would take care of Libby and Gram?

Charise had prayed a really caring, thoughtful, faith-filled prayer. Of course, Josie had prayed for Libby, too. Well. Not the getting on your knees for half an hour and waiting for answers kind, like Libby did. Mostly the *Hey! I need some help here!* kind.

So she decided to spend some time praying for her aunt and grandma. When she finally ran out of things to say and did her best to relinquish the women in her life to God, she closed her eyes and tried to go to sleep.

But the journal kept gnawing at her.

She tiptoed to Libby's upstairs room, took out the notebook, then climbed into bed and thumbed through the pages to pick up where she'd left off. A scrap of paper fell out. She held it up to the lamp on the end table. It was a photo of two women, but other people had been cut out on either side. On closer look, one of the women in the photo was a young Libby, maybe late twenties, and strikingly beautiful. Her pale hair hung long and silky straight, and she wore silver hoop earrings. She looked to be about six months pregnant. The other woman—

Josie let out a gasp. It was her mother. Except Geraldine didn't look the way Josie remembered her. Her face resembled Gram a little. And she was smiling. She reminded Josie of a young Audrey Hepburn.

Though two other people in the photo had been trimmed away, Josie could see a male arm around each of the women's shoulders. It looked like two men had been removed from the sisters' photo. And from their lives, apparently.

Josie's heart raced. Was one Libby's husband, Dean? And was the other her disappearing gene donor, N. Norris?

She stared at the photo so long her eyes began to droop. She tucked it back into the journal and flipped the pages, looking for where she'd left off.

> *September 16, 2004*
> *Nadine came home from middle school today with a*
> *fat lip and a murderous look in her eye that would send*
> *a pack of bikers running. She's not talking, so I'll have to*
> *see if her sister knows what happened. Well, that's dumb,*
> *of course Josie knows. The question is, will she tell me, or*
> *is she sworn to secrecy, as usual?*

Yes, there had been a time Josie and Nadine had sworn to keep one another's secrets. But at some point, they had outgrown that. Sometime between middle school and high school, when Nadine started hanging out with lowlifes and developing a glacial chip on her shoulder.

Josie flipped ahead, glancing at the dates. Nothing eventful, a lot of the same day to day stuff, some proud mentions of the twins' achievements in school, but as Josie read some of Libby's entries, what stood out was that her aunt had been far more invested in the girls' lives than she had ever let on.

Josie stopped on a heavily-scrawled block of narrative, dated the year that she and Nadine would have been sophomores in high school.

> *March 14, 2008*
> *I'm so furious I could scream. I just found out why*
> *Nadine has spent an entire week sulking at the river. Be-*

cause of Jake the Snake. As you know, Diary, I never did like that boy. Something about him was too slick. All wit and charm. No substance. And way too cocky for a high school senior. Josie tells me Nadine really liked him— which I still don't get—but the dirtbag just dumped her for some other girl. And that's not the worst of it. According to Josie, Jake told Nadine she wasn't "enough." I guess we all know what that means.

I usually stay out of the girls' social lives, but this makes my blood boil. It's inexcusable. How can a human be so heartless? Nadine already struggles with self-worth. This is just about the worst thing the little twerp could have done. Why not just tell her something like I just want to be friends, blah blah blah? Why did he have to say that?

I don't blame a girl for crushing on some cute, older boy, but why did she have to put herself in the position to be hurt by the biggest jerk around? Well, she's not going to like it, but I'm going to have some words with that kid. I can't undo the damage he's done, but I can sure give him something to think about. It may be a long time before seeing my face doesn't make him wet his pants.

Is it my fault that I despise males who hurt women? They're lower than animals. How can a man do that? It's inhumane. Are there no moral standards that men can be held accountable to?

Diary, I have no use for the male half of the species. I dare you to produce one honorable male who deserves my respect. Just one. I double dare you.
-Libby

Josie was again surprised by Libby's heated response. She'd never mentioned being angry at Jake or that she wanted to go ballistic on him.

But she did remember how Jake had broken Nadine's heart and how her sister had gone off by herself and didn't surface for weeks. She'd taken it really hard. Josie tried to console her, but nothing seemed to help. And then, Nadine suddenly snapped out of it and poured herself into a new social circle. Josie didn't understand Nadine's fascination with the stoner crowd, but by the time Josie could see that Nadine's new friends were doing her dark mood more harm than good, Nadine had become the life of the party and seemed bent on trying everything and denying herself nothing.

She could understand Nadine's hurt. Rejection was a deeply painful subject for them both. And she understood how Jake's saying Nadine wasn't enough (which probably translated as she wouldn't sleep with the ape) would have deeply damaged her sister.

But it didn't explain why Nadine had totally pulled away from Josie.

CHAPTER
-23-

If you need music at the river, you're missing the point.
—William McKnight, age 26

When Josie came downstairs on Saturday morning, she found Libby reading to Kennedy. Two empty cereal bowls teetered on Libby's footrest.

"I was going to make you some breakfast," Josie said, "but I see you've already eaten, and I'm guessing it was way fancier than toast."

Libby nodded. "Yes. It was, what did you call it?" she asked Kennedy. "Can of baloney, I think it was."

Josie grimaced. "Oh, did he give you leftover cannelloni?"

"It was delicious," Libby said with an indulgent smile. "A little cold, but we Buckleys are not wimps."

Kennedy pointed to the page in the book. "That pig looks like Romeo."

Libby cocked her head. "He does, especially around the eyes. He looks kind of..."

"Happy," Kennedy finished.

"You think?"

Kennedy nodded vigorously. "He loves it here. He doesn't want to live anywhere else."

Libby's gaze rose and met Josie's.

Too many thoughts vied for her attention at once. Kennedy's obvious longing to stay here forever, which stung too much to think about. And her aunt's sudden clarity, but for how long?

"Kennedy, do you think you could find Gram outside and see if she needs any help?" Josie said.

"Sure," he said, hopping down.

As he headed for the door, Libby whistled. "Hey, sunshine, aren't you forgetting something?"

No doubt Libby wanted him to remove the dirty breakfast bowls. She was worse than a drill sergeant when it came to clutter.

But oddly enough, she didn't mention the mess. Instead, she opened her arms.

Kennedy stretched up and gave her a hug, then took off outside.

Speechless, Josie could only gape at her aunt, wondering if there was some way to tell if a person had been taken over by an alien.

Libby patted the arm of the sofa beside her, and as Josie sat down, Libby said, "Don't give me that look."

"What look?"

"One day, you'll wake up and realize you've been rearranging the deck chairs when you should be getting yourself and everyone you love into the lifeboats."

Okay, so maybe her moments of clarity still had a few glitches.

"I'm really glad you're home, Aunt Libby."

She inhaled deeply, let it out slowly. "Me too. That place was driving me cuckoo." She chuckled. "How long are you staying?"

"I'm not really sure. It depends."

"On what?"

On how long it's safe for me to be here. "There's something I need to ask you before Kennedy comes back."

"Okay."

Josie winced. "Do you remember the secret we have, just you and me?" She swallowed hard. "About Kennedy?"

Libby's eyes closed. "Secret. Yes, I remember."

"And you remember that he and Gram can't know anything about, you know, the whole mommy thing. Who and where he came from?"

She nodded. "Your secret is safe with me."

Josie stared at her aunt, trying to understand how she could be saying this now, when the night before, she claimed she'd seen Nadine down at the river. From her chair in the living room.

"So you won't mention my sister's name or anything else about his birth around him, right?"

"Right." Libby opened one eye. "My lips are sealed."

"Okay." Josie nodded and told herself to relax. It sounded like Libby was coming back to her senses. Maybe moving home was just the medicine she needed.

"Speaking of sealed, there was a letter that came for you. It's…" Libby squeezed her eyes tight, as if trying to remember more.

"Gram gave it to me. It was in her cookbook."

Libby frowned. "Cookbook? Since when does my mother cook?"

Josie chuckled. "She'd had it a long time."

"No, this one's different. It came just the other day and I put it in the book I was reading, and then, the next thing I knew, I was in the nut house with Miss Ellie, the bus driver."

Could there be a more recent one? If so, it was probably in the book Josie had been reading to her.

"And I have something else for you." Libby rested a hand on Josie's arm. "I've been keeping a diary of sorts. A whole string of them, actually. They were intended to be for you and your sister one day. Sort of a chronicle of our lives since you came to us." She lifted her gaze and looked into Josie's eyes. "I want you to have them. They're on a shelf in my closet."

Josie's heart raced. She'd already read some of them without permission, of course, feeling partly justified because it appeared they were meant for her to read one day, but also partly guilty for reading them without asking. Now, the fact that Libby was giving permission both relieved her and nailed her with guilt.

"Thank you."

"So." Libby peered at her. "How long will you stay?"

"I will stay as long as…" She wanted to say *as long as you need me,* but there was no telling how long that was, and therefore, wasn't something she could promise in good conscience. "As long as I can."

Libby closed her eyes. "Okay. Go out and play, the grown-ups need some peace and quiet."

Josie chuckled. Classic Libby.

She excused herself and went upstairs to look through the bag of things they had gathered for Libby while she was at the hospital and

Riverbend. She hunted through the bag of books and CDs, then found the novel.

Sure enough, there was a letter tucked into the back of the book, addressed to Josephine Norris at Gram's address. From Lane County Family Court.

Dread tingled through her, but she pocketed the envelope, and went outside. Kennedy wanted to build more roads for his Hot Wheels town, so Josie found a place where she could read and watch him play in the dirt. She'd grabbed the journals along with the court letter. She dreaded reading the letter, but she knew she couldn't put it off.

She sat near the chess stump and looked around for any signs of Jenny, as she didn't want to scare the woman off. Jenny hadn't been around in a while, and this had Gram worried.

While Kennedy plowed winding dirt roads, Josie leaned against the stump and opened the letter, read it, re-read it, and then crammed it back in the envelope.

Nadine's request to terminate Josie's guardianship had grown horns. Because Josie hadn't appeared at the guardianship meeting, another meeting had been scheduled for October 16—less than two weeks away.

And now there was an added bonus: CPS wanted to investigate her and the child to determine his well-being, and to see if her not responding was a reason for concern and possible criminal charges. Based on their investigation, CPS could make a recommendation to the judge to grant or deny the termination request, with or without Josie's input.

And double bonus: if Josie failed to show up at the next meeting, she would be charged with custodial interference, fines, and possibly contempt of court.

Meaning there would be a warrant out for her arrest. Law enforcement involvement.

All because an erratic woman held all the cards.

An erratic woman Josie still couldn't throw under the bus, no matter what she had done. No matter what choices Nadine had made in her own life, no matter how scary she had become. Because she was still a part of Josie, like a vital organ. She'd heard a story about a guy lost deep in the wilderness who got pinned under a rock and had to saw off his own arm with a pocketknife to save his life. Josie would clearly die if that happened to her because she was positive she wouldn't have the nerve. Turning on Nadine felt like that. Like cutting off a limb to save herself. She just couldn't do it.

So, somehow, without hauling out all of Nadine's dirty laundry, Josie would have to convince the judge that the child was in the best possible hands. That he was well-cared for, emotionally secure, and physically safe.

Surely a judge would see that?

Not necessarily. As Josie was continuing to learn, nothing was certain. Not the love of a mother, the vow of a sister, or the safety of a secret. So how could she expect a judge's ruling to be any different? What if Josie couldn't convince him that being with her was the best thing for Kennedy?

What could she do to make sure? All her life, she'd fought hard to make everything work out for the best, but now, she was faced with something she had no control over.

Kennedy had built an impressive freeway system for his Hot Wheels, and was now drag racing two at once, complete with revved engine sound effects. The kid had no lack in the area of volume.

"God, what do I do?" she whispered.

Pray.

It came out of nowhere, like the memory of a familiar voice.

Pray, and cast all your cares on Me.

Okay. She would pray, because clearly, she had so few options. She would ask God for help and hope he'd show mercy to a girl who had given her heart to him as a teen and then gone AWOL.

Dear God, the judge needs to see what's best for Kennedy. Please don't let this turn into a custody battle. I never intended for this. It's not about custody, it's about protecting a sweet, happy boy from terrible, permanent damage. Please, God, we need your help. Please show me what to do. I am trying to trust you, I really am.

She stuffed the letter in the bag that also held the journals, which she'd brought outside intending to read, but she just couldn't. Not today. She didn't want to hear any more about her sister today.

Will – 12:15 a.m.
Looks like I'll be here another week. Let me know if you want me to ask Mandy to take over Eleanor duty.

Josie – 12:15 a.m.
I'm happy to keep visiting, don't worry. Promise me that you'll take really good care of yourself. That's an order! Miss Ellie doesn't call me Bossy Britches for nothing.

Josie – 12:16 a.m.
How are you?

Will -12:16 a.m.
Hahaha. Okay, Boss, I promise.

Will -12:17 a.m.
I'm okay. Can't sleep. Everything smells like smoke. Brain plays weird tricks on you when sleeping near a fire.

Josie – 12:16 a.m.
So what do you do when you can't sleep?

Will – 12:17 a.m.
Pray, read, roast marshmallows. No one else likes them burnt, so I don't have to share.

Josie – 12:17 a.m.
Roast marshmallows? Like in the fire? Are you serious?

Will – 12:17 a.m.
Kidding. You fell right into that one.

Josie – 12:18 a.m.
Dang it! I did. But I actually LOVE burnt marshmallows, so if I were there, you'd be forced to share.

Will – 12:18 a.m.
As much as I really like the idea of sharing a marsh-mallow with you right now, I wouldn't wish you here for anything.

CHAPTER
-24-

We have to go on long drives sometimes and that stinks. But Mommy lets
me have popcorn for dinner and she plays Avengers and sometimes she
shares her M&Ms with me. She's really pretty and smart and she laughs a
lot. She's Wonder Woman. No, she's better than Wonder Woman.
She's my Mommy.
—Kennedy Norris, age 4

Sunday afternoon, Pastor Dennis and his daughter Kristen dropped by to visit Libby. Kristen brought more homemade bread and a project for Kennedy that she said was a leftover from Vacation Bible School. While the pastor talked to Libby, Kristen offered to read the lesson to Kennedy and then helped him make the craft. She told Josie she was applying for college and wanted to study early education. Josie could easily see her doing that. She was a total natural.

While Libby and Kennedy were occupied with their guests, Josie realized she hadn't seen Gram in a while, so she went looking for her. She finally found her napping in her bed. Gram had never been much of a napper, but lately, she didn't seem to have much energy. Josie closed the parlor door to keep the voices from disturbing her, then joined the others.

The pastor was warm and genuine, putting Josie instantly at ease. It wasn't like she expected the man to see through her, but still, it had been a long time since she'd had a conversation with a minister.

"What a huge blessing for Libby and Gwennie to have you here, Josie," Pastor Dennis said. He was slightly thick in the middle and graying, stood a good inch shorter than Libby, and wore a tidy little goatee. His blue eyes were kind and inviting. "It's really great to know they have someone here helping out. How long are you able to stay?"

"Not long, I'm sorry to say," she said slowly. She braced herself for questions she couldn't answer. "But I hope to stay at least until she's back on her feet."

Fortunately, Kennedy and Kristen were in the kitchen constructing a lava lamp out of a water bottle. The less Kennedy heard that they weren't staying forever, the better.

"I understand you're a graphic designer?"

"Yes. Freelance."

He smiled. "That sounds like an excellent way to work. Probably allows you a lot of flexibility."

"It definitely has its perks." Like the ability to work from a playground park bench, inside a pillow fort, or the back row of a kids' matinee.

"Are you taking on new clients? We've been looking to update our church logo. What we have now has been around since the Nixon administration."

"Wow! Yeah, it might be time for an update. I'd be happy to."

He gave her his card, then invited Josie to join him as he wrapped up his visit by praying for Libby. His voice was so steady and calming, and his words so caring and full of faith, that Josie found herself choking up.

After the pastor said his goodbyes, Josie walked him out to his car.

"It was so good of you to come," she said. "It's really nice to meet people who care. And having you here praying for Libby is really…" She couldn't get the words out around the lump in her throat. Tears stung her eyes. "It means a lot to have someone praying for her. You know, someone who actually knows how to do it right."

"I'm happy to be of help." He smiled. "But I hope you know that the Lord loves to hear your prayers, too, Josie. They're every bit as important and effective as mine or anyone else's."

"But I'm not very good at it. I don't know the right words."

"There's no such thing. It's not about being perfect. It's about having a heart-to-heart conversation with your Father who loves you. And we may as well be honest with him, because he already knows our thoughts before we even say them."

Her eyes widened. "Then, why pray, if he already knows our thoughts?"

"Do you know Libby well enough to predict what she might say?"

"Yes, unfortunately," she said with a chuckle.

"And yet, you still talk to her, right? Just like with friends and loved ones, we have a relationship with God. We talk and we listen. We take part in what he's doing. And when we spend time in prayer, we draw peace, strength, and guidance from being with him. I don't know anyone who couldn't use more of those things." He smiled. "Don't be shy, Josie. The Lord knows you better than you know yourself. He's a good Father. And he's always there, ready to listen."

She nodded. "Thank you," she managed to say.

Since Kennedy was at the kitchen table coloring the solar system one planet at a time, Josie grabbed a cup of coffee and grabbed the next journal that began with the fall of 2008, and then plopped down on the window seat.

November 5, 2008

Josie has her nose to the grindstone, working like a maniac to maintain her 4.0, while Nadine's grades are sinking like the Titanic. The school counselor called, again. Nadine lipped off to the gym teacher and then stormed out of class. I told her Nadine's been having a rough time and I'd talk to her. Thank heavens the counselor is cutting her some slack.

Okay, Diary, I'll be honest. I'm running out of patience and ideas. I'm not throwing in the towel, but I sure wish I could get some help. Sometimes I really wish their mother had stuck around to raise them, but even if she had found the courage to live, and even if the girls hadn't been emotionally shortchanged by abandonment, I doubt Gerry would have had the stamina to raise two strong-willed girls. She couldn't even stand up for herself, much less for a sullen, sass-mouth teenager.

It wasn't easy to read. Josie found herself holding her breath, turning the pages slowly, as if she needed to brace herself for what was to come. But it didn't seem as if Libby had any more answers about Nadine than Josie did.

> *February 14, 2009*
>
> *I can't take much more of this. Mom and I made the traditional double decker chocolate birthday cake, and Nadine, the brat, didn't even show up. Josie tried to act like Nadine missing their seventeenth birthday was no big deal. Josie and Mom sat in the kitchen and ate cake in silence. I went for a very long walk.*
>
> *It's been obvious for some time now that Nadine and Josie have grown apart. If it hurts me to see them like this, I'm sure it has to be ripping Josie to the core. She doesn't understand, but then who does? Nadine won't talk to anyone. I've tried, but trying to get anything out of her is like trying to crack a safe. She's angry. But life has taught me that anger is usually a cover for something else. Hurt, maybe. Or fear. If that's true, what is Nadine afraid of? The only thing she's ever genuinely cared about is Josie, and Josie is the one person she's avoiding like the plague. God help us. I don't think I can survive another repeat of me and Ger.*

Josie let out an exhale and studied her sweet boy; his dark, shaggy hair long overdue for a cut, his long-lashed brown eyes, the way his mouth pursed to the side when he colored. He had such a sweet, trusting nature.

Was he a sample of what Nadine might have been like at that age if she hadn't been discarded by their mother? And could Josie protect him from being scarred the same way?

The more Josie thought about the upcoming court meeting, the more she struggled with the possible outcomes and consequences—of both appearing and *not* appearing.

There was a very real possibility that Nadine could somehow twist things and convince the judge to revoke Josie's guardianship and take him from her. That simply could not happen. Kennedy was too young, too vulnerable. But the thought of ignoring the court twisted Josie's stomach in knots. Deliberately doing something that could get her into trouble—especially legal trouble—was so entirely against her nature.

As she watched him color, she knew. It was risky to skip the meeting, but the risk of harm to Kennedy was far greater. The idea of being in serious trouble terrified her, but she just couldn't put her personal freedom or comfort over his. It was never about her. It was all about Kennedy. Any consequences for Josie were nothing compared to the alternative.

If she was lucky, maybe once Kennedy was old enough to handle the truth, she would contact the judge, explain the situation, and appeal for leniency for the missed meetings. She just couldn't risk exposing herself right now. She needed to buy a little more time, a few years, at least. She had to protect Kennedy as long as possible, come what may. Hopefully, it wouldn't mean anything too serious for her.

Josie stared at the journal in front of her, the elegantly penned words a blur.

Surely it wouldn't mean anything as serious as criminal charges?

She glanced at Kennedy. Even if it meant jail down the road, it would be worth it if she succeeded in guarding his heart. He needed to be emotionally mature and confident of his worth.

Her head was beginning to pound, but she focused on reading one more entry. Why, she had no clue. Maybe she was hoping to turn the page and find that Libby had discovered some secret that could magically solve everything. Like some shining epiphany about her twin nieces, some nugget of hope.

Which was dumb, because Josie already knew how the next decade of the *Josie and Nadine* story played out.

September 30, 2009
We're in the home stretch now, senior year. I wish I had better news. Josie is working at DQ part-time and laser-focused on maintaining her GPA. She's been burning the candle at both ends trying to get that special Governor's scholarship for orphaned kids. On the other hand, Nadine is partying like it's 1999. I truly fear for her.

I suspect she's drinking and running with a dangerous crowd. The more I try to talk to her, the more she pushes me away. It breaks my heart to watch, and it angers me to feel so helpless. There's no one I can go have it out with. I need to have a heart-to-heart with Nadine, but my niece doesn't give a flying rat's tail what I have to say anymore.

I'm afraid I've lost her. And I don't know what to do. For the first time since I ran away from that monster I married, I'm scared. Scared she'll end up like Gerry. I don't even want to think about what might happen to her. I wish there was someone I could talk to. And sorry, Mom, I won't be appealing to your woodland friends. I need real answers. Something solid that I can count on.

If there is a God, I think it's about time for him to show himself, because we need a miracle.

"Mommy? What's wrong?"

Josie wiped her wet cheeks and looked up. Kennedy stood staring at her, his frown a blend of caution and concern.

"Hey, bud," she said, her cracking voice barely audible. "I'm fine."

"Are you sad?"

She wanted to say no and make up some excuse, but a voice in her heart said *don't do it. Don't keep choosing to lie by reflex. Kids need to know it's okay to feel emotion. Don't box him up with the rest of your baggage.*

Her breath caught and she had to fight a fresh wave of tears. She nodded slowly, a little wary of how he'd respond. "Yeah, bud, I guess I'm a little sad."

He hopped up beside her and rubbed her arm. "It's okay. Just have a nap and when you wake up, ta-da! Everything's magically okay."

Josie chuckled. It was a line he'd heard at least a hundred times.

"No, I know—an ice cream cone at DQ. That'll make you feel better."

"Really." Her brows rose. "Wow, you're so smart. How do you know so much?"

Kennedy shrugged. "I want banilla, and we gotta get a strawberry milkshake for Miss Ellie."

Josie checked the time on her phone. It was past dinnertime at Riverbend, and she hadn't been to see Eleanor yet.

Miss Ellie was in the TV room when Josie and Kennedy arrived. The older woman tilted her head up and peered at them as they approached. Each of them carried a DQ cup. Josie had learned that it was best to have a backup option in case she had a sudden aversion to the offering. If she didn't like the food or the milkshake, an ice cold root beer was usually a sure bet.

Eleanor accepted the shake and took a deep tug on the straw, then eyed Kennedy. "There you are, Magoo. Hallelujah, it's about time! Are you riding in this rodeo tonight?"

He shrugged. "I don't know. What's a rodeo?"

The old woman peered up at Josie. "Well, the more, the merrier. Have you been up to see Lois today?"

"Not today," Josie said cheerfully. She didn't know Lois from the Cat in the Hat, but she'd learned from the staff that with memory care patients, it was best to just roll with the conversation and not try to correct them.

"She's lonely, poor gal. She forgets sometimes."

Josie pulled a chair closer and sat beside Eleanor, then whispered to Kennedy to pick a book for Eleanor to read to him. "What does Lois forget, Miss Ellie?"

"That Jesus is always right beside her."

Kennedy brought the whale book, as usual, and another one about Australia. Eleanor always liked reading to Kennedy, and it seemed her mind was a little clearer when she read.

"Read the one about the Orcas," Kennedy said. "I want to catch one next time I go fishing on Ranger McNugget's boat."

Josie doubted there would be a next time, but she didn't want him to know that.

"Well, just remember the rules when you fish around here. My son Keith knows all the best places. He fishes whenever he gets a chance."

"For orcas?"

"Salamanders."

"What about narwhals?"

Eleanor frowned at him. "North Pole?"

Kennedy shook his head. "No, narwhals. They have a long, beaky horn on their nose. Like a swordfish."

"Sofas? Sonny, you're not making a lick of sense."

Josie tucked her lips and bit them to stop a giggle, but it exploded into laughter. She slapped both hands over her mouth. Mercy, but it felt good to laugh, it had been too long.

"What's taking so long to dock this ship, anyway?"

Kennedy looked up at Josie. "What ship?"

Josie shrugged. She decided to try a diversion. "Miss Eleanor, didn't you used to teach school?"

The old woman nodded. "Oh, yes. White River School District. I didn't give an easy A, either. But every one of my students always passed. That's the mark of a real teacher. You have to find the key that unlocks a student's way of learning. The path to the brain is like a maze. They don't all learn the same. The brain is a miraculous machine. You have to figure out what it takes to flip on the power switch for each one."

Josie's jaw dropped. It took a moment for this complete change in Eleanor to register. She was so clear now. It was as if going back into history helped her skip past the cuckoo stuff and find some clarity. Like she could connect with reality if it was in the past—in history she was familiar with.

Okay. Josie smiled. "Tell me more about your school."

Eleanor huffed. "We had the best test scores of any school in Skamania County." She went on, at Josie's gentle nudging, for a full fifteen minutes about teaching and events in world history, and then she declared she was too pooped to dance anymore and needed to hang up her hula skirt and call it a night. "Come back again, though," she said with a vague smile. "I always enjoy a visit from the Avon lady. Bring some hand cream next time, will you?"

The Avon lady? Josie just shook her head and stood. "Goodnight, Miss Eleanor."

"Goodnight. Bring your hula skirt next time too, Avon lady. You can dance with me next time."

"I'll see if I can dig one up," she said on a chuckle. As they headed out, she felt a rush of joy that she had found a "key" that fit the lock of Eleanor's brain. She couldn't wait to tell Will. In fact, she wanted to text him before she headed home.

She pulled out her phone and started a new message while she walked to her car, following on Kennedy's heels.

Just as she opened Kennedy's door, he yelled, "Hey, Ranger McNugget!"

Josie's head snapped up, text message forgotten.

Will was walking toward her, and every thought fled, except for an acute awareness that he was wearing a week's worth of grimy soot and a look in his eyes that made her heart stutter.

CHAPTER
-25-

It's better to have loved and lost than to never have loved at all.
—Gwendolyn Buckley, age 80

This was insane. *He* was insane.

What were the chances that just as he drove by Riverbend on his way home, her Outback would be there? He was in serious need of a shower and about a year of sleep, but he couldn't help himself.

And what were the chances that as he pulled into the lot, Josie would be coming out? She was walking toward her car and looking at her phone, so she didn't see him get out of his truck until Kennedy hollered out a greeting.

She saw Will and froze, the look on her face pure shock.

He couldn't blame her. He probably looked like something that just crawled out of an apocalypse.

"Hey, Ken," he said as the kid came running to him, beaming. Then he drew a steadying breath and nodded to her. "Hello, Josie. I know—I'm filthy. I don't know what I was thinking, stopping like this." *Yes, you do. You know exactly what you were thinking.*

"I was just about to text you."

And then she smiled, her expression filling him with pure joy.

Lord help him, there it was again. That weird clash of calm and longing that sucker-punched him whenever she was near. And that sweet, freckly smile was all it took.

He swallowed hard. Forgot words.

Get a grip, McKnight. If you give a woman that much power over you, you'll be toast.

"I thought you weren't coming home for another week," she was saying.

"After the week we've had, the captain cut me a 72-hour pass. I go back Tuesday night."

"Wow, that's not very long." She regarded him from head to toe. "You must have come straight from the fire zone."

He winced. "How'd you guess?"

She smiled. "I hate to tell you this, but Eleanor is most likely asleep. I'm pretty sure we wore her out today."

"That's okay. She doesn't need to see me if you were just there. I really appreciate you looking out for her, Josie."

"My pleasure. And speaking of which, I'm really excited. I just discovered something about Eleanor, by accident." She frowned. "But maybe you already know."

"What's that?"

"When I asked her about being a teacher, she suddenly got really clear in her conversation. And when we went on to talk about world history, she was clear on that, too. Did you know that happens when you get her talking about the past?"

"No, I didn't. But I knew she was an avid history buff. She read constantly and she used to tell us all kinds of stories. She was always my go-to for history homework." He smiled at her. "Good detective work. So what did she say?"

"She talked about teaching students and different methods she would try if they weren't catching on. Not only was she clear, but it sounds like she was a really good teacher."

Will nodded. "She was. She received a special award from the governor for her innovational teaching techniques."

"I'm not surprised." Josie smiled. "Of course, she did end our time thinking I was the Avon lady—whatever that is—and invited me to go hula dancing with her tomorrow."

"Yeah, Miss Ellie forgot who Mommy was," Kennedy said, frowning.

Josie shrugged helplessly. "That's what you get for being forgettable."

"Josie," he said slowly, "you're a lot of things, but forgettable isn't one of them."

Her smile faded and her green eyes went round.

Kennedy tugged on his sleeve. "Hey, Ranger McNugget. I like your hat. I wanna get one like that."

"I bet I can get you one," Will said, unable to take his eyes from Josie. She was still staring at him, lips parted now. Probably trying to figure out just what kind of Neanderthal would stand there covered in grime blurting out cheesy pick-up lines.

"Sorry," he said, giving himself a mental shake. "I'm so filthy I even offend myself. I need to go get cleaned up."

"I'm not offended, and I'm glad we ran into you." A tiny frown punctuated her smile. "It's really good to see you, Will."

"It's good to see you, too." Massive understatement. She was one of the reasons he'd driven two hours to McKenzie Bridge to spend his precious little time off.

No. In flat out truth, she was the *only* reason. Well, her and Grandma.

His pulse ticked faster. "Listen, since I have to head out again Tuesday, I was wondering if you might be free tomorrow. For dinner."

"Dinner?" She blinked, then glanced at Kennedy. "You mean, like a date?"

He stilled, except for the beat of his heart, which had doubled. "Did you want it to be?"

She opened her mouth but didn't answer. Closed it. Looked confused.

Idiot! He had to be high on smoke fumes to ask her now, looking and smelling like he did. "I was just going to throw burgers on the grill, nothing fancy," he said. "And, maybe…" Brows raised, he rocked his head from side to side.

Her eyes got huge.

"…burnt marshmallows."

"Ah!" She smiled, her look relieved. "I love the burnt ones. But I'm afraid I can't."

He nodded, forcing down his disappointment.

"I couldn't leave Kennedy with Gram that long," she said. "And certainly not with Libby, in the shape she's in."

"Oh, no, sorry. I meant to say he's invited, too."

"Really? Wow." A slow smile spread across her face. "Okay, we'll be there."

"Good."

He waited while she finished buckling Kennedy into his car seat. Then she opened the driver's door. "I can bring stuff for s'mores if you want."

"Sure, that'd be great. So I'll see you tomorrow."

"Okay." She climbed in and then winked, adding, "It's a date."

For a day that was so full of things like hanging Gram's laundry outside on the line and taking Libby to her therapy appointment and helping Kennedy hunt for tree frogs, Monday had crept by painfully slow. When she told Gram that she and Kennedy were going to a friend's house for dinner and s'mores, Gram broke into a big smile. It was the first smile Josie had seen on her in a long time.

Libby told her not to rush home. And then with a laugh, she'd added, *Have fun and smear some in your hair.* Okay, that did not sound like Libby. It also sounded gross.

Fact: The New Libby was just one surprise after another.

And Libby wasn't the only one. Will McKnight was also full of surprises. He pulled off a yummy dinner of juicy burgers, chips, and root beer. Josie brought stuff to make s'mores, and while the sweet, smoky aroma of a real wood fire was like a balm to her soul, she was surprised that Will had a campfire in his backyard. If he was sick of smoke and flames, he didn't show it.

The fire wasn't quite low enough yet for roasting marshmallows, so he and Josie kicked back on wooden deck chairs and watched Kennedy play. Will had rustled up some Tonka trucks, including a dump truck and an excavator, which thoroughly fascinated Kennedy. The scoop even worked. He was in heaven moving twigs and pinecones and creating roads.

"Those trucks are a hit," Josie said. "I didn't think they made them out of metal anymore."

"Yeah, they're ancient," Will said. "They were my dad's, then mine.

I guess we McKnights don't believe in throwing away a perfectly good rig." He smiled, watching Kennedy.

Josie took advantage of his attention being on Ken to steal a nice, long look at Will. He certainly cleaned up well—literally. He'd managed to scrub away the layers of soot he'd worn home. He was now dressed in tan cargo shorts and a white T-shirt—a combo that clearly said *not* that *kind of a date*. And though it wasn't a serious, couple-only date, Josie didn't want to show up in an outfit she'd worn a million times, so she borrowed a soft pink boatneck sweater and a pair of faded denim capris, the only pants of Libby's that weren't too long for Josie.

Citronella candles in tiki torches put off ribbons of pungent aroma to ward off mosquitos. The river surged along the banks with an endless rushing sound, several dozen yards beyond the cabin. The sun was sinking, turning the sky into a gradient washboard of orange, pinks, and deep turquoise. She snapped a photo with her phone, already thinking of ways to incorporate the colors and textures into a new design.

She continued her scrutiny of Will. He seemed at ease, which baffled her. Wasn't he exhausted? Instead of catching up on much needed sleep, he was spending his one day off from a blistering war zone with Josie and Kennedy. Whether or not it meant anything to him, the realization stunned Josie. The fact that he wanted to spend his valuable time off with her whispered something thrilling she was downright scared to believe.

She was worth having around.

"So, whatever happened between you and Ken's dad?" Will asked quietly.

And there went her hopes of his valuing her. Telling him the truth was not an option. She scrambled through every possible answer but there wasn't one that wouldn't send Will packing. The truth was bad. But the alternative was a lie, and also bad.

"Were you married to him?"

Gut clenching, Josie shook her head slowly, not making eye contact. Maybe twenty questions was the way this line of questioning would have to go. And the way their friendship would end.

He didn't say a word.

She braced herself, then met his eyes. Didn't see disgust. His expression was hard to read, but he seemed to be quietly processing what her answer meant.

"I'm not the type who sleeps around."

"No, you don't strike me as the type. I'm guessing you loved him."

She inhaled deeply. "I'd rather not talk about it."

"Okay," he said, a slight frown on his brow.

A dull ache squeezed her heart. But she wasn't sticking around and she certainly wasn't free to get involved, so what did it matter what he thought of her?

But it *did* matter. A lot.

"A child was not part of my original plan." Her cheeks cooked, and not from the campfire. "I only had one semester left at U of O, but then he came along, and..." She shrugged. "He took total precedence." It wasn't the whole truth, but it *was* true, and at least she didn't feel like a complete fraud.

"A lot of women in those circumstances would," he glanced at her boy and lowered his voice, "end an unexpected pregnancy."

She stiffened. "Well, I'm not one of them."

Great. Will was one of those guys. The kind that would drive his girlfriend to the clinic and maybe even have the chivalry to fork over a wad of cash to pay for it.

Anger drumming double-time in her veins, she trembled, debating on whether or not she should just leave now.

Will looked her in the eye. "No, you're not. I can see that. You could have chosen to think only of yourself, but you chose to think of him."

She stared at him. Swallowed hard, tried to calm her heart rate. "Well, he didn't have a choice, did he?" She heard the edge in her voice, but she couldn't help it. She had advocated hard for Kennedy. Harder than anyone could possibly know.

"If you had a do-over, would you do it again?" Will kept his gaze on Kennedy, but he seemed to be holding his breath.

She felt her blush creeping higher. He was thinking of the intimacy that had conceived Kennedy, and for once in her life, she wanted to shout without shame that she was a virgin. She drew a deep breath. "The way it happened was not ideal," she said slowly. "But him being here, in the world, under the right circumstances? Absolutely."

"What would be the ideal circumstances, for you?"

A glance showed her his strong profile, and while he seemed relaxed, and like he was just being conversational, she could see that he was waiting. Like her answer mattered.

"A real family. Two parents who love each other no matter what."

Dream on, Cinderella. There's no such thing as "no matter what."

He nodded. "I never knew why my parents split. Apparently my mom changed her mind about the kind of life she wanted. And the people she wanted in it." His lips went tight.

Without thinking, Josie laid a hand on his arm. "I'm so sorry. But I feel even more sorry for her. She missed out on you."

His breath hitched, and he stared at her hand. "I used to think that a mom was the one person who was wired to want you even if no one else did, but I found out that's not true."

She knew that searing pain and disappointment all too well. She withdrew her hand, smiled gently. "But you and your sister turned out great, in spite of your parents' divorce. So that tells me there's hope."

Will shook his head. "Well, if not for the Lord, I don't want to think about how big a jerk I would have turned out to be."

"Really?" This was not the response she would have expected. "Your faith is strong. I envy that."

He searched her eyes. "Do you believe in God?"

"I do, but—" She drew a deep, cleansing breath, lifted her head, listened to the rushing river. "When I was in high school, I went to church camp and finally understood what Aunt Libby had been trying to tell me about Jesus, how he loved me and died for my sins. I wanted that. I wanted what she had. So I asked Jesus into my life."

"And that's the point where faith begins for all of us," he shrugged. "All we can do is trust him one day at a time. *He's* the reason I trust him, not me. Any strength I have is his, not mine."

She nodded.

"I take it you don't feel like your faith is all that strong."

"I feel like a little raft that came untied and floated down river. Way out of sight."

He chuckled. "But you forget, God owns the river. He sees you no matter where you go. He's always right there with you."

"Ugh." She huffed. "Why does everyone keep saying that?"

"You can't hide from God. I know sometimes we feel like there's this huge distance between us and him. We sometimes think God pulled away, or feel like we drifted away from him. But God doesn't operate in the limited kind of physicality we do. I think we mistake the sensation as distance, when actually, I think it's more of a disconnect. Like a severed artery that suddenly loses blood flow. We may be suffering a loss of connection and a feeling of weakness, like spiritual anemia, but I believe he never leaves us, not for a nanosecond."

If God had been right there with her, all this time, then why did she always feel so alone?

Kennedy came over and climbed up onto Josie's lap. "Mommy, I'm still hungry," he said, leaning against her with a yawn.

Will rose and got sticks, then brought them back, along with the bag of marshmallows. "Sorry, I'm a total slacker. Here you go."

He offered her a stick, but when Josie looked down, Kennedy was already asleep. She shook her head. "Typical."

"I've got this," he said, smiling. "Double order of blackened marshmallows, coming right up." He speared the marshmallows and found a glowing red spot in the fire, while Josie unwrapped enough chocolate for two s'mores.

Will brought the flaming blobs over to her and let her do the honor of blowing them out, then he slid them onto the crackers and gave her one of the oozing treats.

"I see disaster written all over this," she whispered. She took a bite, then moaned. "Oh, man, I haven't had one of these in forever."

Will smiled.

Her little honey bear must have smelled melted chocolate and woke, so she gave him hers and Will fixed her another one. By the time they'd had their fill, the sky had grown dark, and the campfire's flames created a mesmerizing display of shadows dancing against the dark, tall trees surrounding the clearing.

Kennedy wanted another s'more and then whined when she said he'd had enough.

She turned to Will. "And there's my exit cue. I need to take him home and put him to bed. You don't want to be around for the second show if he doesn't get to sleep soon."

Will nodded slowly but didn't say anything. Didn't offer a comfy spot for Kennedy to doze so she could hang out a little longer. Didn't try to coax her, or put the moves on her. Not that she had expected him to. Or wanted him to.

Because she didn't need involvement. Didn't need to get attached.

Oh, girl. You're waaaay past that.

Will offered to carry Kennedy to the car. He buckled him into his seat while Josie gathered her stuff.

She opened her car door, then turned to say goodbye and nearly bumped into Will, not realizing he was so close. She met his eyes and saw something there that took her breath away. Tenderness. Vulnerability. Need.

"I'm...uh..." he said, faltering.

She waited, heart racing.

"I really appreciate your help."

Why did he feel the need to thank her again? He must have thanked her at least a dozen times already. "It's no problem, Will. Really. I enjoy spending time with Eleanor."

His gaze met hers and held fast, like a long, warm, embrace. "So... I'll see you in about a week."

The low, rumbly tone of his voice warmed her midsection, turned her knees to jelly. A week. It sounded like a punishment.

He stepped back so she could close her door, then waved and watched her drive away.

Later that night, staring at the ceiling, she kept replaying the evening, and especially that tangibly charged moment when they had said goodbye.

Had he wanted to kiss her?

Had she wanted him to?

Would she have kissed him back?

Don't answer that!

Was she going to spend the next week driving herself nuts wondering and wishing for a do-over? If she had a do-over, would she have the nerve to ask what was really on his mind?

She stared at the ceiling until she finally came to a solid, definite conclusion.

Fact: Do-overs were highly overrated.

CHAPTER
-26-

I have to watch my mom's spending like a hawk. She loves to buy things like bird boxes and hummingbird feeders. And now, Lord help us, she's discovered the internet. Amazon just delivered a whole case of bat houses. It's time for an intervention.
—Libby Buckley, age 54

Tuesday was dumb.

It was the day Will was heading out of town for another long week. Josie went through the motions of making meals and catching tree frogs and reading with Libby and rigging up a Slip N Slide for Kennedy, but throughout the day and even now, as she watched her little boy shoot across the lawn like a squealing bowling ball, the questions kept spinning in her mind.

Last night, Will clearly had something more than *thanks for your help* on his mind. Something weighty. Unless she was just imagining it, and she didn't think she was. But what?

Giving herself a mental shake, Josie helped Kennedy change out of swim trunks and get into dry clothes, curiosity driving her to distraction.

No, this was going to drive her into therapy.

"Mommy, I need a bigger jar for my frog. What's for dinner? Do we have dram crackers? Ranger McNugget said we need dram crackers next time we have a bonfire."

She tugged him close for a hug and tackled the easiest one first.

"How does peanut butter celery boats and a cheese bagel sound? And I'll see if Gram has a bigger jar, okay?"

Kennedy nodded, already wriggling out of her grasp. Apparently *dram crackers* wasn't a high priority, which was fine. She needed time to figure out what to do about her *Ranger McNugget* obsession anyway.

That evening, once everyone was settled in and asleep, Josie pulled out Libby's journal.

> *October 24, 2009*
>
> *I don't know how or where to begin this, so I guess I'll just dive in. Today is the anniversary of the day Leo died. He would be eighteen now. I've grieved and I've moved on. Or so I thought. But apparently, I've had this deep down, burning ache, like a coal fire smoldering silently along a hidden vein inside the earth. This morning, I could hear a terrible sound echoing in the abyss that formed in my heart the day he died. It was the agonized sound of my own weeping.*
>
> *Diary, I'm going to be brutally honest. With Nadine's dreadful attitude and the twins' last year of high school and then heading off to who knows where, and the awful heaviness in my heart, I couldn't take another second of it. I wanted so badly to shut it up that I was considering my options: an entire fifth of Jim Beam or following Ger's lead and jumping off a cliff (which I promised Mom I would never do, so don't get your knickers in a wad).*
>
> *Then I remembered Helen, the ER nurse who talked to us the day Leo died, telling us it was no one's fault, it could have happened on anyone's watch. She also told me that Leo was in the arms of God now. I still remember how badly I wanted to spit in God's face that day. I told her that God didn't need my baby, he had plenty. Leo was my one and only joy. Mine. How dare God take him away from me? Helen wept and told me God hurt for me far more than I hurt for myself. Then she had the nerve to tell me she attended a church near me in McKenzie*

Bridge and that I was welcome anytime. Right. You can imagine how thrilled I was to hear that.

Well, it only took me 18 years to take her up on the invite. I found out today that Helen passed away a few years ago, sadly, but her church is still there. Pastor Dennis welcomed me as if I was some long lost friend. Well, lost, anyway. After the service, he sat down with me and let me pour out my anger. All of it. He sat there and kindly took it all without flinching. We talked, and then I listened as he talked about God's love for me, and then, Diary, you probably won't believe this, but I asked Jesus to forgive my sins and come into my heart and make me new.

And guess what? He did. I can't explain it, but I know that God did something in my heart and life today. Something has changed. Grief is still a lingering pain, but no longer a consuming one. I feel something I don't think I've ever felt in my life. Joy. Pure, unrestrained joy. I feel something humming inside me, like a powerline buzzing with electricity. I feel free, and clean, like a surgeon has cut away rotting tissue and I'm finally on the mend, free of decay, and becoming whole again. No, not again, but for the first time.

I'm 46 years old and here I am, crying like a baby. I've been born again! Mom was onto something all along. There IS Someone watching over us all. Someone loving and forgiving and wise and strong. Someone who will never hurt me or run away or let me down.

Now, if only I could get Nadine and Josie to meet him. God, please, do a miracle in the twins' lives. Please. They're everything to me—aside from You.
-Libby

Josie covered her mouth, tears flowing. How little she had actually known her aunt. And yet, if she were being honest, which Libby's diary was nudging her to be, she had to admit that her ignorance of Libby's feelings was no one's fault but her own. That year, Josie was so focused on achieving her goals and getting a college scholarship that she didn't notice much of anything else beyond the wall of ice between herself and Nadine, and her aunt's sudden preoccupation with going to church every chance she could. How little Josie had understood what was happening in Libby's heart. How clueless she was about Libby's hurts and how deep her feelings ran.

Drawing a steadying breath, she read on.

November 7, 2009
Ha! Today Pastor Dennis said there's a lake of fire prepared for the devil and his demons. Dean Allen probably has a smoking seat in the front row with his name burned into it. He has to. I hope it's a blistering inferno.
-Libby

December 19, 2009
Okay, I guess it's not very Christian to wish hellfire and eternal torment on anyone, even Dean. Pastor Dennis said God gives us the grace to forgive (or to at least choose to forgive one day at a time, with his help). I did wish hellfire for Dean. With a passion. But Pastor Dennis said that God wants everyone to be right with Him, and unfortunately, that includes Dean Allen. Ugh.
So, I am going to pray God gets a hold of him before it's too late. Don't get all excited, Diary. I'm no saint. Dean doesn't deserve heaven, but then, none of us do. Just to be clear, I DON'T want to share heaven with him, but God, if You decide to turn Dean around, that's Your choice. I just have one request: If he does turn his life over to You and You do save his soul, please, please make sure his place in heaven is far away from mine, okay?
-Libby

March 13, 2010
I've been chewing on something the pastor said, and I feel like a glacier is suddenly melting inside me. He said

life doesn't always work out the way we want, and it's okay to mourn our losses and missed dreams and unmet expectations, but then, we need to wash our face, breathe deep, and embrace the life and the gifts and the blessings that God HAS given us. Embrace life and live.

The Bible says we don't grieve like those who have no hope. We grieve, because we're human, but the hope we have in Christ and in eternity changes everything. There will be loss and disappointment in this life, but in God's love and sovereignty, he gives good things, and gives them generously. Psalm 84:11 says, "No good thing does he withhold from those who walk uprightly."

There will be amazing joys in eternity that we can't even comprehend now. So with his help, I'm going to walk upright, and rest in his love, mercy, and grace. I am going to wash my face and embrace the good things. I choose to embrace life.

-Libby

April 4, 2010

It's Easter Sunday and I'm reminded of God's goodness. It takes my breath away sometimes. And while I worry myself sick about our girls—especially Nadine—I do have hope that God will turn things around for them. I know he can do anything.

But there is still one thing that haunts me: Geraldine. There's no hope for her, it's too late. Out of the three of us, I believe she lost the most. Mom has her wacko utopia and I've had the twins, and now, my Savior. Poor Gerry had nothing but constant torment. No matter how hard I tried, I couldn't remove her pain or her sorrow. I couldn't fix it, and that has always been a source of guilt. But now, I understand that I couldn't have helped her anyway. No one could have healed her except God. Oh, Lord, how I wish she had known You. I'm so sad for my little sister that it breaks my heart, even now, after all these years.

Lord, have mercy on her soul.

-Libby

Josie closed her eyes and laid back against the pillows. Her mother had suffered some terrible grief that Josie didn't understand, a grief for which there was apparently no relief. Josie had never seen Geraldine Norris through an adult's eyes, only through the eyes of a wounded, confused child. And though Josie was now an adult, it felt as if a part of her, the part that was wounded by her mother's abandonment, had not grown up with the rest of her. It was as if there was still a child inside her, one that still viewed select pieces of her life through childish eyes. That inner child saw her mom's departure as a decisive blow to her worth.

But what if Geraldine's desertion had nothing to do with Josie and Nadine?

Maybe Josie needed to learn more about her mother's state of mind and the things that had driven her to take her own life.

Maybe.

Maybe Josie also needed to allow the child inside her to grow up, and try to understand her mother through the eyes of an adult.

But while Geraldine had lost the battle with her personal demons, Libby had suffered her own losses, and had finally dealt with them, with the Lord's help. Looking back, Josie could see the transformation in Libby. She had pursued God, and he had changed her.

Josie wanted to grow, both in faith and in character. But would God be willing to come in and work in Josie's life, after the choices she'd made and the lie she'd chosen to live?

Her phone dinged with a text. Her breath caught, and she checked the notification. It was Will. Smiling, she dried her face—like he could see her—then opened his message.

Will - 11:47 p.m.
Hey, Josie. Are you up?

Josie - 11:47 p.m.
Yes. How are you?

Will – 11:48 p.m.
I'm here.

She waited. The little dots that meant he was typing danced a moment or two, then disappeared. Like he started to say something, then changed his mind.

Josie – 11:49 p.m.
Are you okay?

Will – 11:50 p.m.
Yes and no.

Josie – 11:50 p.m.
Do you want to talk about it?

Will – 11:50 p.m.
Yes and no.

Josie – 11:50 p.m.
Do you know you're kind of redundant, Ranger McNugget?

No answer.

Josie – 11:51 p.m.
Sorry, I'm being a dork. Let me know if you want to talk about it. Promise I'll listen instead of mocking you. Mostly. 😊

Will – 11:52 p.m.
But I like how you mock me. Most of the time. 😊

Oh. Josie stared at his words, smiling. She started to reply when another message popped up.

Will – 11:52 p.m.
I also like how your nose puffs out a little laugh when you're amused.

And the way you turn slightly pink when anyone
praises you.
And I loved the way your whole face lit up when
Kennedy caught his first fish.
And I especially loved the way you let him think
he'd caught it.

She gasped. Then another message popped up.

Will – 11:53 p.m.
I like a whole lot of things about you, Josie.

Heart drumming out a staccato beat, she froze, unsure what to say. Return the compliment? Bask for a heady, tingling moment in this declaration? Be bold and press for more?

Josie – 11:53 p.m.
I'm turning three shades of pink right now. So
when I was leaving last night, it seemed like you
had something on your mind that went unsaid.

She waited, and waited, worried that she'd pushed too far, then finally saw his reply.

Will – 11:54 p.m.
Yes.

That was it? Seriously? He could be such a male. That was probably all the answer she'd get.

Will – 11:55 p.m.
I was trying to figure out how to tell you that I'm
really going to miss you.

Her heart stuttered.

Josie – 11:55 p.m.
Would it help if I told you I'm really going to miss
you, too?

Will – 11:55 p.m.

Yes and no.

She laughed out loud, then whispered, "Aaaand?" and held her breath.

Will – 11:55pm
Yes, because you made my day. And no, because this week's going to go by like a month-long grounding.

CHAPTER
-27-

Memory is not what the heart desires. That is only a mirror.
—J. R. R. Tolkien

Libby was restless, in spite of her three times-a-week therapy sessions, which always wore her out. For a diversion, Josie decided to take Kennedy up to the attic and rummage around in Gram's theater trunk. They fell over themselves laughing at some of the getups Josie created. Kennedy found a black cape, which he decided would make him invisible. Josie grabbed a handful of dresses, shawls, and hats, then they took it all downstairs to Libby. They turned the living room into a stage. The only thing missing was their very own thespian, the legendary Gwendolyn LaPlante.

Josie left Kennedy and Libby coming up with stories for their awful ensembles and went in search of Gram. She wasn't anywhere in the house, so Josie went to look for her outside. She checked the barn, the potting bench, and the shed out front, but saw no sign of her. She went back to the barn and then around it to the little meadow leading into the woods, and stopped.

From where she stood, she could see the stump where the chess game was set up, but now, Gram and Jenny sat at the stump on opposite sides. There was a teacup in front of each woman and a tiny teapot between them, and though Josie couldn't hear her, she could see that Gram was talking. Jenny fidgeted but stayed put, her tattered bundle nestled squarely in her lap. Josie decided to slip out of sight before the woman saw her and bolted. If Gram could coax the poor woman to visit and maybe talk some sense into her, so be it, and all the better for Jenny.

Josie went back inside and found Libby laughing her head off. Kennedy was in a cape, a pointy hat that looked like something from Rapunzel, and a sagging red sash.

"All he needs now is an eye patch and a sword," Libby said, still laughing.

Josie even got Libby to wear an Elizabethan gown, but the velvet made her too hot. They tried on a few more combos, then Josie heard Gram come in the back door.

They joined her in the kitchen and found Gram with a small bucket full of huckleberries—the same bucket she usually left out with a note for Jenny to gather pinecones.

"See what providence befalls us, oh noblest knight and fairest maids!" Gram trilled. "We shall have huckleberry pie tonight."

Libby shot a sideways glance at Josie. "The only way that's happening is if Josephine makes it."

"Me?" She grimaced. "I suck at baking, which you know. All I can do is make toast, and even that's a gamble."

"Oh, simmer down, sister," Libby said. "I'll walk you through it."

Josie cast a doubtful look at Kennedy, who threw it right back with a shrug. He knew that sometimes Mommy's cooking attempts meant they'd end up with popcorn for dinner, and he was fine with that. But Josie agreed to give it a try and followed the instruction Libby delivered from her kitchen stool. Gram sat at the table with Kennedy to watch.

Nothing like an audience.

Libby explained about cutting the lard into the flour with a pastry blender, then told her how to add ice cold water a spoonful at a time until the dough was "just right."

"Yeah, but how do you know when it's right?" Josie asked.

Libby shrugged. "You know by how it looks."

Josie rolled her eyes. "Right, but how do you know what it's supposed to look like?"

"Didn't I teach you anything when you were growing up?"

"Yeah," Josie said. "How to fish, shoot, change a tire, and clean the rototiller blades. You didn't teach me anything in the kitchen."

"That's because you and your—" Biting her lip, Libby stopped herself just in time.

Josie locked on Libby's gaze, fingers planted in dough.

"You spent every minute you could outside and down at the river. Now sprinkle flour on the cutting board and smash the dough flat, then give Kennedy the rolling pin."

"Me?" he asked, eyes wide.

"Of course. We can't have you grazing around here all day like a cow not knowing how to feed yourself." Libby winked at Josie.

"I'm not a cow," Kennedy said, frowning.

"Well, you sure eat like one."

Josie chuckled. The old Libby was definitely back.

After a dinner of spaghetti with meatballs and huckleberry pie—which turned out surprisingly well—Josie cleaned up the kitchen with Kennedy's help, while Gram went to lie down. Libby watched from her chair at the table. When Kennedy decided he was done doing housework, he pulled out his LEGO bricks while Josie finished drying the dishes.

"Have you shown him all your favorite places?" Libby asked.

"Well, most of them. We saw—" she glanced to the rug where he was concentrating on his LEGO kingdom. "My old fort."

"What was that like?"

"Weird." Josie cast a meaningful look at Libby.

"I bet."

Josie scrubbed the spaghetti pot and rinsed it.

"Have you finished reading the journals?"

Taking a dishtowel to the pot, Josie turned around. "No, but I've read quite a bit."

"I imagine you have questions."

"Yes. But some questions I'm not quite sure I want to ask. And others, I'm not sure you'll want to answer."

"Oh. You've read quite a bit, then."

Josie hung the pot on the hook above the island. "I read about a baby boy." She turned and studied Libby, waiting. Was Libby prepared to discuss Leo now?

Libby heaved a sigh. "He'd be eight months older than you."

"My cousin," Josie said softly. "I wish I could have known him."

"So do I." Libby's eyes glistened. "I had a million wishes for Leo."

Josie fought back tears. "Oh, Libby, I'm so sorry. I can't begin to imagine how devastating that must have been."

Her aunt just shook her head.

"Was it SIDS?"

Libby rearranged the napkins in the napkin holder, making them all square up in the same direction. "That's what the ER nurse told us."

How awful that trip into town must have been. "You and Gram drove him to the hospital?"

Libby pondered Josie for a long, quiet moment. "No, not Gram. I guess you haven't read that far." Libby drew a deep breath, glanced out the window. "My sister and I took him in. Ger was a wreck and insisted the doctors had to do something…" her voice trailed off. "Geraldine was also living here at the time, but only for a little while. Nick had vanished on her and she was carrying a double batch." She glanced at Kennedy.

So her mother had also stayed here while she was pregnant.

"I got a job at the fish hatchery because we desperately needed money." Her voice faltered.

Josie came to the table and pulled out a chair opposite Libby.

"Ger watched Leo for me while I worked." Dark blue eyes glistening, she fastened her gaze on Josie.

Understanding hit her like a jolt of electricity. Josie gasped. "Oh my gosh! She was watching him that day," she whispered.

Libby nodded dully.

Josie stared at Libby, processing all the pieces of a puzzle that should have been as obvious as a neon sign. How devastating for Geraldine that the baby's death had happened in *her* care.

She covered her mouth with a hand that trembled.

"She never got over it," Libby whispered. "Never."

Tears rushed to the surface and spilled over. "Oh my word. She thought it was her fault."

"She blamed herself. It probably didn't help that I didn't try very hard to correct her. It could have happened on anyone's watch. At least, that's what the nurse said."

She'd read that, but she hadn't realized it was meant to reassure Geraldine.

Libby leaned closer. "I should have tried harder, I see that now. If I could have convinced her that it wasn't her fault, things might have been very different. She might not have fallen apart."

"I'm sure you did your best—"

"And you might still have a mother."

Josie's breath caught. She stared at Libby. "And then you wouldn't have been stuck raising someone else's kids."

"No." Libby looked her square in the eye. "Let's get one thing straight right now. That is not why I wish she'd gotten better. I do not for one second regret having you here, to raise and to love as my own. Okay?"

Josie swallowed hard. Her throat was thick with tears. "Okay."

Now, Geraldine's mental torment made all kinds of sense. Her guilt. How agonizing and endless it must have been. And after all that Libby had already lost. Even though the child's death might have happened no matter who was with him, it was easy to see why Geraldine would have borne such deep, unappeasable guilt.

"I wish I'd known," Josie whispered.

Libby shook her head. "Some things are just..." She stared out the window. "Just impossible to wrap your heart around and still be able to breathe." She looked Josie in the eye. "I've made my peace with her and with Leo's death. But there are still so many things you need to understand. And I don't have the heart or the energy to tell you everything there is to know. That's why I wanted you to have the journals. Both to read, and to give you time to process things."

"Okay," Josie said. She wasn't sure she wanted to read any more just now. "I do have one question. I found a photograph of you and my mom, and what looks like two men cut out of the picture. Was one of them my father?"

Libby nodded slowly. "Yeah. Nick Norris. Don't bother trying to find him, though, he's long dead."

"How did you find that out?"

Libby shrugged. "Mom and I looked for him when you and— when you came to live here, and it took a while, but we eventually found out he'd died."

She had never really wanted to meet the guy who bolted at the first sign he needed to man up and be a father.

"He was a green-eyed charmer. And your mother was a quiet, natural beauty, although you couldn't convince her of that. Aside from hair and eye coloring, you take after her."

"From the photo I saw, you were both gorgeous."

"Yeah. Well. Fat lot of good that did either of us." Libby sniffed. "All right, I'm beat, I need to go to bed."

Later that night, Josie dreamed she was at the river again. She stood at the water's edge, scanning the bank on the opposite side, searching, seeing no trace of Nadine, but certain she was there. She could feel her. She listened, but only heard the rush of water, the steady flow of its power, its endless churning.

Josie turned and then screamed.

Nadine stood directly behind her, staring at her with black-rimmed, loathing eyes.

Josie sat up in her bunk, heart thumping like a bass drum. Had she screamed aloud? She listened but didn't hear anyone stirring.

She lay awake a long time, not wanting to visit the river again, and definitely not wanting to run into Nadine—in person or in her dreams.

CHAPTER
-28-

I wouldn't have a man in my life for all the tea in China. Men are worthless (Daddy and Pastor Dennis excluded). And even if there was a decent man, I'm no spring chicken. I'm more like a gristly old turkey. What man worth his salt wants to wake up to that every morning?
—Libby Buckley, age 52

On Thursday, Libby asked Josie to pick up her supplements at the store in Blue River, five miles west, so she decided to drive there after her visit with Miss Ellie. Kennedy was perfectly happy to stay with Libby, who seemed to be up and around enough to watch him for a little while.

The Blue River store had Libby's order ready, so all Josie had to do was pay for it. She counted out the cash Libby had taken from her cookie jar and handed it over, but the cashier was eyeing Josie with a frown.

"Sorry, did I get it wrong?" Josie asked.

"No," the woman said, shaking her head. "I was just trying to figure out why you look so different. Did you change your hair?"

"Have we met?" She didn't recall ever meeting this woman, but as she racked her brain to place an old acquaintance, a terrible tingle stole over her.

"I guess not," the woman said slowly. "I could have sworn...but they say everyone has a lookalike in the world. What do you call it? A doppelganger."

Josie froze. "W-where did you see my lookalike?" She could hardly breathe.

"In Eugene, at the Joker's Den."

"When?" Josie barked.

The woman looked at Josie like she'd just brandished a set of fangs. "Couple days ago."

Josie gasped. Ignoring her change, she grabbed her package and raced out of the store. Heart hammering, she sped out of the parking lot.

Could it have been Nadine?

Eugene was only an hour away. If it had been Nadine, she could easily be here now.

Josie floored it at well above the speed limit, praying no one pulled out of a side road or driveway.

She turned in at Gram's place, heart racing.

There was no car at the house, but that didn't mean anything. She ran inside, found Kennedy and Libby just as she'd left them, exhaled, then barreled outside and checked all around the property—the barn, the woods, and everywhere she thought someone could hide.

Seeing no sign of Nadine or any hint that she was there or had been there, she relaxed, but not completely. Had it been Nadine? If she had been in Eugene a few days ago, where was she now?

Did she know Josie and Kennedy were here? If so, how? Had someone told her?

Not likely. The only people acquainted with Nadine who also knew Josie was here were Gram and Libby.

At the end of his shift on Friday morning, Will called the director at Riverbend for a quick update. Grandma was doing well, they said. They noted a marked improvement to her weight as well as her mental clarity. The director mentioned that Josie had been there every day, and not only did she make sure Eleanor ate and drank, she also spent time engaging with her.

He didn't like having to depend on Josie, but he had no choice. It wasn't that she seemed burdened by the daily visits—she had reassured him several times that it was no trouble at all.

No, something else about her being there so faithfully bothered him. He wasn't comfortable depending on a woman, not since his mom and Mandy had left. Of course, Mandy was reliable, and now that they were on such good terms, he didn't mind leaning on her once in a while. But Josie?

Depending on Josie made him feel so...

To be honest, Josie made him feel a lot of things that had him twisted in knots, but what he was struggling with at that moment was how vulnerable she made him feel.

No, worse than vulnerable. She made him *need.*

It was a haunting kind of need that he couldn't remember ever feeling for anyone, and it rattled him. It felt wild, totally out of his control. And he didn't like feeling out of control. Especially when it came to women. The last time he surrendered himself to a woman's control, he found out just in time what an idiot he'd been. The fact that Kristi had played the part of a smart, outgoing, genuine Christian well enough to fool him—and everyone who met her—was a testament to both her duplicity and his stupidity.

Of course, Josie was about as opposite of Kristi as a woman could be.

But still.

There were a ton of reasons he needed to get a grip on the way he was feeling about Josie. First, she was a single mom, and he wasn't looking for a ready-made family. Although Kennedy was a really great kid.

And second, Josie was leaving soon.

He rubbed his tired eyes. That was only two reasons. There'd been more, hadn't there?

Okay, third reason: She was female. Reason enough. Too many women in his life had been shallow, dishonest, and self-centered.

Josie is none of those things, and you know it.

Did he know her?

Yes. Obviously not in every way there was to know her—and Lord help him, but the lifetime it would take to know her intimately was intoxicating just to think about—but he knew enough. And what he knew about her had created a need so deep and so powerful that it scared him.

That was it, the straight-up truth, in a nutshell: He was scared.

Ranger McKnight was scared of a freckled, green-eyed girl.

No, he wasn't scared of Josie. He was scared of needing her badly and of being left empty. He was scared of trusting in the things about her that brought him joy only to find it was all an act, a façade. He was scared of feeling things for her she might not return, of feeling energized when she was near only to feel that energy slip through his fingers and disappear.

He was scared of loving her and not being loved back with the same sleep-stealing, thought-consuming, desire-producing intensity he felt.

He was scared because he'd fallen in love with Josie Norris and there wasn't a blasted thing he could do about it.

"The weird fairy lady is out there," Kennedy said on Saturday morning, peering out the kitchen window.

Frowning, Josie put down the peanut butter knife and went to look. Jenny was hovering near the back porch, wringing her knobby hands, rocking back and forth on her feet. Definitely distressed and not happy to be there. She had to need something pretty bad to come that close to the house.

Josie winced. Gram and Libby were still asleep.

"Stay here," Josie said to Kennedy. "Don't go outside or answer the door."

"Or play in the windows. Or talk to strangers." With an overblown sigh, his whole body sagged.

Josie took a deep breath but said nothing. She knew his complaint was valid, but she didn't have time or inclination to deal with it at that moment.

She slipped out back through the mudroom, wondering if she should make a sound to alert the woman, or if that would only scare her off. So she stepped onto the back porch and waited for Jenny to see her before going down the steps.

Jenny looked startled but kept hovering, still wringing her hands, her stance rigid, wary.

"Hi, Jenny. Do you need something?"

Jenny peered beyond Josie's shoulder at the house. "Are the others sick?"

"No, Gram and Libby are still asleep. Can I be of help?"

The old woman peered at Josie, then turned and pointed into the woods. "I saw goblins."

"What?"

"In the woods. And along the river."

"Goblins?"

Jenny frowned at Josie. "Yes. But you can't see them. Only I can."

Ah. Delusion at its finest. Poor lady.

"You tell her. Tell them both. I saw goblins—right here—in these woods."

The way she said *right here* gave Josie goose bumps. "I'll tell them." She felt like she was talking with Eleanor, rolling with her demented speak like it was perfectly normal.

Jenny nodded and hurried off, looking over each shoulder and all around her as she ambled away.

Then Josie saw Jenny's tattered bundle lying on the ground. The woman was almost to the woods, so Josie picked up the ratty baby and hurried after Jenny, calling to her.

Jenny turned, but when she saw what Josie held, she shrieked and ran at Josie at a faltering but surprisingly fast gait.

Josie trembled but stood firm, holding the doll out in front of her.

Jenny yanked it from her and clutched it to her chest, wailing, "You can't take my baby! You lie! All of you!" She turned and ran into the woods.

Shaking, Josie watched the place where Jenny had disappeared, then forced herself to move.

Later when Gram and Libby were up, Josie told them about the "goblins" and asked them why they couldn't get Jenny into a home.

"The last time we brought it up, she hid herself inside a culvert for over a month," Libby said, her voice weary. "Barb from the diner said her boys were fishing and found her sleeping in there. They had a heck of a time getting her to come out." She shook her head. "You can't force someone to take help if they don't want it."

Gram whispered, "She's too scared. In her world, there is no safe place."

Libby rose slowly. "Convincing her will take a miracle." She grasped her footed walking cane and looked to Josie. "Sorry to be a pest, but it's time once again for my occupational torture. Are you ready?"

Josie took Kennedy, in spite of Gram's disappointment that he wasn't staying home with her. Josie was not about to take any chances, not with doppelgangers and goblins at large. Of course, she was probably just freaking herself out, but she didn't care. Better safe than sorry.

That evening, Josie debated whether or not to read more of the journal, wondering why Libby was so insistent she read the rest. Did Josie even want to know what else it contained? She suspected that her aunt wanted Josie to see her mother in a different light. Through a sister's eyes. Which Josie would normally dismiss as biased, if not for the fact that the sister in this case was the one least inclined to paint Geraldine in rosy hues.

But reading herself to sleep each night had become her new bedtime routine, so she heaved a sigh and looked for the spot where she had left off.

> *February 24, 2011*
> *Well, apparently all that scrambling to get Josie accepted at U of O was all for nothing. I just found out she's not even enrolled. And after all the blood, sweat, and tears she put into graduating with honors? I'm stumped, Diary. But that explains why she's been avoiding my calls. I told Josie to get her little hiney into school. She can get "life experience" some other year. I'm afraid she'll lose her momentum and miss her shot at life and wind up a pathetic spinster like me. I don't know what she's trying to do, but I doubt it will come to anything good. Kids. Why is youth wasted on the young? I can't understand what happened to her. She was all nose to the grindstone one minute, and then wandering around like a bum the next. It's a mystery. But I suspect it has some-*

thing to do with the fact that Nadine tried to get into the
university but was denied. Those two. Even when they're
barely speaking, they still carry out these bizarre, unspo-
ken acts of loyalty. It's weird. Whatever Josie's reasoning,
though, this nonsense needs to end now. One juvenile
delinquent in the family is one too many.

Josie remembered the chewing out she'd gotten from Libby that spring, so this journal entry came as no surprise. She'd never put a lot of thought into why she had suddenly decided to wait a year, or why she had hidden it from Libby, or that there might have been a connection between her foot-dragging and Nadine's being rejected by the university. Libby was far more intuitive than Josie—even when it came to Josie, apparently.

Her phone dinged with a message from Will. Basking in a little rush of joy, she opened it.

> Will – 10:43 p.m.
> I saw a doe today and she reminded me of you.
>
> Josie – 10:43 p.m.
> Let me guess. She had freckles.
> Josie – 10:43 p.m.
> She talked waaay too much.

She waited, but there was still no answer. Then she remembered: the night they met.

> Josie – 10:44 p.m.
> Oh, right. The deer I swerved to miss before I drove off the road. You're SO funny.
>
> Will – 10:45 p.m.
> No, it wasn't that. I saw a beautiful creature in the middle of all this destruction. I held my breath, not wanting to scare it away, wondering how she could be there after fire has ravaged the land, and it hit me.

Will – 10:45 p.m.
Even though forest fire destroys so much, it can't destroy the beauty and the power of life that God set in motion when he created all this.

Will – 10:46 p.m.
It'll take time, but the forest will heal. The trees and the wild huckleberry will grow back, and the deer and beaver and bear will return, and the damage that was done will become nothing more than a distant memory.

Her heart thundered. She read his messages three times, mesmerized by his words. She didn't want to read anything into his message that wasn't intended, but even at face value, she couldn't help but be drawn to him, his heart, the lyrical way his thoughts traveled, especially in the middle of a fierce and dangerous battle.

Josie – 10:46 p.m.
WOW. So beautiful. That you can see the potential for new life and beauty and goodness in spite of the devastation and the danger you're dealing with right now.

Will – 10:46 p.m.
What I see is YOU. You chose to pick up the pieces and make something good from your life. You remind me that beauty can come from ashes.

Tears stung her eyes as she read and re-read his words. Could Will really see her? Could he see through her like that? Was it possible? And why did that idea both thrill and terrify her?

Will – 10:47 p.m.
Josie? Hope I didn't offend you.

Josie – 10:47 p.m.
Offend? My gosh! I'm not worthy of such praise, but just knowing you understand means so much more than I can say.

Will – 10:48 p.m.
Good. I have to go back to work, but when I get
home, is there any chance we could talk over dinner? Just the two of us?

Josie bit her lip. The Voice of Reason whispered *bad idea*. But her
heart screamed *YESSS!!*

Josie – 10:49 p.m.
Do you mean like a date? 😊

Will – 10:49 p.m.
I most definitely mean a date.

She couldn't leave Kennedy with Gram or Libby. But maybe Kristen Brooks would be available and willing to watch him for an evening.

Josie – 10:49 p.m.
If I can get a sitter for Kennedy, then yes. I'd love
to.

Will – 10:50 p.m.
Great. Can't wait. See you soon.

Josie stared at her phone, baffled by what she had just done. She
had agreed to go on a date. With Will McKnight. There were a hundred
and forty-seven reasons she shouldn't have accepted, but she plugged
her ears and shut them all out. It wasn't marriage. It was one date. It
wasn't permanent. It was two people who connected really well and
had things in common and admired each other's character. No need
to bring up that when she was with him, she felt a powerful attraction
that was downright dangerous to think about.

Fanning her warm cheeks, Josie resumed her reading.

September 30, 2011
That sound you hear is me heaving a ginormous
sigh of relief. Josie is now enrolled full time at U of O
and is settled into the dorm. It took some string-pulling
and some serious arm-twisting—she has NO idea what
it took me—but she's on track now. I just spoke to Josie,

and while she was feeling really good about her courses, she's still anxious about Nadine.

I was right. She feels guilty whenever she gets something that Nadine doesn't. So I reminded her that whatever consequences Nadine is facing right now are solely her own doing, not Josie's fault or responsibility. Josie gets it, but that doesn't change the way she feels. I told her to try talking to Nadine, but she said she's been trying to reach her for months. So I told her the best thing we can do for Nadine is pray for her. (I also told her that prayer is not the last resort; it's the BEST resort.) God will not let his precious little green-eyed sparrow slip through his fingers. I pray He gets ahold of Nadine before it's too late. I'd hate to see her wind up like her mother, battling demons until she can't fight them anymore. Mom has already lost so much. She doesn't need to lose anyone else.

-Libby

July 9, 2012

I'm 49 today, which means I'm almost 50. Yay. Before you know it, I'll be dead. Which I made the mistake of saying to Josie. She freaked out and suggested I get on one of those stupid dating sites, but there's absolutely no way I'm getting involved with a man. Mom and Daddy had the best love story ever, even if it ended way too soon. But their daughters were not so blessed. Both Geraldine and I headed straight for the world's biggest jerks like moths to flame. And I'm still not convinced that there's a man on the planet who isn't a total loser. Well, Pastor Dennis is a really good man, but he's rare. Plus, he's been widowed for over a decade and clearly not interested in marrying again—not even to Charise Duncan, who bakes him a pie every week. No, there just aren't many men like him, and even if there were, I'm WAY too stubborn to appeal to a man of any real worth. What good man in his right mind wants an old bird like me?

Good grief, would you listen to me? No, Josie Lee, I am not "hooking up" with some toothy Poindexter on some idiotic dating app. I am content with my garden, my mother's absurd menagerie, and my church family. I am blessed. I'm content!
-Libby

CHAPTER
-29-

Sweet are the uses of adversity.
—William Shakespeare

On Sunday, Libby asked Josie if she could take her to church, which Josie was happy to do. With a little extra help, Libby was dressed and ready in time. She wore slacks, a sapphire blue sweater, and a look of effortless beauty. The bruising was gone now. It was hard to tell she'd even had the accident.

At church, Kennedy was all wiggles and shy smiles when he saw Kristen, who welcomed him to her Sunday school class. And when Josie asked about babysitting, Kristen said she'd be happy to come over, just name the day.

Libby was quickly surrounded by a crowd of people excited to see her back, all asking how she was doing, remarking on how marvelous she looked. She looked amazing, actually. Getting out was good for her. Her cheeks even had a slight pink glow. Pastor Dennis greeted Josie and then seemed to be waiting patiently for a chance to greet Libby, but she was trapped by a mob of gushing women until it was time for the service to begin.

During the message, the pastor asked them to turn in their Bibles to Psalm 139. As they read the first dozen verses, Josie wondered if Pastor Dennis had somehow been eavesdropping on her. It was almost word for word the same conversation she'd had with Will. This passage was all about how God saw her and was always with her, and how she couldn't flee from his presence. He was everywhere.

Okay, point made. She could neither hide anything from God nor run away from him. Somehow, this wasn't as comforting as the pastor probably meant for it to be.

As the congregation read on, Josie's pulse kicked up.

> *For you created my inmost being; you knit me together in my mother's womb. I praise you because I am fearfully and wonderfully made; your works are wonderful, I know that full well. My frame was not hidden from you when I was made in the secret place, when I was woven together in the depths of the earth. Your eyes saw my unformed body; all the days ordained for me were written in your book before one of them came to be.*

It was strange and reassuring and a little unsettling that God was privy to every secret there ever was. Every dream, every hope. The inner workings of every human soul. The potential that each person had. He saw it all. And apparently, he not only saw each person as they were being formed, but he had a plan for every person's life long before they were born.

It was strange but also struck her with a kind of awe that God was so intimately involved with every life. With Kennedy's life. With her life.

With Will's life.

She needed to remind herself that Will had a life of his own, and a future. A God-designed future. She didn't have to wonder if that future included her, because it couldn't possibly. Not now, not with the way things were. And by the time Kennedy was old enough for the truth to be known, Will would be far along the path of his life.

She mulled this over throughout the rest of the service, barely joining in with the songs at the end, keenly aware that God was speaking to her. As Pastor Dennis said the closing prayer, Josie said a prayer of her own.

God, I guess you see me and the lie I've been living, but I don't know what else to do. How can I fix this? This isn't the life I envisioned, and I'm pretty sure you're not thrilled about it, either. But it's all for Kennedy. You know that, right? I don't want to keep this up any more than you do, but I don't know what else to do. He has *to be protected from irreparable damage. Is there any other way? Do you have a fabulous plan B? If you do, I'd really like to know.*

She collected Kennedy from his class and smiled as he chattered non-stop all the way to the car about the guy Daniel who didn't get eaten by the lions even though they were starving, but while he talked, Josie felt as if God was drawing her close, inviting her to listen to him.

And what he seemed to be saying was *Tell Will the truth.*

What? No. Sorry, but no.

As Josie helped Libby into the Outback's passenger seat, she shook her head again. Not possible. Will would hate her for lying. And worse, he might even have to get involved with that little contempt of court issue, if things got to that point, which was a definite possibility since she had no intention of attending the judge's meeting.

Fact: Any felon with half a brain knew better than to fall in love with a cop.

Later that afternoon, Will texted to ask if she could go to dinner the next day, on Monday. It turned out Kristen could babysit, so Josie accepted. Will promised to pick her up at 6:00 p.m.

Great.

She stared at her phone, torn. She was tempted to cancel, tempted to tell him she couldn't get involved with him, even half tempted to tell him why.

She was also tempted to spend a couple of hours in the company of a strong, brave, big-hearted guy who turned her insides to mush just by being near him, who really saw her and still found her very much worth his time. Was that too much to ask? She just wanted to feel like Cinderella, just for a couple of hours. Just until the clock struck midnight and the magic ended and Cinderella had to flee, back to her lonely reality.

While Libby was at her therapy appointment Monday morning, Josie and Kennedy popped in to visit with Eleanor. Josie was tempted to tell Eleanor about her upcoming date with Will but decided against it. Josie didn't want to take any chances on confusing her. The one time she told Eleanor she was leaving because she needed to go to the store, Eleanor hollered at the nurse to fetch her pocketbook because she and the Avon lady were going out on the town. It took two aides to convince the poor woman she wasn't going anywhere. It just about broke Josie's heart.

When Libby was finished with therapy, Josie drove all three of them back to the farm. On the way, she gathered her nerve, then finally spit it out. "Kristen Brooks is coming over tonight to hang out with Kennedy," she said casually. "I'm going out for a couple hours."

Libby turned and regarded her with rapt curiosity. "Out?"

"With Ranger McNugget," Kennedy piped in from the backseat. "But me and Kristen are going to make fish sticks and dram crackers and kaleidoscopes."

"Cool," Libby murmured. "Who's Ranger McNugget?"

"He's a Ranger and he saved us from the volcano and he took us fishing and we made s'mores and he has a dump truck and a es-cavator."

Josie didn't need to look at Libby to know that her brows were sky high.

"So is this Ranger McNugget the same friend you two had dinner with last week?"

Josie blew out a hissing breath, then glanced at her aunt, who was grinning. "Stop it. It's McKnight, not McNugget, and it's just one date, that's it. I'm not...available. Which you know."

"Wow, no need to get all feisty." Libby eyed her with a look like she'd just discovered the hottest bit of gossip ever. "When's the last time you actually went out on a date?"

Josie bit her lip. She hadn't had a real boyfriend—the kind that actually took her out—since before college. "Seven years."

"Seven? Holy Archimedes, you're like a Disney film coming out of the vault. This is great! Does he know about, you know, the full story?"

"No," Josie said slowly, glancing at her boy in the rearview mirror. "And he never will. That's why this will be our only date."

"One and done? Better make it count then, sis. Look in my closet. There's a pale green sundress that will do just the trick."

Josie stared at her aunt. "What trick?"

"Just a little fairy godmother magic." Libby winked.

"Oh my gosh." Josie rolled her eyes. "You've been drinking Gram's tea, haven't you?"

Libby chuckled softly. "The lady doth protest too much, methinks."

With a groan, Josie turned into Gram's drive.

While Kennedy ate lunch, Josie went upstairs, pulled out some of Libby's clothes, and held up various outfits in the full-length mirror, thankful that Libby couldn't quite make it up the stairs yet. She didn't need a fairy godmother, a Shakespeare-quoting dating coach, or any other absurdity. She just needed to feel comfortable in her own skin, and she needed to figure out how to do that by herself.

She found a pretty sage green sundress, and Libby was right. The color on her was like throwing a switch that electrified the color of her eyes. She took some extra time with her makeup, upping her usual dash of mascara and lip gloss with some added blush and a little eye color. The time she and Ken had been spending outside had added a few more freckles, to her dismay, but it had also added a warm, peachy glow to her complexion.

After adding some loose waves to her hair, she studied the results in the mirror. When was the last time she had taken time to really care about how she looked? Life had been a whirlwind of caring for and protecting Kennedy, and that had left room for little else. Had she neglected herself? Okay, dumb question. She had totally neglected her heart, her faith, and, if she were honest, her self-respect. Not good.

She stared at the face of the girl in the mirror. She wouldn't turn any heads in Hollywood, but she wasn't half bad to look at. She and Nadine had been called *cute* and *pretty* all their lives, but even so, she knew *cute* and *pretty* didn't get you anything that really mattered. Like parents who stuck around.

Josie gave herself a shake. Smiled. Drew a deep, cleansing breath. Turning Will's head was not her goal, so she needed to stop worrying about being a disappointment. Her only goal was to spend a little time basking in the warmth of his smile, melting at the depth of his voice, and soaking up the strength of his faith and character.

And then, to move on with her life.

His palms were sweating.

Why? It was just a date. It wasn't life and death. It wasn't a stand-off with a gang of armed thugs or rappelling off a cliff into the middle of a blazing forest fire.

So why did he feel like so much was riding on this?

As Will turned in at the Buckley place, he glanced at himself in the rearview mirror.

Why on earth was he so nervous? It was just dinner. Just two people chatting and laughing over steak and roasted baby reds.

Just him and Josie and no interruptions.

Just him and the girl he'd been thinking about non-stop, day and night. The woman who rocked him with needs so powerful he thought he'd lose his mind. The woman who could at any moment walk out of his life for good.

This was nuts. He'd known her barely more than a month. He didn't know her middle name or what month she was born or if she moved her lips when she read.

But one thing he knew without a doubt was that he wanted to be with her for as long as he drew breath. And tonight might be the only chance he'd have to do something about that.

No pressure, McKnight.

He pulled to a stop in front of the house. He checked his watch—he was a few minutes early. He wiped his palms, then headed for the door. He knocked and waited. There was a VW parked near the shed—probably the babysitter's—and beyond that, an old two-tone Ford pickup and Josie's Outback. He glanced around the property, vaguely taking note of a small koi pond and a well-worn rope swing.

The door opened finally, and Josie's grandma stood there with a long, white braid draped over her shoulder, wearing a tie-dyed dress, a tangle of turquoise necklaces, and grasping a gnarly walking stick.

He smiled. "Hi. I'm here to pick up Josie. I'm a little early."

"O gentle Romeo! If thou dost love, pronounce it faithfully…or if thou thinkest I am too quickly won, I'll—"

"Mother!" Josie's aunt, also leaning on a cane, joined Josie's grandma in the doorway, shaking her head. "You must be Ranger McNugget." She smiled. "I'm Libby. Sorry if I should know you, I have brain damage. Come on in."

He exhaled and stepped inside. Animated music in another room punctuated by kid laughter sounded like Kennedy was having a blast with his new friend, Kristen.

Josie's grandma leaned on her stick and just stood there, smiling up at him. Normally, that level of rapt fascination from a white-haired old woman would creep him out, but at the moment, nothing could make him feel any more unnerved than he already was.

Kennedy saw him from the kitchen doorway and ran to him. "Hey! Ranger McNugget!"

Kristen joined him. "Ken, we still have—" She saw Will and smiled. "Oh, hi. I should have known a Ranger beats decorating cookies."

He grinned. "Wow, I beat cookies? I'm—" He froze as Josie appeared at the bottom of the stairs.

When she saw him, she smiled.

The power in that smile hit him like a sudden shaft of sunlight, warm and enveloping. But as she came closer, she looked a little hesitant.

"Is this okay? Hope I'm not overdressed. You didn't say where we were going."

Slowly, he shook his head. Swallowed hard. Tried to remember her question and some sort of appropriate answer. But all he could do was drink her in. Her long, dark lashes framed a pair of eyes so remarkably green they shimmered. Her face glowed, adding pure warmth to her already heart-stopping smile. She was, in a word, beautiful.

"Will?" Worry filled her face.

A sudden desire to kiss her nearly leveled him. He forced himself to snap out of it. Everyone was staring at him, even Kennedy.

"Uh, sorry. You look amazing." Understatement of the year.

"Bippity, boppity, boo," Libby said with a wink.

Josie ignored her aunt. "Thank you. So do you."

The hippy grandma was still ogling him. Libby tugged the older woman away, saying over her shoulder, "Okay, you two, have fun."

Josie kissed Kennedy and said goodbye, then Will escorted her to his truck and opened her door.

Dang it! The forgotten bouquet lay on the seat.

She turned to him, a question in her eyes. "Flowers?"

236

"Sorry, those were supposed to greet you at the door." *Idiot!*

She picked up the bouquet and smelled the blooms. "Wow, this is a first."

He studied her. "Are you serious?"

"Yep, first bouquet I've ever gotten. Well, not if you count all the dandelions Ken brings me." She climbed into the truck, then gave the flowers another inhale and turned to him with another smile. "These are beautiful, Will. Thank you."

He frowned. "I can't believe no one's ever given you flowers."

She just stared at him, eyes wide, glossy lips parted.

Heart pounding so loud she could probably hear it, he closed her door, then went around and climbed in, started the motor, and prayed for strength. Truckloads of it.

CHAPTER
-30-

Love looks not with the eyes, but with the mind,
and therefore is winged Cupid painted blind.
—William Shakespeare

The hostess at Milton's Riverside Bar and Grill led them to their reserved table overlooking the McKenzie. The restaurant, sitting on a cliff above the river, had been around since the 1920s, but the new owner had gone all out reinventing the crumbling old pancake house into something with a rustic but upscale, fishing lodge sort of feel. Windows filled the entire wall on the river side, giving the place a marvelous panoramic view. Everything was done in pale pine with touches of old copper and deep forest greens. The walls were tastefully decorated with artwork depicting a rich history of angling and northwest river life.

Will pulled out Josie's chair, and while the chivalrous gesture thrilled her, it was the faint touch of his hand on her shoulder that sent warm quivers down her spine. She needed to get a grip if she was going to make it through the evening.

As Will took the seat opposite her, she took an extra second to compose herself. But the hungry way he'd been looking at her from the moment he'd arrived to pick her up had made it hard to breathe. She opened her menu to buy a little more time, then scanned the words, but everything was a blur. Which made zero difference, since she doubted she could eat anyway.

She peeked over the menu.

He was still staring at her.

A little gasp escaped her. Hopefully, he hadn't heard it. But the way he was looking at her… Lord in heaven! It was almost as if he couldn't get enough of her.

Ridiculous. She'd been single so long she was delusional. As intoxicating as it was to think that Will was somehow overcome with madness just by being near her, she knew better than to feed such a fantasy. Best to spill something or snort-laugh or *something*, just to break the spell.

Spell? You're a mess. What next, a glass slipper and a clock striking midnight?

"Well, I don't know about you, but I'm starving," she lied. "What's good here?" She worked up a serious scrutiny, pretending to study the menu.

"I honestly don't know. I pretty much just order steak wherever I go."

"Really? Way to live large."

He chuckled.

Josie relaxed—a little. He seemed slightly more at ease. Which was good, because a smoldering, intense Will was not the Will she wanted to spend the evening with, nor the Will she wanted to remember.

"So, I've been wondering if you know how much longer you're going to be staying," he said. He hadn't touched his menu.

Josie closed hers and met his gaze. "Aunt Libby is doing a lot better now," she said. "But she's still not able to do a lot of things for herself and she definitely can't help Gram. She still needs someone to take her to therapy. A nurse comes by a couple of times a week, but they can't transport, so she's depending on me until she can drive again. And we don't know how long that might be." She shrugged. "I'm sorry, that doesn't answer your question, but it's all I know, at this point."

He nodded. "No, that's okay. I just—"

The server came, so Josie picked the first thing that came to mind and then sipped her ice water while Will gave his order.

When the server left, Will huffed. "Cheese fries? *That's* what you're having?"

She shrugged. "What's not to love about cheese fries? You start with a layer of French fries, a basic food group, and then smother it with cheddar cheese, another equally, and might I add, classic food group. Then broil it until it's a pile of bubbling, golden goodness. Hello, what could be more perfect?"

Grinning, Will put up his hands in surrender. "Hey, no judgment here."

"Please don't tell me you're one of those gourmet foodie types. I don't need that kind of pressure in my life."

"In your life?" he asked softly, his tone deep, thoughtful. He captured her with a searching look.

She tried to smile, but the intensity between them was back again, in surf-pounding waves.

He turned away and fixed his gaze on the river, now a deep, inky blue. "Josie, to be in your life, I'd be just about anything you want me to be."

Her jaw dropped.

He turned back, gaze on her face, and frowned. "Sorry, that was…"

"Really sweet," she finished softly.

Will studied her for a long, quiet moment, the entreaty in his expression impossible to escape. "What are the chances you could stay here? I mean, for good? Instead of going back to Idaho."

Wincing, she drew a deep breath. "There isn't any chance of me staying much longer, I'm afraid."

He looked pained. "So your heart's set on going back? Is there… someone there?"

"No. It's not that. I just…" She swallowed hard. "I don't have a choice, Will. If there was any way, I'd be right here, bugging the daylights out of you, using up all your bait and eating all your marshmallows." She tried to make her tone light, but she just sounded breathless. She met his gaze and held it. "Honestly, there's nowhere in the world I'd rather be than right here."

Will's expression sobered and his eyes searched hers. He reached across the table and took her hand, enveloping it gently in his. The warmth of his touch spread through her like fire. "Is there anything I can do that would help make that possible?" He spoke softly, his voice dangerously deep. "Is it money, is it—?"

"No." Josie closed her eyes, shook her head. Why in heaven's name had she agreed to this date? Her heart was going to break into a thousand pieces, right there in the middle of Milton's Bar and Grill. "You're incredibly kind to offer. But there's nothing you or anyone can do."

Hurt and confusion flashed across his face. "Can you tell me why?"

Tears pricked her eyes. "I wish I could," she whispered. "But it's really complicated."

Will grasped the back of his neck, then stared out across the river again, looking like he might be sick.

Her heart raced. "I'm sorry."

"No, don't be." He heaved a sigh, then shook his head. "I let myself hope and I shouldn't have."

Their food came, but Josie didn't have the stomach for cheese fries, after all.

They picked over their meal and managed to move onto lighter topics, so by the time the bill had come and gone, they were laughing and comparing notes about who was kookier, her grandma, or his.

When they stepped outside, the fading sun had turned the sky a clear, dark blue tinged with shades of orange and pink. A string of lit bulbs outlined the deck that wrapped around the restaurant, a soft glow of dotted light against the deepening dusk.

"Nothing like a perfect sunset to end a perfect evening," she said.

"There's a path along the river here," Will said. "Want to take a walk?"

"Sure," she said, and shivered. The air had taken on a definite chill. Will jogged to his truck and returned with a zip up jacket for her—a gesture that moved her more than he probably knew—then they strolled along the bank, drinking in the colors of the sky. The river's song crooned over them like a sweet serenade.

"Just so you know, I kept my word and didn't ask Eleanor about you," Josie said, smiling. As they followed the river, she lifted a shoulder and sniffed her borrowed sweatshirt. It smelled amazing, like clean air, woods, and Will. "But it took superhuman effort."

He glanced at her, then chuckled. "Thanks."

"She had nothing good to say about your last girlfriend, though."

Will huffed. "She doesn't even know the half of it."

The trail was rough in places, and just rocky enough that Josie had to watch her step, since sandals weren't the best for uneven ground at night. "What happened, if you don't mind my asking?"

He drew a deep breath, let it out slowly. "I fell for a girl who did and said all the right things. On the surface, Kristi appeared to be the ideal woman. What I couldn't see was how rotten she was on the inside. I found out she'd been sabotaging co-workers' sales accounts and then making it look like she rescued the company. She was a total manipulator."

"That's awful!"

Will nodded, then slowed his pace. "When I questioned her on it, she acted like *I* was some kind of fraud. She said anyone with an ounce of drive and ambition would have done the same. And if one of us was a fake, it was me."

Wincing, Josie just listened.

"I asked if her claim to be a Christian was a lie too. She just laughed and said, 'Well, I'm no fanatic, like you.'"

Josie gasped.

"And she was pressuring me to move my dad out of his own house and into a nursing home, instead of taking care of him myself. But even then, I still didn't see how self-centered she was."

Will took her hand and helped Josie over a rocky mound, then followed. "She was really smooth," he went on. "She tried to make it sound like she cared about Dad, like a nursing home would be better for him. But it turned out she just didn't like having to share my attention with anyone else."

Josie wanted to empathize, but saying anything about the woman's duplicity felt like pure hypocrisy, so she just murmured in sympathy and kept walking, soaking up her surroundings, letting the clean, damp air and the peaceful beauty of the canyon settle over her.

"I can't believe how blind I was," Will said. "I was even thinking of proposing. I'm glad I found out before it was too late."

Josie nodded. "But still, what a painful lesson."

He stooped down, picked up a rock, and sent it flying out into the river. "Yeah."

Heart sinking, Josie longed to take him in her arms and soothe him, kiss away his hurt, love him past it.

Just love him, period.

She moaned inwardly. *God, I get that you aren't into magically fixing my mistakes, but I love this man. I absolutely do. And I don't want to hurt him. Please, tell me what to do.*

After a few more yards, the trail led up the bank and away from the water's edge to a knoll overlooking the river. There, the ground leveled out, and when she saw the view, she gasped.

They stood at the edge of the cliff, awed into silence by the burgeoning power of the water below, and above and beyond them, the day's grand finale of orange and magenta glowing on the western horizon.

She had never seen such amazing colors outside of nature. But tempted as she was to start snapping photos, she held off, and instead, just stood still and drank in the stunning beauty and the breathtaking view.

Will stood beside her and also surveyed their surroundings. He was quiet, but he seemed relaxed. Content.

Josie breathed deeply, then she turned to Will and smiled.

He met her gaze and held it.

"Perfect," she said softly. "It's too beautiful for words."

Nodding slowly, he watched her.

The deep greens bordering the river, dotted by the golds and reds of autumn, were a photographer's dream. She pulled out her phone and snapped a few pictures, then asked Will to stand beside her for a selfie at the edge of the cliff, with the multi-colored horizon a backdrop behind them.

He made a cross-eyed face in her camera.

"Oh, that's perfect. I'm going to send that one to your dispatcher and have her post it on the bulletin board at the Ranger station."

"Hey!"

"I'm kidding. Okay, I'm not tall enough to get both of us and the sunset. Do you mind?"

With an amused look, he shook his head. "What, forget your selfie stick?"

She put on her best begging puppy face. "Please? You're way taller than me."

His smile faded, and as he studied her, his expression sobered. His chest swelled with a sudden intake of air. He took her phone without a word.

Josie stood beside him and aimed a bright smile up at the screen, which he held high above their heads.

Squinting, he angled it a few different ways, trying to capture them and as much of the fiery night sky as he could. The air felt thick, suddenly charged.

Ignoring the crazy way her heart was drumming, Josie focused on the screen. But the camera angle didn't quite fit enough of the skyline in the shot, so she took a half step back.

"Watch it," Will growled, darting an arm around her. "That's a nasty drop."

Electricity surged through her at both his touch and the depth of his voice. She looked up, and what she saw made her gasp, forcing away every other thought. She swallowed hard, arrested by the smoldering of his eyes, his nearness. The way his strong arm enveloped her waist. The way his gaze traveled down to her lips.

Propelled by instinct, she turned and faced him.

His encircling arm didn't loosen, but captured her all the more in its warmth. "Josie," he breathed, his rumbling voice unsteady. Longing darkened his eyes.

Josie had no idea if the thumping bass drum she felt was her heart or his, or a duet of both. Swallowing hard, she reached up and lightly touched his cheek.

He gasped at her touch, then wrapped both arms around her and tugged her closer.

"Josie." It was an agonized whisper.

She let her gaze fall to his mouth.

With a moan, he lowered his head and brushed her lips with his, softly at first, testing, then he was kissing her long and deep. Desperately, yet tenderly. There was such pure devotion in his touch, such perfect union of desire and sweet affection, that she couldn't think straight. Couldn't hear anything but her heart answering, booming in a silent but fervent, resounding *I love you.*

I love you...

She'd never felt such desire for anyone. Ever. A toe-curling desire that was as tender as it was powerful. But it wasn't purely physical. She never dreamed it was possible to love someone so instantly and fully. Heart thumping like a wild thing, her mind spun with all that he was, and all that she wanted to be to him. To give to him. To share with him.

His hands slid into her hair and he was kissing her again. Asking. Searching. Needing.

She kissed him back, lost in pure, blinding light and adoration, in wonder at this gift, this moment so full of trust, like a crazy good dream. Like heaven, maybe. She wanted to stay right here, on this bank, in his arms, forever.

With each heartbeat, she felt more and more certain. *If I could, I would move heaven and earth to be with you.*

"I love you, Josie," he whispered against her skin.

Her heart sang. Elation tingled across her nerves, instant and electrifying, rocking her world, seizing her breath.

He felt it, too? Love?

He *loved* her?

She pulled back and stared at him, gripped by the reality of what was happening. This was no dream; this was real, and there was no going back. His heart was as thoroughly entangled as hers.

Heart thudding, Josie fought to catch her breath. "I love you, too," she whispered. "But…"

"I know," he said, his voice raw. "You can't stick around, and you can't tell me why."

"I—"

I can't tell you why because I'm lying and you hate liars.

What had she been thinking? She might as well have been sitting on a pile of dynamite playing with matches. One kiss was all it took. Now, the blast would turn both their hearts to rubble.

Somehow, she had to tell him the truth. She owed him that, didn't she? If he loved her…

"I'll tell you why, but then…"

Then everything will change. You'll never want to see my face again. Eleanor will chalk me up as another piranha.

Her breath came unevenly, her heart still roaring like thunder. Everything in her wanted to go on kissing him until she couldn't see straight. But that wouldn't be fair to either of them.

I'll tell you because you deserve to know the truth.

She caressed his face in both hands, her heart nearly bursting from an ache too big to contain. All too soon, whatever love Will felt for her would be destroyed.

"Tomorrow," she whispered, throat too tight to speak. "Can I tell you tomorrow? Can we just keep today as it is? This amazing, perfect gift?"

Will looked deep into her eyes, searching, then his gaze fell to her lips.

Her breath fled. If he kissed her again, she'd lose it. Glass slipper and all, gone.

"Hold me?" she whispered.

With a shuddering sigh, he pulled her close and held her tight for a long, long time.

CHAPTER
-31-

No one is without sin, and yet we're so quick to judge the sin in others. We see the sliver in someone's eye while there's a two-by-four sticking out of ours. We're prepared to stone a woman for a sin we just committed. We are blind judges. It's wrong and it grieves God.

—Eleanor McKnight, age 65

Josie sat with Libby at the kitchen table after breakfast, head in her hands. Once Kennedy was safely outside helping Gram feed her critters, Josie recapped the entire date with Will, who Libby now insisted on referring to as Prince McCharming.

Libby sipped her coffee thoughtfully. "So when are you going to tell him?"

Josie groaned. "I don't know! But I have to. And then..." The very thought wrung her heart like a sponge, bringing a fresh sting of tears. She groaned again. "Then he'll hate me."

"You don't know that. Give him time. If he's half the man you say he is, he'll look past the end of his own nose and see the girl he loves."

"I could never hope for that," Josie whispered. "You know that. If there's one thing I've learned, it's that you can't count on people to keep loving you no matter what. Well, besides you and Gram." She met Libby's steady gaze and held it. "Another thing I've learned is that sometimes, the people you love would rather jump off a bridge than be with you."

Libby gazed out the window, shook her head. "Oh, Josie. You still think everything's black and white. But it's not."

The Secret Place

Josie lifted her palms. "Enlighten me."

Her aunt heaved a sigh. "Did you give up on the diaries?"

"Are you going to make me read them all?"

"Not if you don't want to," Libby said. "And anyway, there's something you need to know that the diaries won't tell you." She straightened the already straight napkins in the holder. "We never did get any official word that your mom actually took her own life."

"Yes, you did, I remember—"

Wait. What did she remember?

Libby shook her head. "We always assumed she did. Because everything she did and said and the way she vanished all pointed to it. But it was never confirmed."

"So you're saying she died of natural causes? Or—" Josie froze. Her hand lifted slowly and covered her mouth. "Or are you saying there's a chance she could still be alive?"

Because that would be an even harsher low blow. A living mother who simply chose to leave her kids and disappear was a lot worse than a dead mother.

When Libby didn't answer, Josie rose and went to the big kitchen window, arms crossed tightly, thoughts reeling. She watched Gram outside at her bird feeder and felt her blood pressure start to rise.

She turned to Libby. "But you were the one who kept saying she took the coward's way out. Bailed on us."

"Like I said, we assumed."

Josie frowned, trying to order the whirling jumble of too many thoughts crashing in on her all at once. Something was off. Way off. Something was—

She looked out the window again. Gram was feeding birds, but Kennedy wasn't with her.

Josie peered at the chicken coop but could only see part of it from the window, couldn't tell if he was gathering eggs.

She searched what she could see of the property, and beyond. No sign of Kennedy.

Heart thudding, she spun and headed for the door.

"What's wrong?" Libby's voice trailed her and dissolved as she hurried out back to the porch and down the steps to the back yard. She went straight to Gram. "Where's Kennedy?"

Gram stared at her, then shielded her eyes with her hand and peered at the barn. "He wanted to see the kittens."

Right. Of course. She heaved a sigh, then went to the barn and threw open the door.

He wasn't with the kittens.

"Kennedy?" She looked around the stalls and climbed up to the loft. "Kennedy!"

Not a sound.

Heart pounding, she doubled back and checked every corner, but he wasn't anywhere in the barn. She ran outside and spun circles in the center of the yard, calling his name.

No answer.

Icy fear stole over her. "Kennedy!"

Gram tottered to her. "He just wanted to see the kittens," she said, frowning.

"He's not in the barn, Gram. Where else—"

The river.

No. NO!

Josie sprinted to the edge of the woods and stumbled down the trail to the river. She clambered over rocks and along the bank, searching the water and all along the shore, heart hammering her ribs so hard it felt like they would break. She scanned up and down as far as she could see but didn't see him or any sign that he had been there.

She doubled back and searched the dirt mound near the stump, then the edge of the clearing near the woods, then back to the front yard. She searched the shed, the koi pond, the trees where they'd caught frogs.

Maybe she had simply crossed paths with him when he went back into the house.

She ran inside and called for him, went upstairs to search, then back down, looking in every room, every cubbyhole. With each second that ticked by, the blood turned to ice in her veins. With every step she took, terror mounted.

"Kennedy!"

She sobbed.

Oh God oh God oh God where is he?

With hands that shook, she took out her phone and punched in Will's number.

She stood on the porch, both numb and shaking uncontrollably even with Libby's arm around her, while Will and a half dozen search and rescue volunteers, including forest service workers pulled in from battling the nearest fires, circled Will's USFS truck and pored over a map spread across the hood. Then people dispersed, vehicles fired up, and everyone headed out.

Will was walking toward her, talking on his phone, but in Josie's mind, all she could see was a movie playing over and over of Kennedy crying, scared, wounded, alone.

And other things. Far, far worse things, horrible things.

It was so, so wrong that she was just standing here, doing nothing. She needed to be out there looking. She needed to find him, to get to him, wherever he was. What if...

She moaned and shook her head, already throbbing from crying and from trying again and again to shake away horrifying images. *Please, God, please, please, please. He has to be safe. Please...*

Will came up the steps to her. "Josie, we've got the very best search and rescue people here. They know what they're doing. I know it's hard, but just sit tight, okay?" Gently, he took her face in both hands and coaxed her to look at him. "I promise, this is the best place for you to be, right here. He might come wandering back from chasing a squirrel, okay? So just hang tight."

Josie's chin puckered. "What about the river?" She could hardly say it.

He nodded. "We're on it. River Rescue is on their way."

Please, God. He can't be in the water. Please...

A sob escaped her, and she clapped a hand over her mouth. "Will," she breathed. That was all she could say. She covered her face and broke down.

He pulled her to him and held her tight, stroking her hair. "Shh. I know, but just try to hold on. We've got a lot of well-trained people out there, and they're combing every inch of the area. They don't miss a thing."

He held her for a while, then took her face in his hands and dipped his head to meet her gaze. "The best thing you can do right now is hang tight and pray. We'll find him."

She closed her eyes, but images of him lying hurt, scared, falling from a bridge, and all other sorts of terrifying, shadowy possibilities circled her mind like fiendish wolves. She shook her head again, trying to scatter them.

Will let her go and touched her cheek. "I'll text you updates, and I'll let you know the second I have any news, okay?"

Numb, she nodded. As he left, her eyes drifted closed and she began to pray like she'd never prayed before.

Gram was inconsolable.

After sobbing for nearly an hour, she finally allowed Libby to put something in her tea that they'd given Libby in the hospital, and Gram fell asleep on her cot.

Meanwhile, Josie paced the yard, inside the house, and outside again, calling his name even though each time she said it, panic stabbed a little deeper into her heart.

What happened? Had he wandered off? Why? Where would he go?

She and others had searched up and down the highway and throughout the adjacent woods.

The fort? She'd been so rattled, she'd forgotten that he had been there. It was over a mile away, but what if he thought he could find it?

She texted Will and asked him to check the road leading to the bridge and all around it, just in case, then forced herself to wait, even though it felt like she was wasting precious seconds. Seconds that could mean life and—

No.

"Sweet baby boy, where are you?" she whispered. Was he hurt? *Please God, please...*

Minutes felt like hours, and though Will updated her every ten minutes, the reports were the same: no news, no sign of him, no one had seen or heard anything. Will's voice was calm, steady. At least someone could keep their head.

Within the hour, more people had joined the search, including volunteers from town, Libby's church, and Lucky Jack, who came by boat to patrol the river. Pastor Dennis came and asked if he could pray, which Josie accepted, though it did little to help her relax. He also offered to stay in case he could be of help, then waited quietly in the front room with Libby.

Josie paced some more, forced herself to breathe. Fought off a full-blown panic attack.

Ninety minutes passed.

More searchers arrived. Josie was too numb to be encouraged by the added numbers, but just kept watching, kept trying to remember to pray and stay calm. Kept checking the perimeter of Gram's property every ten minutes, just in case.

As she came inside through the kitchen door, she heard Will's voice in the front room and rushed to him. She searched his face. "You found him!"

He gently took hold of her shoulders and looked into her eyes. "No, but you might want to hear what your grandma's friend Jenny has to say. Sounds like she saw something."

Jenny?

Hope leaked from Josie like a hissing balloon. Of course the homeless woman had seen something—goblins, dragons, and fairies, no doubt.

"She's out front."

Will led Josie outside, and Libby and Pastor Dennis followed.

Jenny stood near the big oak with the rope swing, wringing her hands, eyes darting from one person to another. Her stance was wobbly, but braced, as if ready for quick escape.

Josie felt her blood boil. "Jenny?" Sheer willpower kept her from shrieking at the woman and demanding she tell Josie what she'd done with him. She knew that would just send Jenny bolting like a rabbit.

The woman pointed to Libby. "I'll talk to *her.*"

"Find out if she took him," Josie croaked to her aunt.

Libby stepped closer to the woman. "Jenny, what do you want to tell us?"

Jenny glared at Will and Josie, then glanced around at the others.

Her narrow shoulders hunched. She whispered to Libby. "You'll be mad."

"Why?" Josie couldn't feel her legs. Will's hand caressed her shoulder, probably reminding her to let the woman speak.

"Why would I be mad?" Libby said.

"Because of...what happened. To the baby," she said, her voice husky.

"What?" Josie's body shook all over. Will's caress turned to a gentle squeeze. It took all she had to hold her tongue.

"What happened, Jenny?" Libby urged.

Everyone stilled. The air suddenly felt thick and weighty.

Jenny's hand wringing intensified. "I'm sorry," she whispered.

"What did you do?" Josie bolted forward, ready to shake the woman, but Will tugged her back.

"Sorry," Jenny went on. "I put him down for a nap and he...never woke. He was so still." Her face puckered. "I'm sorry." She broke down and wept in dry, rasping sobs.

Also crying, Libby went down the steps slowly and joined her. "It wasn't your fault, Jenny. It happens sometimes."

Josie's jaw dropped.

A baby who never woke?

She couldn't breathe.

Dear God, what is going on?

"The baby is safe with Jesus now," Libby whispered through her tears.

Jenny shook her head.

Will turned to Josie, confusion creasing his brow. "What baby?"

But Josie couldn't speak. Couldn't move.

No...

Jenny lifted her face to Libby. "But you have no baby now." She lifted her doll. "Here. I want you to take mine."

Face streaming with silent tears, Libby shook her head slowly. "No, Jenny. I already told you. Remember? You don't have to give me your baby."

No. *No.* This could not be happening. It had to be a dream—a nightmare—one Josie needed to wake from—

She stared at the two women as the freakish reality continued to take shape. Similar bone structure. Voices. Builds.

Sisters.

Josie burst out in a loud gasp.

Startled, Jenny turned and narrowed her gaze at Josie, then pointed a bony finger at her. "She took the boy. I saw her. First she was in the woods. Then I saw her hiding in the barn and when he went in there to see the kittens, she said she knew where there was a litter of puppies, and they left together."

Josie's heart thundered in her chest.

No no no NO NO NO!

Jenny was Geraldine.

And Nadine had Kennedy.

Light flashed in Josie's eyes, swirling together with dark splotches, and the earth tipped. Someone caught her before everything went black.

CHAPTER
-32-

Whoever said the truth will set you free never had to look a four-year-old in the eye and tell him his mommy never wanted him. Not even after she felt his velvety toes and saw his beautiful little face. Anyone able to shred a child's heart by telling him that has a much thicker skin than I do.
—Josie Norris, age 26

Josie's eyes fluttered open and it took several seconds to realize she was lying on the sofa, staring at the living room ceiling. Her head felt like someone had taken a hammer to it.

"What...?"

"You fainted."

Oh...no...NO...

It was all coming back. Jenny. Geraldine.

Nadine.

Kennedy—

She bolted upright with a gasp, her heart slamming into her rib cage.

Will crouched in front of her and took both of her hands in his. "Josie, can you hear me?"

She nodded, wincing at the dizziness the movement caused.

"Your aunt said we need to call off the search and that you have something to tell me." He plowed a hand through his hair. "I have search and rescue along with fire crew out combing the woods and river. What's going on, Josie? Do you know where Kennedy is?"

As she tried to grapple with the answer to that terrible question, Libby came in.

"Jenny's gone," she said, her voice hoarse. "But I believe her." She sat beside Josie and met her gaze, her face and eyes puffy and red. "You need to tell him."

Josie drew a shuddery breath, then turned to Will. "I think my sister has him." And God only knew what she was telling him now, what horrible things she was exposing him to—

"Sister?" Will's brow furrowed. "What sister?"

"Nadine," she whispered, but inside, she was sinking. "My twin."

His frown deepened. "You have a twin?"

Josie nodded.

"And you believe she may have kidnapped him."

Closing her eyes, she nodded again.

"Why do you think that?"

"Because she's been threatening to steal him since he was a year old." Slowly, she opened her eyes.

Confusion warred on Will's face as he studied her. "Why?" he said. "Is she mentally ill?"

She stared at him helplessly. Tried to form the words, but couldn't.

"Why would she do that?"

"Because she's his mother."

Will's face blanched. "His *mother?*"

In the dreadful silence, the grandfather clock ticked away, an endless urging to keep moving forward.

"You said you were his mother."

"I was going to tell you."

He rose and went to the window, his back to her. Shook his head as if to clear it. Turned back with a frown. "But you have custody of him, right? If so, we need to put out an APB."

"I only have temporary guardianship. Legally, she has the right to take him back."

Will's face flooded with disbelief. "So you've been lying? All this time?"

Libby touched her arm. "We need to try to reach her."

Flustered, Josie took out her cell and hunted for Nadine's number. Her hands shook so hard she nearly dropped the phone.

The call picked up on the first ring.

"Wow," her sister said. "What took you so long?"

"Where is he?" Josie could barely breathe out the words.

"Now *there's* a question. Why does it sound so familiar? Oh, I know, it's the one I've been asking you for years."

Will's phone buzzed. He stepped away to the door and answered it, talking in low tones.

"Do you have him?" Josie said.

Silence.

"Nadine!"

"Yes, I have him. And he's fine. He's eating French fries and watching *Paw Patrol*. And by the way, he went with me without even batting an eye. Some mom you are. Doesn't he know about stranger danger?"

Fear snaked down Josie's spine. She pulled her phone aside and said, "He's with Nadine."

Will glanced at her and then spoke into the phone that the child had possibly been located.

"Thank God," Libby whispered.

No. Okay, yes. Thank God that Kennedy wasn't at the bottom of the river or hit by a truck, but still, this was bad. So horribly bad.

"Bring him back." Josie's voice shook.

Still on his phone, Will nodded, then turned to her, his look grim. "I'm going to need you to get proof. Have her put him on speakerphone."

Josie pressed the speaker symbol and then set the phone down, hands trembling. "Let me talk to him."

"Um, I seem to recall making the same request of you lots of times." It was eerie to hear Nadine's phone voice suddenly filling the room for all to hear. "What was your answer? Oh yeah. 'You can't talk to him. You'll only confuse him.' So. How does it feel not being in control?"

Josie couldn't breathe. "Why are you doing this? This was never about me."

Silence.

Her heart raced. What if Nadine disappeared with him? Who knew what she was capable of? Josie needed to keep her on the line. "Nadine, talk to me. Please, don't do anything…"

"Crazy?" A dark chuckle. "Thanks, sis. As always, your belief in me warms my heart."

Another wave of fear surged through her.

Will stiffened, still waiting for proof that Kennedy was alive and well, forearms crossed, listening. His face was stone, lips set in a grim line, dark eyes impossible to read.

"I need to talk to Kennedy."

Nothing, just the sounds of Gram's ancient clock and Josie's racing heart.

"Please."

"On one condition. Don't upset him."

Josie fought the urge to fire off a hot *Me? Are you kidding?*

Nadine lowered her voice. "He's fine, but if you say anything to get him upset and crying for you, you'll never see him again."

Josie closed her eyes. "Okay. I'll…do my best."

She couldn't control how Kennedy would react. She didn't know if he was scared or confused, or if hearing her voice would set him off. She needed to do everything she could to make sure he stayed calm so Nadine wouldn't follow through on her threat.

The phone put off scratchy, muffled sounds, then Kennedy's distant voice saying, "Who is it? Is that Mommy?"

Josie stifled a sob with both hands over her mouth. Drew a breath. Forced her voice light. "Hi, buddy. How's it going?"

"Mommy? Your friend Deenie has freckles too and she looks just like you. That's weird. When are you coming to get me?"

"Um…just as soon as I can, bud." Her heart raced. *Think, think, think. Keep him calm. Make this fun. Lie if you have to. Don't mention anything about being apart.* "Are you having fun?"

A hesitation, just long enough to tick up Josie's pulse. "Deenie got me another Captain America, and a es-cavator, and a buncha Hot Wheels. But, Mommy? I don't have my toothbrush and she said…" His voice wavered. "Do I have to sleep here?"

Oh no, don't cry, bud.

She had no choice but to lie—again—for his sake, for the critical situation at hand. "It'll be fun. Like a sleepover."

Silence.

"I don't wanna sleepover." His voice trembled.

Her heart raced. "Well, just pretend it's like taking a nap when you get too tired. Remember? After you wake up, ta-da! Everything's magically okay. Okay?" She held her breath, listening, heart pounding.

"O-kay," he said slowly. Not his usual chipper self, but not crying or scared, at least.

"I'll see you soon, bud. I love you lots." Tears blinded her.

"Love ya, Mama."

More muffled sounds, then Nadine's voice. "See you at the court-house."

The call ended.

Josie stared at the phone, willing it to tell her this was all just a typical Nadine prank, or a bad dream that she would wake from. But it was neither. This was real.

She was completely at Nadine's mercy.

Her throat ached with unshed tears. She looked up. Libby was headed to Gram's room to tell her, and Will was almost to the door.

"Will…"

"I need to dismiss the searchers and fill out a report."

"I was going to tell you, it's just…really complicated."

"I got all I need here," he said coolly, without turning. He slapped on his ball cap and walked out the door.

Alone, numb, and blinded by tears, Josie tried to piece together what was happening. The courthouse…the meeting with the family court judge.

She dug through her bag and found the letter from Lane County and re-read it.

October 16th. The meeting she had determined not to attend was tomorrow.

How could this be happening? How could she have lost the child she had vowed to protect at all cost? And now, not only did Nadine have him, but she wanted Josie to come to the courthouse. Which didn't make any sense. If Josie didn't appear, the judge would probably give Nadine whatever she wanted. So why would she want Josie there? What was she trying to pull?

She had to want something else, something that required Josie to appear in person before the judge.

Maybe revoking Josie's temporary guardianship wasn't enough. What if she wanted to get some kind of restraining order? Could she do that? Could she somehow convince the judge that Josie was some kind of threat?

She gasped. Did she want to have Josie arrested?

What would the judge base his actions and decisions on? Josie knew what Nadine was capable of. She was strong-willed and could be very convincing. She might try to use Josie's frequent moves against her. Josie could easily counter that Nadine was a known drug addict and her lifestyle was totally unstable, if not flat-out unsafe for a child. Of course, she had no proof, just her own observations.

But then, Gram and Libby had also observed it.

Josie tiptoed to Gram's room and found Libby sitting on the edge of the cot, rubbing the older woman's back. Josie entered cautiously.

Gram startled at the sight of her. "Oh, blossom," she sobbed. "I'm so sorry...so very sorry." Her shoulders shook and she wept harder.

"No, Gram, it's not your fault." Josie hurried to her grandmother and hugged her. "You didn't do anything wrong. I'm sure Nadine has been waiting for just the right moment."

Waiting, watching, and planning, apparently. Nadine now held all the cards. She had Kennedy. She was in a position to take away what little legal rights Josie had. And who knew what else. Was she doing something to make sure Josie never saw him again?

That thought hit her like a sucker punch. That could *not* happen. Not after all that Kennedy and Josie had been through, after all she had done to guard his little heart, after all she'd done to nurture the fragile seeds of confidence growing in him.

Josie cringed at the glaring mental picture of uprooting him countless times and dragging him around the country to live like fugitives. Though she'd had no choice, it still pained her every time she thought about it.

She hated living that way, but she had provided as best she could. Short of giving birth to him, she was as real a mom to Kennedy as she could possibly be.

She was his mom.

A voice in her heart whispered, *So is that "Mom" title for Kennedy's sake, or yours?*

Josie went cold. What difference did that make?

She had no choice now but to attend the meeting, and to go prepared to appeal to the judge. If Nadine was planning to sway his decision, then Josie would do the same. She had raised Kennedy from birth entirely on her own, so shouldn't she have some say in his life? The judge would also have to listen to her side, right?

If the fact that she alone had raised and provided for him wasn't enough to establish her as the rightful mother, then she would pull out the big guns and bring up every irrational, reckless, illegal, intoxicated thing Nadine had done.

Josie shared her thoughts and concerns with her aunt and grandma.

"If it comes down to it," Josie concluded, "would the two of you be willing to tell the judge about how strung-out Nadine was when she came here to stay?"

Libby glanced at her mother, then back at Josie. "If you think it'll help."

"I mean, I don't want to get her in trouble with the law," Josie added, "but Kennedy comes first. His life and future are at stake."

"Do you want me to go with you?" Libby asked.

"I don't know if you'd be allowed. It's not a hearing, but a meeting in the judge's chambers. I have no idea how that works."

"Well, I'm here for you, either way."

Josie nodded but felt like the bottom was falling out of her world.

"Kiddo, there's something else we need to talk about."

Josie studied her aunt and waited, but she had a feeling she already knew. "Jenny."

Libby sighed. "She's—"

"Geraldine." Josie's eyes drifted closed. "I don't even know what to think or how to feel about that. Why didn't you tell me?"

Gram laid a wrinkly hand on Josie's arm. "Frailty, thy name is woman."

Josie could only stare at her grandmother.

"She means Geraldine," Libby said. "My sister's mental state is extremely fragile. Mom and I learned the hard way that if we're going to be able to keep an eye on her, we have to be very careful not to scare her off."

"How long have you known she was alive?"

"She showed up here three years ago. About the time you went into hiding from your sister. You had a lot on your plate at that time."

One sister goes into hiding from her twin, and another sister comes back from the dead. All in the same year. No wonder people thought the Buckleys were cuckoo.

"So why didn't you tell me?"

"Well, we thought the news of her being alive and in such a frail mental state would be too much to deal with. We weren't sure you'd be prepared to…give her the space she needs."

Space? They'd withheld an earth-shaking truth like that because of what her AWOL mother needed? What about what Josie needed? What about answers?

"There is so much you don't understand, Josie."

"Clearly." What other secrets had they kept from her—that her dad was a pirate? That she had a half-brother in the circus?

Josie's phone buzzed. Startled, she pulled it from her pocket and nearly dropped it when she saw the name on the screen.

Nadine.

CHAPTER
-33-

The wide world is all about you: you can fence yourselves in,
but you cannot forever fence it out.
—J. R. R. Tolkien

Heart racing, Josie stepped out of Gram's bedroom and answered Nadine's call. "I'm listening." She held her breath, heart pounding.

"I'm not trying to hurt anyone," Nadine said, her voice low. "But I don't expect you to believe that."

Josie scoffed. "I wonder why."

A huff rattled the line, then nothing.

"Everything you're doing is hurting him," Josie said, unable to hold back. After more thick silence, she said, "How did you know we were here?"

"Libby called me from a nursing home. I'm guessing she thought I was you. She wasn't making much sense and then she said something about you and your son coming to see her."

Libby. Josie should have monitored her better.

"Good old Josie, still everyone's golden girl. Still lying to everyone, I see."

"You don't want to go there."

"Oh, I'm going there. You have no idea."

"What are you talking about?"

"Don't play the dumb blonde with me, Jose, you can't pull it off. You do brainy tomboy much better."

Frustration burned through her. "I don't know what you're talking about."

"You've never so much as jaywalked. You'd never do anything rebellious, especially blowing off a circuit court judge. I can't believe you pulled a no-show."

"I didn't know about the meetings until recently."

"Oh, well lucky you. Because if you miss tomorrow's meeting, you'll have more than losing a child to deal with. Ever heard of contempt of court? I'm sure you don't want the judge ordering a warrant for your arrest."

Josie gasped. As bad as *fugitive* and *arrest warrant* sounded, her life on the run had never been about saving herself or avoiding the law. It had only been about protecting Kennedy.

"I'll be there," she said evenly. Then she braced her heart to be shattered into a hundred pieces. "So what have you told him?"

A long silence stretched across the line. "I haven't told him I'm his real mom, if that's what you mean. Not yet, anyway."

Josie nearly collapsed with relief. She let out the breath she'd been holding. "Okay, but what about when we talk to the judge? He'll hear all that and then he'll—"

"Kennedy's not going to be there."

"What? Who's going to have him?" She could barely squeak out the words. A picture formed in her mind of the guys she'd seen Nadine with downtown. The image paralyzed her.

"He'll be in good hands. You're just going to have to trust me."

Trust? Josie stared at the paneled hallway, fighting panic.

"Look, I didn't call to fight. I called because I wanted to tell you something."

"Just tell me you're bringing him back."

Silence.

Or maybe she was pregnant again.

"I'm saved."

"What?"

"Born again. You know, a Christian."

Josie's mouth hung ajar. "That's not even funny."

The thick silence that met her seemed to agree, and for a second, she entertained the possibility that Nadine was telling the truth. But how could it be true? How could Nadine be a Christian now? Where in the Bible did it say kidnapping a child was the Christian thing to do?

"But I don't expect you to believe me," Nadine muttered.

"I haven't been able to believe you for a long time."

The line connecting them seemed to pulsate, like it had taken on a heartbeat of its own.

"Do you have any idea what a jerk you are?" Nadine said, her voice low.

"Me?" Josie's heart pounded. "All I ever did was try to help you."

"Right. Because you're the *perfect* sister."

"Oh, so I should be more like you?" Josie huffed. "Reckless, breaking rules, hell-bent on coloring outside the lines? Using people, and then tossing them behind you like a trail of candy wrappers? Always looking for the next thrill? Needing someone to constantly bail you out?"

"You loved being better than me, and you know it."

"What? You know that's not true. It's just that someone had to be the responsible one. With you acting like a lunatic, it was up to me to try to hang on to some kind of normal life."

"Normal?" Her sister's scoff was sharp, followed by a stretch of silence. "Did you ever think maybe I was trying to blow the heck out of normal because I never fit into anyone's normal and never will? Did you really not see that?"

Josie had no answer for that.

"The reason I never colored inside the lines is because I can't. It's like everyone gets a box of puzzle pieces for their life, only my box didn't have a picture on it, and I had no idea what my life was supposed to look like. I kept trying to toss my pieces out there to see what I could make out of it, and you kept gathering up the pieces and stuffing them back in the box. Trying so hard to appear the part."

She was almost afraid to ask. "What part?"

"The part of a normal girl with a normal life and a normal family and not the grubby little stray that some crazy woman decided she didn't want and tossed out with the trash."

Josie gasped, her face burning.

Nadine huffed. "You really don't get it, do you?"

"What?"

A long silence stretched from two heartbeats to three, then four. Then a sigh.

"Forget it. See you in the morning."

He was done.

There was no way a woman would ever make a fool of him again.

Will turned off the truck but just sat in the staff lot, staring at the station's rear entrance. He didn't doubt that Josie's sister was all kinds of trouble or that Josie loved the boy. He didn't care about some twisted custody battle between two sisters. The thing that knocked the wind out of him was that she'd lied to him. She'd flat out lied by telling him she was Kennedy's mother. That the boy was *her* son.

She was also lying to a kid. And the cherry on top: She was keeping a boy and his mother apart.

Women were secretive, devious, and two-faced. Was it part of their nature? What was that infernal Hamlet thing his dad used to say?

Frailty, thy name is woman.

What troubled Will even more than Josie's deceit was how easily he had been fooled. He'd fallen for Josie like a seventh-grader high on hormones. How had he missed it? Some award-winning investigator he was. The fact that he'd been fooled disturbed him. Was he just blind when it came to women? Was he some kind of liar magnet? Or was he just stupid?

That was it. He was stupid for falling for a liar, again.

Stupid for telling her he loved her.

Except, Josie Norris was the truest thing he'd ever known. She'd made him feel whole, like she held the missing piece of his puzzle, a piece he hadn't even known was missing.

Josie and Kennedy had brought joy into his life and made the picture complete.

But apparently, that joy was just an illusion.

Which meant what he thought he and Josie felt for each other was also just an illusion.

Unfortunately, his emotions hadn't gotten the latest update. His heart was gullible. Easily deceived.

And flat out ached now because of her duplicity.

No, the truth was, his heart ached because he'd fallen for Josie—hard. And finding out she wasn't what she appeared was a brutal blow.

Will dragged a hand over his face. He needed space. Maybe he could pull a couple stretches of fire duty back-to-back. Stay out with the crew indefinitely. Get away for a month or two.

He went inside, slipped past the dispatcher, and ducked into his office to file reports.

A half hour later, his phone buzzed, and Mandy's name appeared. He did not need his sister's perk, her pity, or anything else. He muted his phone.

Seconds later, he got a silent text alert. With a growl, he read it.

> Mandy – 12:32 p.m.
> Any updates? The girls and I are still praying that Kennedy will be found 100% okay soon. Keep me posted when you get a chance. xoxo

Dang it. He'd forgotten that he'd sent out an SOS to Mandy asking her to pray when Kennedy first turned up missing. With a sigh, he replied.

> Will – 12:33 p.m.
> He's been found with a family member.

> Mandy – 12:33 p.m.
> Oh, praise the Lord! I bet Josie is beside herself with relief! That's awesome!

He stared at the words. Didn't answer.

> Mandy – 12:34 p.m.
> Will? This isn't like a baby-daddy kidnapping thing, is it?

Will didn't want to do this. Didn't want to get involved with Josie and her double-identity games and he definitely didn't want to get sucked into some drama over custody.

She lied to me.

He deleted that.

She's not what she appeared.

Delete.

She's two-faced.

With a groan, he deleted that, too. If the kind, selfless, freckled girl who filled the vacancy in his heart wasn't real, then nobody was.

Mandy – 12:37 p.m.
Call me when you can.

With a growl, he punched his phone off.

When he had finished composing and sending his daily reports, he took his Hydro Flask out to the front office to refill it while he checked the weekend duty roster. Two of the three fires were nearing containment, which was a massive relief. The Willamette crew had been working triple time.

"Hey, McKnight," Darcie said as Will passed her desk. "How did everything turn out with that boy you were searching for?"

Will stiffened. Even at work, he couldn't escape thinking about Josie and her son. Or her nephew, as it turned out. An innocent kid who had been kidnapped by his estranged mom and was now in the middle of an ugly tug-o-war.

Darcie knew the boy had been found, but she also knew that Will was acquainted with the boy's family. The middle-aged woman wanted tidbits. He suspected that she loved working dispatch because she loved being in the know.

Well, she didn't need to know that the boy's mom had been lying to everyone and pretending to be something she wasn't. Or that it still ate him up that he'd fallen for her duplicity.

Or that he'd fallen for her, period.

Or that a fierce battle between hurt and longing still raged inside him.

Darcie didn't need to know that Will couldn't stop thinking about Josie, couldn't stop hearing her voice. Couldn't stop remembering the silky feel of her lips against his, or the way she begged him to hold her beside the river, or how good she felt.

How incredibly good.

Just thinking about her ignited traitorous desires inside him that were ludicrous and totally unwanted. He didn't know what to do with them, so he continued doing what he'd been doing all day: Fight them, suppress them, extinguish them.

"Are you okay?" Darcie was looking at him oddly.

He frowned. "Yeah. What do you mean? I'm fine."

The woman's brows rose. "Yikes, forget I asked."

Growling, he took his Hydro Flask back to his desk, where he discovered it was still empty.

CHAPTER
-34-

Love is not love which alters when it alteration finds.
—William Shakespeare

Later that night, as Josie lay on Kennedy's top bunk, smelling his pillow and ignoring the tears trickling into her ears and hair, she heard someone slowly thunking up the stairs. When Libby finally came in the room, a sheen of perspiration covered her face.

Josie wiped her swollen eyes. "I'm sorry you took the trouble to come up the stairs, but I don't want to talk about Jenny. Or Geraldine. Or Nadine."

"Okay. How about we talk about Josephine?"

Josie didn't look at her aunt. She wanted to bury herself beneath the covers until she woke from this nightmare. "No, thanks."

Libby sighed, then pulled the desk chair over to the bunk bed and sat. "You and your sister used to be totally inseparable."

"Yeah, and then we grew up. But oddly enough, I'm not in the mood for fondly reminiscing about Nadine."

"I can see that."

Josie sucked in a deep breath. "I don't know what to do, Libby. Everything in me wants to call her and scream at her to bring him back. Or make her tell me where he is so I can go get him and make sure he's okay. I'm praying, but I don't even know if God is listening."

"Sure, he is."

She shook her head. "I don't think you tackled a flight of stairs just to tell me God is in control."

Libby handed her a Kleenex. "I didn't. But you're right, he is."

Josie rolled toward her. The pillow felt lumpy. She reached beneath and pulled out Captain America, which set off a fresh batch of tears. "Why did you come up here, then?"

"Just to say that it's easy to look out across the horizon and assume we know what we're looking at. In the foreground, we see a huge, rushing river and deep green canyon. In the distance, we can see the Three Sisters and a vast, blue sky. But we forget what we're seeing isn't the whole picture. There's more to the world that we don't see. A lot more to the story."

"Okay…?"

"There's a lot more to people than what we think we see, Josie. We're all guilty of making assumptions. Drawing our own conclusions, whether they be emotionally rash, childish, or just uninformed. We all do it, it's human nature. And we have unspoken expectations of people. Big ones, and sometimes impossible ones we don't even realize we've assigned to them. And neither do they. So they don't even know they're failing us."

Josie shook her head, trying to grasp how Libby could be discussing Jenny a.k.a. Geraldine now, of all times. Libby was a wise woman, but her brain had recently gone through a blender and spent several weeks as a smoothie. She couldn't possibly be thinking straight.

"You can't tell me a mother doesn't know what's expected of her."

Libby's brows rose. "In whose book? See, that's the problem. We each have our own list of things that we believe make the perfect mother, or sister. Or Christian. Or spouse. I'm not saying we shouldn't have expectations and even hold people accountable to certain standards. But sometimes we can get ourselves stuck in a bitter rut because we can't forgive people for not being who we need them to be."

Josie stared at the ceiling. As much as Josie dearly loved her aunt, she couldn't see how this was helping her immediate and far more dire situation.

"It's human nature to hold others accountable for their failings and forget the strengths in them. No one is perfect, and we all need supernatural grace. Not a once and done job, either, but a never-ending river that begins with us. God loves you, Josie. He has poured out all sorts of grace on you. Sometimes, you have to remember the grace you've received and give it to others."

Josie heaved a sigh. "Okay. I'm going to assume you've come up here preaching because I need to figure out how I feel about my dead mother being alive, homeless, and apparently clueless about who I am. I get it. But I'm going to need you to give me some space to even begin to process all that. I can only deal with one smart bomb at a time."

Especially when her stolen child was already one bomb too many. She had to force herself to block out what Kennedy might be feeling right now, because if she allowed herself to go there, the tidal wave of panic lurking at the edges of her heart would drown her.

"I'll be praying for you."

"Thank you. I have no idea what to expect tomorrow, or what to say. Or what my sister is really up to." She turned and met Libby's sapphire gaze. "But I'll do whatever it takes to protect Kennedy, and at this point, I don't care who I have to throw under the bus."

Libby let out a slow exhale. "Are you sure about that?"

Josie blinked at her. "You don't think I will, or that I should?"

Her aunt studied her carefully. "Hopefully, you won't have to find out."

"You're the one who always told me to hope for the best and be prepared for the worst."

Her aunt nodded. "What are you hoping happens tomorrow?"

That was a no-brainer. "I want the judge to give Kennedy back to me, and I want Kennedy protected from the truth."

"And what about Nadine?"

Josie shrugged helplessly. "What about her?"

Libby shook her head. "She's still your sister."

For a moment, all Josie could do was blink at her aunt and wonder if her brain was starting to curdle. "This is about Kennedy. This is about what *he* needs. He needs to be protected. He needs—"

His mommy. He needs…

Me. I'm needed.

Josie gasped.

With an arched brow, Libby looked her square in the eye.

Heart pounding, Josie glanced away. Everything she'd been doing these past four years was solely about protecting Kennedy. That was it, nothing more.

"I trust you'll do the right thing, Josie." Libby rose to leave. "Call or text me the minute you're done tomorrow."

After Libby left, Josie tried to sleep, but her mind kept circling around Kennedy. Nadine. Jenny. She prayed for help and wisdom. She asked God to move mountains because quite frankly, she was trapped beneath several, and they were suffocating her.

One of those mountains was Will.

She had promised him at the end of their date that she would tell him the reason she couldn't stay in McKenzie Bridge, that sticky, complicated part of her life that she'd been holding back. Or more accurately—lying about. But after today's revelation, it was clear he didn't want to know anything more. He'd heard enough. But now, she wanted to tell him. Not just because she'd promised, but because he only knew part of the story. She needed him to know her reasons, the history that had led up to it. To see the rest of the picture, as Libby would say.

If he would even listen.

All Josie could do was offer the truth and try not to hold out hope that he would understand or forgive her.

Yesterday, he said that he loved her. Today, he stormed out of her life, which tore deeply at her core. It was a crushing pain she knew all too well.

So was this a case of a man who spoke too soon, or a man whose love was easily lost?

Was there ever such a thing as love that never gave up, no matter what?

Did *Love No Matter What* only exist in fiction and poetry?

Gram had quoted the Shakespeare sonnet so many times that Josie knew it by heart.

> *Love is not love*
> *Which alters when it alteration finds,*
> *Or bends with the remover to remove…*

Was there even such a thing as an unbendable, unalterable love in the real world?

Yes. As far as Josie was concerned, there was, because she felt it. She no-matter-what, no-turning-back, without a doubt, loved Will. Even if he never truly had, or no longer felt the same way.

And because she loved him, and owed it to him, she would tell him the truth.

> Josie – 10:46 p.m.
> Can we talk?

She waited several minutes with no response, which, while heart-wrenching, was no surprise. It could have been that he was working, asleep, or outside of cell service. Or just not interested in hearing what she had to say, which was more likely.

Ten minutes later, he replied.

> Will – 10:56 p.m.
> I'd rather not.

Fine. She could text just as well as she could talk. No more wishing for do-overs.

> Josie – 10:56 p.m.
> I understand why you don't want to talk to me.
> But I'd like to know how you're feeling.

> Will – 10:57 p.m.
> Deceived. And disappointed. You're lying to a child.

She winced, tears filling her eyes. She wasn't surprised, but still, it hurt to see his words in black and white. His response was a cold, swift reminder that she couldn't count on being loved, couldn't trust an *I love you* from anyone.

Josie swallowed the ache in her throat.

> Josie – 10:57 p.m.

I am. And as much as it kills me to do it, I'm doing it because the truth would hurt him far more than the lie.

Will – 10:58 p.m.
And you lied to me. It's not just the lies, though, Josie. It's that you wear it so easily, like a mask. I can't trust someone who can lie that smoothly. You're a real pro.

His words sank deep, crushing her to the bone. Wiping fresh tears, she read the next text.

Will – 10:58 p.m.
You told me things that aren't true, that he's your son. You let me believe that you're this complete-ly devoted, selfless mom.

Josie – 10:59 p.m.
Those things are all true, except I didn't give birth to Kennedy. But I have loved him since the mo-ment I knew he existed. I fought for his life three times when my sister would have aborted him. I was there when he was born, and I worked like crazy to give Nadine everything she needed to mother him. But she never wanted the job, so she gave him to me and then vanished. I never in-tended to lie to Kennedy, or anyone else, but too much time, and Nadine's irrational behavior, and my naïve mistakes grew into a situation I didn't know how else to solve. By then, it was too late to fix, and I had to go on letting him think I'm his mother because I know how painful and devas-tating it is to find out you're worthless in your mother's eyes and she didn't want you. You know that feeling, Will. I hope you can understand why I never, ever want him to suffer the same pain that you and I have.

Josie waited a few minutes, but he didn't respond.

Josie – 11:02 p.m.
I'm sorry for lying to him, to others, and to you. All I ever wanted was for Kennedy to never doubt his worth, to know he's loved without question or wavering, forever and ever. If I'm wearing a mask, the only thing beneath it is just plain old Josie doing whatever it takes because I love no matter what.

She sent it and waited, wondering if he would respond. Wondering, hoping, and then kicking herself for hoping because she knew he wouldn't and besides, it was late, and she really needed to get some sleep if she was to have any kind of functioning brain in the morning.

She plugged in her phone, then re-read her message to him and stared at the last line.

I love no matter what.

The words pulsed, like they were beckoning to her, daring her to prove it.

Did she love no matter what? Did she love her mother even though she'd tossed Josie away like a bag of trash? Even though she never once checked on her kids? Even though she had never been the mother Josie needed her to be? Even though she didn't know who Josie was now?

Did Josie love her sister no matter what?

With a hand that shook, Josie put her phone down. She had no answers.

CHAPTER
-35-

Can a mother forget the baby at her breast and have no compassion on the child she has borne? Though she may forget, I will not forget you! See, I have engraved you on the palms of my hands.
—Isaiah 49

The meeting was set for nine o'clock at the Lane County Courthouse in Eugene, a little over an hour away. Josie wanted to be there with plenty of time to compose herself, so she got up early, dressed carefully in a borrowed gray pencil skirt and pink silk blouse from Libby, then hit the road and arrived a little after eight. Waiting at the corner Starbucks sounded supremely tempting, but she didn't need to add caffeine to her already jittery nerves.

Instead, she went inside the courthouse, found the floor where the Family Court judge's chambers were, then spied a row of chairs in the hall nearby to wait. As people passed by, she spent some time praying. She had no idea what the meeting would entail, or how well she'd be able to hold it together. She probably should have taken Libby up on her offer to come and lend support. But if Josie couldn't stand on her own two feet to fight for Kennedy, she probably had no business claiming she was the best person to raise him.

If she ever saw him again.

She inhaled deeply, willed herself not to cry. Not now. A meltdown before she even went in there was the last thing she needed. She closed her eyes.

Dear God, I really need your help. You know how I'm hoping this meeting will go. And you probably know how scared and alone I'm feeling. And maybe you even know how much I could really use a friend right now. Could you just stay with me? Help me know you're there? And give me strength? Give me the words? Help this meeting to go—

She was about to say *the way I need it to go,* but something in her heart checked her.

Help this go the way you *want it to go.*

That concession made her heart cinch up like too-tight shoelaces. It was a familiar feeling. It was that same panicky feeling that always fueled her with adrenaline and kept her moving from town to town. The same feeling clutched her heart now like a huge claw, like the talons of an eagle carrying away her young.

Trust me.

Tears stung her eyes. But what if…

I love you and will never leave you. Place Kennedy and everyone else you love in my hands. Let go and trust me.

She wanted to trust him, but…

Either she trusted him, or she trusted her wimpy self to do things her own way. And based on her track record, her own way pretty much sucked. Despite her doubts, fears, and her habit of drifting downriver from God, she knew she couldn't keep going like this. Doing things her own way, she'd made a mess of her life and Kennedy's.

How many other lives would she mess up?

She longed to talk to Libby. What would her aunt say? What wisdom would she offer?

That was easy. Libby would whip out her Bible and quote scripture.

Josie pulled up the Bible app on her phone. The passage she'd looked up during church last Sunday appeared first on the screen:

> *Where can I go from your Spirit?*
> *Where can I flee from your presence?*
> *If I go up to the heavens, you are there;*
> *if I make my bed in the depths, you are there.*
> *If I rise on the wings of the dawn,*
> *if I settle on the far side of the sea,*
> *even there your hand will guide me,*

your right hand will hold me fast.
If I say, "Surely the darkness will hide me
and the light become night around me,"
even the darkness will not be dark to you;
the night will shine like the day,
for darkness is as light to you.

Josie closed her eyes again.

I love no matter what.

No. Even at this, Josie had failed. But God had not. No matter where she went, God was there. Not only there, but he was holding her. Loving her. No matter if everyone else left her or stopped loving her.

I love you, Josie. And I will never leave you. No matter what.

She sucked in a sharp breath.

Okay, God, I'm letting go of control and putting my life and everyone I love in your hands and I'm going to trust you. But just so you know, I'll probably change my mind and come back for a few rounds of tug-o-war. But I don't want to do it my way anymore. And I can't do it alone. Please help me learn to run to you instead of away. Help me fully trust you.

She felt like she was no longer alone. When she opened her eyes, her heart skipped.

Two chairs down, her twin sat very still, watching her.

"You came." Nadine didn't sound surprised.

It took Josie a few seconds to adjust to seeing her sister, face to face. Nadine was also dressed in a skirt and blouse. And was too thin.

And was alone.

"Where's Kennedy?"

Her sister's expression turned stony. "You really need to chill. He's fine. He's with my rehab mentor. She watches her two grandkids every day, and he's having a blast playing with them."

Rehab? Josie took a closer look at her sister. Nadine was thin, but didn't look strung out. Her eyes were bright, her skin pale, but clear. Her hair was no longer black, but was now a soft, light brown, slightly darker than her natural honey blonde. She looked good.

"I don't use anymore," she said, as if she could still read Josie's mind. "I'm even careful about over-the-counter stuff." She tucked a lock of hair behind one ear. "I've been working on finding healthy ways to deal with pain instead of medicating with drugs and alcohol."

"Good for you," Josie said slowly. Maybe she was clean. But for how long…

"And you still don't trust me."

It wasn't really a question, and therefore didn't need an answer.

"That's ironic." Nadine folded arms across her chest.

"Why?" Josie checked the time. The meeting with the judge would begin in a few minutes.

"You were the first one to break our trust."

"Me?" Josie stared at her sister, trying to decide if she wanted to spend energy fighting with Nadine before they saw the judge. But maybe that was Nadine's plan. To get Josie flustered and throw her off. "As I recall, you were hell-bent on having nothing to do with me. And after years of chasing you from one crazy stunt to another, I guess I just couldn't keep up anymore."

Nadine answered with a cool, steady stare. "At least I'm not lying to a kid."

Josie's jaw dropped. "That's low, coming from the one who—" *Wanted to end his life.* Josie clamped her lips to avoid saying the last part, but Nadine's narrowed eyes said she didn't have to. "You were always about the adrenaline and shocking the daylights out of everyone," Josie went on. "Do you know how exhausting it is to be your sister?"

A thick silence fell between them, stirred only by the sound of Nadine's quickened breathing. She didn't say anything, but Josie could see that she'd hit a nerve.

She went on. "I was constantly trying to keep you from being a social outcast and trying to make sure you didn't kill yourself. You didn't care about anything. You didn't even care about your own life as much as I did."

Nadine's face reddened. "I never asked you to do any of that. I never asked you to rescue me or defend me or fix me. Ever."

"What else was I supposed to do?"

Nostrils flaring, Nadine just glared at her. "How can someone so smart be so stupid?"

Josie sucked in a sharp breath.

"You really don't get it." Nadine shook her head. "I didn't ask you to be my mother or my chaperone. All I wanted was one person I could really count on. Just one. You were supposed to be that person." Her eyes glittered.

Count on? That was all Josie had ever done. Been there for her sister. She could only stare at her twin, her thoughts spinning. How could she, with their unique connection, not comprehend?

Nadine gave herself a brisk shake and inhaled, chin high, holding herself stiff, as if that would keep her from crying. She dabbed at her eyes.

"How was I not there for you? What did I do?"

"You broke your promise. And after everything else, that was the last straw. Don't pretend you don't know."

"What promise?" Josie frowned. "When?"

Nadine leveled her gaze on Josie, then heaved a sigh. "That just shows you how much it meant to you."

Josie waited, at a total loss.

"Tenth grade. Jake Miller broke up with me."

What? Their estrangement was over a stupid high school boy? She didn't want to voice her confusion, mainly because it didn't make sense. Nadine was the toughest girl Josie knew. She never gave a rip if people didn't like her.

Nadine went on. "The breakup really hurt, but I was getting over it. Until one day about a week after he dumped me. Jake and a bunch of his friends were hanging around outside the gym. When I passed by, he mocked me in front of everyone. You know what he said?"

Josie shook her head slowly, feeling a prickle of dread.

"He said, 'There's the little crybaby who sicced her psycho aunt on me like an old junkyard dog.'" Angry tears welled in her eyes. "He even barked at me. His friends cracked up like that was the funniest thing they'd ever heard. But you know what, Jose? I didn't care about that. I didn't hear any of the taunting. All I could hear was the sound of you telling Libby something I told you in confidence. For your ears alone."

Heart racing, Josie racked her brain, trying to remember exactly what she had told Libby. Josie frowned. "Are you sure I told her?"

Nadine scoffed. "Libby knew the exact reason he broke up with me. Word for word. That I wasn't 'enough.' That was something I told no one but you."

"I didn't know Libby talked to him," Josie said slowly. "But I'm not surprised. I just found that the way he treated you made her furious." She studied her sister, but Nadine's eyes, now red, looked even more stricken.

"You swore to me you'd never share our secrets. You broke your promise."

Josie's mouth fell ajar. Clearly their childhood oath was far, far more important to Nadine than Josie had realized.

"You were my rock," Nadine said, her voice low. "But after that happened, I realized no one had my back. There was nothing solid beneath me. Nobody I could count on. Your loyalty was to Libby, not to me. You had Libby, and I had no one. I was all alone." Tears rolled. "When you broke our promise, you…" Trailing off, Nadine just shook her head and looked away.

"What?" Josie whispered.

Nadine swiped her cheeks. Wouldn't look at her.

Josie waited.

"You broke my heart."

Josie gasped. Memories and feelings spun like leaves in a whirlwind until a single thought came to a dead stop in her mind: *Josie* was the reason they'd split apart. Nadine had grown distant and pushed her away, but Josie had caused it.

How had she not seen this?

Nadine plucked at a thread on her purse strap. "You were always bent on damage-control and trying to make me more socially acceptable, but there was only one thing I ever wanted from you."

Tears blurred Josie's vision.

Her sister leaned closer, her face suddenly full of passion, her gaze intense. "And when I had it, Jose, I could do anything. I could fly. I could take on the world."

Josie shook her still reeling head. "What one thing?"

Nadine wiped mascara from beneath her eyes. "I shouldn't have to explain this to you."

Throat too thick to speak, she whispered, "Tell me."

Crying now, her twin stood. "The only thing I ever wanted was for you to love me." Nadine shouldered her purse, walked to the judge's door, and disappeared.

Josie felt the blood drain from her face.

What had she done?

A bailiff stepped out of the judge's chambers and motioned her inside.

CHAPTER
-36-

Friendship with oneself is all-important, because without it,
one cannot be friends with anyone else.
—Eleanor Roosevelt

The bailiff indicated two upholstered chairs facing an enormous mahogany desk, then left the two women alone in the wood-paneled room. Nauseous and shaken, Josie took a seat and glanced at Nadine. Her twin was blowing her nose and checking her totally wrecked makeup in a little compact.

Great. If Josie looked as bad as Nadine, which she probably did, they were both toast.

A weird form of panic swept through Josie, a reeling sensation that left her feeling ten kinds of sick. Just when she needed to be strong, her world was collapsing. She had failed Nadine. She had broken trust with the one person whose feelings she should have valued more highly than anyone else.

The gulf that had formed between them had been Josie's doing.

When the judge stepped into the room, she was surprised that he wasn't wearing some kind of official robe, but a regular suit. He took a seat at his desk, then took a painfully long look at the two women seated before him. He was an older, fatherly-looking black man, graying at the temples, wearing bifocals and an air of authority that scared the socks off Josie.

"Miss Norris and Miss Norris."

Nadine's chin lifted an inch.

"And, Josephine Lee Norris is…?" he said, his enquiring look ping-ponging between the two.

"Here," Josie said, raising her hand halfway, then dropping it. This wasn't third grade.

"Ah." He leaned forward and studied her with a piercing gaze. "Thank you for finally accepting my invitation." He turned to Nadine. "You wish to revoke Miss Norris's temporary guardianship of Kennedy Charles Norris, is that correct?"

Nadine nodded.

"Do you have the documentation?"

"What documentation?" Josie gasped, then covered her mouth.

The judge peered at her above his glasses.

"It's all in my file." Nadine cast a sidelong glance at Josie, then looked straight ahead at the judge. "I have a job, money in savings, and a safe home."

Could Josie object?

But she held her tongue, heart racing. Everything Josie had come prepared to say about Nadine in order to shore up her own case suddenly seemed like a giant wrecking ball—with spikes.

While the judge pored over pages on his desk, Josie raised her eyes skyward in silent prayer, then caught sight of a large plaque on the wall behind the judge, which read, *Love is patient, love is kind. It does not envy, it does not boast, it is not proud. It does not dishonor others, it is not self-seeking, it is not easily angered, it keeps no record of wrongs. Love does not delight in evil but rejoices with the truth. It always protects, always trusts, always hopes, always perseveres. Love never fails.*

Love rejoices with the truth. It always trusts. It never fails.

Love doesn't quit, no matter what.

Josie fought hard to contain her tears. She wanted to reel in the years, reel in the past, retract every one of her mistakes. She wanted to go back to the time when she and Nadine had been soulmates, to the promise they had made in their secret place, and renew her vow with all her heart, and then make absolute sure she kept it.

If only.

"Miss Norris, er, Josephine? Are you still sole care provider for the minor child?"

"Uh, well, I was, until she…" She glanced at Nadine. "Reclaimed him. Yesterday." Without permission, warning, or Josie's knowledge.

"You have repeatedly failed to respond to your sister's request to terminate guardianship. Are you aware that CPS has made numerous attempts to contact you to investigate the child's living conditions?"

"I didn't know, but I do now. I moved a few times, so I didn't—"

"And since you have not responded to or made any attempt to contact this court, this raises concern for the safety of the child, which now authorizes me to defer the case to Child Protective Services."

Shockwaves numbed her.

"It's my duty to inform you that I am also authorized to charge you with custodial interference and contempt of court, as I see fit."

Josie stilled, barely able to breathe.

He eyed her. "I am a firm believer in seeking the best interest of the child." He pushed his glasses higher on his nose and read over something in front of him. "From what I can gather, neither of you has much to say for yourselves regarding Kennedy's best interests. One has a history of drug abuse, and the other can't show up to a simple meeting. One is a good caregiver but appears to be in contempt of my court—of which I take personal offense—and the other is the biological mother but is a total stranger to the child. You've both shown pitifully poor judgment, and apparently, you can't even be friends, let alone sisters."

Josie glanced at Nadine, but her sister kept her gaze fixed on the judge.

"With the way you two are behaving, I have half a mind to have the child remanded to protective custody and leave the two of you to go squabble over something else."

"No!" Josie slapped both hands over her mouth.

Judge Levine drilled her with a frown.

"I apologize, your Honor," she said. "But Kennedy has only known me as his mother his entire life. If you take him away and place him with strangers, he'll be terrified and he'll feel—" A sob burst from her. She fought for control of her voice. "He'll feel scared and lost and completely abandoned." She shook her head. "Please, don't do that to him."

The judge looked at Nadine, who had gone deathly pale. "I need to inform you that I am prepared to defer my final decision to whatever

CPS recommends." He addressed Nadine. "Do you have any objections to CPS—"

"I object!" Josie said, half rising from her seat.

Judge Levine stared at her like she'd just produced horns.

Josie slowly lowered herself. "Sorry. Please, may I say something?"

The man's left brow rose. He folded his arms across his chest. "I'm flattered that you're actually offering me a choice. Proceed."

She glanced at Nadine, heart sinking. *God, please, I can't do this, I really can't, but if you help me.* "We were both abandoned at Kennedy's age by our mother, and I know the damage it does. I know what being sent to live with strangers would do to him. If you have to choose someone, and you can't choose me, then…then just…" A tingle of dread stole over her. She sucked in a breath and forced out the words. "Let him stay with Nadine and leave CPS out of it."

Nadine stared at her, eyes wide.

Josie focused on the judge—she didn't dare look at her sister. "Please. I know what I'm saying. If you send him to complete strangers, it will tear that sweet little boy apart."

The judge cocked his head and studied her, his examination long and thoughtful. "And you would rather give him up than see him 'torn apart'?"

No, she would rather not give him up in any way, shape, or form, but he left her no choice. Tears blinded her and her throat felt too thick to speak. She nodded faintly.

The judge wrote on the paper, signed with a flourish, then said, "Temporary guardianship is hereby revoked. Custodial parent retains full, exclusive guardianship. This meeting is adjourned."

She and her sister waited for the judge to rise, then both women stood.

Buttoning his jacket, Judge Levine turned to Josie. "You know, I've read about a similar case of two mothers who each claimed a child as theirs. They also appeared before a judge. Do you know the case?"

Josie shook her head, too numb to speak.

"Interesting story. The judge's solution was to cut the child in half to appease both women, but at that suggestion, one of the mothers immediately relinquished her claim on the child in order to spare him harm."

He gave her a wink as he left.

Josie spun and stared at the bailiff who held the door open for them, but she couldn't make her feet move.

Oh God, what have I done?

"Josie…" Nadine said.

She stiffened but didn't turn, didn't look at her. She couldn't.

"I'll come this afternoon for his things. And I'll bring him with me, so you can, you know…"

"Say goodbye?" Josie whirled around to face Nadine, feeling like she would be sick. "He won't say goodbye, he's four. He'll fall apart and cry and ask why he can't stay with me. He'll beg me not to let you take him." She could barely get words out around the lump in her throat threatening to choke her. "What are you going to tell him?"

Nadine looked her in the eye. "I haven't thought that far ahead yet."

Great. Josie nodded slowly, fighting back monster panic. Of course Nadine didn't have a clue what she was doing. "Will I ever see him?"

Her twin met her gaze and held it. "Yeah. I'm not you, remember?"

Josie stilled. "Meaning you wouldn't hide him, like I did."

Nadine studied her without answering, then took out her keys and left the room.

Josie stared at the empty doorway, numb from head to toe. She needed a cold shower, a slap in the face, something.

No. What she needed was a do-over. To rewind and go back to that meeting and not hand Kennedy over to a completely alien life. An erratic, crazy life with Nadine that Josie did not want to even think about.

No matter how carefully this ripping away was handled, he would be scared and confused, at the very least.

Dear Lord, please do a miracle in my sister's life. Please help her take the absolute best care of him. Help her want the very best for him, help her know how to care for him. Help her be…

No. She couldn't ask God to help her sister be a *good mom.* Not yet. She wasn't ready to ask for that just yet.

Please, Lord, I don't know how to let Kennedy go and trust him into your hands. I really, really don't. I need some help here. An impossible amount of help, actually. Please, God.

Crying, she headed to her car, fumbled with her key fob, and unlocked the door. This wasn't the way it was supposed to go. Well, it wasn't like she'd ever had a really good, solid plan, but she had pictured going on for a while longer avoiding interference from Nadine until Kennedy was old enough and had the emotional tools to process the truth. Now, an ugly seed of self-doubt would be planted in his sweet little heart, and it would grow deep roots and choke out the confidence and security that she had so carefully nurtured in him.

Kennedy fully believed that Josie was his mother. He would be so confused about who he was now. Scared of the unknown, and insecure about what other rugs would be ripped out from beneath him. He would be hurt that his mommy had—

Josie gasped and nearly doubled at the impact of the realization. Kennedy would think she had abandoned him. Gave him away, just like her mother had done.

"Oh dear God, what have I done?"

Sobbing, she couldn't even open her door, and it was all she could do to keep from crumpling to the ground.

CHAPTER
-37-

Son, it looks like I won't be around for your birthday, so here's my gift to you, one last bit of advice from your old man: always remember to be slow to anger, quick to forgive, and never cling to an earthly joy if it brings pain to another.
—Keith McKnight, age 57

His first day off in more than a week was also the first frost of the season. Will kicked it off with a crackling fire, a day-old fritter from Wally's, and his favorite old sweats—a pair he'd had since college that Kristi had tried to throw away more than once. He stared into the flames dancing in the stone fireplace, mesmerized by the way they shifted and leapt, intense and consuming. For something so mindless, fire wielded so much power. For a person facing hypothermia, it could save a life. And just as swiftly, fire could take a life. It could destroy all the life in an entire forest in the blink of an eye.

How crazy that something so simple had the power of life and death, that it could cause two completely opposite outcomes.

Much like love.

A long sigh escaped him.

He studied the flames, then glanced at Mandy's photo album on the end table beside him, untouched since he brought it home. A day off left him alone way too long with his thoughts. He had no calls to respond to, no reports to file, nothing to distract him. He really needed to get his heart and mind off yesterday's emotional roller coaster. He needed to stop wondering what was happening with Josie at court today and worrying about whether or not Kennedy was safe. He needed something totally mind-numbing to do.

He scowled at the album.

Blasting out a sigh, he picked it up and started at the beginning. The first page was a collage of photos of Dad growing up, then several of Keith as a teen, fishing with Grandpa McKnight. Then more of Dad at his high school graduation standing between his parents. Seeing Grandma Eleanor so much younger was weird. She was even small back then, but her smile for her son was big and beaming with pride. His parents had every reason to be proud of their son; they'd raised him well. Keith was tough but kind, courageous to a fault, quick to help and slow to complain.

He spied another photo from the same day—this one of both his mom and dad in caps and gowns. Will didn't know they were high school sweethearts. What had his dad seen in Linda Shaw? Maybe she was different back then. Or more likely, maybe she was pretending to be someone she wasn't and showed her true colors later.

Sorry things turned out the way they did for you, Dad. You deserved better.

Will turned the pages, giving scant attention to his parents' wedding day. His mom wore a simple gown, flowers in her hair, and a smile.

With a frown, he flipped the page and kept turning. His sister had painstakingly organized the book in chronological order, adding captions and dates to some of the photos.

He stopped on a photo of Mandy and himself, probably around nine and eleven years old, swimming near the shore of a large lake surrounded by huge evergreens. He studied the rest of the photos on the page and realized they were from a family camping trip. His gaze paused on a picture he'd never seen before: his mom working a jigsaw puzzle on a weathered picnic table. She was poking out her tongue with a playful, sidelong glance, as if she knew she was being photographed. Dad must have taken the photo.

Will studied the background carefully. The family's 24-foot travel trailer was set up nearby. Beyond the camp, he could see a bit of lake beyond the thick trees.

He remembered. They'd been camping at Ochoco Lake in Central Oregon. Will and Mandy had been out the entire day riding his little Honda Trail 70 around and around the lake, much to the irritation of neighboring campers. He still remembered how Mandy had clung to him as he gunned it through the minibike's gears, and how she screamed in sheer panic, and then hollered at him to go faster.

Will smiled faintly.

There were more camping trip photos Will had never seen, and in several of them, Mom was smiling. Those were probably the ones Mandy had gotten from her. He wasn't sure how he felt about that; both the fact that she had kept them all this time, and that she'd given them to Mandy for Keith's memorial album. He also wasn't sure how he felt about his mom appearing to be happy at one time—*if* the photos were to be believed.

He pulled out his phone.

> Will – 9:26 a.m.
> Hey, Sis. Question: Did Mom ever love Dad?

> Mandy – 9:28 a.m.
> Yes, I believe she really did. She was happy for a while. But she had problems. The longer she stayed, the harder she had to fight to be happy. Eventually, she lost the battle.

> Will – 9:28 a.m.
> I don't get how she could have been unhappy. Dad was the best guy any woman could ever hope to find.

> Mandy – 9:28 a.m.
> Sad, right?

> Will – 9:28 a.m.
> What?

> Mandy – 9:29 a.m.
> How a person can lose the best thing that ever happened to them.

Will shook his head. If his mom felt loss, it was entirely her own fault. He had zero sympathy for her. He and his dad had been left to fend for themselves. And then later, Dad had to face a terrible battle with cancer all alone.

> Will – 9:30 a.m.
> I don't care what she lost. She made her choice. You do the crime, you do the time.

> Mandy – 9:30 a.m.
> You know I love you. But I need to say something and you're not going to like it.

> Will – 9:31 a.m.
> You already know there's nothing you can tell me about her that I want to hear.

> Mandy – 9:31 a.m.
> It's not about her. It's about you.

Frowning, Will muttered his reply as he typed it.

> Will – 9:32 a.m.
> What about me?

> Mandy – 9:32 a.m.
> I don't know how or why it happened, but you've become really hard. And it's not the job. You didn't always think every skinny guy driving a beater car is a scumbag up to no good. You used to have compassion. I'm sorry to have to say this, but you're turning into a real jerk.

He glared at the last word of her text. Who made *her* the personality police?

> Will – 9:33 a.m.
> Wow. You don't beat around the bush.

> Mandy – 9:33 a.m.
> I'm only telling you because I love you.

He tossed his phone, then flipped through the album with a vengeance, barely glancing at the arranged photos, each page decked out with stickers and artfully doodled words. When Mandy had given him this album, he expected it to be a photoshopped fairy tale that didn't tell the real story, but that wasn't the case. His sister couldn't have invented what Will was seeing now. Of course, pictures could lie. People could pose, use trick photography, create the impression they wanted others to see. But these photos weren't fabricated. What he was seeing was a story he'd forgotten. It was a history—and not just his dad's, but Will's also. The book was like a key that unlocked a buried chest of truth.

He'd forgotten the laughter and good times. Forgot them, walled them up, sealed them off. But there had been a time when the four of them were happy, including his mom. So was the McKnight family not enough for her? Or was it just Dad and Will who weren't enough? What was so bad that she had to walk away and destroy what the four of them had?

Dad had said something before he died about letting go of things that bring you joy if they cause others pain. Will hadn't made the connection then, but he wondered now if Dad was describing his own marriage. For whatever her reasons, Dad had put Mom's wishes first. He'd let her go for the sake of her happiness. He'd been sad, but he had never once been resentful.

Why not? Why hadn't rejection and abandonment hardened his heart?

The next page displayed a picture of himself in full-dress uniform. It was taken at his swearing in ceremony when he was hired as USFS law enforcement. It had only been five years ago, but he looked like a kid. An eager, naïve kid who had no idea what a brutal schooling the world was about to throw at him.

True. The last five years had been hard. A lot harder than he liked to admit.

Squinting, he looked closer. The younger Will stood proud, solemnly swearing the oath of honor like someone who meant it. Someone prepared to care for the land and serve the people, guided by integrity and compassion.

As he stared at the photo, a strange, burning sadness washed over him. After five years, he had the integrity part down tight, but the compassion that once guided him had quietly withered.

He stood and walked into his bathroom, flipped on the light, and studied himself in the mirror. The grim reflection staring back bore little resemblance to the younger Will in that photo. He remembered that guy. But the guy he was seeing now, he didn't know. Not really.

And what he was seeing, he didn't like.

"Okay, Lord," he whispered. "I'm listening."

Get rid of all bitterness.

Right. The Bible had a lot to say about the dangers of harboring bitterness. The trouble was, he'd taken to skimming past that verse in Ephesians, like somehow, it didn't apply to him.

Be kind and compassionate to one another.

He studied his reflection again. The man staring back had no compassion for people who did wrong. It was true; he had become hard-hearted. He'd been acting as judge and jury.

Mandy was right—he was a jerk.

Will's eyes closed.

Be kind and compassionate to one another, forgiving each other, just as in Christ God forgave you.

Forgiveness was a gift from God for those who repented. Even the scumbags. But it wasn't the scumbags or the looters or even his mother who needed to repent. It was Will.

"Forgive me, Lord," he whispered. "I need your help. Please."

God had always been faithful to meet him whenever Will yielded in surrender, and even now, he sensed the Lord's nearness, his pleasure.

I will give you a new heart and put a new spirit in you; I will remove from you your heart of stone and give you a heart of flesh.

CHAPTER
-38-

I can't wrap my mind around it. I'm having not one but two babies and I'm all alone. I don't know what to do. Mom says come home, it'll be just like old times, but the good old days are gone, and Lib has enough problems of her own. I don't want them to know that I'm losing my mind.
I'm so scared I can't breathe.
—Geraldine Norris, age 25

Josie dialed Libby and put her on speaker phone, then turned onto the McKenzie River highway and headed east.

"Is the meeting over?" Libby asked. "What happened?"

As best she could between shuddering breaths, Josie gave her aunt a stilted replay of the entire day, both her private meeting with Nadine, and the meeting with the judge. Libby listened quietly, and even waited patiently for Josie to cry, pull herself together, and continue.

"I'm so sorry, Josie," Libby said when Josie finally stopped, unable to say any more. "Are you okay to drive?"

"I think so," she murmured. She was basically on autopilot at this point.

"Are you coming home?"

"Yes."

"Okay. I'm going to ask Pastor Dennis to come over and pray with you, if that's okay. He's really good at that sort of thing. He's so wise and caring."

Along the winding road, spent leaves in gold, orange, and red dotted the highway, but even far brighter colors burst from the trees at intervals like random wildfires. She had always loved the beauty of nature, and yet now, the vibrant colors somehow heightened her pain. As if nature was throwing a party while her soul was being ripped in half. "I don't mind. Pastor Dennis seems really kind."

"Oh, yes, he is. He's amazing."

It suddenly occurred to Josie how different her aunt seemed when the pastor was around. Like a little more at peace. But not just that—there was something unusual about her demeanor around him. Something...*soft*.

"Libby," Josie said slowly, grateful for a bit of distraction. "If I didn't know any better, I'd say you were crushing on Pastor Dennis."

"What? No. You've been sniffing Mom's brew. No."

Josie puffed out a tiny nose laugh.

"What are you going to do now, kiddo?"

"I don't know. I don't know what to do." She teared up again. "Oh, Libby, I really don't think I can do this."

"I know you feel that way now, but you will get through it, because we're going to ask God to help you and Kennedy both."

Josie could only stare at the spent confetti on the road ahead, wanting to somehow absorb Libby's strength of faith, desperate to believe the impossible.

"Sometimes, when everything around us looks awful, the only thing we can do is develop tunnel vision and fix our eyes on Jesus," Libby said quietly. "Like Philippians 4."

"Tunnel vision," she murmured. Yes. Great. Maybe she could try that. Because what the future held was a sad, lonely blur. When she thought of a future without Kennedy, she couldn't breathe.

"What am I going to say to him, Libby?" Josie asked. "And how can I be sure that Nadine is going to stay clean? What if she—"

"We can't be sure of anything except that the Lord knows and is in control. What we can do is pray. We can place those we love in God's hands and trust him. And we can find ways to stay involved in their lives. In case you haven't noticed, I pretty much interfere whenever I want."

"I've noticed."

Josie ended the call and focused on the road, but grief flooded her again. She needed to get a grip, and she needed to psych herself up to see Kennedy and face the heart-rending ordeal when he learned he would be leaving without her into the unknown.

She needed to prepare herself to say goodbye.

The rest of the way home, she poured out her heart to God and then tried to listen as best she could between bouts of crying. Tried not to ask why, though her mind screamed the question.

Because in her heart, she already knew the answer. She had taken matters into her own hands and tried to fix everyone and everything. She had fought to give Kennedy a secure identity. And if she were to be truly honest, she'd been using him to secure her own worth.

The truth wasn't pretty.

"Are you there, God?" she half whispered, half sobbed. "Do you see what I've done?"

I see you. And I know you. I know everything about you.

A powerful sense of God's presence surrounded her. More tears fell.

"Right. There's no keeping any secrets from you," she whispered.

I knew you and loved you before you were born, Josie. Your name is engraved on the palm of my hand.

Stunned that he would even speak to her heart, she drove on, marveling at the way he met her when she quieted herself before him. He was bigger than her mistakes, bigger than the circumstances, bigger than her fears. He knew everything about her and still loved her. He wouldn't leave her. He was in control, and she didn't need to be.

She prayed some more, and by the time she pulled into Gram's driveway, she felt a little calmer than when she left the courthouse.

A white sedan was parked in front of the house. Apparently Pastor Dennis wasted no time when called upon for help.

Josie drew a deep breath. She had to do this. She had no choice.

When she went into the house, she found Libby's visitor was not the pastor, but an older woman she didn't recognize. Probably someone from Libby's church.

Josie was just about to pass on through to the kitchen to give them their space when the woman rose to greet her and smiled. "You must be Nadine's sister. I'd know you anywhere."

Josie stiffened. Being an identical twin left no doubt about whose sibling you were.

The woman held out a hand. "I'm Selah Stewart. I'm Nadine's mentor in the addiction recovery program at our church."

Taking her hand, Josie greeted her politely, but confusion jumbled her thoughts. What was she doing here?

"I've so enjoyed Kennedy, he's such a sweet, smart little boy. He and my grandchildren have had the best time playing together. Oh, and he's been telling us some very interesting stories about someone named Ranger McNugget." She smiled. "I'm not sure if he's real or a superhero."

Josie nodded, still confused.

Selah glanced at Libby. "I was just telling your aunt that Nadine asked me to say she has some pressing business to take care of today, and that she'll be in touch to arrange to meet up with you on another day."

Another day. Awesome. This was so Nadine. She'd had Kennedy less than twenty-four hours and was already changing the plan, prolonging his trauma. This was a really bad sign.

And you turned him over to her.

Selah was still smiling, so Josie forced herself to stay calm.

Libby sent Josie a meaningful glance as she spoke to Selah. "Did she give you any idea of when? So that Josie knows how much time she has?"

"Time for what?" Josie asked.

The woman smiled gently. "Nadine didn't want to rush you, so she asked me to bring Kennedy to you. She'd like to meet back here in a couple of days."

With a gasp, Josie looked around the room. "Kennedy's here?"

"He's outside with Gram," Libby said. "He wanted to check on his chickens."

Josie's heart raced. "So, I have him for a couple of days?"

"Yes. And Nadine also wanted me to tell you…" the woman trailed off, looking slightly uncomfortable. "She wants you to know that she trusts you not to take off with him."

Nadine trusted *Josie?*

The sound of voices burst in from the other room.

"Kennedy!" Josie bolted toward the kitchen.

When Kennedy saw her, he shot at her like a torpedo. "Mommyyyy!" He wrapped himself around her legs.

Don't cry. Don't cry. Don't cry.

She hugged him, despite his protests, then swooped him up in her arms and held him tight, kissing his face.

He giggled at her kisses. "Ow, you're squishing me!" Looking at her, he frowned. "Did you see a spider?"

She wiped her cheeks and smiled. "No, I just missed you like crazy."

"Mommy, we drove bumper cars! And Deenie took me to the races and it was really loud and then we had ice cream and we got a kite and we went to the park. Can we go do that again?"

Reluctantly, she put him down, then forced a smile. "Sounds like you had a blast," she said, trying to keep her voice light but failing miserably.

Gram came to her aid. "Methinks the noble knight has returned. All is well that ends well."

Sorry, Gram, but this one doesn't end well.

Selah and Libby joined them in the kitchen.

"Josie, it was lovely to meet you," Selah said. "I just want you to know that your sister is doing really well. And she knows to take her victories one day at a time, and that it's only by the grace of God."

Josie nodded but didn't trust herself to say anything kind or useful, so she said nothing.

"I know how difficult family estrangement can be. I'm praying that you and your sister can work things out."

"Thank you" was all she could say.

Over lunch, Kennedy talked non-stop about Deenie's cat Fergie, her tropical fish tank, and Selah's grandkids, Oliver and Lexi, who had wasted no time making Kennedy an official member of their rescue pup team. Captain America was so yesterday. He was now obsessed with *Paw Patrol.*

Josie nodded and exclaimed at all the right spots, but all the while, she fantasized about buckling Kennedy into her Outback and driving somewhere far away. Like Bangladesh. Of course, she wouldn't. But it was mighty tempting.

Josie spent every moment with Kennedy, reading, baking cookies, building forts, and taking care of Libby's garden and Gram's critters. Kennedy wanted to visit Miss Ellie, and while Josie wasn't sure visiting Will's grandmother was a good idea, she promised to take Kennedy to see her tomorrow. It would probably be the last chance he would have to see his "funny" friend.

Throughout the day, a little voice nagged at her, reminding her that she still needed to tell him he would be leaving her and this place. She needed to prepare him. But she had absolutely no idea how to do that, and whenever she thought about it, she felt sick.

After Kennedy was asleep that night, Libby asked Josie when she was planning to tell him. She couldn't pretend things were going to stay the way they were, but she desperately needed just a little more normal time with him. Just for a little while longer. Libby was clearly not on board with that plan, but, thankfully, she didn't lecture. She knew Josie well enough to leave her alone and let her work it out on her own.

On Thursday morning, Nadine texted to say she would meet her at Gram's on Friday evening, if that worked for Josie.

Of course it didn't work for her, but what choice did she have?

So she had Kennedy for thirty-two hours. Until then, Josie would do like Gram and lock the pain away and make every last minute she had with her little boy count.

CHAPTER
-39-

Grief is like climbing a mountain carrying four boulders and a flag. Of the five stages of grief—denial, anger, bargaining, depression, and acceptance—the last one is the hardest. Acceptance is the flag you plant at the pinnacle, the reward for reaching the top, one foothold at a time, with no one but God at your side. Planting that flag can be lonely, but it's still a victory.
—Libby Buckley, age 56

After his shift Thursday evening, Will changed into jeans and a sweatshirt, stopped at the mini-mart, then headed to Riverbend. Grandma was in the TV room reading to a deaf lady who was working on a jigsaw puzzle.

Grandma took the jelly donut he offered, then peered up at him. "What's eating you, Eeyore?"

He opened his mouth, but all the came out was a terse huff. What was it with everyone? "I'm fine. You doing okay, Grandma?"

"I think someone stole my pocketbook. I want to talk to the ship's purser."

"I'll take care of it, don't worry."

She bit into her donut, then offered some to him.

"No, thanks."

While Grandma licked jelly from her fingers, Will noticed a book on the table beside her with a howitzer on the cover. He picked it up and thumbed through the glossy photos of cannons and old war weaponry.

"Yes, you should check that one out. It's all about the artillery used in the Civil War," Grandma said. "Good pictures. But if you're going to write a book report, you need to know that some of the facts are incorrect. There were twice as many casualties from disease than there were from weapons. But don't tell my young friend. She was tickled pink to bring me that book. She practically begged me to tell her all about it."

Will stared at his grandmother. "What young friend?"

"The green-eyed one. And that funny little Mr. Magoo."

Josie and Kennedy? Impossible. Grandma just had things mixed up, as usual. "When did she bring you this book?"

Eleanor shrugged. "Oh, a little while ago. Did she leave already?" Frowning, she peered around the room.

He sighed. Grandma was definitely delusional. Josie couldn't have come with Kennedy recently, since the boy was no longer in her custody. And besides, Josie had no reason to visit Eleanor now.

He looked through the gun book again. Eleanor's name had been written inside the front cover in big, loopy cursive. Labeling personal belongings was necessary in a memory care facility, as things often had a way of turning up in other residents' rooms.

The shift nurse brought apple juice for Grandma to take her meds, and while she sipped it, he slipped out to the foyer and looked at the visitor's logbook.

And there it was, under today's date: Josie and Kennedy Norris had checked in to visit Eleanor McKnight at 10:15 a.m. Exit time: 12:00 noon.

He stared at the big, loopy way Josie had signed her name, stunned. Josie had come today.

But why? She was no longer bound to their agreement and under no obligation to visit Grandma. And Kennedy had come too, so apparently he was back with Josie.

Safe.

A wave of relief washed over him.

Josie had come to see Grandma today and brought her a book. Why? She had no reason. Unless she was simply being kind to an old woman.

He swallowed hard.

As he returned to his grandma, he told himself it didn't matter what Josie did. It was none of his business.

So, if her life didn't matter to him, why did it feel like a giant cannonball had hit him square in the chest and ripped a gaping hole?

By Friday morning, Josie was starting to get a handle on her new skill: tunnel vision. Of course, Libby meant to tunnel focus on God, which Josie was trying to do, along with reminding herself that he loved her no matter what. He would never flake out or turn cold or run away and hide from her. And whenever despair pressed down on her like a lead blanket, she read Philippians 4 and prayed for focus.

But she was also determined to focus on the time at hand, on just breathing in the moment. It was about the only way she could function and avoid dwelling on things too awful to feel. She tried not to think about what was being ripped away from her. Or how she had lost not one, but two people she loved with every bit of her heart.

Kennedy was leaving tonight, and she didn't know when—or if—she would ever see him again. All throughout the day, the thought of losing him came in waves of stabbing pain that threatened to take her breath away.

Don't think. Just soak in his funny little voice and his sweet baby face.

Meanwhile, it had been three days since Will found out Josie had been lying to him, and he hadn't contacted her at all. His silence spoke loud and clear about the radical change in his feelings. Knowing he despised her only amplified the pain of losing him. She longed to tell him why she'd made the choices she had, but he clearly wasn't interested in hearing any more of her story. And as tempting as it was to beg him to listen, she couldn't burden him like that. She knew how he felt about honesty, how important it was to him.

She heaved a tearful sigh. Wasn't this exactly what she feared would happen when Will learned the truth? Yes. But for once in her life, just once, couldn't one person—besides Gram and Libby—love her no matter what? Or was she stupid to hope for such a thing? For all her impressive grades in school, she was dumb. Dumb to hope, dumb to set herself up for a broken heart.

Maybe Will no longer found her worth keeping, but God did, and that would never change. That was a truth she was learning to accept, to take hold of, to lean on.

And today, she and her broken heart were leaning extra hard on that one.

Since Friday was to be their last day together, Josie took Kennedy fishing in the morning, to the same spot where she had helped him catch his first fish. Every once in a while, she glanced up the bank toward the road. Thanks to her ridiculous imagination, she could see Will coming down the trail toward them, wearing that heart-stopping smile and teasing her about poaching.

But he didn't.

Back at Gram's place, Kennedy helped Josie make lunch. Gram asked if they could make an extra sandwich. Josie didn't ask who it was for—she could guess.

She avoided watching the clock, and instead, helped Gram and Libby take their lunch in a basket out to the back yard. The sky was a clean slate of autumn blue, the temperature a perfect seventy-eight degrees. October in Oregon could be so moody; raincoat cold one day, flip-flops warm the next.

They gathered around the big oak stump to eat and watch Kennedy play with his cars. Josie noticed that the chess pieces were gone.

"Did you and Jenny finish your game?" she asked Libby.

Her aunt peered into the woods. "Yep. She beat me fair and square."

Josie watched her aunt and grandma. Chess wasn't the only game people played around here. How long would this family continue playing hide and seek with Geraldine? Would she ever come around and allow them to help her?

"Do you think she'll ever get better?" Josie asked.

Libby shrugged a shoulder. "I don't know. But she has made strides. For the longest time, she wouldn't even show herself. Now, she'll actually sit and carry on a conversation." She heaved a sigh. "As long as we don't bring up things she isn't equipped to deal with."

Things like reality, apparently. It seemed that Geraldine, like Gram, was too emotionally frail to deal with the past and the traumatic events that had so deeply scarred her life.

"Most women eventually get back to normal after giving birth,"

Libby said softly. "But for some, it's so severe they never recover. Ger was one of the less fortunate ones."

Gram nodded.

Josie frowned. "What's so severe?"

"Post-partum depression. She had it bad, and she never had a lot of stamina to begin with. It was completely debilitating. That, combined with Leo's death, totally broke Ger's spirit. She never got it back. And she knew it."

A rustling in the trees pulled Josie's attention to the woods. She could see that Jenny was hovering in the shadows, causing goose bumps to rise on Josie's arms.

Gram motioned to her, but Jenny hung back like a ghostly wall-flower, just watching them.

Right. She had a feeling this was why they wanted to eat outside.

Jenny crept into the clearing, eyes shifting from person to person, then lingering on Josie and Kennedy. She came a little closer, clutching her baby tighter. When Libby offered her a sandwich, Jenny peered at it, then shook her head.

"Give her the bucket, dearest," Gram said softly, gesturing to Josie.

Josie picked up the small, empty bucket, then rose slowly and took it to Jenny.

The woman cast a wary glance at her. "You need more pinecones?"

"Yes, please," Josie said, uncertainty tinging her words. This was too surreal, knowing who this woman was, seeing her up close, viewing her through new eyes. Now that she knew, she studied the woman's features. Yes. She could see it, beneath the weathered, strained look of her face. There was a similarity about her cheeks and nose, the shape of her shoulders.

As Jenny went about her task of gathering pinecones, Josie turned to Libby, her throat so tight she could barely speak. "This work she does, it isn't just about earning food, is it?"

Libby shook her head slowly.

Josie swallowed hard, then whispered, "Do you think she's trying to pay penance for Leo?"

Eyes teary, Libby glanced at Gram. "I think so."

"So," Josie faltered. She gathered a breath and braced herself. "Was her giving me and Nadine to you part of that penance?"

Gram's gasped softly, her eyes glittering. "Oh, no, blossom, no. That wasn't penance."

Josie stiffened, swallowing back tears. "So I was right. She didn't love us enough."

"It was certainly no lack of love," Libby said quietly. She met Josie's gaze and held it, her dark blue eyes imploring for Josie's full attention. "It was lack of strength. She knew she couldn't even take care of herself, much less two little girls. She loved you. So much that she wanted the best for you. She was too weak, too emotionally frail to keep you safe and protected. She gave you girls to me because, in her mind, I was the strongest person on earth."

Josie stared at Libby as the words bumped against her heart like a newborn kitten, searching for a way in.

"And only the strongest would do for her babies."

Tears filled Josie's eyes.

"My sister wanted the very best for you and knew she couldn't give it. She was caring for you the best way she knew how."

Josie pressed a hand to her mouth to avoid alarming the woman who was collecting pinecones several yards away. Tears rolled down her cheeks. Her mother had loved her, in her own broken way. She had done the best for her children that she knew how. Giving them up had been *for* them, not because of them. Not because she didn't love them.

Geraldine had been incapable of being what Josie and Nadine needed her to be, so she found a way to make sure they got what they needed.

How had Josie been so blind?

Josie watched the frail woman, her ratty bundle under one arm as she clutched the small pail, bending down to pick up pinecones one by one.

Slowly, Josie rose and made her way to Geraldine. The older woman stopped and watched Josie, wide-eyed, but still.

"May I help you do that?" Josie said gently.

Her mother squinted at her. "Are you trying to trick me? I won't let you take my baby."

Josie shook her head. "No one wants to take your baby, Jenny. You're the mother." She swallowed hard and willed her voice not to break. "You're doing a great job."

Geraldine squinted at her, then thrust the bucket at Josie. As if to say *yes, you may help me.*

Josie held the bucket while Geraldine filled it to the top with pine-cones, then Josie sat in the grass while her mother took the bucket to Gram and exchanged it for a sandwich.

Josie sat cross-legged and watched.

And wept.

CHAPTER
-40-

A true friendship is one in which everything can be told,
and nothing will be judged.
—Unknown

Nadine – 4:00 p.m.
meet me at the bridge
alone

The bridge. Not Gram's house.

Josie stared at her sister's text, confused and a little alarmed. She hoped like crazy that Nadine's switch-ups and strange requests weren't an indicator of the kind of parent she would be or the life she would lead with Kennedy in her care.

She left him doing dishes under Libby's watchful eye and drove to the bridge alone. She parked on the shoulder and looked around. She didn't see anyone, so she walked to the covered bridge and stepped inside. It took her eyes a moment to adjust to the dark, contrasted sharply by the stripes of sunlight peeking in from the large vents along the bridge's wooden walls. The droning sound of water below instantly took her back twenty years. The bridge had withstood every storm and had remained unmoved and unaffected by the powerful current passing below.

Her sister's slender silhouette appeared at the other end of the bridge.

Josie swallowed hard. Breathed. Dug deep.

I love no matter what.

They met in the middle. Nadine no longer wore smeared make-up. In fact, she wore none at all, and without it, she looked ten years younger. Much like she had when they were a matched pair of freckle-faced, green-eyed tomboys.

Seeing her sister in this place, looking so young and vulnerable, struck Josie with a powerful sense of déjà vu. How long had it been since they were in this place together? How long since they had treated each other as sisters and friends?

Nadine studied her. "You've been crying."

No kidding. Josie blinked her burning eyes and told herself to suck it up, hold it together. *Lord, please. I really need your help.*

"There are some things I need to say to you," Nadine said quietly.

Josie braced herself as best she could.

"I need you to know that since I asked Jesus into my life three months ago, I've done a lot of soul searching. He's making me new, but I have a lot of work to do. I know that. I've spent a decade self-medicating pain, and it messed me up bad. I'm still learning how to untangle all that."

While Josie knew about the drugs, she didn't know about the pain. Nadine had hidden it well behind a mask of devil-may-care indifference.

"Part of that pain was because I was jealous. Of you and Libby. You didn't need me because you had her. I felt totally left out."

Josie opened her mouth to argue that it wasn't true but sensed the need to hold her tongue. This wasn't the time for arguing. It was Nadine's turn to talk, and Josie's turn to listen. She nodded. "I'm really sorry you felt that way."

"And I always felt like…" Frowning, Nadine dropped her gaze to the wooden flooring, scraped at a wet leaf with her boot. "I was never good enough for you. No matter what I did, you were always rushing around trying to fix everything. Trying to fix *me*."

How had Nadine read her so wrong? "I needed to take care of you. I guess I developed a mother hen disorder. I just didn't want you hurt."

Nadine lifted her head, her lips pressed in a grim line. "And all that time, I thought you were ashamed of me."

Josie gasped. "No, it wasn't that. I was just trying to help." She blinked as fresh tears pricked her eyes. "I guess all I did was ruin your life."

Her sister shook her head. "No, Jose. *I* ruined my own life. But that's all in the past. I just needed to get this stuff off my chest, because after we talked at the courthouse, I realized that you never knew any of that. We both thought we understood each other when we didn't. At all."

A breeze picked up and brought a whirl of yellow and gold leaves inside the bridge.

"What I want to say to you is that there's something both of us never understood growing up. That it's okay not to be okay. And we're not. My gosh, look at us! We're both a mess—the judge even said so. There's no shame in being imperfect, or broken, or being raised by two kooks on a fairy farm. But, Josie, you were always trying to get us to be perfect, like we had to earn our place in the world or something. You worked so hard to reach some level of worthiness, but there's no such thing. We're never going to be good enough to make sure no one throws us away. No matter how hard we try, we can't."

Nodding, Josie just stared at her sister, vaguely aware that she was crying again.

"It sucks that our mom dumped us, but that doesn't matter now. I'm sure she had her reasons. I don't know what they were, but it probably wasn't even about us."

Josie nodded. Her sister had no idea how right she was.

"Maybe our own mother didn't want us, but God did. There's this verse in Isaiah that says, 'Can a mother forget the baby at her breast and have no compassion on the child she has borne? Though she may forget, I will not forget you! See, I have engraved you on the palms of my hands.' Don't get me wrong, I struggle with this stuff every single day. It's a battle to stay clean and focused and dependent on God for help, but one thing I know is that Jesus died for me because he loves me. This is about him, not me. His goodness, not mine. He won't ever dump me or hide from me or leave me behind. Ever."

A sob caught in Josie's throat. She swiped away tears.

"I can't earn his love and I can't lose it. I have to remind myself every day that his love is like this old bridge. It's unshakable. It's not going anywhere."

Who was this person who looked like her sister but sounded like Libby?

A bolt of anger rushed through Josie's veins. "Okay, I'm really glad for you, Nadine, really, but for someone so enlightened, that was a really, really crappy thing you pulled. Sneaking in and taking Kennedy like that. You scared us all, and gave Gram a total breakdown. Why didn't you just call and come over?"

Nadine's steady gaze faltered. "You're right, that was totally crappy. I'm sorry. I needed to get your attention, and…I was desperate. I didn't know what else to do."

"Well," Josie replied, arms crossed to ward off the chill. "You definitely got my attention."

They just stood there in the center of an ancient wooden bridge, facing off in silence above the deafening sound of water.

"Honestly, Josie, would you have talked to me? Or would you have packed up and split before I arrived?"

Josie couldn't answer that.

"I'm just trying to walk in faith with the Lord's help, but I'm going to screw up, so I need you to be patient. I need you to pray for me. And to just be there." Her voice broke. Fat tears rolled down her face. "And I need you not to turn your heart away from me," she whispered.

Tears blurred Josie's vision. "I never stopped loving you, Deen. Ever."

Nadine swiped her cheeks.

Josie shook her head, baffled. "Why didn't you tell me any of this?"

Her sister shrugged. "I thought you knew. Because back then, I thought we were so, you know, in tune, so I figured you would have just known how alone I felt. I thought you knew I was hurting. I was stupid. And a total jerk. I never stopped to think about how I was hurting you. I'm really sorry."

Josie nodded. "Me too. I'm so sorry."

Nadine inhaled sharply. "Selah told me I needed to do this, even though it's the hardest thing I've ever done. Harder than withdrawals. I'm being super vulnerable, here, Feen. I just really need to know that you have my back now."

"Always."

Nadine nodded, sniffling. "Okay."

On impulse, Josie moved toward her sister, and before Nadine could recoil, Josie pulled her into an embrace. Nadine hugged her back, stiffly at first, then she clung to Josie like they were two souls lost and separated in a scary time-warp and finally reunited.

A sense of rightness flooded through Josie, settling in her bones, steadying her footing on solid ground. Like something had been way off kilter and was finally level again. Like she wasn't alone anymore.

Nadine pulled back and looked at her. "Do you think we could start over?" She drew in a deep breath, lips trembling. "I mean, do you think we could ever be friends? Or maybe even...sisters?"

Slowly, Josie nodded. "I'd like that."

Nadine sniffled. "There's just one more thing."

Josie braced herself again.

"Kennedy's a really good kid." She stepped back and stood up straighter, as if gathering every bit of nerve into her spine, then met Josie's gaze and held it. "You've done an amazing job. He's the luckiest kid in the world to have a mom like you."

Mom. In the last few days, those three small letters had suddenly taken on profound weight and inexplicable meaning.

Nadine's face crumpled. "I'm so sorry, Josie. I never meant to hurt you. Honestly. I'm so, so sorry for all the crap I put you through."

"I forgive you," Josie whispered. Forgiveness was easy, but trust would take time. "And I'm sorry, too. For everything I've done that hurt you. I love you, Nadine."

"I love you, too." She drew a deep breath. "Promise me you'll raise him to be a good man."

Josie's heart raced. "What?"

"I went back and talked to the judge. As of now, you have permanent guardianship, if you want it. And Judge Levine is prepared to give you full custody. Or discuss adoption." Her green eyes softened. "It's completely up to you. Whatever you want."

"*What?*" Josie gasped and pressed a quivering hand to her heart, as if that would keep it from bursting. "Why?"

"Because you're his mom. You know it, I know it, and apparently, Judge Levine knew it all along." Tears rolled down Nadine's face unchecked. "Kennedy belongs with his real mom. The one who would do anything for him, including ripping out her own heart if that's what it takes to protect him."

"He's really going to stay?" Josie could barely get the words out. "With me?"

"If that's what you want."

"Yes! My gosh, yes! But what about all your plans? All the documentation you put together for the judge?"

Nadine shook her head. "I was only giving them that stuff to keep the meeting on the judge's docket." Shame clouded her eyes. "I never was planning on keeping him, Jose."

Josie's jaw sagged. "Then why did you take him?"

Nadine wrapped her arms around herself. "I just wanted to see him. Talk to him. I wanted him to meet me without anyone's jaded input and let him get his own impression of me. And I was going to bring him back, but then our phone conversation got ugly. So, I decided the only way you'd hear the rest of what I had to say is if you were forced to come to court."

"Really, Nadine?" Tears prickled her eyes. "He's a child, not a chess piece."

A choked sob escaped. "I know, and I'm sorry. It was stupid. Really stupid. Selah told me..." She smeared away tears with both palms. "She said after that little stunt, I'm going to have to work even harder now to gain back your trust. I know that."

Josie studied her sister carefully. She wanted to believe her. And yet she couldn't simply ignore her sister's reckless past, which included the last couple of days. But Josie had a choice. She could continue to keep her sister at arm's length and maintain the gulf between them, or she could listen to Nadine's heart. She could keep believing she knew her sister better than Nadine knew herself, or she could try to get to know who Nadine really was.

"I have to agree with your mentor. Trust is a bridge that's going to take some time to build, but I'm willing to work on it, if you are."

Nadine nodded. "I am. I want to be...part of the family again. Part of your life."

"And what about Kennedy's life?" She watched her sister carefully.

Her sister drew a steady breath, then shook her head. "I had the honor of bringing him into the world. But you nurtured and cared for him. You've taught him to be strong and confident. You're raising him to be a really good man. And God knows the world needs more good men."

Josie nodded.

"I told the judge that you fought for his life from the very start. You're that little boy's hero."

"But you let him live," Josie said softly. "That makes you a hero, too."

Nadine shrugged. "I carried him for a few months while I waited tables. That was the easy part. You sacrificed your degree and any hope of a social life. You loved him and rocked him even when he wouldn't stop crying, and now you're teaching him and equipping him for life. Because of you, that little boy has a choice, and a voice, and a chance to be whatever he wants to be. We both know you've always been his mom, right from the start." Tears glittering in her eyes, she beamed a broad smile. "Now, it's going to be official."

A breathless laugh slipped out. "Nadine, are you sure—"

"Absolutely. You have my word, and I won't go back on it. Tell him whatever you think is best, whenever you think he's old enough to handle it. And I'll…" Her voice faltered. "I'll be around, if you want me to be part of that. Whenever you're ready."

They hugged again, and even when they parted, Josie couldn't shake the dreamy fog she was in. She hadn't lost Kennedy. And she got her sister back, and they were making a fresh start.

When they arrived at Gram's house, Josie and Nadine parked their cars, then walked up the steps together. A gentle drizzle had begun, the first rain in a long time.

Nadine paused at the top step and turned to Josie. "I've been working really hard at recovery and with the Lord's help, I've been winning the battles, but now, knowing I have my best friend and warrior fighting for me, I know I can do this."

Josie teared up again. "You've got this. And you've got me." She hugged Nadine long and hard.

Libby stepped onto the porch, then gasped. She covered her mouth. "Oh, my heavens!"

From the corner of her eye, Josie notice movement in the little orchard beyond the garden. It was Geraldine, hobbling through the apple trees, carrying her little bucket.

Nadine frowned. "Who's that?" she whispered.

"You'd better sit down, sis," Josie said. "There's something we need to tell you."

CHAPTER
-41-

Faithless is he that says farewell when the road darkens.
—J. R. R. Tolkien

L ibby took Nadine inside, but Josie lingered on the porch. She needed a moment to think, to compose herself. To let the weight of everything she'd just learned sink in.

She was going to keep Kennedy. She was going to be his mom.

His *real* mom.

She would adopt him as soon as possible. Not only would adoption solidify the mother-son bond that had existed since before he was born, but it might also, in time, make it easier for Josie to explain to her son how very much he was loved and wanted.

Smiling, she went inside and found Gram in the kitchen teaching Kennedy how to speak Pig. She scooped him up and hugged him until he squealed and tried to wriggle away. She kissed his face and spun him around before finally setting him down.

When Libby heard the news about Kennedy, she cried—something Josie still couldn't get used to seeing.

Nadine said her goodbyes, then left with a promise to come back in a few days, because now that she knew about Geraldine, she was determined to do everything in her power to get help for their mother.

After telling everyone goodnight, Kennedy brushed his teeth and put on his pajamas while Josie hunted for a bedtime story. He had three new books that "Auntie Deenie" had bought for him, along with a basket of new toys. She let him choose a story, and he picked the

Three Little Pigs—with the understanding that Mommy had to do the pig voices the right way. Tamping down her giddiness, Josie acted affronted, but agreed to try if he promised to help.

Glad that the pigs learned their lesson and got their happily ever after, Kennedy settled into his pillow and fell asleep while Josie lingered, watching him as the rain drummed hard like impatient fingers against the old windowpanes. She marveled at how things had turned out for him, and wondered how she could have been so fortunate, shown such favor. She didn't for a minute think she deserved it, but she was beginning to believe that God had heard her prayers. He had turned her sister's heart around, and so much more. He had changed Nadine, and was healing her and making her whole, little by little. He was doing a miracle.

Thank you, Lord. For hearing me, and for helping my sister. Thank you for all that you've done and all that you are restoring. It's all so incredible. Thank you.

So much was being restored, and she had been given so much more than she'd ever dared to hope for. Almost every single desire of her heart, all pouring over her at once, like a shower of blessings. And for all of these gifts, she was truly grateful. She'd been given far more than she deserved and didn't dare long for anything else.

Even though an enormous part of her heart still ached.

No. Longing for anything else at this point was just greedy.

She kissed the top of Kennedy's head, then went downstairs to the kitchen. Libby was at the table reading sonnets aloud while Gram brewed a pot of nastiness.

Josie grabbed an apple and sat at the table beside Libby.

"I told your sister that I'm proud of her for getting clean and for working so hard to get her life straight," Libby said, placing a ribbon in the small leather-bound book. "But I also let her know that the choices she made in this situation make me seriously question her judgment."

Josie nodded. While she and Nadine had discussed this, nothing Josie could say to her sister would ever sting like a scolding from Aunt Libby. "How did she take it?"

"She agreed, which about knocked me off my chair. She knows she has a long way to go, but this little stunt made that painfully real."

Josie was relieved that Libby would also be reinforcing the trust issue. "I'll totally support her in her recovery. But I agree, trust will take time." She kept a watchful eye on Gram as the old woman lifted a hot tea kettle off the burner. "I thought she took the news about our mom well. A lot better than I did."

"Yes. Quite frankly, your sister surprised me."

"How?"

"She was very compassionate. It seems she felt an instant connection. I think that, because of the things she has struggled with, she can empathize with her mother. I believe she really wants to help her."

"Do you think our mom will let her?"

Libby shrugged. "I don't know. I told her my sister is easily spooked, so Nadine hopes to get some advice from one of her counselors who specializes in mental illness. Who knows, Nadine may be just what Jenny needs to face being Geraldine again."

"A splendid plan," Gram said as she poured steaming water into her teapot.

Rain continued its steady pitter-patter against the house, a welcome reprieve for the crews battling forest fires, but it only added to the heaviness in Josie's heart. One thing still dampened her joy, but she set it aside. She and Kennedy were going to be legit! A *real* family. No more living on the run. She would count her blessings. She would remind her broken heart to take a deep breath and bask in the incredible joy that this day had brought.

"Now, my question for you," Libby said, leveling a gaze at Josie. "What happens now? Are you and Kennedy going to go back home to Idaho?"

"Home?" Gram turned with a frown, tea strainer dripping green goop everywhere. "But this is home."

Josie glanced at Gram, then looked her aunt in the eye. "Well, now that I don't need to avoid crossing paths with my sister…" The massive relief of no longer living on the run was still sinking in. "Would you two be interested in a couple of roomies?"

Libby gasped and broke out in an enormous smile, which she quickly tamped down. "Well. I guess so. As long as you two freeloaders are willing to pull your own weight."

Josie chuckled. Classic Libby.

Gram brought her teacup to the table and took a seat. "'There is a divinity that shapes our ends, rough-hew them how we will.'"

Yawning, Josie started a sink full of soapy water before her motivation to scrub pots faded. A couple of sleepless nights was all it took to turn her into a zombie. She inhaled the scent of rain wafting in from the kitchen window and basked in the tranquility of this place. Even the rain was peaceful here.

Lord, I am at peace. Really. I'm so, so thankful for all you've done. It's just that—

Her phone vibrated in her pocket. She dried her hands and checked the screen.

A text from Will.

Her knees turned to jelly. Heart racing, she opened the message.

> Will – 8:33 p.m.
> Can we talk?

Josie froze, thoughts pinwheeling. She sucked in a deep breath and replied.

> Josie – 8:33 p.m.
> Okay.

> Will – 8:33 p.m.
> Can you come outside?

What?

She hurried to the front room and peered out the window. Will was standing in the middle of the driveway, in the dark, in the pouring rain.

Heart thumping, she slipped outside, then felt wet wood beneath her bare feet and hesitated at the edge of the porch.

He just stood there, not saying a word, not moving.

Josie stared at him, baffled, then glanced around. Where was his truck? And why was he completely soaked? She chewed her lip. And why would he show up unannounced? And on foot? As much as she was dying to ask, she chose to wait. Let him explain.

Will took a few steps closer, eyes never leaving hers, and came to a stop near the bottom step.

Not breathing for fear of missing something, she studied his glistening face in the porchlight's glow, but his somber expression gave no clue what he was thinking or why he had come.

Inhale, you fool.

"Would you like to come up here and get out of the rain?"

He climbed the steps slowly and joined her under the eaves, his running gear dripping all over the place. In the three days since she'd last seen him, he had somehow gotten taller. Broader. His eyes were darker. Way darker, and he looked sort of…hollow.

And his chest was working as if he'd just run six miles and was still catching his breath.

Wait…

Josie gasped. "Did you run here? From your house?"

"Yeah."

The fact that he was standing in the middle of her porch looking like he'd just taken a shower fully dressed rattled her so much she couldn't think straight.

"Why?"

His gaze roamed over her face and hair and then rested on her mouth. "I don't know." He winced. "I went for a run and I was thinking about you and the next thing I knew, I was here."

Heart kicking against her ribs, she searched his eyes, knowing how easily she could get lost there. "What were you thinking?" she asked, barely above a whisper.

"I…" He frowned. "I can't stop thinking about the day Kennedy disappeared and how you found out he'd been taken, and how you told me some things about your life that didn't set well with me."

Don't cry.

Josie wrapped her arms around herself to keep from shaking, a pitiful attempt to hold herself together. "I'm really sorry you had to find out that way. And I'm sorry that I'm a disappointment to you." She swallowed down the knot gathering in her throat. "Just so you know, I've wrestled with my conscience every day for the past four years. I'm sure the really good, competent moms would question my choices, and frankly, so have I. It's a terrible way to raise a child. I hate that I've hurt the person who was supposed to be my best friend forever, and I really hated lying to a child. And some days, it was really hard, but at the end of the day, you know what? As much as I value and respect the strength of your integrity, I have to stand behind what I've done. Because I love him. And if I had a do-over, I have to say, for Kennedy, I'd do it again."

Will shook his head, sending droplets from his hair flying. "Josie, I don't—"

"And the reason I didn't tell you the truth up front is because I didn't dare tell anyone. I was terrified that Nadine would find us." She rushed to finish before she broke down and lost the ability to speak. "I'm so sorry that I lied to you, Will. I understand how you feel about dishonesty." She forced out the last of what she needed to say around the burning knot in her throat. "I wish with all my heart that things were different, but I can't change it."

"Josie." He stepped closer, wet face gleaming in the porch light's glow. "I'm the one who owes *you* an apology." His jaw rippled. "What I said that day, the way I walked out on you in the middle of your worst, darkest moment, I'm the world's biggest jerk. I should have never done that. I'm so sorry."

She nodded, grateful that he understood how hurtful his leaving had been, especially in that moment of anguish and pure fear. She gave a one-sided shrug. "I understand why you did it."

Shaking his head slowly, he studied her. "No, Josie, I don't think you do." His gaze darted beyond her, toward the river, like he was searching for the right words in the water's steady flow. The crease in his brow deepened. "These past couple of days, I've been taking a long, hard look at myself and to be honest, I don't like what I see. I've been angry for a long time, longer than a person claiming faith in Christ ought to. And that anger had burrowed in a lot deeper than I'd like to admit. I'm afraid bitterness has altered me. Hardened my heart. And it's made me forget really important things, like how most people are just trying to do the best they can, sometimes lacking the right tools, sometimes making mistakes. Some people are just desperately trying to figure out how to get by."

She thought of Geraldine. "And some are scared and totally alone and have no idea what to do."

"Right." He swallowed hard. "And sometimes, people do strange things out of love."

Yes, they do. Tears blurred her vision.

"Even lie, if they're desperate to keep someone from being hurt," he said softly. "Push their own desires and needs aside to protect someone they love."

She nodded, swiping away tears.

He blasted out a breath. "Josie, if anyone ought to be wrestling with their conscience, it's me. I'm an insensitive jerk, and I've deeply wounded the one person on earth I would never, ever want to hurt."

"Will—"

"I don't expect you to forgive me," he said softly, "but maybe someday—"

"I can forgive you."

He stilled, eyes on hers. "You can?"

She nodded, mesmerized by the way he was drinking her in suddenly, ignoring the rivulets still trickling down his face.

"I've been so afraid." His deep voice faltered.

She searched his face. "Of what?"

Moist heat radiated from him like a sauna. "I'm afraid I've destroyed the best thing that's ever happened to me."

"No." She reached up and brushed a soaked lock of hair out of his eyes. "You didn't."

His breath caught at her touch. Hope and desperation mingled in his dark eyes. "Really?"

Speechless, she nodded, throat thick with emotion.

"I've been going out of my mind not knowing what's happening with you and the court, or if Kennedy's okay, or what's going to happen to him." He hesitated, his features soft, his expression solemn. "The only thing I know is that every day we're apart, the worse I feel."

"Me too," she whispered.

Misery darkened his face. "And I miss you," he said simply.

Teary, she nodded again. A calm, peaceful knowing washed over her. "Ditto," she smiled. "Like crazy."

He moved closer and leveled his tender, caramel gaze on her. "And I'm in love with you."

"Me too." Her voice mingled with the gentle, steady patter of rain. "I love you, Will."

He pulled her close, wrapped his arms around her, and held her tight, burying his face in her hair.

Her eyes drifted closed, heart cartwheeling, her mind too numb to think of anything except that she loved him, and that he was here—really here—holding her like he would never let her go.

Really, God? Is this even possible?

She melted into his embrace, joy exploding like fireworks.

He pulled back to see her face, arms still encircling her. "I saw that you and Kennedy were at Grandma's yesterday. Does that mean he's back with you?"

She smiled. "Yes! It's a long story, but he's going to be mine for good. No more living on the run, no more hiding from Nadine. She's clean and doing well—and she feels really bad about taking him and scaring us all. She and I talked about a lot of things, things I should have seen, and I'm..." She trailed off, unable to trust her voice. "Will, I'm so ashamed of the things I did that hurt her." She blinked away tears. "We'll have some work ahead to restore our relationship, and it's going to take time to rebuild trust. But we worked it all out about Kennedy. I'm going to adopt him, and she and I will explain everything to him when he's a little older."

He smiled. "That's incredible, Josie. I'm really happy for you. You're an amazing mom." He dipped his head and searched her eyes. "More than amazing. There's no 'competent' mom who can even hold a candle to you. Kennedy is a really, really lucky kid."

A sudden rush of tears nearly blinded her. "Thank you," she said, shaking her head. "But I'm pretty sure I'm the lucky one." She looked into his eyes and smiled. "And, we're not going anywhere. Kennedy and I are staying right here."

Air whooshed from him. He studied her carefully, as if he needed to make sure he'd heard right. "You're not leaving?"

She shook her head, unable to stop smiling. Then slowly, she laced her fingers around his neck and pressed her lips to his, warm and sure, a sweet, lingering promise.

A low sound came from deep inside him, and he pressed her closer, kissing her again and again, until everything was a heady swirl of blinding light.

They kissed until she had to break free to catch her breath. She studied his face. His broad smile and the love burning in his eyes nearly knocked her flat.

"I hope you have a lot of patience, because I've got some things to work on," he said softly. "Like learning to let go, and keeping my heart open. And..." One brow lifted. "It sounds like I need to learn Shakespeare."

Waves of bliss forced her smile wider. "Probably. But you're quite the expert on plenty of other things. Like treating a girl to a perfect sunset."

As he studied her face, love illuminated his. He let out a deep sigh. "Your smile is worth a hundred perfect sunsets."

Later that night, Josie lay wide awake, staring at the underside of Kennedy's bunk. Why, why, why had God blessed her with so much? His favor had to be something he chose to give, not something a person earned, because she certainly didn't deserve it. Despite her mistakes and flaws and taking matters into her own hands, he had steered things to work out so that the people she loved were headed in the direction they needed to be, in spite of her interference, and he was working in all of it. His mercy and grace were so clearly evident.

Thank you, Lord. For everything. Thank you for loving me and never leaving me. Please help me do things your way, every day, one at a time.

Her phone dinged with a text.

Will – 10:45 p.m.
Can you talk?

With a chuckle, she slipped out of the bedroom to the landing at the top of the stairs and called him.

"Hi," Will said softly. "I just wanted to tell you that I love you, and I'm really proud of you."

She smiled.

"And that I'm onto you. I figured out who you really are."

"And that is?"

"Wonder Woman."

"Shoot!" She grinned. "My secret's out."

He chuckled. "It was really kind of you to take Grandma that book. Thank you. That means a lot."

"How did you know?"

A huff sounded across the line. "Are you kidding? I'm a professional investigator."

"Right, I forgot, your detective powers are insane." She smiled. "And so are your eyes, by the way. Sometimes, the way you look at me does things to my heart that I'm pretty sure in some cultures means you have to marry me now."

Silence.

Wincing, she caught her lower lip in her teeth. If there was a program for people who blurted out things at the wrong moments, Josie probably needed to check herself in.

"Uhh," he said slowly, the rumble of his voice crossing a half dozen miles. "Is this a proposal?"

Her heart thumped. "Do you want it to be?"

"Do you always answer questions with questions?"

She sighed. "Sounds like you have more investigating to do, Ranger McNugget. But I'll make it easy on you. Come at sunset tomorrow for a campfire at the Buckley place. It'll be you, me, a mini superhero, a Shakespearean pig, some fairies, and a couple of kooky senior citizens."

"Wow, sounds romantic," he said with a wry chuckle. "I'll bring the marshmallows."

Unable to keep her joy from bubbling over, she laughed.

"Ahh, Josie..." Will heaved a sigh. "You have no idea how much I love that sound."

CHAPTER
-42-

When I grow up, I'm going to live in the woods and eat huckleberries and catch trout and salamanders. If I ever get married, my wife better know how to fish and make huckleberry pie and she has to have a really good laugh.
—Willie McKnight, age 8

Autumn turned to winter, and on a pristine, snowy day in January, as family and friends looked on, Josie, wearing a simple white gown, walked down the aisle with Kennedy's hand tucked into hers. Her son's job was to escort her to Will, and it was a job he took seriously. He wasn't giving her away, of course. There would be none of that.

Josie wanted to be kept.

When Josie and Kennedy reached the front of the sanctuary, Will, wearing his full-dress uniform, crouched level with the boy. He shook his hand and thanked him, then spoke privately to him for a minute, man to man. Then, as Kennedy scurried away to sit on his Auntie Deenie's lap, Will straightened and took Josie's hands. Love shone in his eyes as Pastor Dennis spoke about marriage, advising that there would be good days and bad, times of joy and sadness, but that there was a secret to weathering every storm; a solid foundation that would make a marriage continue to grow strong and unshakable in the years to come.

The secret, he said, was grace.

Winter turned to spring. Will, Josie, and Kennedy McKnight spent a weekend in Sisters with Mandy and her family, even though Will suspected his sister had ulterior motives. He was right. Mandy pulled him aside and told him that their mother was hoping for a chance to talk to him in person. Linda McKnight wanted to apologize to her son, and to give him the explanation she felt she owed him. She also hoped he might allow her to meet his new family.

Will had suspected the request was coming, and though he wasn't thrilled with the idea, he knew he needed to take some tangible steps toward letting go of bitterness and toward softening his heart. It began with the ability to accept that sometimes people had reasons for the choices they made, and that what we see is often only part of the picture. And that sometimes an apology wasn't an expectation of forgiveness, but simply because it was owed. And even if the apology made no one but Linda McKnight feel better, allowing her to do it was an act of compassion that probably wouldn't cause him any regrets.

As it turned out, the meeting went better than he expected, and in the weeks and months following, conversations between mother and son began to open Will's eyes to his mother's depression and other issues she had struggled with in her younger years, and to build a bridge where none had existed for a very long time.

Another bridge was formed when Nadine, Libby, Gram, and Josie watched Geraldine take a huge step in her personal health by accepting her half of Miss Ellie's room at Riverbend, with the understanding that she could "work" for her keep by doing dishes and folding linens, for as long as she wanted to.

Spring turned to Summer. One day in July, when Josie came home from visiting both Grandma Eleanor and her mom at Riverbend, she walked around to the back of the cabin that Will and his father had built and headed straight for the river, knowing exactly where she would find her guys.

And there they were—one tall and one small, sitting at the end of the dock, just as she had suspected. But the sight of them, both in cargo shorts and a tank top and holding a fishing pole, filled her with a rush of joy that stole her breath. She pulled out her phone and snapped a photo of father and son, heads together, discussing something. Will pointed to a spot way out in the river, then made a casting motion. Kennedy gave it a try and cast his line as far as he could. Will said something Josie couldn't hear and then gave their son a *way-to-go* pat on the back.

She snapped a couple more frame-worthy photos, then joined them.

Will turned to her and smiled.

Kennedy saw her then. "Mommy! Look how many we caught!" He pointed at the fish swimming in the bucket. "We're gonna fry 'em for dinner!"

"Excellent. I was hoping I could count on you two to feed me." Josie dangled her feet off the edge of the dock, and then leaned back on her elbows, eyes closed, drinking in the mingling scents of pine and moss and leaves, and allowing the river's endless song to relax her.

And above the soothing, steady rush of water, she heard the sound of a grown man taking a deep breath and letting it out slowly.

Josie opened her eyes and found her husband watching her. She smiled.

Will stretched out and reclined on the dock the same way, mirroring her, and reached for her hand. He wove his fingers between hers, then lifted her hand to his lips. Kissed a knuckle, then another. Caught her gaze and held it, inquiring something with his eyes she couldn't quite read, but whatever it was, it sent warmth curling all through her insides.

Will eyed her. "Are you okay?"

She nodded.

Fact: Josie McKnight was so okay she could hardly speak.

"How is she today?"

"Mom seemed really good. They let her fold the laundry, and while she was super focused on doing all of it, she was really calm, not at all antsy. The diet and meds are definitely helping."

"That's good."

"Yeah. But I think most of her improvements are due to Nadine. She still comes to see her three times a week, like clockwork. She's been totally faithful to her commitment."

Will smiled. "Turns out your sister has a caregiver's heart, too."

Josie heaved a sigh. "She does. I'm just sorry it took me so long to get out of her way."

Will shook his head, studying their joined hands. "Or maybe God knew all along that one sister would have Wonder-mom skills, and the other would have an overcomer's patience and compassion, and he shaped each of them and guided them to be at just the right place at just the right time. To be there for the one priceless soul who needed those superpowers the most."

Two sets of sisters, shaped by human weakness and failings. Weaknesses that God had turned into strengths.

Josie turned her gaze toward the east end of the canyon and pictured her and Nadine's secret place a few miles upriver, beneath the bridge where she and her sister had taken a giant step toward each other and began to close the gulf between them.

Grace was like that, like a bridge. Bringing together those on distant shores, separated by a gulf too wide to cross. Bridging gaps that seemed impossible.

Grace was a bridge that says *I love you no matter what.*

Josie turned to Will, struck by how powerfully she loved him.

He reached over and tucked a lock of hair behind her ear and then searched her face for a long time. Just as Josie was about to ask what he was thinking, he said, "Do you have any idea how much I love you?"

"Not a clue." She tried for a chuckle, but it was more of a breathless little sigh.

"Hey! I got one!" Kennedy leapt to his feet.

"Reel that sucker in—"

"You got this, son—"

Will and Josie spoke at the same time.

Kennedy reeled like mad, laser-focused on the fish at the end of his line, oblivious that his slacker parents were still reclining on the dock behind him, sharing a long, deep kiss.

EPILOGUE

Dear Little One,

I didn't know.

When you were forming inside me, I thought you were just a lump of tissue, a human pea in a uterine pod, a freeloader hijacking my body and making me tired and screwing up my hormones.

I didn't know how to feel about your sudden, unexpected existence. I didn't know how terrified I would be that you would somehow know, even in the womb, that I was totally unfit to be a mom and had no idea what to do. I didn't know that when I walked into that clinic, they would offer me options that made "terminating" you sound so routine, so easy. So painless.

I didn't know that you were asking so little of me. You weren't asking for the moon or for me to make you a world-changer. You weren't asking me to be a good mother. Or to even be a mother at all. All you needed from me was a fighting chance. You could be raised by anyone. There are countless women who would beg for the chance to love you, sight unseen.

I didn't know much, but what I did know was that one day, for your sake, I would need to turn you over to far more capable hands. What I began, another would continue.

You were formed in the secret place, long before I ever knew you existed, by Someone who has a perfect plan and purpose for your life, who has gifts and talents for you to use and inventions and discoveries for you to make and worlds for you to explore. You weren't asking me to draft a plan for your life—that's God's job. What you have the potential to become was never up to me. The choice was never mine.

All you were asking of me, the only person on the planet with the power to give you a choice, was to simply be patient for nine months. I could at least do that. And I'm so glad I did. It's the most courageous thing I have ever done.

I didn't know that the greatest joy I would ever have is knowing that the world is a better place because I got out of the way and simply allowed you to be, for, as Tolkien said, "Even the smallest person can change the course of history."

I thank God that he loves you and fashioned you for a purpose, and I'm honored that he allowed me to be a small part of your big, bold, beautiful life.

Signed,
—Mom

AUTHOR'S NOTE

Ah, the constancy of life, so like a river. Little did I know as I wrote and later turned in the manuscript for this novel that I would suddenly experience things in this story that I could only imagine as I wrote them. After I turned in the manuscript to my editor, my dad died unexpectedly. When I re-read the story later, the scenes in which Will mourns the loss of his dad, and the memory-stirring photographs that change his perspective, suddenly rang with an eerie sense of reality. Since I had no idea, I'm really glad that the story went the way it did, that the photographs of his dad led Will to have a moment of clarity that helped him seek and listen to the Lord's leading, because this reaction turned out to be similar for me. Looking back over my dad's whole life startled me, snapped me to attention, taught me that time passes much too quickly to invest it on things that have little eternal value. Rather than ask God to help me in my endeavors, I'm asking, *Lord, what do you want me to do today?*

The Secret Place touches on some very sensitive topics, and as always, my hope is to help shine the light of Christ's love and mercy into the real-life struggles that so desperately need his touch. While addiction, unplanned pregnancies, bitterness, broken relationships, abuse, grief, and pain are part of the imperfect world we live in, grace, healing, and hope are found in Christ. For thirty-three years, Jesus walked amongst sinners while resisting temptation, taught much-needed truth, healed, and showed love and compassion to the sick and unlovely, lived a perfect life in an imperfect world, and then willingly suffered a cruel death, all for the joy of making wholeness, hope, and forgiveness available to a broken and hopeless world. Where we struggle and fail, he is successful and victorious. Where we are lacking, he supplies everything our hearts need. When we are faithless, he remains faithful. His love is real, and I hope to always share of this awesome, unchanging, life-giving truth.

ACKNOWLEDGMENTS

I want to say a GINORMOUS thank you to my husband, Dan, for his endless patience, for road-tripping with me (twice) to visit the McKenzie River, and for lending help from his lifetime of fishing wisdom. Thanks to those who provided legal input about family court and custody proceedings, and to local USFS LEO Ross Gamboa for helping me understand the duties and challenges of serving as Ranger in Oregon's National Forest. Thanks to my fabulous writer friend, Beth Vogt, expert on sister and relationship stories, and to Cara Grandle and David White, for lending first eyes and valuable insight and encouragement to make this story shine.

Another ginormous thank you goes to my "Blue Pool Hiker Chicks" including Wonder Woman Waynette Stotts, who still hasn't forgiven me for dragging her over four-or-was-it-really-eight-miles of rocky terrain; Cara Grandle, aka Author and Rockstar Publicist (and Wife and Mom of five and Prayer Warrior and Farmer and Artist and seriously, is there anything she *can't* do??); and my SUPERCOOL pal & heart-sister Meghan Yow, who not only adores a good hike, but who had the nerve to climb down a 50-foot vertical rock-face for a closer look at the pool.

Okay, there are two things about Meghan that you need to know: (1) Josie's character is *loosely* based on her. I can only say loosely, because Meghan is *incredibly* witty, killer smart, fun, and someone you cannot help but love to be around, and though I tried really hard, I could not write Josie to be even half as cool as her. But Meghan did generously provide helpful inspiration for Josie by patiently answering really random, late night questions via text. And (2) after our hike to see the Blue Pool on my birthday so that I could describe an important scene firsthand, Meghan gently burst my bubble by reminding me that the Very Important Romantic Scene in question takes place in October, and in the evening, so at that time of day and year, the pool (and hike) would be in total darkness. I had to totally rewrite the Very Important Romantic Scene. But the birthday hike was still awesome and amazing, even though I nearly killed Waynette's poor feet. Note: If you are ever near the Willamette National Forest in summer and if you're like Will McKnight and love nature and water, the Blue Pool hike is a must see. The water is a vivid shade of neon turquoise, especially when the sun is high overhead. An absolute MUST SEE.

Thank you, Jesus, for continuing to shower me with your patience, grace, unwavering persistence, mercy, love, nearness, help, strength, joy, and so much more. Thank you to my sisters and daughters for loving me anyway, imperfect sister and mom that I am. And thank you to MY sweet mom for giving me life, and for all that you sacrificed for me.

And to my Dad in heaven: Thank you for being the most stubborn human I've ever known, for not letting me push you away out of my deep disappointment in fathers, and for making me a believer in *Love No Matter What*.

DISCUSSION QUESTIONS

1. Have you ever entrusted a secret to someone who was suddenly unable to keep it?

2. Which characters did you admire? What characteristics about them stood out?

3. What motivates Josie to shield Kennedy from the truth about his real mother? Do you think her actions are justified?

4. Which characters' actions or reactions surprised you?

5. Which characters grew during the course of the story? In what ways?

6. Protecting Nadine is an ingrained part of Josie's identity. Why do you think she assumed that role?

7. Have you ever felt compelled or duty-bound to protect someone from the consequences of their choices or actions?

8. What motivates Gram's "utopian" outlook? Did she strike you as frail, wise, or a combination of both?

9. Josie often dreamed of Nadine. What do you think Josie's subconscious was trying to tell her about her sister and their relationship?

10. How did believing in "twinsy-telepathy" backfire for Josie? For Nadine?

11. Josie struggles with guilt for lying to Kennedy and others, but she also struggles with another form of guilt. Can you identify it? Relate to it?

12. What created Will's black and white outlook? Do you think

his behavior when he learned the truth about Josie was understandable?

13. What factors led to Will's change of heart?

14. Were you surprised by Nadine's news that she was "born again"? How did you first respond?

15. Josie wonders if *Love No Matter What* exists outside of fiction or poetry. Does it? How have you experienced it?

16. If you could meet one character from *The Secret Place*, who would it be? And at what time in their life?

17. Does the book resonate with your own life in any way?

18. When did you first know or suspect Jenny's true identity?

19. Consider the ending. Did you expect it or were you surprised?

20. Which character in this story do you relate to the most, and why?

21. Have you ever discovered the "bigger picture" about someone that radically changed the way you felt about them?

22. Libby told Josie about the unspoken expectations we have of others, the standards we can hold people to, standards they may not be aware of. Do you think it's fair to hold people accountable to unspoken standards? Why or why not?

23. The bridge is a recurring motif in this story. Did any symbolism come to mind whenever you encountered a bridge in this story?

24. The term "Secret Place" has multiple meanings in this story. How many did you come across, and what do you think they symbolize?

CPSIA information can be obtained
at www.ICGtesting.com
Printed in the USA
LVHW031644310321
683083LV00005B/932

9 781946 531995